Master of
Formalities

ALSO BY THE AUTHOR

Help Is on the Way: A Collection of Basic Instructions

Made with Recycled Art: A Collection of Basic Instructions

The Curse of the Masking Tape Mummy: A Collection of Basic Instructions

Dignified Hedonism: A Collection of Basic Instructions

Off to Be the Wizard: Magic 2.0, Book 1

Spell or High Water: Magic 2.0, Book 2

An Unwelcome Quest: Magic 2.0, Book 3

Master of Formalities

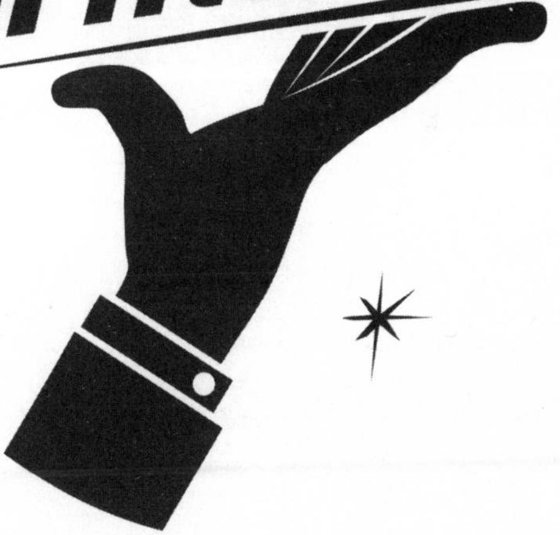

AN EPIC SCI-FI COMEDY
OF MANNERS

Scott Meyer

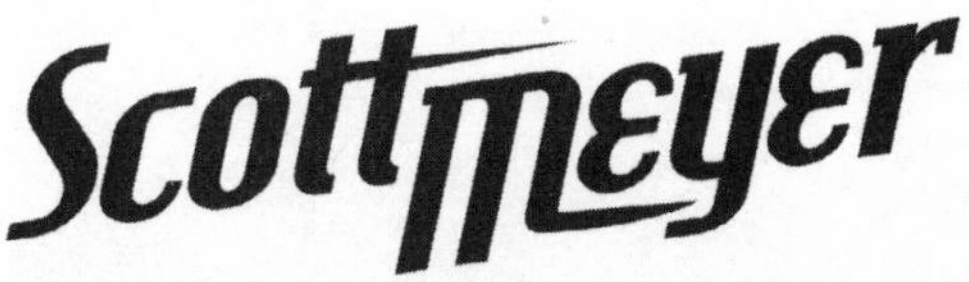

47NORTH

This is a work of fiction. Names, characters, organizations, places, events, and incidents are either products of the author's imagination or are used fictitiously.

Published by 47North, Seattle

www.apub.com

Amazon, the Amazon logo, and 47North are trademarks of Amazon.com, Inc., or its affiliates.

ISBN-13: 9781477830918
ISBN-10: 147783091X

Cover design by Cyanotype Book Architects
Illustrated by Maciej Rebisz

Library of Congress Control Number: 2015930385

Printed in the United States of America

PART 1

It is often said that the most majestic tree starts as a mere sapling.

It is less commonly noted that when viewed by an insect, the sapling was majestic in its own right.

-Excerpt from the *Academy of Arbitration Instructional Supplement: Aphorisms to Distract and Placate*

I.

"Know that two thousand, one hundred, and seventy-one conventional years have passed since the Terran Exodus. Today is the fifty-sixth day of the third month," the pale man said. He had slick black hair and a sleek black suit, which served to accentuate his lean, gangly frame. "We meet on the planet Apios, in the servants' hall of Palace Koa, the ancestral home of House Jakabitus and its matriarch, Lady Joanadie Jakabitus. I am Wollard, Master of Formalities for House Jakabitus, and I am currently delivering the daily meeting to the palace staff."

Wollard recited the full formal greeting, as was customary. The younger members of the staff rolled their eyes and looked bored, as was also customary. The full formal greeting was designed long ago, in the days when interstellar travel still involved time distortion and suspended animation. Back then, it was common to greet travelers who didn't know where they were, when they were there, or in some cases, who they were.

Of course, those days were long past. In these more modern times the full greeting was only used at the most formal occasions or by the most formal people. The daily staff meeting was delivered by the Master of Formalities, so it always started with the full formal greeting.

Now that the greeting was complete, Wollard looked up from his papers, and his entire demeanor softened. He studied the staff with keen eyes and a warm smile.

"Good morning, all."

The staff wished him a good morning, more or less in unison, their voices echoing in the cavernous servants' hall. Like the full formal greeting, the room had been crafted for a less advanced time, a time when it took a staff of dozens to maintain the palace. Things were different now. The ruling family's personal quarters were maintained quite well by seven people. This made it much simpler to manage the staff and operate as a coordinated team, but it did give the servants' hall an empty, lonely feeling. The room, like all of the more utilitarian spaces in the palace, had been crammed in wherever it would fit, making an irregularly shaped chamber with one end much smaller than the other. Wollard and the rest of the staff were gathered at the narrower end of the room, with the dual result that they were cozier, but the room looked far emptier.

Greetings out of the way, Wollard moved on to the day's agenda.

"Today is a momentous day for House Jakabitus," he said, glancing back down at his papers. "Lady Jakabitus will not be enjoying breakfast with her family this morning. Chef Barsparse has already provided Her Ladyship with a small repast, which should keep her going until lunch. Her Ladyship's military advisors have requested a supplementary briefing this morning, during which Lady Jakabitus will be updated on the status of this planet's ongoing war with the forces of the detestable Hahn Empire over the planet Ophion 6. My protégée and I shall attend this meeting, as the Formalities dictate."

A young woman raised her hand and said, "Query."

Wollard stopped reading from the agenda and addressed the young woman. "I recognize Shly, deliverer of liquid refreshment."

Shly was a young woman, pretty by most conventional standards, and confident in a way that either made her seem slightly less attractive or much, much more attractive, depending on the observer. Her hair was light for an Apiosan, which meant it was almost black. She had it pulled back, in keeping with the appearance guidelines for palace staff, and she wore the staff uniform, which was simple, functional, cut to be gender flattering, and made of the absolute finest materials.

Shly lowered her hand and smiled. “Where is your student? Don’t the Formalities dictate that she attend the daily staff meeting?”

“First,” Wollard said, “her title is *protégée,* not *student*, as I’ve told you before, Shly. You are correct that in most cases she would be here; however, one of Lady Jakabitus’s ministers will be attending the briefing in person this morning. My protégée is awaiting this minister’s arrival while I deliver the daily meeting.”

“Do they have news of the war?” a second young woman blurted. “Did something happen?” She was roughly the same age as Shly, with essentially the same coloration, but she was a bit less pretty and a bit less confident, and as such, was totally overshadowed by her friend

Wollard smiled benignly at the woman, but said nothing.

The woman blushed slightly and said, “Sorry. Query?”

Wollard said, “That’s quite all right. I understand your anxiety. I recognize Umily, tender to personal needs. To answer your question, I have no information, nor could I tell you if I did. I doubt, however, that anyone would request a special briefing, travel to the palace, and stand in Lady Jakabitus’s presence in order to tell Her Ladyship that there is nothing noteworthy to report. That said, Umily, we mustn’t get our hopes up. The House Jakabitus has been at war with the Hahn for generations. I don’t see that changing any time soon.”

No one voiced disagreement, and the moment of silence following Wollard’s statement cast a pall over the staff. Wollard cleared his throat, returned his gaze to his papers, and continued.

“Master Rayzo, the heir to the Jakabitus Dynasty, has a sports practice session this morning with his tutor, Hartchar.” Wollard looked up to acknowledge Hartchar, who nodded, signaling for Wollard to continue. She wore the same uniform as the rest of the staff, but it rode differently on her tall, muscular physique. Her flaming red hair caused her to stand out further. Like Wollard and his protégée, she was an import from a different world, so she lacked the distinctive dark coloration for which the people of Apios were known and envied.

"After sports practice and lunch, which will be attended by the ruling family, who will have no guests, Master Rayzo will be competing in a sports meet, which his father, Lord Frederain Jakabitus, will attend. I'm certain we all wish him good fortune."

The instant the word *fortune* left Wollard's lips, a male voice cried out, "Query?"

Wollard grinned slightly, in spite of himself, but spoke without looking up from his papers. "I recognize Ebbler, food delivery."

Ebbler sat between Shly and Umily, which accentuated the broadness and solidity of his build, but also made him look shorter, as both Shly and Umily were relatively tall, and Ebbler was not.

Ebbler smirked at Shly, then asked, "Will Master Rayzo require extra portions at lunch and dinner to recover from his training in the morning and his game in the afternoon?"

Wollard grimaced at Ebbler. "As you know, the official, sanctioned term for what you refer to as *training* is, in this case, *sports practice.* As you are also aware, the official name for the type of sporting event in which Master Rayzo will be competing is a *sports meet.* I know that in more casual circles, other words are employed, but I must remind you that this household is not a *more casual circle.* Is that clear?"

Wollard's words were stern, but his voice was not. Ebbler nodded. Wollard continued.

There was a brief discussion of dinner, followed by a discussion of the importance of standards. Wollard attempted to end the meeting early so he could make it to Lady Jakabitus's briefing in a timely manner, and was only slightly delayed by a minor debate as to the officially sanctioned term for *hurrying.*

As Wollard made his exit, Glaz, the palace expediter, turned to face the group and clapped her hands together. She was an older woman of average height and weight, with unremarkable graying hair. She wore the same palace uniform as the rest of them. Nothing about her appearance set her apart, but she spoke with an easy authority, and everyone paid attention.

"All right," she said. "It looks to be a good day, full of work to be done. We'd best all get to it."

The group dispersed. They knew where they needed to go, and roughly how long they had to get there, so their pace was brisk, but not urgent. Only Ebbler seemed to hurry, jogging a few steps to catch up with the white-clad figures of Barsparse, the palace chef, and her sous chef, Pitt.

"Pardon me, Chef," Ebbler said as he slowed to match their pace.

"What do you want now?" Pitt asked before Barsparse could reply.

"I just wanted to say that the family's dinner last night was amazing. I didn't get to taste it, of course, but just seeing it and smelling it was more satisfying than most of the meals I've eaten."

"Thank you, that's very kind," Barsparse said, not looking at him. She was thin and graceful, but radiated determination. Her manner was not unfriendly, just uninterested. She was all business, and her business was making food, not conversation.

"I was wondering," Ebbler said, "what are you planning to make tonight?"

"Thank you for the compliment, but we don't really have time to go over my meal plan with you. We need to get breakfast on the table. I'm sure you understand."

"Of course," Ebbler said, trying not to sound disappointed or embarrassed.

"Good," Barsparse said. "See you at service."

Ebbler slowed his pace. His duties called for him to assist Umily until it was time for breakfast service, and Umily's job was not in the kitchen. Barsparse's pace didn't slow, so she quickly pulled ahead of Ebbler. Pitt, however, paused and turned to face Ebbler. The two were roughly the same age and height, and Ebbler had worked in the palace much longer, but Pitt didn't let any of those facts interfere with his sense of superiority.

"You will not pester the chef—or *me*—with your questions again," Pitt snarled.

"Am I bothering her?" Ebbler asked, concerned.

"Another question. It is not your place to question the chef. It's not your place to even speak to the chef."

"I just wondered what you were cooking today. What's the harm in that?"

"It's not your place to question me either. You carry the food. You take what we cook to the people for whom we cook it. You're a beast of burden. You don't need to know what you're carrying any more than a cargo hauler needs to know what's in his hold."

"A cargo hauler does need to know what's in his hold, doesn't he? He'd need to know lots of things about it. Is it legal? Is it dangerous? How much does it weigh? How its weight is distrib—"

Ebbler was interrupted by the distant sound of a clearing throat. Barsparse had reached the passage to the kitchen, and was looking back toward Pitt, waiting.

Pitt nodded and started moving toward her, but he glanced back at Ebbler and said, "I'll get you for this."

"For what?" Ebbler asked.

Rather than speaking, Pitt bit his lip and turned away, running to catch up to the chef.

Ebbler caught up with Umily as she was maneuvering a large, hovering grav-platter down the service corridor to the high-speed lifts that would take her to the Jakabituses' personal chambers. The platter supported a bin to collect used toiletries, sheets, and other detritus for recycling, as well as a small portable bulkfab unit to replace what had been collected. The platter supported its own weight, but it could be quite cumbersome.

"Sorry for the holdup," Ebbler said.

"That's fine," Umily said. "Talking to the chefs, I assume?"

"Yeah."

"How'd that go?"

Ebbler shook his head. "Let's just say I miss the old sous chef."

"So do I," Umily said.

Ebbler said, "I'm sure you do. How is Gint doing?"

"I'll find out soon. I got a letter from him this morning. I probably won't have time to read it until tonight. He's through training by now."

"That must be exciting."

"Exciting," Umily repeated in a flat, dull tone.

Ebbler said, "I know that being conscripted into Lady Jakabitus's military was a surprise for Gint, but you have to admit it was very generous of her to reward his new battalion for their service by assigning them a chef trained in the ruler's own palace."

"I have to admit that," Umily said. "You have to admit that it would have been even more generous if that chef hadn't just gotten married . . . to *me*."

They reached the door to the lift. Umily started to enter, but Ebbler stopped her.

"Look," he said, "I can get us started on the morning rounds. Read your letter from Gint, and when you write him back, tell him I said *hi.*"

The morning rounds mostly consisted of distributing fresh bedding and towels. While it was true that technology had long ago eliminated the need for something as primitive as bedsheets, the fact remained that one of life's great luxuries was the use of brand-new, perfectly clean sheets, and the same went for towels. Technology also made it possible for sheets and towels to be self-cleaning, but knowing that the linens you were using for the most intimate of purposes had never been touched by anybody before only added to the sense of luxury.

Umily thanked Ebbler profusely as he took the grav-platter of linens and disappeared into the lift. As soon as she was alone, Umily sagged against the cold, gray wall of the service corridor and pulled out her papers.

Umily's papers were the standard sheaf issued to all members of the household staff, not as fancy or official looking as those possessed by senior staff like Wollard or Glaz, but still superior to the single dull-white rectangles issued to ordinary citizens. Umily's papers were four large sheets of thick, cream-colored parchment. They felt stiff and brittle to the touch, but no matter how hard you tried you could not rip or crease them beyond the three neat folds that allowed them to fit neatly in a pocket or purse.

The front sheet always contained her name and the full formal greeting, updated daily, as well as any news bulletins or personal alerts, printed legibly in a hand that spoke of the dignity of the Palace Koa. Page two was the official schedule of the Jakabitus family and the palace staff, updated as conditions warranted. Page three held any correspondence, either personal or official. Page four displayed research material, pleasure reading, and other pertinent information.

She turned to page three, scanned the options, and selected the waiting letter from Gint by running her finger along it, as if reading it carefully. The contents of the page faded away, replaced by a page of text rendered in Gint's familiar handwriting.

> Dearest Umily,
>
> How are you?
>
> I know, that's a simple way to start a letter, but I can't think of anything more important. Not a moment goes by that I don't think of you. The fact that I know where you are and what you're doing somehow makes it both better and worse. Every time I see a clock, I calculate for local time and remember the daily schedule at the palace. I can see you

performing your duties in my mind's eye, as clearly as if I were there with you.

I'd rather not tell you about my life since we parted, but you asked, and we swore that we'd never keep secrets.

The war is not as I'd been led to believe, at least not anymore. While it is true that all hostilities are restricted to the surface of one world, Ophion 6, I'd believed it was a war in name only. Because of the huge fortifications that have been built and the power of the weapons both sides have placed in orbit to neutralize those fortifications, I'd thought any organized military action would guarantee unacceptable mutual losses. I was told, as were we all, that until something drastic changed, neither side would dare make a move.

When I arrived at my battalion's outpost everything was as I'd expected. This planet is a scorched, uninhabitable waste, save for the twin lines of entrenched fortifications—one Jakabitus, one Hahn—that run parallel to each other and encircle the planet like a belt.

My new home started long ago as a trench on the border of no-man's-land, but over decades of warfare, it has been widened, deepened, roofed, reinforced, and eventually, carpeted. I was shown to the mess hall, which has wood paneling and a shelf where all of the soldiers in the battalion have their own handcrafted metal cups, engraved with their names. The cups were made out of spent bulk-ammo containers, the very same kind of containers they had bent and welded in their off hours to make the statue of Lady Jakabitus that had won them her favor . . . and my services. A few of the soldiers seemed embarrassed. They merely took up sculpture to pass the time. They didn't expect it to get Her Ladyship's attention, and certainly didn't expect her to be touched enough to send one of her kitchen staff to cook for them. They seem like good people, all in all, but they make me terribly uncomfortable. Of course most of them are much taller than me (most people are taller than me), and all of them outweigh me, more because of my lack of muscle then their surplus of it.

I mentioned that they seemed to go through a lot of bulk-ammo. I think my commander could tell I was nervous. She explained that the cups were made from containers of ammo that had become too old to use.

The next day I supervised my first full dinner service for the platoon. I used recipes that Barsparse taught me, and the troops all seemed pleased. I was enthusiastically welcomed and given my own engraved cup, which was kept full of the strongest liquor available until late in the evening.

Then, the Hahn attacked.

I've since learned that our commanders thought we'd be obliterated from orbit if we were ever attacked. They never expected a hundred Hahn soldiers would walk across no-man's-land, enter our trench through the front door, and start beating us physically. They caught us unaware, drunk, and full of heavy food. Those swine had a field day until we finally snapped out of our stupor and mounted a defense.

I'm ashamed to admit that my first instinct was to run, not for cover, but to the kitchen, where I feel like I know what I'm doing. Several of the brutes pursued and cornered me, though luckily it was near the meat carving station. The Hahn didn't know the mistake they'd made. Most military outposts, like most households, rely entirely on bulkfabs for their sustenance. Only the wealthy, the lucky, or their servants, have ever seen an actual kitchen full of kitchen tools, and these men were none of those things.

Please thank Barsparse for encouraging me to work on my knife skills. Ghastly as that sounds, they saved my life.

By the time I had dispatched my attackers, the soldiers out in the mess hall had driven those Hahn jackals back out into no-man's-land. We found no call for celebration though. Several of our number were killed, some apparently beaten to death with their own cups.

That was three days ago, and we have had precious little peace since. The Hahn continue to attack at irregular intervals, but always by the same means. We are overrun by foot soldiers. They use heavy weapons to breach our walls, but they never use them to attack us personally, so our leaders insist that good form prevents us from firing our weapon as a means of defense. The attacks are never enough to destroy us outright. They just weaken us and prevent us from resting. Our commander believes that they are softening us up for a big attack that will wipe us off the map, but that's madness, as such an attack would surely elicit an equally deadly response from Her Ladyship. Indeed, we are told that reinforcements are on their way now. None of us see any sanity in the Hahn's conduct, which is the most frightening part.

Try not to worry about me, Umily. Just know that I long to see you again. I want to spend my life with you, but for now my only goal is to return to you in one piece.

Love always,
Gint

Umily watched the words scroll slowly up the page until they stopped at the end of the letter. When she was done crying, she put her papers away and went back to work.

2.

Wollard walked at his fastest pace, which was barely discernable from his slowest pace. He lived by the rule: *Walk as if you have somewhere to go.*

It was not the only rule he lived by, but it was one of them.

He didn't run, because to run gave the impression that one was running *from* something, and as such, was a form of negativity. Negativity was bad form, for which Wollard had no tolerance.

The daily staff meeting was held in the servants' hall, on the ground floor in what was called *the New Palace.* It was as grand and ornate as any other part of the palace, but was built only a thousand years prior, and as such, it felt immature and inelegant to Wollard compared to *the Old Palace*, where the briefing was to be held in Lady Jakabitus's offices. The Old Palace was essentially a three-hundred-foot-tall cylindrical atrium, with various rooms dispersed around its outer circumference in four rings, spread equally along the four levels of the towering space.

The grand gallery through which Wollard walked was on the ground floor. He navigated around the columns that supported the upper levels like an ant weaving through tree trunks, emerging into the empty expanse in the center of the gallery, pointedly not looking up to see the sunlight streaming in through the rows of ancient windows that towered above his head. To do so might slow his stride, and with Her Ladyship waiting, that would be very bad form indeed.

He mounted the grand escalator, a graceful line of ponderous, polished stone slabs the size of dinner tables. They moved swiftly and silently, via no obvious mechanical means, floating upwards in a lazy spiral, transporting Wollard through the full, dizzying height of the atrium, pausing at each of the three upper levels. To the uninitiated, riding the grand escalator was terrifying. This was a deliberate design decision on the part of the long-dead Jakabitus ancestor who'd ordered its construction. Once you learned to trust that the same invisible forces that moved the slabs also prevented any passengers from falling off, it became a bit easier to relax and enjoy the ride.

Wollard disembarked on the fourth level, near the top of the atrium. After he stepped off the stone slab, it followed a similar lazy spiral, this time descending back to the Grand Gallery below.

He walked past the empty meeting rooms and lesser offices before entering the antechamber to Her Ladyship's primary office. He found his protégée, Phee, awaiting his arrival. Her posture was impeccable, and she was wearing a slim, high-collared black suit with distinctive narrow lapels and cuffs, identical to his. One might expect it to look odd on a woman of her youth, but she seemed utterly relaxed, as if she had been born in her uniform. This pleased Wollard greatly. If the Master of Formalities were to look uncomfortable, it would affect everyone with whom he or she interacted, and to make people uncomfortable was always bad form.

Phee smiled slightly and bowed her head. She was slim, but not tall, so when she bowed she gave Wollard a fine view of the back of her head. Her blonde hair was slicked down exactly like the hair of every other Master of Formalities galaxy-wide. She said, "Wollard. I greeted Her Ladyship and her guest as you requested. They've been inside for less than five minutes. I suspect the briefing has only just begun."

"Splendid, Phee. Thank you," Wollard said, returning her nod. He glanced at the wallpaper.

An undetectable coating of nano-engineered machines called *utilitics* coated every surface of the palace, both inside and out. Each utilitic was designed to perform a specific task, but all bore limited computational power. As they were mixed so evenly, cooperated so effectively, and coated the palace so thoroughly, they made the palace, essentially, a gigantic self-maintaining computer. The utilitics' ability to clean surfaces and repair microscopic damage to the structures they covered was one of the principal reasons for the palace's greatly streamlined maintenance staff. The coating also ensured that every flat surface in the palace was usable as a display, meaning that such details as the wallpaper patterns could change, not only to reflect the changing seasons and time of day, but (thanks to the intervention of a skilled artist who worked somewhere in the palace's new addition) the fluctuations of Her Ladyship's mood. Most importantly to Wollard, the décor in this antechamber was tied to the décor in Her Ladyship's office suite, allowing him to judge Her Ladyship's mental state before entering.

This morning, the wallpaper was a repeating pattern of flowers, stippled with what appeared to be rampant birds of prey.

All in all, a mixed bag, he thought.

Wollard paused in front of the office door and glanced back at Phee, who was waiting for him to ask her a question before offering the answer, which was usually good form, but not in this case. This was excusable. She was young, and the Formalities were complex.

Wollard turned, his hands still on the door, and looked at Phee. "With whom is Her Ladyship meeting?"

Phee shrank, realizing she should have offered the information. "I'm sorry, Wollard. Her Ladyship is with The Weeper."

Wollard stiffened. He didn't want to delay joining the briefing, but this infraction made it necessary. Phee shrank even more and looked at her feet. To her credit, she said nothing.

"*Who* is with Her Ladyship?"

Phee winced and said, "The supreme commander of Her Ladyship's armed forces, General Kriz."

Wollard said, "Better. I know that you are from off-world, as am I. And I know that on other worlds, and even in the less respectful quarters of this world, certain members of the ruling class are called by names their parents never intended, but we who tend to the Formalities do not use those other names. Is that clear?"

"Yes, Wollard."

"Good, and while we're discussing it, the fact that General Kriz was with Her Ladyship is information one might have chosen to offer, rather than waiting to be asked. After all, if I hadn't known that Her Ladyship was meeting with a representative of her military, and thought to ask which representative it was, his presence might have come as a complete surprise."

"Yes, Wollard. I see that."

"Good." Wollard turned back to the door, made sure his suit was straight, then added, "Now come along. As always, stand behind me and have your papers ready. You may need to refer to them or take notes."

As Phee was standing behind Wollard, she did not bother to hide her relief. As Wollard's back was to Phee, he did not bother to hide his smile.

Without any additional delay, he pushed the doors open and entered.

As was befitting of her post as the sole ruler of one of the galaxy's more influential planets, Lady Jakabitus's office was larger than many entire buildings. Just beyond the center of the room stood Lady Jakabitus's desk, which itself was larger than most offices. Behind the desk, Lady Jakabitus stood across from a general who was larger than most desks. The general was a precariously balanced slab of muscle and scar tissue draped with a dizzying tangle of medals, braids, and buttons. Lady Jakabitus herself was petite but solid. Her jet-black hair was pulled back in a style that somehow managed to look elaborate despite being, essentially, a bun. Because of the early start and short notice, she was dressed for work in her least formal uniform. Her shoulders bore the barest hints of golden epaulets. The front of her jacket was cunningly designed to suggest aglets and brass hardware without any of those items actually being present. She was, in truth, the least ornamented thing in the room, as the truly important things usually are. That said, she was always dressed well, because she understood that certain standards needed to be upheld. Even her most impromptu and informal meeting was still an audience with the ruler of a planet.

Behind her, a bank of floor-to-ceiling windows offered a stunning view of the capital city of Koa, as seen from the very tip of the Old Palace tower. The walls on either side of the office were usually decorated with immense framed paintings depicting great moments in the history of the planet Apios, as well as notable members of the Jakabitus family, stretching all the way back to the original Terran Jakabituses, who had cemented the family's claim to rule Apios by funding the initial colonists. For this briefing the frames had been repurposed through the use of utilitics to display real-time feeds of Her Ladyship's generals and ministers, all who might have information to share, or a need to hear that information. The surface of the desk displayed a tactical map of the disputed world, Ophion 6.

The war had been a fact of life for generations—so long that few people could say why it had started in the first place and even fewer held out hope that it would end within their lifetime. Lady Jakabitus and her generals did not have the luxury of such pessimism. They were in charge of the war effort, which meant they worked each day to bring it infinitesimally closer to a successful end, or at least to keep an ignominious end at bay.

"Conventional wisdom holds that our orbital weapon platforms and automated defenses have rendered direct, manual violence obsolete," General Kriz said. "As such, it is the one form of military action for which we are not prepared."

"And the Hahn have exploited that weakness," Lady Jakabitus said, nodding to Wollard as he approached the desk, followed by Phee.

"Yes. They breached the frontier zones in numerous places, infiltrating our forward installations unannounced and engaging our soldiers in undignified close-quarters combat."

Lady Jakabitus studied the general for a moment, then asked, "And what have we done to eliminate that weakness? Surely our defenses have been recalibrated to fend off these incursions."

General Kriz said, "That approach has certain challenges. Our airborne weapons can level buildings and render large areas uninhabitable. Our ground-based weapon systems are designed to repel an air attack. Neither is effective against a small group of unarmed soldiers, unless those soldiers are launched through the air somehow. We weren't prepared for the Hahn to simply walk over and physically attack us man to man. In a sense, the war has grown too civilized for that."

Lady Jakabitus frowned at the tactical map, lost in thought. Kriz and Wollard both had the good judgment not to interrupt.

"We could retaliate by reducing one of their bunkers to ashes," she said, "along with all the soldiers inside. Or we could just vaporize their next raiding party. It's a hateful thing to even consider, but it would deter them from further attacks."

Wollard cleared his throat and said, "It might indeed; however, there would be a price to pay for such a response. The Hahn would undoubtedly claim the reaction was disproportionate to their action, giving them the rights of the aggrieved party. Form would dictate that they respond by destroying one of our installations, and as our position is that we are the wronged party, we would be forced to destroy another of theirs. Of course, one side or the other would be forced to see reason and stop this chain of events before all life on the planet is destroyed. Sadly, if the Hahn were well known for seeing reason, we would likely not be having this discussion. Many of the ruling houses would take our side, but many would not, and in the end House Jakabitus would lose face, if not the entire war."

Lady Jakabitus nodded. "You're right, of course. I had to consider it, though."

Wollard bowed slightly. "Of course, Milady."

Lady Jakabitus stared down at the map, and Wollard took the opportunity to check on Phee, who was looking at her papers. She quickly glanced up to show that she was paying attention to the meeting.

"All right," Lady Jakabitus said. "Aerial bombardment is out. How do we defend ourselves, General?"

"That's where the news gets better. While our soldiers are not currently as well trained in hand-to-hand combat as we would like, it would appear that the Hahn aren't adept at it either. Their technique is haphazard, and their discipline is lacking."

"Are you saying that the Hahn are using a method of attack for which they themselves are not well prepared?"

"So it would appear. That means that the skirmishes almost always devolve into a combination of grappling and wrestling. When that happens, our soldiers are invariably on their own home turf, which, combined with their experience with sports, gives them an edge. As such, Hahn casualties have been consistently higher than ours."

"What are the losses?" Lady Jakabitus asked.

General Kriz exhaled, paused, and inhaled. "Milady, it has been one day since the Hahn began their irrational offensive. In that time we have lost three hundred and twenty-three soldiers, and the Hahn have sacrificed five hundred and thirty-one."

A single tear rolled down Kriz's cheek as he delivered the figures. Wollard turned to make eye contact with Phee. He didn't approve of referring to Kriz as *The Weeper*, but he understood how the name had been earned. To Wollard's disappointment, he found Phee with her quill out, writing something in her papers.

"Terrible," Lady Jakabitus said. "More than we've lost in decades to this ridiculous stalemate." She paused for a moment, then turned to Wollard, her eyes wide. "Gint!"

"Yes," Wollard said.

"I sent him to the front."

"You had no idea how dangerous it would be, Milady."

"We have to get him out of there," Lady Jakabitus said.

"A tempting idea, to be sure," Wollard said. "But think of the message it would send. You would, essentially, be telling the very soldiers you were trying to honor that their reward is being rescinded because it's exposing someone you know personally to the exact danger you expect them to endure."

"I'm afraid I agree," Kriz said, "but I shouldn't be too worried for the boy. When taken as a percentage of the forces we have on the ground, our losses have been quite manageable. Besides, the Hahn have lost nearly twice as many soldiers as we have." Kriz's voice was stern and composed, but tears continued to trail down his cheeks, just as they did whenever he discussed fatalities on either side of the conflict. "We've already begun enhanced training, and with your permission, we'd like to enact the emergency loss-retardant measures our research branch created."

"Of course," Lady Jakabitus said. "It's just so utterly senseless. Why would the Hahn persist when it's costing them so dearly?"

Kriz smiled. "It's cost them more than you know, Milady. I didn't come here to deliver statistics. I have good news as well—news I wanted to tell you in person. For reasons that are beyond my understanding, one of the incursions was led personally by a member of the Hahn ruling family. We managed to capture that Hahn alive, along with one of his personal servants."

"We've captured a Hahn?" Lady Jakabitus asked, astounded.

Wollard heard Phee's papers shuffling behind him. He expected that she was looking up the protocol for such an event. He lifted his papers to do the same.

"Yes, Milady," Kriz said. "Hennik Hahn, the son of the undisputed ruler of the Hahn home world, Lord Kamar Hahn, and his spouse, Inmu Hahn. The prisoner is also, as you know, the brother of the leader of all Hahn armed forces, Shimlish Hahn, popularly known as *Shimlish the Pig*."

"I still can't fathom making your teenage daughter fight in a war, let alone as the commander of your entire military," Lady Jakabitus said. "It's horrific."

"What can I tell you, Milady? They're our enemies for a reason."

"Are there any other offspring?" Lady Jakabitus asked.

"No, just Hennik and his sister."

"Kamar Hahn's only son," Lady Jakabitus said quietly, while looking at the far wall. She was mostly saying it out loud to make sure she understood what she'd heard. "And we have him. This is great news."

Kriz agreed. "Yes. The boy could be a powerful tool. We could use him to end the current violence, maybe the entire war."

"How?" Lady Jakabitus asked.

"Well, there are various options, Milady." General Kriz took out his own papers to refer to what was clearly a prepared list.

"I bring these first few up only so you can dismiss them," Kriz said. "That way, you can later say you honestly considered all of the options. A few of my more reactionary commanders have suggested that we could retaliate for the Hahn's recent uncivilized attacks by taking it out on the boy and his servant, then sending their remains back to Kamar Hahn."

Wollard looked to Kriz's eyes. No tears, which was good. He didn't seriously hope for the indecorous plan to be approved.

"Why would we do that?"

"It's thought that it would send a message, Milady."

Wollard shook his head so subtly that the gesture was obvious to all who could see him. "Undoubtedly it would, and the choice is yours to make, Your Ladyship, but I know you don't need to be reminded that it would have serious ramifications. Perception of House Jakabitus could be seriously damaged. Such a message reaches not only one's enemies, but one's allies as well."

Lady Jakabitus said, "Of course that's true, Wollard. And what if the Hahn failed to get *the message*?"

"Then we're back where we started," General Kriz said. "A plan like this is sort of a one-shot deal, Your Ladyship."

"All right," Lady Jakabitus said, "I've considered that proposal, and am rejecting it. Next idea?"

"It's a modification of the first idea. We'd avoid the all-or-nothing nature of the first proposal by sending a substantial portion of the boy back to the Hahn. That way, we'd have more portions to send if—"

"I reject that proposal as well," she said before he could continue.

"The next proposal stipulates that we start with the servant—"

Lady Jakabitus waved her hand dismissively. "I hereby formally reject any proposal that calls for the murder or mutilation of the boy or his servant. We are not savages, General. Is that clear?"

"Indeed, Milady. All options that involve harming the boy or his servant are off the table."

"Good."

Kriz took a moment to skip a great many lines down in his list, then said, "We could keep the lad and his servant in a safe secure location, then lie to the Hahn and tell them that we've killed—"

Lady Jakabitus said, "General!"

Kriz cringed, crumpling his papers slightly. The instant his hands unclenched, any creases they'd left in the papers smoothed out, seemingly on their own. The days of objects becoming worn with age were long past. Of course, some items were allowed to remain worn simply to remind people of their age. Those items were rare, and the majority of them were located in the Palace.

Wollard coughed, theatrically. He would never interrupt Lady Jakabitus or the general, but to divert their attention now, when they were interrupting each other, could defuse the situation, and as such, was perfectly acceptable.

"If I may interject," Wollard said, folding his papers and tucking them in his pocket. "I have a suggestion, one supported by multiple precedents, which may end the active hostilities on Ophion 6, ensure the safety of both the Hahn boy and his servant, and send the message we want to send—both to the Hahn and to the other great houses."

Wollard glanced at Phee, who had been scanning the same list of protocols he had, and judging by the amazed look on her face, had recognized the same possibility. This was not a surprise. Phee was a very fast reader, which was a necessary skill for any Master of Formalities.

"What is it, Wollard?" Lady Jakabitus asked. "What is your suggestion?" Now that she had officially asked, he could continue, but he'd need to choose his words carefully.

3.

Over an hour later, the doors to Lady Jakabitus's office swung open as Phee and Wollard walked backward out of the room.

"Yes, Milady," Wollard said, bowing. "I will begin making the arrangements."

"Thank you, Wollard, and please tell Frederain to come see me. He should hear this news directly from me."

Wollard stopped at the door's threshold. "Indeed, Milady. His Lordship will be in the training room, preparing Master Rayzo for his sports meet this afternoon. I'm certain His Lordship will ask if you plan to attend.

"Please tell him I cannot, Wollard."

"Of course, Your Ladyship. I understand, but His Lordship will be disappointed."

"I know," Lady Jakabitus said, "but I can't bear to watch Rayzo compete. I just feel so . . ." She trailed off, trying to find a word that would be neither insulting nor dishonest. Eventually she settled on, "Embarrassed." She did not look happy with her choice.

"I understand, Milady."

"Thank you, Wollard."

Wollard stepped backward over the threshold. The door swung shut, and he turned to face Phee, who could finally drop her carefully curated façade. She looked amazed.

"She's going to do it!" Phee gasped.

"So it would seem," Wollard replied.

"This is tremendous!"

"Potentially," Wollard allowed. He walked out of the vestibule at his usual pace. Phee had to rush to keep up.

"Wollard, you may have just ended the war."

"No, Phee," Wollard said as he stepped onto the escalator for the trip back to the tower's lower levels. "I did nothing of the kind. Her Ladyship may well have just ended the war. I merely suggested a possible course of action that would allow House Jakabitus to make the best of this situation without breaching etiquette."

"Of course, there was no way that Lady Jakabitus would have ordered the Hahn boy's death."

"I sincerely doubt it."

"If she had harmed him, it would have been a disaster."

"Most likely, both in the long run for House Jakabitus, and in the short term for the Hahn boy."

Phee said, "You were wise to let Lady Jakabitus dismiss General Kriz's suggestion about harming the boy on her own. Of course she knew that she couldn't do such a thing."

Wollard looked at her, but said nothing.

They reached the circular promenade that formed the tower's second level and disembarked. Phee had assumed that they were going to the training room, as they'd told Her Ladyship, and was unprepared when Wollard abruptly stopped walking. Phee took two full steps before she noticed, then stopped and turned to see why her mentor was no longer beside her.

Wollard stepped toward the nearest door, which led to the library.

He opened it and said, "Phee, would you please step in here for just a moment?"

Phee's cheeks blazed a bright red as she walked into the library. Wollard followed her in, closing the door behind him.

The library was, like all of the rooms in the palace, so ornate as to overwhelm the senses. When decorating a room, it was commonly agreed in Apiosan society that adding no decorative detail gave the impression of a deliberate choice to avoid ornamentation. Adding a little gave the impression that a little ornamentation was all the builders could afford. Adding too much made a room feel cheap and desperate. Adding four times that amount created the overall aesthetic effect achieved in the palace. The grand-scale, extravagant design and opulent finishes were taken to such an excessive degree and applied so uniformly to every surface that one simply stopped noticing it, perceiving it as an extremely fancy shade of beige.

The library was a large room filled with comfortable chairs, many of which were astonishingly old and valuable, and bookcases made of rare, exquisitely carved wood. The leather-bound paper books that lined the shelves were all far too valuable to risk damaging by putting them to their intended use.

Wollard loved the library. It was the perfect place to have stern discussions with his protégée. It reminded her of the amazing history and importance of their post, the incredible privilege they had in executing that post, and it also had the advantage of being private, as nobody else seemed to remember it was there.

Wollard said, "Phee, I am displeased."

Phee blanched as if she had been struck. "Wollard, I'm sorry! What have I done to displease you?"

"To start with the most recent incident, what did you just say?"

"That I'm sorry?"

"Just before that."

"I said that you were wise to let General Kriz make his suggestions."

"Wise because?"

"Because Her Ladyship knew . . ." Phee trailed off, seeing her error.

Wollard stepped forward and lowered his voice. "You said that Lady Jakabitus couldn't do a thing. Do we ever tell anyone that she or he cannot do a thing?"

Phee said, "No."

"Are you telling my shoes, or are you telling me?"

Phee looked into Wollard's eyes. "No, Wollard. We never tell anyone that she or he cannot do a thing."

"Why not?"

Phee recited the most basic yet crucial tenet for a Master of Formalities, passed down by the Arbiters from when the great houses had first agreed to Arbitration. "Because anyone is free to attempt anything, as long as she or he is willing to accept the consequences."

"And what is the duty of a Master of Formalities?"

"To inform those around us of what those consequences will be, and at times, to suggest a course of action that will be less . . . consequential?"

She knew all of this, of course, but she was flustered, and everyone needed a reminder from time to time.

Wollard said, "I would have said *damaging,* but the point stands." He turned his back and pretended to study the spines of some books on a shelf, but Phee had his undivided attention, whether he was looking at her or not.

"We deal in etiquette, Phee. We see to it that proper form is maintained and the Formalities are respected. Why is etiquette important?"

"Because it maintains civility, making it possible for people from different worlds to interact with a minimum of unnecessary conflict."

"No," Wollard said. "That is what etiquette *does.* Why is it important?"

Phee felt a renewed pang of embarrassment when she realized what Wollard was getting at. "Because everyone agrees that it is."

"Yes," Wollard said, turning to face Phee. "The only reason etiquette is important is that everybody has agreed it is important. Would it have been difficult for Lady Jakabitus to have Master Hennik Hahn killed?"

"No, Wollard."

"Correct. It would have been trivially easy. She could have said a word, and it would have been done. Of course, she wouldn't have. We are fortunate, Phee. Lady Jakabitus is a genuinely decent person. Not every Master of Formalities is so lucky. I hope you don't learn that the hard way when you move on to your own assignment. My point is: the people we deal with have real power. Those kinds of people don't react well to being told that they can't do things. If you tell the ruler of a world that she can't do something, she may well do it just to show everyone, including herself, that she can."

Wollard studied Phee. She looked mortified, as well she should. Here she was, a protégée in one of the great houses of the galaxy, and her mentor had to reexplain the basic facts of their profession to her.

Wollard took a breath and softened his tone. "Phee, it was long ago that the great houses agreed to Arbitration and created the Arbiters, who in turn created the Masters of Formalities. The cultures of the different worlds had grown so distinct that interplanetary communication was becoming impossible. Our job was to keep them from offending one another in order to prevent pointless conflict. We may have broadened our scope a bit since then, but that is still the core of our job, and we do it solely by talking to our leaders. If we ever give them a reason to stop listening to us, we're finished. Understand?"

"Yes, Wollard."

"Good. While we're discussing the importance of listening, I noticed how enthralled you were in your papers during the early portion of the briefing. Were you tracking down some interesting historical precedent that I may have missed?"

"No, Wollard. I mean, yes, I was trying to find precedents, but I found none."

"When I first noticed that you were preoccupied, General Kriz had not yet told us about the capture of young Hennik Hahn."

Phee said nothing.

"So, for you to be searching for precedents would itself be rather . . ." Wollard paused and leaned in toward Phee. "Unprecedented."

Wollard was quite pleased with this little joke. Phee showed no sign of amusement, which made it even more amusing for him. He was not a cruel man, but when he knew the person he was observing would come out unscathed, he had no qualms about enjoying her discomfort.

"One might have thought that you were reading some sort of personal correspondence during an official briefing, which would be quite bad form indeed."

"That's not possible," Phee said, with weakly feigned confidence. "All of my correspondence filters through you. You'd know if I'd received a message, and if I'd read it."

It was true. Wollard couldn't read her messages, but as her mentor he was alerted whenever she received and read a message. The mentor/protégée relationship wasn't meant to rob the protégée of privacy, but it did damage his or her autonomy.

"Of course. And I know that you would not have been reading an official message during an official briefing. I wouldn't be wasting my time mentoring you if you weren't smarter than that."

There was a silent moment while Phee tried to figure out how to respond. Finally she said, "Thank you, Wollard."

"You're most welcome."

They stood looking at each other for a long moment. Phee was mortified and was having difficulty hiding it. Wollard was enjoying himself and also having difficulty hiding it.

"You know," Wollard said, "there is a rumor, one that has never been officially verified, that it's possible for protégées to send and receive short, informal messages to one another without their mentors being alerted."

Wollard watched the color drain from Phee's face once again.

"It seems one protégée can edit another's official curriculum vitae, causing the second protégée to receive an alert, which is not shared with their mentors. These minor edits can be approved or rejected, allowing two or more protégées to effectively have a remote conversation in real time without supervision. It's a nasty little flaw in the system that the Arbiters have not seen fit to repair, but if a protégée is caught letting the abuse of this flaw interfere with his, or *her* official duties, the ramifications could be most severe."

Wollard stared down at Phee, who was pointedly staring anywhere but back at him. He thought, *Every generation believes that they are the first to ever misbehave. They don't understand that the reason their less-honorable activities upset we who are older is that we know from experience where those actions may lead.*

Wollard made a deliberate effort to give his voice a bouncy, non-threatening tone. "So, hypothetically speaking, might the person with whom I'm certain you weren't communicating be the same person with whom you've never confirmed or denied having a romantic relationship at the Academy of Arbitration? I believe this individual's name may or may not have been Keln."

After a short pause, Phee said, "If such a person existed, they could be someone with whom I might chose to communicate."

Wollard nodded. "Ah, I see. Or not. And, if such a person existed, would he or she understand that when you both graduated from the academy you forswore any future romantic relationships, as such an entanglement would inevitably result in a Master of Formalities having greater loyalty to his or her partner than to the ruler with whom he or she works?"

"Keln knows—" Phee stopped herself, then said, "That hypothertical person would know that."

Wollard said, "To know and to understand are not the same thing."

Phee looked Wollard in the eye and said, "*I* understand that."

The frustration in her voice and the emphasis she'd put on the word *I* told Wollard the whole story. "Ah, I see. One person doesn't have the strength of will to stop contacting a second person, and the second person has enough strength to not initiate contact, but not quite enough to ignore the first person's overtures. Do you also understand that such a situation will only become more painful the longer it persists?"

"I'm beginning to."

"And do you comprehend how much you have to lose, Phee? Apios is the most influential world in this sector, arguably in several sectors. Her bulk farms supplement the supplies of countless worlds. Lady Jakabitus is the unquestioned ruler of Apios, I am her Master of Formalities, and you are my protégé, for the moment."

Phee stiffened, then looked up at Wollard and asked, "Sir, am I to be rebuked?"

Wollard laughed, which didn't reduce her tension. Then he put a hand on her shoulder, which did.

"Of course not, Phee. That would be a punishment far greater than the crime of which you have not even been formally accused. You won't be reprimanded either. I don't even intend to note this conversation in the log. I am only trying to impress you with the importance of being attentive and undistracted whenever dealing with others. Looking up precedents, consulting the Formalities, and referring to related correspondence are all acceptable uses of your papers in a meeting. Anything else is bad form, and if we don't adhere to the Formalities, how can we expect others to?"

4.

His Lordship Frederain Jakabitus sat in his customary ringside seat in the gymnasium, where his only son, Rayzo, was training for his sports meet that afternoon. The meet meant that this day's practice was more important than most, but it made no difference in Frederain's demeanor. Rayzo was the most important thing in the galaxy to him, and he took a keen interest in his training.

"Come on, boy! You must be better than this! Pitiful! You look pitiful!"

The palace training facility was absolutely state of the art, but the game that the Apiosans had dubbed *sports* was, in fact, fairly primitive.

The room had long ago served as the palace's formal dining hall, and was still ornately decorated around the edges. In the middle, there was a large circle, meant to simulate a sports arena. A protective railing surrounded the sports mat—a raised, padded, circular platform with a five-foot gutter between it and the row of seats for any spectators who might be present. The mat was painted with three concentric rings, and several lines radiated out from the center.

In the middle of the mat, Hartchar stood in her light, loose-fitting training attire, her red hair tied back in a long ponytail. One of her feet was planted firmly on the mat; the other was planted on Rayzo's throat.

She looked down at him impassively, watching as the boy, who was pinned on his back, failed to escape despite his squirming.

Rayzo was young and was not blessed with a large frame, but his physique showed that he spent a great deal of time training, not that it was helping him at the moment. His black hair was saturated with sweat. He wore only a pair of shorts, which were emblazoned on both the front and back with a prominent number one. Rayzo switched tactics and grabbed Hartchar's ankle with both hands, trying to shift her foot with all his might. Then he kicked his legs wildly, trying to gain some leverage. It was all to no avail; she didn't move an inch, and neither did he.

"Pitiful!" Frederain shouted again, through his prodigious moustache. He rose from his seat and leaned his ample, middle-aged bulk over the railing to get his head closer to his son. "I refuse to believe this is the best you can do. A boy your age, this is pathetic!"

Rayzo looked away from Hartchar's calf, casting a glance at his bellowing father.

Frederain continued, "When I was fourteen, I could have cast her into the gutter long ago!"

Hartchar shifted her gaze to His Lordship as well.

"You're a Jakabitus!" Frederain shouted to the boy. "Act like it!"

"Pardon me, Your Lordship," Wollard said. He and Phee had entered the room unnoticed.

Lord Jakabitus stopped midshout and sagged back down into his seat. He was not an old man, but he was neither as young nor as energetic as he claimed to have once been, and the exertion of Rayzo's training had taken its toll. His uniform was askew, and his thinning black and gray hair and sizeable all-black moustache were disheveled, though not as disheveled as his son's hair.

"Ah, good morning, Wollard," Lord Jakabitus said.

"Good morning, Milord. I trust Master Rayzo's training is going well."

Lord Jakabitus leaned closer to Wollard and lowered his voice, lest Rayzo overhear. "Yes, the boy's doing well."

"Good," Wollard said. He lowered his voice as well, but made a point of smiling broadly to increase Rayzo's chances of sensing the congenial tone of the conversation. "Here's hoping that his hard work pays off at the sports meet."

Lord Frederain Jakabitus raised his voice back to a normal level. "Yes, I certainly hope he does well. We have a prophecy to fulfill."

"Indeed," Wollard said.

"So, what can I do for you, Wollard?"

Wollard braced himself. "Her Ladyship has requested that you come to her office as soon as possible."

"Fine. Tell her I'll be there after practice." Lord Jakabitus turned back to the mat. "Come on, boy! Do something! Anything! I mean, really . . . well, not that! That didn't work before, why would it work now? Think!"

Wollard coughed, then said, "My apologies, Your Lordship, but Lady Jakabitus was quite clear that you should come as soon as possible."

"Was she?"

"Yes, Milord."

Lord Jakabitus watched his son writhe beneath his trainer's heel for another moment, groaning halfheartedly when Rayzo's next bid for freedom failed.

"I promise, Milord, it is a matter of highest importance," Wollard assured him.

"So is this. Joanadie should remember that this is her son's life I'm supervising here. And it looks," he added loudly, "like he's going to spend that life entirely under Hartchar's right foot!"

Wollard and Phee exchanged a quick look, then Wollard leaned down to speak quietly to Lord Jakabitus.

"Milord, the topic Her Ladyship wishes to discuss involves your son."

"Does it?" His Lordship asked, interested.

"Indeed, Milord."

Lord Jakabitus stood up, smoothing the material and straightening the epaulettes of his formal training attire. "Well, that's good. Nice to see her taking an interest. Perhaps she'll even attend the sports meet today."

"Perhaps," Wollard said, "but one shouldn't get his hopes up, I'm afraid. I believe the implications of the topic Her Ladyship wishes to discuss are a bit more long-term in nature."

"I see. Well, off I go. Mustn't keep Joanadie waiting. Wollard, may I ask a favor?"

"Always, Milord."

"Rayzo's training is going to go on a bit longer. Will you stay and shout encouragement at him, you know, like I always do?"

"I'll do my best, Milord."

"Thank you, my friend." Lord Jakabitus turned back to Rayzo and Hartchar. Neither of their situations had changed.

"Boy, I'm afraid I have to go. Wollard has agreed to take over for me. I'll see you at lunch, and don't worry—if you're not there, I'll tell Barsparse that you'll be taking all your future meals under Hartchar's instep!"

Lord Jakabitus left. Phee turned to Wollard.

"I know, Phee, but I assure you, I did not lie to His Lordship," Wollard said in a hushed tone. "The matter Her Ladyship wishes to discuss *does* directly involve their son."

"Yes, Wollard, I quite agree. That was very well handled on your part. I'm just looking forward to watching you *encourage* Master Rayzo in His Lordship's stead."

"Yes," Wollard said. "I did tell His Lordship that I would, didn't I?"

"Indeed you did!"

Wollard smiled in spite of himself. Knowing what he had recently put Phee through, he didn't blame her for enjoying his discomfort. In fact, he was more than a little pleased that she seemed to have shaken it off instead of dwelling on her embarrassment.

Wollard took a deep breath, faced Master Rayzo, who was still struggling fruitlessly, and said, "I must say, Master Rayzo, that seems a difficult predicament!

"Yes! Yes, um, try pushing her ankle the other direction," Wollard continued after a moment. "That might . . . oh, no it did not. It very much did not. Apologies, Master Rayzo. Take heart, you will emerge from this trial a stronger person, I guarantee it!"

On the mat, Rayzo's head turned away from Hartchar's lower leg, his gaze seeking out Wollard. Wollard worried that he was being a distraction, but he had agreed to fill in for His Lordship, and a Master of Formalities must keep his word. Rayzo's eyes then shifted to the door.

"I must admit," Wollard said, "I would fare no better were I in your shoes, or—in this case—under Hartchar's shoe."

Wollard became aware of the sound of feminine laughter. He looked at Phee, but she was containing her mirth, if just barely. Shly, the deliverer of liquid refreshment, had appeared beside Phee and was holding her small silver grav-platter, her portable bulkfab, and several empty glasses. Wollard noted with satisfaction that Shly's high degree of training was asserting itself. Neither the tray nor the beverage was moving in the slightest, despite the fact that she was convulsing noticeably with laughter.

"Phee," Wollard said, "you take over for a moment, but bear in mind the dignity of our post."

Phee winced but did as she was told. "Master Rayzo," she shouted, "you are displaying great endurance! That is to be commended!"

"Can we be of any assistance, Shly?" Wollard asked.

"I hope so, Wollard. I'm here with Lord Jakabitus's post-training restorative beverage. Encouraging Master Rayzo always leaves him parched, but I see that His Lordship is not here."

Lord Jakabitus liked to finish every training session with a glass of a specific concoction of his own devising. It was a unique blend of fruit juices, electrolytes, and mild intoxicants that helped him recover, physically and mentally, from the rigors of Rayzo's training.

Rayzo drank water, as per His Lordship's orders.

"Your current course of action seems ineffective," Phee called out helpfully. "A change of strategy is crucial!"

Rayzo struggled with Hartchar's foot, but his eyes were locked on Shly, and had been since she entered the room.

Phee continued, "I would point out that Hartchar's weight is not evenly distributed between her feet at the moment! Perhaps that can be used to your advantage."

It was enough to transfer Rayzo's attention from Shly to Phee, then up to Hartchar.

Hartchar shot Phee a quick smile. Then Rayzo's hands pulled at the knee of her weight-bearing, non-throat-crushing leg, causing it to buckle. Hartchar rolled gracefully and sprung right back up, ready to attack, but Rayzo had already regained his feet and adopted a defensive posture.

"Well done, Master Rayzo," Hartchar said. "Now you know how to get out of that problem. You made the classic error of trying to attack the foot I was using to hold you down. Remember, strike your opponents where they are weak, and they will seldom use their weaknesses as a weapon."

They circled each other warily, Rayzo dividing his attention equally between Hartchar across the mat from him and Shly standing behind the rail.

Shly pointedly kept her attention focused on Wollard.

"Do you know where His Lordship has gone?" Shly asked.

"Yes, I apologize, Shly. I became distracted. His Lordship is on his way to Lady Jakabitus's offices. Her Ladyship and His Lordship have important business to discuss. I doubt you can beat him there, even if you use the servant's lift, but you may yet reach him before their meeting gets started."

Shly curtseyed. "Thank you, Wollard. Phee." She nodded to Phee. Before moving to leave, she glanced at the mat, where Rayzo was standing in a posture designed to both help fend off Hartchar and look as manly as possible from Shly's point of view. He glanced over to see if Shly had noticed him, then promptly looked away to hide the fact that he had noticed her. His attention refocused on the empty space where Hartchar had been standing, but it was too late. His legs were swept out from under him and he was plummeting face-first toward the mat. The air was forced from his lungs as he hit the ground. He immediately felt the familiar pressure of Hartchar's foot, this time pressing against the back of his neck.

"There, Master Rayzo," Hartchar said. "You're pinned again, this time facedown. What now?"

Rayzo looked at Shly, who was looking back. Without comment, she silently turned and carried her drink tray to the exit.

"One might have predicted that, Master Rayzo," Phee yelled, "but there's little to be done for it now! What's past is past!"

5.

As with the servants' hall and every other part of the palace, the kitchen was designed for a bygone era when a far larger staff was needed to fulfill the needs of the ruling family. It was a cavernous space, the mirror opposite of the servants' hall. Every surface was covered in gleaming tile and filled with shining cooking apparatuses. The vast space echoed with the busy sounds of two chefs working.

Much of the equipment was seldom used; in fact, the majority was never used. One small corner of the room contained the tiny fraction of the devices that saw regular use. There, amid clouds of steam, waves of heat, and flashing knives, Chef Barsparse and Sous Chef Pitt were preparing the ruling family's lunch. Nearby, grav-platter at the ready, Ebbler watched in rapt attention, waiting to do his part.

Shly entered, stopped next to Ebbler, and said, "Pardon me, Chef?"

Barsparse continued stirring a pot with one hand and shaking a pan with another. She didn't look up, but said, "Yes?"

"Her Ladyship has requested that you meet with Wollard at the soonest opportunity."

"About?" The question was brusque and direct, but Shly knew that Barsparse was not a rude person, just busy.

Shly said, "It's not for me to say."

Barsparse's hands kept moving, but her head swiveled to look at Shly. Pitt stopped chopping whatever root vegetable he was breaking down before doing the same.

"But do you know what it's about?" Barsparse asked.

"I think it has to do with a change in meal arrangements."

Barsparse frowned, but her hands continued working at full efficiency. "The meal arrangements?"

"Yes," Shly said, "And perhaps some sort of feast."

"What makes you say that?"

"Something His Lordship said."

"His Lordship?"

"Yes, you see, I was delivering His Lordship's post-training restorative, but His Lordship wasn't in the gymnasium—"

"It's good that you were there anyway," Ebbler said. "Master Rayzo's training day isn't complete until he's watched you deliver the beverage. How'd he look?"

Shly muttered, "Distracted, as usual," then continued. "His Lordship was meeting with Her Ladyship in her offices, so I followed. They were having a pretty intense conversation. I gave His Lordship his drink, and as I was leaving, His Lordship said, 'If you think this is what's best, it is what we'll do, but I don't know how Rayzo will react. We should tell Barsparse about the change in the meal plan and the feast.' Her Ladyship agreed, and told me to ask you to meet with Wollard."

Barsparse nodded. "Yes," she said, "I'd say your supposition is correct." Her hands were still working furiously, but her face was calm and contemplative now, as if she were already planning the menu for the mysterious feast. Pitt looked angry. He sneered at Shly before shifting his eyes to Barsparse, who merely glanced at the vegetables he was not chopping and raised her eyebrows. Pitt's knife flashed into furious action.

After thanking Shly for the information, Barsparse went back to the work she had never fully left.

Ebbler and Shly watched the chefs work for a moment, then Shly leaned in close to Ebbler and said, "All of this effort, three meals a day, every day. It's a wonder the Jakabituses don't just get their food from bulkfabs, like everybody else."

"All of the ruling families and most of the wealthier Bulk-Barons have chefs, Shly. It's one of the few big luxuries left."

"You've said that before, but I still don't get it. A bulkfab can make any food, or almost anything else you want, and it's the same every time."

"That's the whole point," Ebbler said, his voice raising. "If you order the same dish twice from a bulkfab, it will fabricate the dish identically both times, right down to the molecules. They can give you anything but a surprise. There's no creativity, no insight. Those are things only a real person applying real expertise and real heat to your food can give you."

"But if it's real food they want, why do the chefs use a bulkfab?" Shly asked.

"They only use it to create raw ingredients. That way they know they'll get high-quality stuff. The chefs want to surprise the diners, but they don't want any surprises themselves."

Pitt slammed down his knife. "We don't want to listen to you two yammering all the time either. Unlike you two, our job requires concentration, so shut it!"

Ebbler jerked as if he'd been slapped. Barsparse continued manipulating her pots and pans, but said, "You're right that their conversation isn't particularly productive, Pitt, but if you were really concentrating, Ebbler could shout in your ear and it wouldn't slow you down."

"Yes, Chef," Pitt said. "Sorry, Chef."

"Is there any reason you can't chop while you apologize?"

"No, Chef."

Pitt resumed chopping, glaring at Ebbler between cuts.

6.

The city of Koa's official sports arena was bustling, but that went without saying. The arena bustled every day.

The building itself was a vast, flattened dome, but the traffic patterns around the arena caused disruptions so complete and predictable that a large area around it was referred to with dread as *the Arena District.* Anyone who didn't feel a deep need to get to the arena avoided the entire district as if it were quarantined. There were people who had lived in Koa for decades without ever seeing the arena in person, not because they weren't allowed to go, but because they didn't want to waste the time, exert the effort, or endure the frustration that was part of the admission price of attending a sports meet.

Since only powerfully motivated individuals would brave the Arena District, it was constantly full of powerfully motivated individuals, all trying to achieve the same goal. That might have been productive had they been willing to cooperate, but such was not the case. The men who brought their sons to the arena wanted to get them there before the disqualification cutoff, and if everybody else missed the mark, that was not a bad thing.

If a boy arrived after the cutoff, he couldn't compete, which in turn meant he couldn't improve his standing until the next meet, ten days later.

There were hundreds of sports arenas on Apios, one for every major population center on the planet. Each arena served a specific region, and each region was split up into ten districts, and each district had one meet every ten days. On meet day, registration remained open until eighty percent of the young men who had preregistered arrived, at which point it closed. No exceptions or special cases were made, and lining up in advance was not allowed. If you wanted your son to compete, you had to deposit him at the competitors' entrance as close to (but not before) the opening of the registration period as possible. Thus, the competition began well before the meet started. There was a booming industry in the sale of strategy guides that contained hints as to the best traffic channels to take and landing zones in which to park. Fathers invested considerable resources in selecting the perfect transport, some going so far as to retrofit their conveyance with special equipment to scan for parking or adapt it to be wider and taller, making it easier for them to spot parking places or holes in the traffic while simultaneously making it harder for everyone else.

Like most sports fans, Lord Frederain Jakabitus considered getting to the arena to be a nightmarish grind. Unlike most sports fans, His Lordship was able to avoid the nightmarish grind altogether. He had access to transportation that could fly outside of the legal traffic channels, cut through the channels it couldn't avoid, and deposit him and his son Rayzo directly in front of the competitors' entrance mere seconds after registration had begun.

Frederain stood and watched the boys and young men stream into the arena. He looked down at his son and gave him their standard pep talk.

"Remember, son, do well."

"I will, Father."

"I'm sorry your mother couldn't be here again."

"That's all right, Father."

"No, really, it isn't."

Rayzo peered into the competitors' entrance. Boys as young as ten and as old as nineteen were crowding in. At fourteen, Rayzo was noticeably taller than the smallest competitors, but most of the boys towered over him.

"No, Father, really. I don't mind."

Frederain took his son's head into his hands. "Son, look at me. I need you to understand that you are the most important thing in the world to me."

"I know that, Father."

"And your mother loves you very much. It's just hard to tell sometimes."

"Yes, Father. Because she has to love a whole planet's worth of people."

"Yes." He squeezed Rayzo's head to his chest and said, "Yes, my boy. That's right." Frederain pushed Rayzo's head back again and stared into his eyes.

"Son, you must understand, no matter what happens, no matter how things change, you will always be the most important person in the world to me. Do you understand?"

Rayzo looked more concerned than touched. "Father, what did you and Mother talk about when you left training today?"

"Nothing, Rayzo."

"It must have been important for you to leave practice."

"It was nothing, Rayzo. Nothing important. I'll tell you all about it after the meet. We don't want you to be distracted."

"Distracted by the unimportant nothing," Rayzo said.

"Exactly." Frederain straightened himself and let go of his son's head. "Now, you had better get in there. We don't want you to miss the cutoff."

Rayzo looked again at the torrent of boys entering the arena. It was true that they'd spent longer than usual talking, allowing many other boys to enter in the meantime, but they were early enough that Rayzo had no doubt that he would make it in well before the cutoff, no matter how much he dragged his feet.

Rayzo started to walk away, but stopped when his father said, "Oh, and Rayzo, do well."

Rayzo said, "You already told me to do well, Father."

"And I'll always be here to give you that advice," Frederain said. "Remember that."

Frederain watched as Rayzo disappeared into the throng of boys and young men entering the arena. *Who knows,* Lord Jakabitus thought. *Maybe he'll adapt better than expected.*

Frederain strolled through the crowd to the fathers' entrance. Everybody recognized him, but nobody let on. He was here every ten days, just like they were, and he relished making as little disruption as possible. If Lady Jakabitus appeared in public, it was a spectacle. She stood apart from the people she ruled, even when standing among them. Her Master of Formalities did most of the talking, both for her and her subjects, who were often too awed to speak.

Lord Frederain preferred to think of himself as a man of the people. He did his own talking, and was accompanied only by a distant detail of elite guards who protected him with ruthless efficiency while doing their best to conceal their presence from everyone around them, His Lordship included. Lady Jakabitus's great-great-great-grandfather, Lord Proprion Jakabitus, had instituted the convention that all services rendered to the ruling family would be made to appear as near to invisible as was feasible, and Frederain thanked him for it. He wanted his family's lives to be as normal as possible, and he also treasured the opportunity to know the subjects as they really were.

He found the subjects to be pleasant, deferential, and easily startled.

Frederain joined the other fathers entering the arena and took a moment to enjoy his surroundings. While the competitors' entrance was a rough, Spartan affair, the spectators' entrance was a grand cathedral to the importance and majesty of sport. Vaulted ceilings decorated with murals depicting great moments in the history of sport hung above suspended statues of legendary competitors. In the middle of it all, a bronze plaque on a massive pedestal bore the words of the most important document in sports history, *the prophecy.*

Beneath all this splendor, as progress slowed to an awkward, crowded shuffle, another father recognized His Lordship. To the poor man's horror, Frederain noticed before he could look away.

"Hello, my good man," Frederain said. "Here to watch your son compete, I trust."

"Yes! Yes, Your Lordship!" The man stopped in his tracks, reflexively attempting to bow. The instant he halted his forward shuffle, he was bumped by the man behind him. The bowing man leapt straight up in the air, letting out a staccato yelp. By the time he landed, he was already jabbering.

"His Lordship asked me a question! I've done nothing wrong! Please don't take me!"

The man who had bumped into him looked confused, but then his mind pieced together what it was hearing and registered the sight of Lord Jakabitus. He stopped dead in his tracks and cried out, "Lord . . . er . . . Your Lordship. I'm sorry! I didn't mean to interrupt! Is this man bothering you? Say the word and I'll teach him a lesson. I'm a loyal subject. Loyal!"

"Gentlemen," Lord Jakabitus said, "please relax. I appreciate the sentiment, but I'm just another sports fan like you, here to support my son."

The two men stood in silent horror, not knowing what to say. The three of them had stopped moving forward now, but while most people who held up the line would be abused and trampled, they were left alone. As soon as the fans behind them got within insulting or shoving range, they saw His Lordship and invariably chose to route around the obstruction rather than cause a fuss.

Lord Jakabitus smiled at the two men. They tried to smile back. He laughed. They laughed back at him, then looked at each other and laughed more, then looked back at His Lordship. When they saw that he was no longer laughing, they stopped abruptly.

"Well, we don't want to block traffic," Lord Jakabitus said. "Good luck, gentlemen. It was nice to meet you."

The two men bowed deeply. Lord Jakabitus smiled, turned, and continued into the arena. The two men sagged with relief. Now that His Lordship was no longer standing with them, they were merely an obstruction, and as such, another father who'd only just arrived and hadn't seen His Lordship said, "Oi! Keep moving or—"

The man's voice was silenced midthreat by a black bag that was pulled down roughly over his head. At least three burly, armor-clad arms crossed in front of his torso and pulled him backward, pinning him down to the ground. There was a small, muffled cry as the crowd flowed around the unfortunate man, hiding him from view.

The two men had watched it happen, and were so terrified that didn't even notice that they were clinging to each other like frightened children clutching their favorite stuffed animals.

◆ ◆ ◆

Rayzo and the other competitors formed a single-file line and moved past the registration desk. Their bodies were scanned, their identities were confirmed, and their official standing was calculated. They were issued their regulation sports shorts and led to the changing room.

It was a vast space filled with endless rows of benches and lockers. Each competitor changed out of his normal clothes and into his sports shorts. They were all male, so no accommodation was made for their privacy. They were packed in so tight that their elbows and knees often collided as they changed clothes.

As Rayzo adjusted his shorts, the utilitics synced with the registration database, and his ranking was displayed. In bold, black numerals #5,367 appeared on the front and back of the shorts.

Not bad, he thought. *Nearly halfway through the pack. Considering my age and size, Father should be pleased.*

Once his clothes were stowed and he was clad only in his shorts, as per the rules, Rayzo joined the line to the dispensary, where the competitors finished the solemn premeet ritual by slathering their bare torsos and limbs with the traditional conductive oil.

◆ ◆ ◆

Lord Jakabitus sat in the ruling family's elaborate box. He felt that he was missing a critical part of the experience by not mingling with the other fans, but watching from the box was tradition. It was this sense of tradition that had allowed sports to supplant all other athletic pursuits on Apios, becoming so important to the culture as to subsume the very word *sports* as its name. Besides, he would still get to interact with the common man when Rayzo actually competed. It was only during the other matches that Frederain would be isolated.

From the rulers' box Frederain had a wonderful view of the arena. The floor was a repeating pattern of several hundred luminous white circles. These were the sports mats where the actual sports would take place. Each was rigged with its own lighting and a VIP box, but from this distance all he could see were the glowing circles. The view was both beautiful and dizzying. Spectator seating was arranged around the perimeter of the arena. The distances were so immense that Frederain could not make out individual spectators, just a random wall of muddy, indistinct color, like pixelated noise, except that each pixel was a living person. Only the tracks of the spectator rapid transit system broke the homogenous field of random, moving dots. Once the sports began, fathers would use the system to come to their sons' matches and watch from the mat-side VIP boxes.

Above the mats, there hung an enormous panel. This was *the big screen.* At any given time there were far too many matches going on to follow, and it simply wasn't possible for any one spectator's son to be competing the entire time, so to entertain the spectators an algorithm would select the ongoing match that was statistically most likely to be interesting and show it on the big screen. It was a great honor to have your match displayed. Rayzo had yet to make it to the screen, but Frederain always held out hope.

Using the box's built-in bulkfab, he got some refreshments as he waited for the matches to start. He sipped his sports training beverage and frowned. *It's good enough,* he thought, *but it's better when Shly fabs it for me. Maybe I should bring her with me next time.*

He considered this for a moment, then decided against it, realizing the effect Shly's presence at the arena would likely have on Rayzo's performance.

Soon, the lights dimmed, the crowd hushed, and the big screen displayed the face of an announcer. He was perfectly suited to his audience, good looking and well groomed enough to command the spectator's attention, but not so much as to arouse their jealousy or contempt. The announcer was clearly standing somewhere amidst the mats on the arena floor, but it was impossible to tell where. Despite his improbably shiny suit, he was lost in the pattern of lights.

After reciting the full formal greeting, the announcer moved on to the traditional reading of the prophecy.

This, truth be told, was Frederain's favorite part of the sports meet. He'd always known the prophecy was important, but the words had taken on a deeper meaning now that he was a father. The first time he brought Rayzo to a sports meet, the prophecy had hit him on a deep, instinctual level, and from that day onward, it had never failed to give him goose bumps.

The announcer started with the preamble. It was the same every time, and any person randomly selected from the audience could probably have recited it from memory. Many spoke it under their breath with the announcer, but the only audible sound in the arena was the announcer's voice.

"Long ago," he said, "during the Terran Exodus, mankind spread out into the galaxy, and found countless inhabitable worlds, but no intelligent life with which to share them."

That line always made Frederain a bit uncomfortable. It was consistent with the official history of the galaxy, of course, but the human colonists *had* encountered life. They had simply been left to their own devices to determine whether or not that life was intelligent. Now, thousands of years later, there was reason to suspect that some of the colonists had concluded any life forms that got in the way of heavily armed settlers couldn't really be called *intelligent.*

Frederain put that out of his mind, returning his focus to the announcer.

"One colonial ship landed on Apios. Its survival seemed unlikely, for the winter was harsh, food was scarce, and most of its systems were offline. The colonists huddled together in the hold of their ship with nothing to take their mind off their predicament."

The announcer paused, allowing the crowd to picture the hardships he described before he continued. "Then a simple man named Dilly Glifton, who was blessed with seven children and the gift of prophecy, spoke. Dilly set out the basic rules of what we now call *sports*, and the colonists played sports to pass the time until their food preparation robots and other essential systems could be repaired. As the colonists ate, the navigational systems came back online and showed them that the winter was not as harsh as they'd thought. They'd merely landed on the polar ice cap. Most of the planet was warm and pleasant. As the colonists celebrated, Dilly Glifton stood and uttered this prophecy."

The announcer's image faded from the big screen, replaced with the words of the prophecy.

"Things looked bad, but through sports, we persevered. Now, I deliver unto you my prophecy. We will continue to persevere, and we will continue to play this sport I have invented, for it is a metaphor for our lives. We will fight. We will struggle. And in the end, some of us shall thrive and master this world. Then, one day, there will come a boy. This boy will compete in our new sport. He shall fight. He shall struggle. In time, he shall thrive, and at the age of nineteen he shall stand victorious over all his competitors. He will dominate the sport like none before him. He will be famous, wealthy, and powerful, and his father will be revered above all others, for having created such a glorious son. It will happen. It is the prophecy."

Every spectator, Frederain included, murmured, "It is the prophecy."

7.

With the reciting of the prophecy completed, the sports commenced. Competitors reported to their mats, and their fathers used the spectator rapid transit system. Loud music was piped over speakers, and the big screen displayed various matches in progress.

Hundreds of boys and young men, including Rayzo, stood gathered in the many competitors' lounges—large open rooms next to the arena—wearing their sports shorts, watching the big screen feed, waiting for their turn. At one end of each lounge was a tunnel leading to the arena floor. At seemingly random intervals the music would fade and the announcer would list two numbers and a location. Competitors 3-8-7-2 and 3-8-2-1, report to mat 1-9-3. Repeat: Competitors 3-8-7-2 and 3-8-2-1, report to mat 1-9-3."

Each competitor would look at the front of his shorts to see if his number had been called. The rankings were updated in real time, so memorizing your number was useless. When a competitor's number was called, he would step onto the rapid transit pod that would take him to his ring. In a different lounge, the other competitor would do the same, and up in the stands, both of their fathers would check the official program, which had been delivered to their papers as soon as they entered the stadium. Once each father recognized his son's most current ranking, he would use the spectator rapid transit to reach the appropriate mat.

Soon, Rayzo's number was called. He walked to the pod, acutely aware that every competitor in the lounge was looking at his shorts.

The pod zipped down the dark tunnel, then emerged onto the chaotic arena floor. The music was deafening. All around him hundreds of sports matches were in progress, just beginning, or just ending. At the speed his pod was moving there was no way to actually see what was going on in any of these matches, not that it mattered. He needed to focus on his own match. Anything else was a distraction.

Rayzo was relieved to reach the mat and enter the sound-deadening field that kept out the music and the crowd noise, making it possible to once again focus. His pod was the second to arrive, beaten only by the one carrying his competitor's father, an average-looking man who did a better-than-average job of hiding his terror when His Lordship, Frederain Jakabitus, arrived and sat next to him in the VIP booth.

Once Rayzo's opponent arrived, the two competitors took their starting positions on the mat. Rayzo sized up his opposition. The other boy looked slightly older than him, and he was ranked higher, but only by a little over sixty places, which was practically nothing given the number of competitors. While the boy's father was clearly intimidated by His Lordship, the boy was not intimidated by Rayzo. They were on the mat. Not only was anything that happened during a fair match allowed, this was probably the only chance the guy would ever get in his life to interact directly with a member of the ruling family. He would fight harder to beat Rayzo, just to have the story to tell.

Sports was a fast game, consisting of only two phases, both of which were strictly timed. It began with the *advantage round,* where the two competitors battled to see who would start the challenge round with the advantage.

The advantage round took exactly fifteen seconds, which was quite long enough.

Rayzo and his competitor stood facing each other at arm's length in the center of the mat. The mat began to pulsate and display a countdown from five. When the countdown reached zero, the mat turned red, and Rayzo and his competitor started slapping at each other as quickly as they could. Whichever of them landed more palm-first, open-hand slaps on the face of their opponent in fifteen seconds would win the advantage.

Strategy was involved. One could block, but a blocking hand could not slap, so you had to pick your moment.

The oil with which all of the competitors were coated made attempted blows and grabs slide off more readily. Long ago it had also been used to conduct a very small current that could be measured to detect a hit. Of course, utilitics made this quite obsolete, but the oil's conductive property remained useful for other aspects of the game.

Rayzo and his opponent were both slapping furiously. In the VIP box, Lord Jakabitus was on his feet, shouting, "Slap him, boy! Slap him!"

The opposing father remained silent, sitting on his hands and looking acutely uncomfortable. His discomfort only grew when the advantage round ended in victory for his son.

"No! Ngaah!" Frederain said, flopping down into his seat. He took a deep breath, then turned to the other father and said, "Oh, well. Good for you. You must be proud."

"Yes, My Lord," the other man said, sounding as if he had taken it as a command.

The competitors now had fifteen seconds to prepare for the challenge round. Rayzo's opponent had the advantage. From his slightly superior height, he sneered down at Rayzo as if he were looking at a bug.

Good, Rayzo thought. *He has no idea that I threw the advantage round.*

"What's your dominant hand?" the competitor asked, as was his prerogative.

"Left," Rayzo lied, as was his prerogative.

The competitor reached with his right hand and grasped Rayzo's left wrist firmly. They both bent their knees, hunched their shoulders, and waited for the challenge round to begin.

Again, the mat pulsated and counted from five. At zero, the mat took on the segmented line pattern of Rayzo's practice mat back at the palace. The challenge round was on. Rayzo had one minute to either score more points than his opponent or throw him into the gutter.

Lord Jakabitus was back on his feet, shouting "Beat him, boy! Beat him! Boy!"

The other boy's grip on his wrist forced Rayzo into a slightly awkward stance, meaning he had a bit less leverage than his opponent. The two feinted at each other with their free arms, trying to force a mistake. This only went on for a few moments before Rayzo lost traction and fell backward.

Lord Jakabitus shrieked in horror at the sight of his son tumbling to the mat, but of course, Lord Jakabitus had missed the end of practice. In their post-practice conversation, Hartchar and Rayzo had discussed many topics: subterfuge, strategic withdrawal, feigning weakness to gain the advantage. Rayzo had found it quite enlightening.

Rayzo's back hit the mat. He was careful to keep his face pointed toward the ceiling, and was delighted not to hear the tone that signified a point scored for his opponent. Because of the firm grip he held on Rayzo's left wrist, the opponent was tugged forward by Rayzo's weight and forced to move his forward leg to remain upright. Of course, the opponent had a choice of where to put that foot—on the mat or on Rayzo. He chose to place it on Rayzo's chest, pinning him down.

Rayzo heard his father let out a long, anguished wail. From his father's perspective, all his worst nightmares were coming true.

The opponent sneered down at Rayzo. Rayzo smiled up at him, then used his free dominant hand to strike his opponent in the back of his load-bearing knee. The opponent's leg buckled, and he fell to the mat in a heap. Rayzo moved on top of his opponent and rolled him over. When the other boy's face made contact with the mat, the segment it touched glowed and a chime played, signifying that Rayzo had scored. Not that he could hear it, or anything else, over the sound of Lord Jakabitus yelling in triumph.

Rayzo had his opponent pinned down, of which he took full advantage by lifting and lowering the other boy's head to make his face contact the mat again and again, scoring additional points each time.

When the minute was up, Rayzo was very much victorious. This was signified in the traditional manner by his father rushing onto the mat, holding his son's hand high, and proclaiming, as fathers had for generations, "It is the prophecy!"

Rayzo used the same trick in the next four matches he fought. One of the advantages of there being so many competitors was that it was rare to fight the same opponent twice and next to impossible to watch anyone else compete, so if you found a strategy that worked, you could use it all day.

Rayzo knew he was doing well. You don't win five matches in a row without noticing it. He didn't look at his rankings too often. There were many competitors who did, constantly gazing down at their own shorts, but Rayzo found it unseemly. He did notice a profound change in his father's tone. Lord Jakabitus was still shouting, but instead of commanding him to do things he was already trying to do, he was congratulating him for things he had already done, which was a nice change.

When Rayzo was called for his sixth and most likely final match of the day, Frederain arrived at the mat first. It had been an eventful meet, and Lord Jakabitus was very tired, but in a buoyant mood. He took his seat in the VIP box and waited patiently for his son to come and defeat another competitor.

The competitor's father was next to arrive, a jolly, portly man with a ready smile. He greeted Frederain with a genuinely delighted "Your Lordship," and a deep bow.

It was rare for a commoner to take such a cheerful tone upon meeting Lord Jakabitus, but it never failed to delight him. The other father settled into his seat, turned to His Lordship, and asked, "How goes the meet for young Master Rayzo? He's always seemed a fine lad. He's doing well, I hope."

On the mat, Rayzo was stepping out of his pod. Now they were just waiting for his competitor.

"Yes, quite well," Frederain said. "Thank you for asking. And your son?"

"Today has been hard. His rankings have dropped," the other man answered, his smile not fading one bit.

"You seem to be taking it well."

"That's just the way things go. What can one do?"

"I suppose," Frederain said.

The other father looked at him for a moment, then asked, "May I ask an impertinent question, Your Lordship?"

"We're in the VIP box. Our boys are about to compete. Feel free. Treat me as you would anyone."

"Thank you, Your Lordship. I will. My question is this; Master Rayzo, do you think he's *the one*?"

Frederain looked out at Rayzo. He was jumping up and down to get his blood pumping before the match.

It was a good question.

The prophecy stipulated that *the one* would be nineteen years old, would "stand victorious over all his competitors," "dominate the sport like none before," be "famous, wealthy, and powerful," and that his father would be revered. Those requirements sounded rather specific, but in reality, they weren't quite specific enough.

Over the centuries since Dilly Glifton had first uttered his prophecy, many nineteen-year-old champions had dominated the sport, going on to achieve great acclaim and wealth—and the power that comes with those things. As such, all of them (and their fathers, on their behalf) had laid claim to the title of *the one.* But any hopeful father who could read realized that to "dominate the sport like none before" was a moving target, and all his son would have to do was surpass the preening pretender who was claiming to be *the one* in order to take his rightful place as the true champion.

There had been a great many possible *the ones.* Some of the less gracious off-world sports commentators had gone so far as to suggest that the boys of Apios weren't competing to be *the one* so much as they were competing to be *the next one,* or more to the point, *the last one.*

But the question was: could Rayzo be *the one?* He didn't stand out as a great competitor. Dominating the sport *like none before* seemed an awfully ambitious goal for the lad, but that was only one of the prophecy's conditions. Rayzo was the son and heir of the ruler of Apios. He was already wealthy and famous; one day he would certainly be powerful; and Frederain took it as a given that Rayzo's father was revered, so that gave the lad a huge head start.

"He might be," Frederain said.

"Yes," the other man said. "He might be. I suspected you'd say that. You know, my father thought I might be *the one.* He did everything he could to encourage me and mold me and push me to be *the one.* I don't remember a single conversation with him that wasn't about sports. He wasn't a bad man. He wanted what was best for me, and he thought that was being *the one.*

"Well," the man continued, "as you've no doubt guessed, I wasn't *the one.* My old dad died when I was twenty. In our last conversation, we talked about all the time I had spent practicing and competing, all the time he had spent pushing me to excel. His last words to me were, *It was all wasted, son. All of our time together, wasted.* Then he died."

Out on the mat, the man's son arrived. He was at least two years older than Rayzo, and much more fully developed. The man looked out at his son with obvious pride before returning his gaze to Frederain. "I can't change the past, Your Lordship, but I can learn from it. I have a son of my own now, and I'm making sure that my time with him is not wasted."

Lord Jakabitus nodded sagely. "How are you doing that?" he asked.

"By making damn sure that he really is *the one*." The man stood up from his seat, leaned out as far over the handrail as he could, and bellowed, "You're late, you worthless clod! Fancy boy there has had plenty of time to get warmed up while you've been loafing!"

Rayzo's competitor cringed. "I'm sorry, Father. I got in the pod as soon as my number was called. It took a longer route than—"

"I don't want your excuses! I want results!" the boy's father shouted. "Now you get in that ring, and don't just win. Humiliate him. If that pretty little lad isn't crying when you're done, you'll be crying before I'm done. Understand?!"

Both his son and Rayzo understood well enough. The father turned back and shrugged at Frederain, as if to say, *kids*.

Rayzo lost the advantage round. Rayzo, Frederain, Rayzo's competitor, and the competitor's father would all have predicted this, but for different reasons. The only surprise was that when the round was over, the spectators around the perimeter of the arena cheered. Rayzo and his competitor looked at each other, confused, then looked at the VIP box, where both their fathers were staring upward in amazement. They were on the big screen.

The competitor asked Rayzo about his dominant hand. Rayzo lied. The competitor chose not to believe him, but it mattered little. It only meant that Rayzo would be buckling his opponent's knee with his non-dominant hand.

They took their positions and waited for the match to begin. In the brief moment of calm before the countdown started, the competitor's father shouted, "Humiliate him!"

"You can beat him, Rayzo," Lord Jakabitus said, sounding confident. "Just use your trick."

"Yeah, Rayzo," the competitor said, also sounding confident. "Use your trick."

Rayzo died a little bit inside. The countdown started. He didn't know what to do, and he had five seconds to decide.

Hartchar had trained him to analyze his options, and to do it fast.

I have two choices, he thought. *Do the trick, or don't.*

If I don't do the trick and I lose the match, Father will say that I should have listened to him. Outcome: negative.

If I don't do the trick and I win, Father will say that I would have won faster if I'd listened to him. Outcome: better, but still negative.

If I do the trick and I still lose, Father will say that I didn't do it right. Outcome: negative.

If I do the trick and I win, Father will praise me for winning, or for listening to him. Either way, outcome: positive.

It was a bad situation, but Rayzo's only hope for a positive outcome was to stick to the plan. He started to fall backwards. His opponent's grip on his wrist both slowed his fall and pulled his opponent forward, just as expected. His opponent let go of his wrist, however, which was unexpected. Rayzo fell gracelessly to the mat, then lay there with no wind in his lungs and both hands free.

All things evolve over time, and sports was no exception. Rules had been invented, introduced, debated, repealed, missed, lamented, and reintroduced repeatedly since sports was invented.

Sports started as a simple form of wrestling where you either shoved the opponent out of bounds or pinned him facedown. Scoring was introduced to eliminate draws. The gutter was introduced to prevent people from claiming they hadn't gone out of bounds.

For a long time, slapping during a match was allowed and considered by many to be an important part of the game. It was ultimately judged to be too distracting, so it was outlawed during the challenge round, at which time the advantage round was introduced to placate the slapping enthusiasts. The reward for winning the advantage round, grasping the opponent's wrist, was also introduced to curtail a serious problem—the fact that the first half of every match had devolved into a desperate attempt on the part of one or both competitors to execute one specific move, a move for which you needed both hands.

Nobody knows which competitor first grabbed his opponent's shorts and pulled them down around his knees, but everyone agreed that doing so led to certain victory, as it both restricted the movement of the victim's legs and paralyzed his brain with embarrassment.

Pantsing, as it was called, immediately became everybody's primary goal, until it was outlawed. This led to a long period in which competitors would design moves that would plausibly allow them to *inadvertently* pants their opponent. Over time, sports meets devolved into bad theater, as the winners of matches were often the competitors who most successfully made pantsing look accidental.

This problem was solved in a revolutionary manner designed to protect the dignity of the sport. Pantsing was written into the rules as a legitimate strategy, but only if an alternative method was used—one that gave the *pantser* a similar advantage without forcing public nudity on the *pantsed* or the spectators.

Rayzo lay wheezing on the mat. He knew what was coming, but it was too late to prevent it. The competitor dove for his midsection and thrust both of his hands into Rayzo's shorts, grasping the waistband. Sensors built into the shorts registered the presence of a regulation *pantsing grip* and administered a sizeable shock, which was assisted on its trip into Rayzo's nervous system by his body's generous coating of conductive oil.

Rayzo's body was incapacitated, but his mind and senses were unaffected. The shock caused little pain, not nearly as much as hearing every spectator in the arena shout, "Pantsed!" in perfect unison. The only three people in the arena who were not shouting were Rayzo, Rayzo's competitor, and Rayzo's father.

Rayzo lay twitching on the mat, unable to control his own limbs. He knew exactly what would happen next as if it were a choreographed dance. His competitor grasped him by the ankles and twisted. Rayzo flopped over like a wooden plank, settling facedown on the mat. The segment of the mat where his face made contact changed color and a chime played, signifying points scored. Rayzo was dragged feetfirst to the gutter, his face skidding through various segments of the mat. As each new segment changed color, the chime raised in pitch, telling everyone that not only had more points been scored, but that the point value had doubled for each consecutive cell his face slid through.

The strangest things get one's attention at such times. Here Rayzo was, experiencing the worst nightmare of every sportsman, and all he could think about was that he was unable to close his mouth. His tongue was dragging along the mat with the rest of his face. He pictured all of the bare, oiled feet that had touched that mat. He was actually relieved when he reached the edge and rolled into the gutter.

Rayzo lay there for a moment, waiting for control of his limbs to return. Normally, a competitor in his position would be spared the sight of his opponent's victory celebration, but because they were on the big screen, and because he had landed on his back, Rayzo got to watch as his competitor's father proclaimed, "It is the prophecy!"

Rayzo closed his eyes, and kept them closed until he heard his father's voice.

"Son? Can you move?"

Lord Jakabitus was peering over the edge of the gutter.

"Yes," Rayzo said, sitting up shakily.

"I blame myself, Rayzo. This was my fault."

"Oh, Father, you didn't mean any harm."

"I was just so excited that you were doing so well," Frederain said. "I wanted to encourage you, but I made you overconfident."

"Overconfident? Father, I don't think I was overconfident."

"Sounds like you still are," Frederain said. "Now get out of that gutter. They need the mat cleared for the next match."

Rayzo stood and put up a hand for his father to grasp and pull him up, but Frederain didn't move.

"No, Son. I'd like to help you, but it's better for your self-esteem if you pull yourself up."

8.

"The full formal greeting was invoked at the staff meeting this morning, so we will dispense with it now," Wollard said as he walked briskly into the room, Phee following behind. "Instead, I will simply thank you all for taking a moment from your duties to attend this impromptu meeting. I assure you, it will be worthwhile. Everyone is present, I trust?"

Wollard looked over the assembled group. They were sitting in their accustomed places in the servants' hall, but their mood seemed unfathomably dark, and he didn't know why. He looked to Glaz. She was the palace expediter, and, as such, was the staff's leader and spokesperson.

Glaz glanced at the rest of the staff, all of whom were staring at the floor. "I'm sorry, Wollard. I didn't get the chance to tell you. Umily's not here. She just received some terrible news. I've given her the rest of the day off."

"Gint?" Wollard asked.

"I'm afraid so."

"Injured?"

"Worse."

"Oh, dear. I see," Wollard said. "That is, of course, terrible. I know we all thought very highly of the young man. I don't want to intrude on poor Umily, but please let her know that if I can be of any assistance in the planning of a memorial and the disposition of the remains—"

"She won't get any remains," Shly said, speaking out of turn. "The letter said that they only found one piece, and they're keeping it for something called *loss-retardant measures*, whatever that is."

"Well," Wollard said, "please let her know that Phee and I are anxious to assist her in any way we can."

Phee nodded vigorously at Glaz, who thanked them and promised to pass along the message.

Wollard took a deep breath and barreled on to the topic of the meeting.

"I know that this is hard, but as much as we'd all like to take some time to digest this news, the world isn't going to stop moving because we are grieving." He studied the faces of the staff to see if they were with him, and he was pleased to see that they were. They didn't look happy about it, but given the circumstances, it would be most inappropriate if they had.

"As you all know, Her Ladyship received a special briefing this morning about the state of the war with the Hahn. I can now tell you that the subject of that briefing was the capture of a member of the Hahn ruling family, the ruler's son, Master Hennik Hahn."

Wollard paused to let the import of his announcement sink in before continuing.

"After exploring all of the options put forth by her military commanders and checking for any available precedents, Lady Jakabitus has determined that the best course of action is for Her Ladyship and His Lordship to adopt the Hahn boy and raise him, alongside Master Rayzo, as their own son."

There was a moment of silence, followed by every staff member saying, "Query," in varying volumes and tones of voice.

Wollard said, "I recognize Glaz, the palace expediter." She could speak on behalf of all of them, since the others would likely want to ask the same few questions.

Glaz said, "I have a question in two parts. The first part is, are you serious?"

"Understood, and yes, I assure you that both I and Lady Jakabitus are entirely serious."

"Thank you. The second part of my question is this: Why would Her Ladyship do that?"

"I'm glad you asked. I understand that adopting her sworn enemy's son is not the first course of action that springs to mind. There were those in the military who wanted to injure the boy or worse, but Her Ladyship understands that to harm a defenseless prisoner would be poor form. That sort of thing simply isn't done. If we hurt him, we hurt our standing in the galaxy, and thus, ourselves. Conversely, if we sent him back to the Hahn unharmed, it would show considerable weakness in a time of war, which is also quite unacceptable."

Glaz shook her head. "Treating a Hahn as if he's a member of her own family seems crazy."

"But it is a brilliant tactical maneuver, when you think through the possible outcomes. Despite spending the rest of his adolescence with us, Master Hennik will still be a member of the Hahn ruling family, and may very well take control of the Hahn Empire someday. If that happens, he will think of Her Ladyship not as the enemy, but as a parent, and the war will essentially be over."

"Query," Shly said.

"Recognized," Wollard said.

"What about the Hahn who runs their army? *Shimlish the Pig.*"

"It is true," Wollard said, "that Master Hennik's older sister Shimlish Hahn commands the Hahn armed forces, and is considered most likely to succeed their father, but she is actively involved in the war. It is possible that she will not outlive her father. Whether Shimlish Hahn takes control or Kamar Hahn maintains his grip on the reins of power, any kindness and respect Her Ladyship shows Hennik Hahn may still be appreciated."

"Query," Hartchar said, then continued without waiting for a reply. "Is the general idea that the Hahn are unlikely to attack the palace if we have one of their family here?"

"Her Ladyship's plan has many merits," Wollard answered.

Glaz queried, and when she was recognized, said, "Was this your idea?"

"No," Wollard said, "I can't take credit for it. It is a strategy that has existed for hundreds of years. Phee and I merely found the precedents and brought them to Her Ladyship's attention."

"Follow-up query: In the past, has this strategy led to peace?"

"I would scarcely have brought it to Her Ladyship's attention otherwise."

Wollard said it with conviction, though Phee struggled to betray no emotion. While it was true that this strategy had led to peace in the past, part of the secret knowledge from the Arbiters that all Masters of Formalities needed to understand in order to do their job was that all strategies led to peace eventually. Even defeat leads to peace, if you take a broad enough view.

The two most similar precedents for this strategy had, indeed, resulted in a period of peace in the short term, followed eventually by a lasting peace in the long term, with a brief period of strife in between.

In one, the adopted son had attempted to usurp his older adoptive brother's position and seize control, but his scheme was discovered and thwarted, resulting in his banishment. In the other, the adopted son grew to adulthood, returned to his birth world, and then came back with a small army to seize control of his former adoptive family's palace. He was betrayed by his own men, and eventually captured and tortured by a third great house, simply for belligerence's sake, so it seemed.

Phee and Wollard both understood that these results were less than optimal, but the alternative was continued, uninterrupted war. It was true that neither precedent had worked out well for certain individuals, but another piece of secret knowledge all Masters of Formalities understood was that in the long run, no plan *ever* worked out well for every individual. Even success and happiness ends in death eventually.

Ebbler muttered, thinking out loud, "If he's going to be living here, we might want to get out of the habit of calling his sister *the Pig*."

Wollard said, "I'll recognize your out-of-order comment, Ebbler, because these are unusual circumstances . . . and because I like the way you're thinking. The practice of referring to Shimlish Hahn as *the Pig* was actually started by the Hahn family itself, and it was meant as an honorific, not an insult. Indeed, she's reported to be quite attractive, physically. The name describes her behavior, not her appearance."

"But how could it possibly be meant as a compliment?"

"The Hahn culture is different from ours. As soon as the plan was settled, I requested a report on their home world customs from the Arbiters. Thankfully, the Arbiters made it a priority and had it compiled, organized, and vetted at an accelerated rate. Even so, it just arrived. Phee and I have only had time to give it a cursory glance. It is a given that introducing Master Hennik to our way of life will cause a certain amount of friction. To ease this, Her Ladyship is allowing him to keep the servant who was captured with him. Said servant will act as his personal valet, and will be treated as a member of the palace staff."

There were uncomfortable glances and murmurs. Wollard pressed on.

"Hennik Hahn and his servant were captured yesterday. This morning, Lady Jakabitus settled on her course of action, and word was sent to Ophion 6. The pair was put on a direct warp transport as prisoners. Soon they will arrive as a member of the ruling family and a member of the palace staff. They will be tired and disoriented. They will have eaten on the transport, so they will be shown to their new quarters to rest after a brief welcome ceremony. Tomorrow night there will be an official welcome banquet, for which Barsparse will be preparing Master Hennik's favorite dish from his home world."

Wollard looked toward Barsparse. "I will get back to you as soon as I know what that is."

Barsparse nodded. She and Wollard had met earlier to discuss the addition of an extra family member and an extra staff member to the meals, so she'd had extra time to process the news.

"Now, a word about the Hahn culture. As you all know, Apios has been at war with the Hahn for generations. As such, there has been little cultural interaction between the two worlds. The average Apiosan knows little about daily life on the Hahn home world. Phee and I have skimmed the Arbiter's report, and it seems the primary feature of Hahn culture is their respect for honesty. Theirs is a culture built upon total honesty in all things.

"Oh," Shly said, quietly, "that sounds nice."

"Yes," Wollard said, casting a glance at Phee. "It does."

9.

At the appointed time, the staff gathered in the palace's inner courtyard. It was that brief moment before night falls, when the light of day has dimmed slightly, yet everything seems to be lit from within. The heat of the day had died, and the chill of the night was still ahead. It was as if the day knew this was its last chance to make a good impression and had pulled out all the stops.

The palace was spectacular from any angle and in any light, but in this light, seen from within the inner courtyard, it defied description.

Palace Koa, or *the palace*, as it was commonly called, was one building but had been constructed in three phases. Phase one, the Old Palace, dated back all the way to the dawn of the Jakabitus empire, two thousand years prior. For centuries the Old Palace was renowned for its beauty, opulence, and size. Now it was renowned mostly because of its age and history.

The second phase of construction, the New Palace, took the form of an oval ring that flared outward as it rose, its walls starting out thick at the bottom, then growing narrow and graceful at the top. It had been built a little under a thousand years later, a little over a thousand years ago. Clad in shining polished marble, the ring connected to the rear of the Old Palace. It surrounded and framed the Old Palace like a giant collar. Its outside wall was featureless, but the inside wall held several balconies, offering a view of the courtyard and the city beyond. The ring thinned to a sharp edge, and was embedded with a gate directly in front of the Old Palace. This addition was the part that contained the kitchen and staff accommodations, which had allowed those spaces in the Old Palace to be repurposed.

The final, outer portion of Palace Koa, surrounded and connected with the New Palace. While lavishly embellished and decorated on the exterior, it was essentially a low, hollow rectangle. It housed the security staff, bureaucrats, and fixers whose tireless work allowed Lady Jakabitus to make the leadership of an entire planet look graceful and elegant. It was the definition of thankless work, and the décor of its offices bore that out. This was *the Recent Expansion,* completed a mere four hundred years ago.

When Wollard stepped into the palace courtyard with Phee, he was pleased to see that the staff had taken their assigned positions, lining up as they would to greet any visiting member of a ruling house. He was less pleased to see the empty spot where Umily would usually stand, but perhaps it was best for her not to be present. *This is probably not the best moment to introduce the poor dear to a member of the Hahn ruling family,* he thought.

Though all appeared to be going according to plan, Wollard felt uneasy, which was understandable given the circumstances. In a voice quiet enough that only Phee could hear, Wollard said, "I assume you've taken the time to read the Hahn cultural report in more detail."

"Yes, have you?"

"Of course."

Phee looked up at Wollard. "Shouldn't we warn everyone?"

"No, Phee," Wollard said without turning to look at her. "We should not, tempting though it may be."

"But you saw what the report said about the Hahn."

"Yes, but the report was referring to *the Hahn,* plural, as in all of the Hahn, not *the Hahn,* singular, in this case, Master Hennik."

"But Wollard, surely the category of the Hahn, plural, would include Master Hennik?"

"Not necessarily. There is great variation from individual to individual. Master Hennik could be an unusual Hahn, and if so, we would do him a grave disservice by telling the staff to expect typical Hahn behavior. We must give Master Hennik the opportunity to create the first impression he chooses. People make their own beds, Phee. It's not our place to dictate how they do it. We just advise them on what bedding to select."

The immense entrance doors of the Old Palace swung open, and the ruling family, consisting of Her Ladyship, His Lordship, and Master Rayzo, stepped out of the palace and into the courtyard. They were dressed in their third-finest formal uniforms. The cavernous interior of the Old Palace shone behind them invitingly.

Her Ladyship nodded her approval to the staff, who bowed and curtsied in return, then they all shared that uncomfortable moment where everybody's ready for something, but that something hasn't happened yet.

The staff was dead silent and stock-still. Lady Jakabitus smiled at them, hoping it would help them relax. It did not.

Lady Jakabitus sighed, then looked at her son.

"Rayzo, you look very handsome."

"Thank you, Mother."

"You had a sports meet today, didn't you?"

"Yes, Mother."

"How did it go?"

Lord Jakabitus said. "He got pantsed."

"Oh dear," Lady Jakabitus said. "Still, I'm sure that's not the only thing that happened. How was the rest of the meet?"

Rayzo brightened. "Quite good, actually. I won my first five matches in a row."

"Then he got pantsed," Lord Jakabitus added.

"And, uh, my last match made it onto the big screen."

"Yes," Lord Jakabitus said. "So everyone could see him get pantsed."

Lady Jakabitus glared at Lord Jakabitus, then said to Rayzo, "Your father and I are going to have a discussion about this later."

"Yes," Frederain agreed. "Don't worry, son, we'll think of a way to straighten you out."

Lady Jakabitus ignored him. She put a hand on Rayzo's shoulder and said, "I'm proud of you, son."

"Imagine how proud she would have been if she'd actually attended," Lord Jakabitus said.

Rayzo imagined it, and did not like the result.

"Here they come," Wollard called out, breaking the tension. He was looking to the sky, shielding his eyes with his hand. High in the stratosphere, a black dot was shooting toward them, leaving a white line of fire and vapor in its wake. It slowed as it approached the ground, and the staff and the ruling family heard the distant sonic boom that had been generated while the craft was still high above the city of Koa.

The craft leveled out just above the buildings. It was a streamlined metallic lozenge, devoid of sharp angles or distinguishing details, save for the windows. The craft cruised straight through the palace gates, but it decelerated and yawed sideways shortly before reaching the outer gate. The casual viewer might be forgiven for thinking the craft was skidding to a stop, but it was merely turning to afford its important passengers the best possible view of the palace as it continued its approach.

The craft slowed to a stop, then held its position as firmly as if it were set in concrete, though it was, in fact, untethered and hovering several feet above the ground. Through the craft's windows, several heads were visible, but the interior was too dark for anyone on the outside to make out details.

The surface of the craft rippled. A rectangular portion of the outer skin became fluid and poured down from the craft, hardening into a ramp with steps, leaving an open hole into the craft's interior.

An armored soldier stepped out into the light, and Wollard and Phee walked out to greet him. The two men spoke in hushed tones for a moment, then the soldier returned to the transport. Wollard nodded to Her Ladyship.

The soldier reemerged from the transport, this time with Hennik Hahn. The boy was in his midteens (fifteen, they'd find out later), and tall for his age. His build and features were lean and angular, and his pale coloring was of a type never found on Apios. His hair was so blond it was nearly white. He wore a skintight jumpsuit, colored unevenly in patches that ranged from drab to dark. His bearing gave the sense that he felt in command of the situation despite the facts that he was quite young and his wrists were manacled. Behind him, wearing similar clothes and restraints, followed an adult female with sandy-blond hair, darker skin, and downcast eyes. She too was quite tall and thin, though in her case her gauntness seemed more the product of malnutrition than genetics. Another soldier accompanied the woman, leading her by the elbow.

They walked to the middle of the courtyard in silence. The soldier and Wollard exchanged more words. The soldier shook his head, then manipulated the manacles on Hennik's wrists. Like the skin of the transport, the manacles became fluid and poured off of Hennik, pooling into a metal ball in the soldier's hand. The second soldier did the same with the woman's manacles. The soldiers bowed deeply to Lady Jakabitus, then hustled back into the craft and flew away silently, at great speed.

Wollard stepped toward Hennik Hahn and said, "Know that two thousand, one hundred, and seventy-one conventional years have passed since the Terran Exodus. Today is the fifty-sixth day of the third month. We meet on the planet Apios, in the inner courtyard of the palace of the ruler, Lady Joanadie Jakabitus. I am Wollard, Master of Formalities for House Jakabitus, and I am honored to welcome you, Master Hennik Hahn, to your new home."

Hennik turned to the woman who had been delivered with him and said, "I see the Formalities are just as tiresome on this world."

Wollard let this statement pass, as it was not directed at him. "We are sorry for the manner of your transport here. Under better circumstances you would have been conveyed in a manner more in keeping with your status, and you would have been allowed traditional Hahn formal attire."

"This is traditional Hahn formal attire. We have fewer inadequacies than others, so we don't need to hide them with useless ornamentation."

"Of course." Wollard smiled. "As I said before, I am Wollard. I know you are Hennik Hahn, son of Kamar and Inmu Hahn. Your companion is . . ."

"Irrelevant," Hennik said, "as are you. Is there anybody important I can talk to?"

Wollard gestured toward the ruling family. "Lady Joanadie Jakabitus, ruler of Apios and your adoptive guardian, is waiting to meet you."

"She'll do," Hennik said, barging past Wollard on a direct course for Her Ladyship. The Hahn servant made brief, but distinctly apologetic, eye contact with Wollard, then followed Hennik.

Wollard and Phee moved quickly, and were able to reach Lady Jakabitus at the same moment as Hennik did.

"Your Ladyship, please allow me to introduce Master Hennik Hahn. Master Hennik, this is Her Ladyship, Joanadie Jakabitus, ruler of Apios."

Lady Jakabitus smiled. "Welcome, Hennik. We hope you will be comfortable here."

Hennik made no effort to bow. He looked Lady Jakabitus directly in the eye and said, "My father tells me that you're silly and weak."

If Lady Jakabitus was pushed off balance by this comment, she didn't show it. "Hennik, your father and I have never met."

"Which makes it all the more impressive that he has you figured out." Hennik turned and looked at Lord Jakabitus. "Who're you?"

Wollard deftly ducked around and behind Hennik, moving to his other side before bowing and saying, "This is Lord Frederain Jakabitus, Lady Jakabitus's husband."

"My father never mentioned you," Hennik sneered. "Clearly, he considers you a nonfactor. And you?" he asked, turning to Rayzo.

Wollard said, "I introduce Master Rayzo Jakabitus, Her Ladyship and His Lordship's son and heir." Hennik stepped in front of Rayzo, much closer than any Apiosan would dare. Hennik was a bit older and a bit taller. Rayzo looked up at him and said, "Hello."

Hennik laughed. "No wonder they wanted a replacement."

Wollard said, "Perhaps I should introduce you to the staff."

Disregarding Rayzo, Hennik stalked off toward the staff, followed by Wollard and the Hahn servant. Lady Jakabitus put out a hand to block Phee from following. It was unusual for her to address Phee directly, but Wollard was busy.

"Is this the Hahn honesty we were told to expect?"

Phee avoided eye contact. "I'm afraid so, Milady."

"And Wollard knew about this?"

"No, Milady. It's not my place to say, but at the briefing this morning he had no more reason to expect this behavior than you did."

"Tell your mentor that we will have words. Soon."

"Yes, Milady, but I suspect he knows."

Wollard, meanwhile, bowed, flourished, and said, "Master Hennik, it is my pleasure to introduce the Jakabitus family's personal staff."

Hennik surveyed the six people lined up before him, an amazed look on his face.

"Pathetic," he spat.

"I believe you'll find them more than adequate," Wollard said.

"You're mistaken."

Hennik approached Glaz at the head of the line. She was a woman of substance. Middle-aged, but not old. Direct, but not unpleasant. She was the kind of person who commanded respect from strangers and loyalty from friends. Hennik smiled at her.

"Master Hennik, I present Glaz, the palace expediter."

Glaz bowed and said, "Master Hennik."

"I will never remember your name," Hennik said, then moved on to the next person in line.

Wollard said, "I present Hartchar, Master Rayzo's, and soon-to-be your, chief trainer."

"You are physically intimidating," Hennik said, "We'll see if you can back that up."

"Yes, we will, Master Hennik," Hartchar said.

Moving on, Wollard said, "I present Barsparse, the palace chef."

Hennik said, "I'm told Apiosan food is swill."

"I assure you," Wollard said, "Chef Barsparse is one of our world's finest chefs."

"The best at making terrible food," Hennik said. "You must be so proud."

Wollard gestured toward the sous chef. "I present Pitt, the sous chef."

"I will never remember your name."

"This is Ebbler, deliverer of edibles."

"I will never remember your name."

"This is Shly, deliverer of liquid refreshment."

Hennik took a moment to study Shly before speaking. "You, I may use as a toy. It will mean nothing to me, but it will be a great honor for you."

Wollard changed the subject before Shly could respond. "There is also Umily, who tends to the ruling family's personal needs. Sadly, I cannot introduce you to her at the moment."

"Why not?"

Wollard paused. "Because she's not here."

Hennik said, "She's already my favorite. It's a shame the rest of you didn't follow her example."

"She isn't here," Shly hissed, "because she just found out her husband was killed by the Hahn."

Hennik considered this. "Sorry. I take it back. It's a shame the rest of you didn't follow *his* example." With that, he stepped back from the assembled group and cleared his throat, then launched into a clearly rehearsed statement.

"I understand that I am to be treated as a member of the Jakabitus family. I am aware that this is an alternative to killing me as a punishment to my father, the magnificent Kamar Hahn, ruler of the Hahn home world. I reluctantly thank you, and grudgingly admit that being treated as a member of your ruling family is marginally superior to execution. I accept your hospitality and will expect to be treated well, but know that I despise you, one and all, and will never stop plotting escape and revenge. Now, I am tired. Show me and my servant to our quarters."

Lady Jakabitus nodded, and Wollard led Hennik away. Phee bowed to Her Ladyship and followed. The Hahn servant followed as well, but turned, walking backwards. She bowed so deeply she looked as if she might fall over and mouthed, "Thank you."

PART 2

Communication is unavoidable.

Making a statement tells others about one's thoughts and feelings. Not bothering to make a statement also tells others about one's thoughts and feelings.

-Excerpt from *The Arbiters' Official Guidelines Regarding the Maintenance of Proper Form When Expressing Sympathy to the Sick and Injured*

10.

"Know that two thousand, one hundred, and seventy-one conventional years have passed since the Terran Exodus," Wollard said. "Today is the fifty-seventh day of the third month. We meet on the planet Apios, in the servants' hall of Palace Koa, the ancestral home of House Jakabitus and its matriarch, Lady Joanadie Jakabitus. I am Wollard, Master of Formalities for House Jakabitus, and I am currently delivering the daily meeting to the palace staff."

Wollard looked out over the staff, then plowed into his synopsis of the day's business.

"As we all are aware, Umily's husband and Barsparse's former sous chef, Gint, was killed in action by members of the Hahn military. We all grieve for him. Umily has been temporarily relieved of her duties, and will be given all the time she needs to compose herself."

Wollard took a breath, then moved on to the next item. "Today we welcome a new staff member: Migg, who arrived with Master Hennik last night. I'm certain you will all join me in bidding her welcome."

Unconvincing welcomes were muttered in Migg's direction. She sat at the back of the group, still wearing her skintight, drab yet shiny

Hahn uniform. She took up little space, made no noise, and utterly dominated everyone's attention.

Migg raised a single finger and said, "Query?"

Wollard smiled. "Recognized, Migg."

"May I please say a few words?"

"Of course."

She was a tall woman, but she seemed somehow smaller when she stood up. Her eyes traveled around the room before returning to the floor, where they stayed as she addressed the group.

"I just want to say that I'm sorry for everything. I'm sorry for what happened last night. I'm sorry that I'm making you all uncomfortable in your own home. And I'm sorry your friend's husband was killed by someone from my world. I'm sorry, but I'm also grateful to be here, and to be alive. Thank you."

Migg sat down, and Wollard performed his primary function, knowing how to react when others don't. "Last night's formal introduction was not entirely successful," Wollard continued, "and the situation in general could be described as *suboptimal,* but that should not reflect negatively on Migg. She did not ask for this situation. She is now a member of our team. Migg will be acting as Master Hennik's valet, meaning that instead of interacting directly with Master Hennik, we will often be dealing with her instead. Again, I say, welcome, Migg."

The staff again muttered words of welcome. Wollard noted that this time they sounded more sincere.

"Glaz will be orienting Migg today—giving her the grand tour, showing her how we do things at Palace Koa. Shly and Ebbler will pick up Umily's duties. There will be the regularly scheduled postbreakfast briefing for Her Ladyship, and Masters Rayzo and Hennik will attend sports practice after lunch.

The entire staff pictured Hartchar *practicing* with Master Hennik. The idea of it made them all happy. Particularly Hartchar.

"Query."

"I recognize Barsparse."

"Would it be acceptable if we all rearranged our schedules to be available to watch Master Hennik's first practice? I could whip up some snacks."

Wollard said, "No. I'm sorry, but we don't want to make Master Hennik uncomfortable on his first day." This was a rare instance of Wollard telling an obvious lie, but nobody blamed him for it.

"Indeed, there will be a feast tonight to welcome Master Hennik into the Jakabitus family. Dignitaries planetwide will attend. It will be a formal occasion, and while the Formalities will meet the Apiosan cultural norm, the feast's main course will be Master Hennik's favorite Hahn dish, which will be prepared manually for the Jakabitus family and replicated via bulkfab for the guests, in the name of expediency."

"Wow," Ebbler muttered. "That should be something."

Barsparse mumbled, "Yeah, *something*," then, louder, said, "Query?"

"Again, I recognize Barsparse."

"Do we know what that dish is yet?"

"Sadly, no," Wollard said. "Unless Migg has some idea."

All eyes turned to Migg, who shook her head. "No. I am sorry. Master Hennik has never been anxious to discuss things he likes."

"I see," Wollard said. "I shall discuss the matter with Master Hennik at the soonest opportunity. In the meantime, I have asked Phee to liaise with the Arbiters to acquire information about Hahn culinary techniques."

Phee said, "I will forward the report to your papers as soon as I receive it, Chef."

Wollard said, "Splendid. On that subject of research, Phee and I have had more time to study Hahn culture. It seems there is a fundamental difference in our two worlds' social structures. As I said, they value total honesty, but the differences run deeper than that. On Apios, we measure a person's worth by how useful they are. Migg, it may surprise you to hear that Lady Jakabitus considers herself to be a servant of the people."

Again, all eyes turned to Migg. "That, wow!" she stammered. "Really?"

"Indeed," Wollard agreed, "for it seems on the Hahn home world, one's status is demonstrated expressly by inconveniencing others. The more people you can inconvenience, the higher your status. Have I been misinformed, Migg?"

"No. That's right."

"How many staff members does the Hahn ruling family household employ?"

Migg said, "Several hundred. I don't know the exact number."

"As I thought," Wollard said. "If a person is capable of doing a job, they have another person do it instead. If the job is unpleasant or dangerous, others line up to watch. It's a different culture. This, I think, goes a long way to explaining why Master Hennik was . . ." Wollard paused, looking for the right words.

"Such a hateful little turd," Migg said.

Yet again, all eyes turned to Migg.

She shrugged, "Total honesty flows in both directions."

"Indeed," Wollard said.

After a brief discussion of a few administrative odds and ends, Wollard adjourned the meeting. Glaz stood, rubbing her hands together with relish. "All right. It looks to be a good day, full of work to be done. We'd best all get to—Umily!"

Everyone followed Glaz's eyes to the door, where Umily stood. Though her hair looked slept on and her uniform looked slept in, she did not, in fact, look as if she'd slept. Her eyes, still red and puffy, were streaming with fresh tears.

"Good morning, Umily," Wollard said, keeping his tone level.

"He's alive," Umily said, holding her papers up for everyone to see. "I just got a letter from him, sent this morning. Gint's not dead!"

The palace staff rushed her, expressing delight, relief, and a strong desire to read the letter. Wollard watched the outpouring of emotion from a dignified distance. He was pleased to note that Phee was standing beside him. She was maintaining her decorum, but she was clearly ready to jump out of her skin with excitement. Wollard nodded to her. She smiled and walked over to the group at a dignified pace.

Phee was young, and her role as a protégée who was still learning afforded her a certain latitude that Wollard didn't feel he could allow himself. He continued to stand apart from the rest of the staff. They were all happy, and watching them be happy together pleased him. He cast his gaze around the room, which was when he realized he was not the only one who was remaining separate from the celebration. Migg was standing a distance away from the others too, watching with clear interest, but not interfering. Wollard was impressed with her good sense.

It wasn't a long letter, but everyone was taking his or her time reading it. Some were savoring every word, others had already read it multiple times, and still others were having trouble making headway because of the way Umily's hands were shaking. Shly and Ebbler made room for Phee to squeeze in and read the letter herself. She did so carefully, as she knew that Wollard would want a full report even though he would never come out and ask.

Dear Umily,

I'm not dead.

My superiors tell me it's very important that I make that clear straightaway. I promise, despite what you've been told, I am not dead.

They say they sent you a letter telling you I was killed in action. While I am alive, that letter was not wrong. My superiors believe it's also very important for you to know that, so I will say it again: my superiors were not wrong.

I know. It sounds crazy. I don't really understand it myself. I guess the best thing I can do is just tell you what happened.

When I went through training they did some scans and tests on me. I thought it was just routine medical stuff, but it turns out they were part of an experimental program. "Loss-retardant measures," they call it.

Here's what I remember. I left the palace, went through training, put my head in their scanner, and then woke up this morning in a hospital. Well, it looks like a hospital. They call it a *Recuperation Center,* but I guess it's more like a science lab. They tell me that I was assigned to a battalion, shipped to the front, and killed in combat with the Hahn. They used what was left of me to rebuild my body, and their scan to refill my mind. Seems they've been able to rebuild bodies and reload brains for a long time. They haven't used the technology up until now because they weren't convinced it worked properly. They didn't like the idea of a bunch of people who might be copies of dead people walking around, but I guess they figured if we *were* copies, we could still fight in the war just as well as the originals. All I can tell you is that I feel like I'm still the real me, and that's all the proof I need.

They say the Hahn overran our bunker again, and that I made two errors that led to my death. I hesitated to kill what I thought was an unarmed enemy, and I failed to search him well enough to find the fission grenade he was hiding.

I'm sorry and ashamed to have to tell you these things. The good news is that they tweaked a few things while they were rebuilding me. They also improved my military knowledge and combat skills, to make me stronger and less likely to get killed again. Hopefully they didn't have to erase too many of the recipes Barsparse worked so hard to teach me to make space.

They tell me they've also taken three months off my term of service to make up for the inconvenience, so not only am I now much more likely to come home to you alive, but it will happen sooner!

I know what I wrote you in my last letter. They let me read it before I wrote this one, to get me up to speed. It was a little embarrassing to read something I don't remember writing, particularly since it was so mushy. I hope it didn't make you respect me less.

I have to go. They're shipping me back to my battalion. I love you, Umily, and can't wait to come home to you. Please tell everyone "hello."

Gint

Once everyone had read the letter, they stepped back to let Umily have some air. There was a fresh round of congratulations, which ended abruptly with Pitt saying, "Well, Umily, you'll want to meet our new Hahn."

Having anticipated this possibility, Wollard had prepared for it. He was standing near Migg. Not *with* her. *Near* her. His goal was to give the impression that she was not to be feared or avoided.

Umily said nothing.

Migg bowed deeply.

"Ma'am. My name is Migg, and I am from the Hahn home world. I don't know you, but I can tell that all of these people think highly of you and your man. I'm glad to hear he's alive."

It was inelegant, but Wollard thought it would do. He especially liked that Migg had called Umily *ma'am,* even though Migg was clearly at least a decade her elder.

Umily stared at Migg for a long moment, then said, "Thanks."

Again, Wollard thought this would do.

II.

The wallpaper in the vestibule outside Lady Jakabitus's office was a pattern of thorn bushes and storm clouds, rendered in dark colors. Neither Wollard nor Phee chose to comment on this.

Wollard put his hands on the doors, then paused to look down at Phee.

Phee took a deep breath.

Wollard nodded, as if in agreement, and pushed open the doors.

The wall of windows that usually gave a spectacular view of the capital was darkened, blocking out much of the light. Lady Joanadie Jakabitus sat with the intricately decorated back of her chair facing the door.

"Ah, Wollard. Do come in," Lady Jakabitus said without turning to look at him. "I see you've arrived mere seconds before my morning briefing is scheduled to begin. It's a shame we won't have time to talk privately."

"Indeed, Milady."

The chair spun to face Wollard and Phee. "Perhaps it would be possible for me to free some time in my schedule after the briefing for us to have a little chat? Who manages my schedule, Wollard?"

"I do, Milady."

"Good. Wollard?"

"Yes, Milady."

"Schedule our talk for directly after the briefing."

Wollard looked at his papers and cleared his throat. "Milady, that time is currently set aside for—"

"I didn't ask, Wollard."

"Yes, Milady. How should I categorize the time, for the record?"

"Just put *berating Wollard.* I'll know what it's about."

"It is done, Milady."

"Splendid. It's nice to have something to look forward to."

"Milady, while last night's introduction did not—"

"Ah ah ah," Lady Jakabitus interrupted. "There'll be time for that later. Now the briefing is starting."

The portraits on the walls faded out and were replaced with live feeds of the various ministers, functionaries, and generals who reported to Her Ladyship each morning. Today General Kriz was present as a feed, rather than being there in person.

Most of the briefing was utterly routine. On a planetary level, political change was a slow process. Over time the circumstances could change drastically, but when experienced on a day-by-day basis, each briefing was almost identical to the one delivered the day before, like a single frame in an animation. It was only in retrospect, when an entire year could be compressed into a short paragraph, that history seemed to move.

The only real surprise came midway through the Minister of Health's report: Phee giggled. Lady Jakabitus didn't seem to notice it, but Wollard did. He turned and saw Phee hastily stow her papers away.

General Kriz, who went last, reported that the Hahn offensive continued and had grown even more violent while remaining equally futile. Many Hahn soldiers had started using conventional weapons, though not for offensive—or even defensive—purposes. The invading soldiers would use their own weapons against themselves if there was a risk of being captured alive. He also reported that the experimental loss-retardant measures were bearing great fruit, and would be expanded. Then, with permission from Her Ladyship, he informed the non-military personnel of the capture of Hennik Hahn, and Lady Jakabitus's decision to show the boy mercy. He explained that the palace security staff, maintaining their invisible vigil from the palace's recent addition, had been ordered to keep an extra eye on Hennik to prevent him from either doing harm to, or escaping from, the ruling family.

Lady Jakabitus received a barrage of congratulations on this brilliant and unorthodox move. She was gracious but unequivocal as she put a quick end to the daily briefing.

"That went well," Lady Jakabitus said.

"They did seem to take a favorable view of your adoption of Master Hennik," Wollard said.

"Yes," Lady Jakabitus agreed. "Of course, they haven't met him."

She stood up and rubbed her hands together. "Well, Wollard, I guess we should move on to the next item on the agenda."

"The briefing ended a bit early, so you do have some free time before your next scheduled appointment, Milady."

"Good. We can start early then."

"Indeed."

"Wollard, did you know Hennik Hahn was a monster when you proposed that I adopt him?"

"No, Milady."

"Why didn't you find out if he was a monster before you brought up the idea?"

"I couldn't have known, Milady. The people of Apios know precious little about the Hahn, as you are aware."

"But the Arbiters know all about them."

"Some Arbiters do, yes, Milady. The Arbiters of the Archive get information directly from the Hahn's Master of Formalities."

"And you and your protégée work for the Arbiters."

"On your behalf, Milady. As such, we are seen by the Arbiters as citizens of Apios. We're given only the information they deem necessary to lubricate the interaction between ours and other worlds. Thus, the Arbiters, in their wisdom, only chose to inform me and Phee of the cultural differences between our peoples once you had committed to your chosen course of action."

"So they won't warn us that we're about to make a mistake, but they will tell us how big a mistake we've made after the fact."

"It may feel that way, Milady, but I am not convinced we've made a mistake."

A long silence passed while Lady Jakabitus stared at Wollard. Finally, she said, "Explain."

"I agree that Master Hennik's attitude upon arrival was challenging. He is young, and has been captured by his enemies and told that he cannot leave. One could well expect even the most docile person to be combative under such circumstances, and I think we can all agree that Master Hennik is not the most docile person."

"You're telling me that taking the Hahn boy in was not a mistake because we should have known he'd be awful?" Lady Jakabitus said. "You should have known telling me that would make me angry. Was it a mistake to have told me, Wollard?"

"No, Milady, and as is often the case, you have cut directly to the heart of the matter. I did suspect that saying what I just said would do little to improve your mood, but it was not a mistake. You would not want me tell you anything other than the truth as I know it, so I did so, knowing it might anger you further. Telling you the truth was worth the risk and difficulty."

Lady Jakabitus stared silently at Wollard. When dealing with someone who is both powerful and angry, anything other than an invitation to speak is an order to be quiet, but Wollard felt the occasion warranted the risk of additional words.

"Milady, you are ending a war that has lasted generations. There's no easy way to do that, or it would already have been done. Fate has given you a unique opportunity. You can cease untold bloodshed and waste by enduring the presence of a petulant teenager in your home. Like anyone who has ever been forced to tolerate such a thing, there will be times when you'll wonder if it is worth it. You have far more reason than most to decide that it is."

Lady Jakabitus sat in her chair and considered Wollard's argument. She sighed heavily. "Will he come around eventually?"

"Nobody can say for sure, Milady."

"We are committed. I guess we need to do everything in our power to make sure this works."

"Agreed, Milady. That brings me to the next issue. We must announce to the galaxy that Master Hennik is here, he is safe, and he is being treated as a member of your family."

"How do you suggest we proceed?"

"For your subjects, the usual means of releasing information will suffice. The more pressing issue is how we should inform Kamar Hahn. We don't know how much he knows. It is possible that the last news he heard was that his son was involved in a battle that ended badly for the Hahn."

"You're saying that he might think Hennik is dead?"

"Dead or in danger, Milady," Wollard said. "In a situation such as this, it would be good form for you to make contact with Kamar Hahn personally to deliver the good news."

"Direct contact with the leader of the Hahn?" Lady Jakabitus said. "There hasn't been any direct contact between the Apiosans and the Hahn for over a hundred years other than violent exchanges."

"But there will be, today," Wollard said, "because of your actions, Milady."

"And you can set this up?"

“I’m certain, given the nature of the message, that the Arbiters and the Hahn Master of Formalities will cooperate. It’s because of situations such as this one that the great houses agreed to Arbitration in the first place.”

“Direct communication with the Hahn,” Her Ladyship said, picturing it in her mind. Her expression soured. “He’s going to be awful, just like his son, isn’t he?”

“It is possible, Milady. It is also possible that he may be the exact opposite of his son, and that Master Hennik behaves as he does in an attempt to rebel against his father.”

“You think that’s the case?”

“It’s possible, Milady.”

“But is there any reason to believe it’s true, Wollard?”

“Milady, there’s no reason to believe it, but there’s always reason to hope.”

12.

Wollard walked through the Grand Gallery at his accustomed speed, but with less than his usual energy. Between arranging the communication with the Hahn, planning a strategy for said communication, and entertaining Lady Jakabitus's musings as to how the situation would play out, the meeting had stretched on until lunchtime. It had taken a great deal out of Wollard. Still, he needed to meet with Barsparse as soon as possible to discuss arrangements for dinner. The conversation had already been delayed far longer than he would have liked, but he could hardly have put off Lady Jakabitus for an *important meeting* with the chef.

He walked as quickly as he could without appearing to hurry, but the escalator ride, which he usually used as a chance to talk with his protégée, was instead taken as a welcome chance to rest.

He and Phee walked in silence. Phee wanted to commit every second of the meeting to memory so she could refer to it in the future, when she herself was a Master of Formalities. Wollard, on the other hand, wanted to forget it all. He saw his role as helping other people wriggle out of trouble. He found it undignified to have to wriggle out of trouble himself.

Phee finally broke the silence. "Wollard, that was amaz—"

"Phee," Wollard interrupted, then paused, reinstating the silence for a few steps before continuing. "You laughed. The Minister of Health, the Honorable Seibert Adler, was briefing Her Ladyship, and you laughed."

She inhaled sharply through her teeth, then said, "I had hoped nobody would notice."

"That which is out of place is always noticed, Phee, and nothing is more out of place than a sign of enjoyment when the Honorable Seibert Adler is speaking. If I did not know better, I would suspect that you were reading unrelated materials during the briefing."

Phee said nothing.

"Perhaps messages sent through less than legitimate channels."

Phee said nothing.

"If I were being particularly pessimistic, I might even suspect it was the very type of message you were warned about only yesterday."

"I wasn't sending messages," Phee said. "But I saw that I'd received one."

"Don't say another word, Phee," Wollard admonished her. "I took you on as a protégée because I want to teach you, not because I want to punish you. Don't make me."

"I'm sorry, Wollard."

"Don't tell me you're sorry. Show me, by not doing it again."

Wollard and Phee came to the kitchen, where lunch production was in full swing.

Barsparse held two pots in one hand, using her powerful fingers and forearm to grip their handles. The pots contained two fluids of subtly contrasting colors and viscosities. Four plates were lined up on a prep table, each holding a beautifully formed ball of pinkish meat. Barsparse worked her way down the line, using a spoon to drizzle a thick, dark-blue fluid around the meat, then a thin, light blue fluid in an artistic curve around the dark blue fluid. She applied the sauces to each plate with the precision and regularity of a machine.

Pitt followed behind with a small metal bowl full of sprigs of some herb. He placed a single sprig on each plate, instantly transforming the dish from a piece of meat with two sauces into an edible piece of art depicting a tiny island, surrounded by water, with a single tree.

"That's beautiful," Ebbler said, watching from the corner.

"Dat's beeeeuteeful," Pitt imitated in a slow, slurred voice. "Just be careful lugging it to the dining room. We didn't make a masterpiece just to have it destroyed by the lummox carrying the tray."

"Less talk, more work, Pitt," Barsparse said. "Thanks for the compliment, Ebbler. It turned out all right, but there's definitely room for improvement. There's always room for improvement, isn't that right, Pitt?"

Pitt glared at Ebbler, then looked down at the plates. "I, uh," he stammered, "I don't know what more we can do, Chef."

Barsparse put down her pots and walked back over to the plates. "You don't know what more you can do, but that doesn't mean that nothing more can be done. You should be thinking of ways to improve each dish right up until the moment that Ebbler carries it away."

"Yes, Chef," Pitt said miserably.

Barsparse, Pitt, and Ebbler all stared at the four plates of food.

"And the moment that Ebbler carries it away," Barsparse said, "should have been several seconds ago."

Ebbler leapt as if he'd been prodded with a sharp stick. "Yes, Chef! Sorry, Chef! Sorry, Pitt!" He deftly placed the plates on his grav-platter and left the kitchen.

Pitt looked delighted as he watched Ebbler scramble.

Barsparse said, "Dessert course."

Barsparse looked delighted as she watched Pitt scramble.

Wollard cleared his throat.

Barsparse turned, then nodded. "Wollard. Phee."

Phee nodded back, but stayed silent.

Wollard said, "Chef, I just wanted to make sure the Arbiter's report on Hahn cooking methods was satisfactory."

"Yes, the report was thorough. The Hahn's cooking methods, on the other hand . . . they have an entirely different approach. The quality of the food is secondary to the presentation."

"That's good news," Wollard said. "You've always excelled at presentation."

"But like I said, Wollard, their approach is different. Remember what you told us about how they value inconveniencing others?"

Predictably, Glaz and Migg entered the kitchen just as Barsparse referred to the Hahn as *they*. Barsparse looked chagrined, but if Migg was offended, she didn't show it.

"Glaz, Migg, this is remarkable timing," Wollard said.

Phee was continually amazed at Wollard's ability to describe an unfortunate situation in a positive tone.

"We were just discussing Hahn culinary techniques," Wollard said. "Migg, it occurs to me that you would certainly know more about it than any of us."

"It wasn't my area of expertise," Migg said, "I mainly just tended to the little tasks the Ruling Family didn't want to do themselves, but I'm happy to tell you anything I can. What Hahn dish are you making for the feast?"

"That's a good question," Barsparse said. "Wollard?"

"Her Ladyship intends to broach the subject over lunch, so we should know soon."

Ebbler returned to the room just then, looking both embarrassed and angry. His platter floated in front of him. One plate sat facedown, its contents smeared across the platter's surface.

Ebbler looked ruefully at Wollard, then addressed Barsparse. "Master Hennik, who we have been instructed to treat as a member of the ruling family, has requested that I inform the chef that her work is unsatisfactory, and hunger is preferable. He requests that the chef report to the dining room to receive some constructive criticism."

Barsparse turned to Pitt. "Do you have the dessert course under control?"

"Yes, Chef!"

"Good. I'll try to be back soon. If you need an extra set of hands, Ebbler would probably be willing to help out."

"Yes," Ebbler said. "Yes, I would!"

Pitt said, "Won't be necessary, Chef."

"I'll accompany you, Chef," Wollard said.

"Thanks" Barsparse said. "On the bright side, we should be able to find out what Master Hennik wants for dinner."

"Her Ladyship asked him while I was serving," Ebbler explained. "Master Hennik said that he wanted something made by his father's chef, in his father's palace, on the Hahn home world."

As Barsparse, Wollard, and Phee left the kitchen, Barsparse muttered, "Maybe we can accommodate him."

"Now, now," Wollard admonished her, and then the three of them were gone.

Migg turned to Ebbler, who was still standing with his platter of ruined food. "Let me help you clean that up," she said, reaching out to take it from him.

"That's not necessary," Glaz said.

"Please," Migg said, then stopped, confused. "Is that uncooked meat you served Master Hennik?"

"Yeah," Ebbler said. "It's how the dish is served. It's called tartare. It dates all the way back to before the Terran Exodus. Ancient dish, probably the most ancient if you think about it."

"Yes," Pitt shouted from across the kitchen. "If you want to learn more about it, you could ask a chef, who actually knows about food."

Ebbler gritted his teeth, but his voice remained pleasant. "Of course, Pitt, if you'd like to tell her about—"

"I'm busy," Pitt said.

"You've told me enough, Ebbler," Migg said. "Very interesting. Anyway, I'm sorry for what Master Hennik did to you. Please, I'd like to help clean up."

Glaz said, "We understand, but it's really not necessary. Ebbler, please show Migg how we clean here."

"They don't have utilitics on the Hahn home world?" Ebbler asked.

Glaz said, "I doubt it." Migg looked confused, which reinforced the idea that the technology was new to her.

Ebbler held the platter with both hands and lowered it to the floor, signaling to the utilitics that it was ready for cleaning. The viscous, partially congealed food dripped, then slid, then almost seemed to flow toward the corner of the platter. It poured into a puddle on the kitchen floor. The overturned plate also glided to the floor, landing beside the puddle. Ebbler grasped the plate by a dry corner and slowly lifted it, handing it to Glaz, who held it up to the light to show how spotlessly clean it was.

Ebbler lifted the now-immaculate platter from the floor. The puddle of refuse on the floor thinned and constricted until it was flat and perfectly round, then moved toward the wall of its own accord, where it thinned into a narrow stream and slunk away as if it were ashamed of itself. When it reached the corner, it disappeared into a small drain.

Glaz and Ebbler both delighted in the look of astonishment on Migg's face.

Glaz explained. "The utilitics are billions of little machines, too small to see. They each have certain abilities and a very small amount of intelligence, but they're all connected, so they work together as a whole. Every surface and object in the palace is covered with them."

"Okay," Migg said, talking herself through it. "So, these tiny machines. Are some of them carrying the food away, or are they passing it to each other?"

Glaz shrugged. "That's a good question. I don't know. Ebbler?"

"It works, so I've never questioned it." Ebbler said.

"Fair enough," Migg said. "So, they take away the mess, but is it really clean? What about viruses and such?"

"Oh, they'd never allow a virus anywhere near Her Ladyship. One of the benefits of working at the palace is that the utilitics destroy anything contagious to keep us healthy, because that, in turn, keeps the Jakabituses healthy. You still have viruses at the Hahn palace?"

"Yes. Her Ladyship, Inmu Hahn, usually has some sort of contagious illness."

"Oh," Glaz said. "The poor thing. She must be miserable."

"No, the opposite. She passes them on to the servants for fun. Whenever she falls ill, her goal is to get well in time to enjoy watching everyone else suffer. Then she gets something else so she can be infectious again just when everyone starts to recover. About the food waste, where did it go?"

"What?" Glaz asked, taking a moment to wrench her mind back to the original subject. "Oh, it's collected and broken back down into simple molecules for the bulkfabs to use."

"Bulkfabs?"

"Yes, they're machines that take simple molecules and piece them together into the things we need. Food, drinks, medicine, plates, clothes. Most people get entire meals out of them, but chefs like Barsparse only use them for raw ingredients. Shly carries a small one to serve drinks."

Migg nodded. "Life on Apios sounds very convenient."

"A bit different, I take it, from life on . . ." Glaz paused. "Migg, we really do know very little about your planet. We've always referred to it as *the Hahn home world.* What is your planet's name?"

"The Hahn Home World," Migg said.

"And we call your people *the Hahn.*"

"That is our name," Migg said.

"But, your ruling family are named Hahn."

"We are all named Hahn. Our name is Hahn."

"Your name is Migg," Glaz said.

"Yes. Migg Hahn."

"Is everyone on your planet truly named Hahn?" Ebbler asked.

"Yes. Centuries ago, when the Hahn family first seized control of the Hahn Home World, they cemented their power, both over the planet and their subjects, by changing all names to Hahn, and the name of the planet to the Hahn Home World. All records of any names used before the Hahn have been erased. It is said that there are those who still know our planet's true name, but I don't believe it. Nobody really cares at this point anyway."

"That sounds confusing," Ebbler said, looking up from his work for just a moment. Pitt had finished plating the desserts, and Ebbler was concentrating on arranging them on his platter.

"It's an obstacle to our society's functioning, and any attempted work-around to simplify matters is immediately detected and prevented. It is an awful blight on my people, and the fact that it has been enforced successfully for so long is a testament to the Hahns' will. Keep that in mind as you anticipate Master Hennik's reaction to those delicious-looking desserts."

13.

The mood in the gymnasium was tense. Despite the winning streak at the beginning of the previous day's match, no one was pleased with the outcome. The only thing for it was to train harder. Hartchar had reviewed footage of Rayzo's final match and listened to Lord Jakabitus explain, at length, what needed to be done to fix the deficiencies in Rayzo's performance.

When His Lordship finally tired of explaining, Hartchar summed up his concerns, saying, "If I understand correctly, Milord, you would prefer it if Master Rayzo did not get pantsed in the future."

Lord Jakabitus was glad that she understood.

Hartchar devised a drill to give Master Rayzo the skills he needed to avoid getting pantsed. Rayzo stood in the center of the mat, wearing only his training sports shorts, which were emblazoned on the front and back with the number one, as he was the only active competitor in the palace. Hartchar stood in front of him and tried to get her hands into the waistband of his shorts while he blocked her repeated attempts. Lord Jakabitus assisted, as he always did, by shouting instructions from his mat-side seat.

"Protect your shorts, son! Block her hands! I said block them! Her haaaaaands!" he shouted, encouragingly.

Hennik sat beside His Lordship and smiled, in spite of himself.

Hartchar continued to pose her attack from the same few angles. The goal was to burn the motions required to fend off a pantsing into Rayzo's muscle memory, much as the experience of getting pantsed was burned into his actual memory.

Lord Jakabitus took a break from coaching Rayzo to make an attempt at talking to Hennik. He held little hope of success, but he'd promised Lady Jakabitus to try.

"So, my lad, did you play sports back on the Hahn Home World?"

"Yes," Hennik answered. He was too distracted by the spectacle of his adoptive younger brother defending his pants to concentrate on being nasty to His Lordship. "I played lots of sports."

"Really? What was your ranking?"

Hennik puzzled at the question for a moment, then groaned condescendingly. "Oh, I see the confusion. You were asking if I played *Apiosan sports.* When you asked if I played sports, I thought you meant any of the hundreds of games that the rest of the galaxy refer to as *sports.*"

"Oh," Frederain said. "Yes, I can see where that would cause some confusion. So, did you play Apiosan sports?"

"No. I'm not Apiosan."

Shly entered to deliver His Lordship his training beverage. Normally it was held for the end of training, but His Lordship had requested it early today, fearing he'd need a pick-me-up. She slowly made her way along the back wall of the gymnasium, hoping to escape the younger boy's attention.

"We invented Apiosan sports here on Apios," Lord Jakabitus said, "but the rest of the galaxy knows about it. I've never understood why you all don't play."

"Because we play real sports. We didn't make up our own game, give it a name that makes it sound like it's as important as all other sports combined, then pretend that because we're the best at this one thing nobody else cares about, it means we're the best, period."

Lord Frederain was on the verge of responding when Shly interjected, with timing that would have impressed Wollard.

"Would Your Lordship like his training beverage now?" Shly asked.

At the sound of Shly's voice, Rayzo's eyes darted away from the training mat, finding her in the room.

Lord Jakabitus said. "Yes, Shly. Please."

As Shly started to fabricate His Lordship's beverage, Hennik watched Rayzo attempt to split his attention between blocking Hartchar's attacks and checking to see if Shly was looking at him. His blocks became sloppy, and Hartchar soon managed to get both hands into his waistband. The shorts were set to training mode, so instead of a paralyzing shock, the voltage was tuned to merely cause discomfort. Rayzo leapt straight up in the air, shouting, and grabbed his posterior, where the current had entered his body.

Rayzo bounced on the balls of his feet a few times, trying to work the pain out of his system. By the time he stopped, Shly, Lord Jakabitus, and Hennik were all three looking at him.

Lord Jakabitus shook his head. "No, son. You have to block her hands."

"Yes, Father," Rayzo panted as he limped back to the center of the mat.

Lord Jakabitus sighed heavily. *My son needs guidance, and I'm wasting my time playing host to this little snot,* he thought. *Still, I gave Joanadie my word.*

"Hennik, would you like something to drink? I'm certain that Shly would give you anything you'd like."

"Yes, is there anything you'd like, Master Hennik?" Shly asked.

Rayzo shouted in pain, having lost his concentration again, and received another shock.

"Block, son!" Lord Jakabitus shouted. "Block! I can't put it any more simply than that!"

Hennik watched Rayzo as he limped around the mat again. The younger boy looked at Hennik, then at his father, then at Shly, then back at Hennik.

Interesting, Hennik thought. *There might just be an opportunity to escalate matters here. It would mean being courteous to this fop, which I won't enjoy, but it will increase the son's misery exponentially, and when the fop realizes he's been used, he'll be significantly more miserable as well. I believe Father would approve.*

Hennik held eye contact with Rayzo and smiled sweetly. "Yes, Shly, is it? I would love a drink. I'll have what His Lordship is having. He seems like a smart man, with refined tastes."

"Good," Lord Jakabitus said, surprised. "You might alter the formulation a bit, given Hennik's age."

Shly dispensed a second glass, expecting it to be thrown on the floor, the mat, or perhaps even on His Lordship. The last thing she expected him to do with the beverage was exactly what he did, which was drink it, then smile and say, "I was right. Delicious. Thank you, Shly."

Shly and Lord Jakabitus looked at each other in wonderment as Hennik held his glass high and smiled at Rayzo. Rayzo did not smile, but instead returned to Hartchar, who was ready to resume training.

Having completed her duty, Shly took her leave, and Lord Jakabitus returned his attention to his discussion with Hennik, who was watching Rayzo's training with renewed interest.

"So, you say you played other games before you came to Apios. Were you good at them?"

"Yes," Hennik said. "I was."

"Well, perhaps you'd like to try your hand at *Apiosan sports,* as you call it."

"Perhaps," Hennik said in a loud, clear voice he was sure would carry well. "I've always been a natural athlete. I'd be interested to see how well I stack up against young Rayzo."

Again, Rayzo's concentration slipped, resulting in an invasion of his waistband, a shock, and a pained yelp.

"Block her hands, son! Her hands!"

"Yes, Rayzo," Hennik said. "Do try to block her hands."

As training resumed, His Lordship changed the subject. "So, the dish you requested for the banquet tonight. *Skolash*?"

"That's correct."

"What is it?"

"Irrelevant," Hennik said before he could catch himself. He quickly added, "I'm afraid." His first impulse was to be rude to whomever he was speaking. It was going to take a while to make the mental adjustment to being courteous to Lord Jakabitus, even if the ultimate goal was to torture Rayzo.

"I know that all of this is an effort to make me feel welcome," Hennik said. "Skolash is my favorite dish, but I don't think I'll be here to eat it, or to try your *sports.* Lady Jakabitus is going to talk with my father today, and I expect I'll be on a transport back to the Hahn Home World before dinner."

Lord Jakabitus said, "I doubt that."

Instead of saying what he wanted to, Hennik replied, "Well, Your Lordship, if I'm right, I'll think of you all eating your Skolash as I go home. If you're right, I get to be here to watch you eat your Skolash. It's good either way."

14.

"And that, Pitt, is how you make Skolash." Barsparse set her papers down on the worktable. She'd told Pitt to meet her in the kitchen, and to bring her a stiff drink. She had read almost every word of the recipe, instructions, and stage directions aloud to him, and now she waited while he absorbed what he'd heard.

"That's awful," Pitt said.

"That's Hahn cuisine," Barsparse countered.

"We can't do that," Pitt said.

"It's difficult," Barsparse allowed, "but possible. I've been in contact with Her Ladyship's zookeepers, experts in forensic biology from Her Ladyship's University, as well as the machine shop and seamstresses in the palace's new addition. Getting everything in place before dinner will be tight, but we'll be ready in time."

"I'm not talking about any of that stuff," Pitt said. "Our part, we can't do it."

Barsparse put her drink down. "We must," she said. "Her Ladyship promised Master Hennik he could have any dish from his home world. He chose Skolash. She has commanded us to make that happen, and we will."

"I can't believe Wollard signed off on this."

"He has, in a sense. He handed me the instructions personally."

"Did he read them?" Pitt asked.

"No. Part of the Skolash ritual is that nobody outside of the kitchen staff can know how it's made. Master Hennik told me that, in the original Hahn language, Skolash means something like *surprise.*"

Pitt squinted. "Something like?"

Barsparse shrugged. "It's more nuanced than that. There's no word in the common tongue for it. The instructions said it means *an unexpected revelation that leaves one more knowledgeable yet less content.*"

"And you want to serve that up to the ruling family and their guests?"

"No, but if they want me to, as long as I'm not being asked to make something poisonous, I will, and you'll help me," Barsparse said.

"But they don't know what they're asking for."

"I warned them as best I could, but Wollard was adamant. He said that the Formalities demanded that we welcome Master Hennik properly, and that interfering with Master Hennik's choice in any way would be bad form. I tried to tell him what Skolash was, but he refused to hear it. In the end, all he'd do was promise to make Her Ladyship aware that we were making the dish under protest, and out of loyalty to her."

"Chef, this is a mistake."

"Yes, Pitt, but it's their mistake to make."

"We're the ones making it, Chef."

"At their direction, Pitt."

"Chef, that's just stupid. We can't do this."

Finally, Barsparse snapped. "It will be done, Pitt! We've already started."

"What, because you ordered some stuff?! Cancel it! I'll cancel it!"

"You will not! That's not what I meant anyway. We've already started because the first step in the Skolash-making process, the one that I didn't tell you about, is the delegating of the actual work, starting at the head chef and ending with the lowest-ranking member of the kitchen staff. We aren't going to make Skolash. You are, Pitt."

"What?!" Pitt yelled.

Barsparse sighed. "It's actually written into the instructions. The Skolash is ordered from the head chef, who tells his second to make it, who passes the duty to the third, and it goes all the way down, reminding everyone of exactly where they stand in the pecking order, spreading the misery around. It's all a part of the Skolash ways, I guess. Anyway, I'm sorry, Pitt, but there's only the two of us, so you get the honors."

"No way," Pitt shouted. "There's no way! I won't do it!"

"You are the lowest ranking member of the kitchen staff, and you will do it."

"No. No way. And besides, I'm not the lowest. What about Ebbler?"

"He's not kitchen staff," Barsparse said.

"But you could make him kitchen staff."

There was a long silence, then Barsparse said, "An interesting idea. I can think of at least one way to make Ebbler part of the kitchen staff."

"Yeah," Pitt said, agreeing with Barsparse without stopping to consider her words. "And I bet he'd make the Skolash. He'd probably thank you for the opportunity."

There was another long silence. Barsparse took a sip of her drink, then said, "You know, I bet he would."

15.

Lady Jakabitus sat in her intricately carved chair, behind her expansive desk, in her opulent, historic office, with a stunning view of the capital visible through the massive gilt-framed windows behind her. She wore a heavily decorated blazer and hat that managed to be both militaristic and feminine. The only flaw in the tableau was Her Ladyship's expression, which betrayed her nervousness.

"I'm about to be the first Jakabitus to exchange civil words with a Hahn ruler in hundreds of years," she said.

"Indeed, Milady," Wollard agreed to the words she'd repeated several times that day. He felt confident in his answer, being sure that, at the very least, Her Ladyship's words would be civil. He nodded to Phee who stood beside him, soaking in the historic moment.

"How do you think Lord Hahn will react to the news?" Lady Jakabitus wondered.

"I expect he'll be angered by the loss of access to his son, but I would hope that said anger will be tempered by the relief of knowing that the boy is safe and being well treated," Wollard said.

"Frederain says that he made some progress with Hennik today," she said, looking for any hook on which to hang her hopes.

"That's very good to hear, Milady."

"How are the preparations for the banquet proceeding?"

"Well, Milady," Wollard said. "Migg retrieved the necessary recipe from the Arbiters and we have forwarded it to Chef Barsparse."

"Did the chef seem satisfied with the recipe?"

"She expressed concerns, Milady."

"Concerns?"

"Yes, Milady. I'm led to understand that the dish is rather theatrical in nature, and is designed more for the Hahn's tastes than for our own."

"I see," Lady Jakabitus said. "Maybe I should have a snack before the banquet."

"That might be wise, Milady."

As the meeting time approached, Wollard walked to a spot directly in front of Her Ladyship's desk. He and Lady Jakabitus nodded to each other. They had worked together long enough for each to know without asking when the other was ready to face a challenge. Besides, in this situation, it didn't particularly matter. The conference was going to happen at the appointed time whether they were ready or not.

Wollard turned his back on Lady Jakabitus to face the epic oil painting that took up most of the wall opposite Her Ladyship's desk. The painting, which would soon transform into a feed for the communication with the Hahn, depicted one of the early battles in the war over Ophion 6, which was fitting. Wollard took a moment to appreciate the skill of the long-dead painter in depicting the long-dead soldiers attempting to kill each other.

Such beautiful work, he thought, *with such ugly subject matter.*

Without turning away from the painting, Wollard asked, "What happens next, Phee?"

Phee was standing along the wall where she could see and hear everything, but would be neither seen nor heard herself once the connection was made. She replied, "The link will be established automatically. We will see Kamar Hahn's Master of Formalities first. As it was Her Ladyship who initiated this contact, it will fall on you to offer the full formal greeting. The Hahn Master of Formalities will respond, then you will defer to Her Ladyship, at which point the Hahn will defer to Lord Kamar Hahn. Once the two principals are talking, you will do your best to make everyone forget that you are in the room, unless you are needed."

"Indeed. Well done."

Wollard looked down at his papers and slid his finger around them for a moment. The painting faded to a uniform shade of black, then brightened slightly to display a live feed from the office of Kamar Hahn.

Most of the image was taken up by the Hahn Master of Formalities, a tall, thin man with slicked-down platinum-blond hair. He wore the same sort of shiny, skintight one-piece suit as Hennik and Migg wore, but his was all black, with a collar and cuffs identical to the design of the ones on Wollard and Phee's suits.

The wall of Kamar Hahn's office looked to be covered with detailed carvings of industrial conduits and ducts, all painted a uniform nonreflective black. Along the wall, on the right side of the screen, a short blond man in a skintight Hahn uniform stood silently with some sort of boxy mechanical apparatus strapped to his belly. Further forward, two additional Hahn footmen stood on either side of the Hahn Master of Formalities. They stood sideways, facing each other. Each held two handles, but whatever they were supporting was hidden from view behind the Master of Formalities. All three of the men were standing ankle deep in some sort of gravel, which seemed to completely cover the office floor.

Wollard bowed and said, "Know that two thousand, one hundred, and seventy-one conventional years have passed since the Terran Exodus. Today is the fifty-seventh day of the third month. I speak to you from the planet Apios, in the palace and office of the ruler, Lady Joanadie Jakabitus. I am Wollard, Master of Formalities for House Jakabitus, and I wish to facilitate communication between Her Ladyship, Joanadie Jakabitus, and His Lordship, Kamar Hahn, of

House Hahn and the Hahn Home World, regarding the capture and treatment of His Lordship's son, Master Hennik Hahn."

The Hahn Master of Formalities bowed, but instead of introducing himself, he said, "I formally invoke His Lordship's right to express offense on a line item basis."

Wollard said, "Acknowledged."

The Hahn Master of Formalities said, "We accept and endorse as accurate all of the times, locations, names, and titles listed in the formal greeting, but would remove the words *capture* and *treatment,* replacing them with the verbiage: *unlawful kidnapping* and *continued use as a hostage and human bargaining chip*."

"Noted," Wollard said.

The Hahn Master of Formalities bowed. "I, Kallump, Master of Formalities to His Lordship Kamar Hahn, acknowledge and return your greeting."

"Greetings, Kallump."

"Greetings, Wollard."

"I present Her Ladyship, Joanadie Jakabitus, the ruler of Apios." Wollard stepped smoothly to the side and out of view, revealing Lady Jakabitus at her desk. She looked very much like someone with whom one would not want to mess.

Kallump bowed quite deeply. "Your Ladyship, I present His Lordship, Kamar Hahn, ruler of the Hahn Home World." Kallump turned, and with noticeable effort and loud crunching noises, walked out of view.

The object supported by the two men who had been visible behind Kallump was revealed to be a thick slab of polished stone roughly the size of a large desktop. Behind the slab sat a chair that appeared to be made entirely of nonreflective metals and hoses. The chair had a high back and six arched, folding legs that supported and surrounded it like buttresses. In the chair, there was a man so lanky and thin that Lady Jakabitus doubted whether he could stand on his own. He had a bushy mane of platinum blond hair atop a sickly hide of platinum blond skin. His eyes were bright and lively, and a huge smile stretched across his face.

Lady Jakabitus said, "Greetings, Lord Hahn."

Lord Hahn turned and said, "Well? Don't you know your job? You're even worse than the last one."

Kallump said, "Oh, sorry, Milord!" He crunched his way back into view, this time behind Lord Hahn, and said, "Your Ladyship. His Lordship offers you his greetings."

Lady Jakabitus glanced to Wollard, then said, "I've initiated contact to tell you that your son, Hennik, is in our custody, is being treated well, and is in no danger."

Kamar Hahn leaned over and quietly said something to Kallump, who said, "His Lordship assures you that he had no doubt you would keep Master Hennik safe, as he knows that you are not foolish, and would not dare harm His Lordship's son."

Kamar Hahn grabbed Kallump's shoulder and roughly pulled Kallump's ear down to his mouth. He snarled something, then let Kallump go.

"I apologize. I misunderstood His Lordship's meaning. He intended to say that while you are unquestionably foolish, even you are not so foolish as to harm His Lordship's son."

"Is there some reason Lord Hahn is hesitant to speak with me directly?" Lady Jakabitus asked.

Lord Hahn pulled Kallump back down and spoke at great length into his ear. After a long moment spent listening intently, Kallump straightened back up and said, "Yes."

"And that reason is?"

"He believes that addressing you would be beneath his dignity."

Lady Jakabitus looked directly at Kamar Hahn. "I don't want to inconvenience you more than necessary." She paused until he stopped laughing. "I just wanted to inform you that I have your son, and I'm not giving him back. I intend to raise him as my own."

Kamar Hahn sat motionless for several seconds, then turned to Kallump, who leaned down of his own accord. After more whispering, Kallump rose and said, "His Lordship says that raising a child is one of the most challenging tasks a person can undertake."

"I agree," Lady Jakabitus said.

"As such, his brilliance in tricking his sworn enemy into raising his son for him will become legendary."

Lady Jakabitus turned to Wollard and said, "End this. I've said what I had to say."

Wollard stepped in front of Her Ladyship's desk and initiated the formal closing salutation. "This has been an official transmission of the Apiosan ruling family. Any reuse or re—"

Lord Hahn interrupted him. "Please give Hennik a message."

"What is it?" Lady Jakabitus asked, leaning to see around Wollard.

"Tell him not to let living there make him weak and stupid, or he will not be welcomed back. End transmission."

The feed went dark, and the antique oil painting reasserted itself.

"The rudeness of the manner in which Lord Hahn terminated the conversation will be noted," Wollard said. "Given the tenor of the exchange, the Formalities do not require you to pass along the message verbatim, Milady."

"Right now, Wollard, I do not want you to tell me about the Formalities."

"Underst—"

"Or anything else."

"Have I displeased you, Milady?"

"This entire mess was your idea."

"I couldn't take credit for the idea, Milady."

"*Credit* is not what I was offering."

"Your Ladyship, I do apologize. I recognize that the situation is unpleasant. We are at war with the Hahn. You were presented with the choice between harming a child and weakening your planet's position by delivering him to the enemy unscathed. I found a precedent for a third option, and you, in your wisdom, chose to take it."

Wollard's tone and body language were relaxed, but Phee could see his hands, which were clasped behind his back. They seemed to be trying to kill each other.

"As to what just transpired," Wollard continued, "we contacted Lord Hahn for the express purpose of telling him that we had his son and were not going to give him back. We discussed beforehand that it would be a difficult conversation. Lord Hahn simply made it difficult in a way we did not anticipate."

Lady Jakabitus considered what Wollard had said, then—in a slow, quiet voice—replied, "I suppose that's all true."

Wollard nodded, but said nothing.

"I had a decision to make, and I made it," she said. "After listening to your impeccably worded input."

Again, Wollard nodded.

Lady Jakabitus said, "All I can do now is forge ahead and hope I haven't made a mistake."

16.

Migg stood behind Hennik, holding his Hahn formalwear up by the shoulders, ready to help him wriggle into the garment. Hennik stood in his underwear in front of a full-length mirror, running his fingers through his hair, trying to make it spike up to his standards. She was not comfortable with her new duties as the personal valet of a teenage boy, and Hennik was not of a mind to make her more comfortable.

"What exactly was Father's message again?" Hennik asked, studying his hair in the mirror.

"I wasn't given the exact words, Master Hennik. I was merely told that he said to tell you not to be stupid or weak."

"And that was it?"

"I was led to believe that His Lordship has no intention of interfering with Lady Jakabitus's decision to raise you as her own."

Hennik turned, looked at the formal one-piece, looked at Migg, then simply stood still and held his arms out to his sides. Migg started threading the suit onto his limbs while he offered the absolute minimum cooperation possible.

"That lays things out pretty clearly for me, doesn't it, Migg?"

"I suppose it does, Master Hennik."

"We're stuck here."

"So it seems."

"It's not so bad."

"I agree, sir."

"The palace is large and well-appointed by Apiosan standards, and the people are friendly and helpful."

"Indeed, sir."

"It should be quite easy to escape."

Migg paused in the action of stretching a sleeve over Hennik's arm. "Escape, sir?"

"Of course, Migg. This is no place for a member of the Hahn ruling family."

"No, sir. I suspect you're right."

"And you don't deserve to be stuck here either, Migg."

"I fear that might also be true, Master Hennik."

"Migg, I know what your duties were back on the Hahn Home World, but despite the fact that you're beneath me, we're in this together."

"Yes, Master Hennik."

"Just don't forget that you're in it beneath me."

"I won't, Master Hennik."

17.

On a normal day the Jakabitus family's needs were ably handled by a limited staff, but this was not a normal day. Dignitaries, functionaries, friends, relatives, well-wishers, ill-wishers, and freeloaders from all over the solar system had flocked to the palace to help the ruling family celebrate their new addition as well as Lady Jakabitus's success in capturing the boy.

The festivities were to be held in the banquet hall in the Old Palace's second floor, a space that was large enough to house hundreds, and this night it would be filled to capacity. A small army of staff had been called up on short notice to make the guests feel that they were being served in a manner befitting the Jakabitus family. As a result, the servants' hall was full for a change. Large groups of excited temporary help stood in clusters, listening as they were briefed by their leaders for the evening. Each member of the household staff was in charge of directing those whose tasks for the evening mirrored his or her own. Shly's group was ordered to ensure nobody went thirsty. Umily would see to it that anyone who wanted (or didn't want) a napkin, glass, or utensil had his or her needs fulfilled. Ebbler would have been tending to food delivery, but he was otherwise occupied, so Glaz was supervising the waitstaff. Migg helped wherever she could.

The room was so hectic, and the staff was so busy, that nobody took note of it when Pitt, dressed in civilian attire, entered the room and walked around its periphery. The only person who spoke to him was one of the temporary staff, who asked him to step aside as she came through with a grav-platter piled high with empty glassware.

Pitt was angry, but he held his tongue. He'd talked enough today.

The passing temp added, "Just so you know, this might not be the best place to stand around. There are a lot of people trying to work here."

She didn't know she was piling insult on top of injury, or that the only reason Pitt wasn't one of those people trying to work was because his own big mouth had finally lost him his job.

Pitt watched her go, then made his way out the back of the servants' hall and down the corridor. He paused just outside the door to the kitchen.

He heard Barsparse say, "Make sure we have all of the implements we'll need for the presentation. If we're going to do this thing, we must do it right."

Ebbler said, "Yes, Chef."

Pitt stood motionless for a moment, with his eyes squeezed shut, then walked down the corridor, out the service exit, and off the palace grounds.

◆ ◆ ◆

After the details were discussed and the pep talks were given, the temporary help prepared the room and made sure all the bulkfabs were full and ready.

Shly and Umily hadn't had a chance to talk since lunch, but in the short time they had spent in the same room, always running in opposite directions, Shly had gotten the distinct impression that Umily wasn't happy. Given the great news she'd received that morning, Shly would have expected Umily to be walking on air. Finally, Shly took an opportunity to grab her friend and ask, "Um, what's the matter?"

Umily looked around to see who might be listening. The room was full of people, but the vast majority were strangers, which, oddly, made it feel more private than a mostly empty room with a few people whom she knew well.

"Don't make a big deal about it," Umily said, "but I got another letter."

"Gint?" Shly asked.

"Yeah, he was killed again, but they're already regenerating him, so he'll be fine."

"Good, I guess," Shly stammered. "I mean, I'm happy he'll be okay, but I'm so sorry he got killed again, and . . . wow, I mean, so soon, right?"

"Yes," Umily said. "Poor thing. He didn't even get to enjoy one day back on his feet before he was cut down again. It seems the Hahn are really pushing."

"Poor Gint."

"Yes," Umily agreed. "Poor Gint."

A female voice from behind them asked, "Has there been news about your husband?"

Shly and Umily turned to find Migg, who looked nervous and concerned.

Umily's mouth became a hard, straight line that would not be moved. Shly said, "Can we do something for you, Migg?"

Migg said, "I . . . no. I just wanted to say a word to you about Skolash, the dish Master Hennik requested. I'm forbidden by custom from telling you anything about it directly."

"So we've heard," Shly said. "It's supposed to be a surprise."

"And it will be. I know that you are in charge of drinks, and that you—" she nodded to Umily, "—handle linens and refuse. I can't tell you why, but it would be to your advantages to have far more linens than usual, as well as ample supplies of any drink the people of your world might use to treat an upset stomach."

Shly and Umily thought about this while Migg looked around, as if worried about being seen. She leaned in toward Umily and said, "I think the war is hateful. I hope your husband is all right." Then she walked away at top speed.

◆ ◆ ◆

Before dinner was served, the general consensus was that the banquet was a huge success. The mood was buoyant. The canapés were delicious and light, featuring subtle greens, well-seasoned meats, and small cups of clear broth. Most guests took the lightness as a sign that the chef wanted them to have plenty of room for whatever Hahn delicacy she had prepared.

The only complaint most of the guests had was that they weren't given the chance to interact personally with the new arrival. Hennik was seated at the Jakabitus family table, surrounded by attendants. If a guest approached Hennik, he or she was politely but unequivocally rebuffed for *security reasons.* Some said that it was to protect the Hahn from any guest who might harm him. Others thought it was to protect the guests from the vicious Hahn who might attack them. None guessed the real reason, which was to protect the party atmosphere from Hennik's dangerous attitude.

A little later than usual, the gong rang, signaling everyone to take their seats. There was an unusually long pause before drinks service, then a surprisingly long wait for the food to be served. In a lesser chef, this stalling would be taken as a sign of disorganization or a lack of confidence. Barsparse, however, had an impeccable reputation. If she was moving slowly, it was probably to let the anticipation build before she presented something truly remarkable.

There was a polite round of applause as Barsparse walked into the middle of the hall. The tables were arranged at the sides of the room, leaving a large empty area in the middle for announcements and presentations. Barsparse had given hundreds of these pre-meal explanations in her career, and she seemed cool and composed in her immaculate chef's whites, her black hair tied back and mostly hidden beneath a small white cap. Nobody could tell that she was nervous about this presentation, because nobody knew what she was presenting.

Barsparse acknowledged the applause, then spoke.

"First, ladies and gentlemen, I apologize for the delay. I don't like to keep people waiting, but, when you see what we have for you, I believe you'll forgive me."

She seemed uncomfortable with the fresh round of applause that followed, a clear sign of her humility.

"As you know," she continued, "this banquet is being held to honor Master Hennik Hahn, blood-son of Lord Hahn, ruler of the Hahn Home World. Master Hennik has found himself among us, and Lady Jakabitus has generously taken him into her family."

A fresh round of adulation erupted, this time aimed at Lady Jakabitus, who nodded from her seat at the Jakabitus family table. Her family reflected a range of attitudes—while Lord Frederain Jakabitus looked proud, Hennik looked positively giddy, and Rayzo looked as if he wanted to leave.

"Master Hennik was promised that I would prepare any traditional Hahn dish he selected," Barsparse said. "He chose a dish called Skolash, which can be roughly translated as *surprise.* It is a dish that requires secrecy. Her Ladyship, His Lordship, and the Master of Formalities; none of them have any idea what my sous chef and I will be serving. I want to repeat that: Master Hennik Hahn selected this dish. Only he knows what it is. We were ordered to make it, and proper form dictated that we could not tell anyone what we were making. Not even Her Ladyship knows. Again, we had *no choice*, and she *does not know*."

Fresh applause sprang up to recognize Lady Jakabitus and her staff for maintaining good form and making poor Master Hennik feel welcome. Barsparse looked to the Jakabitus family table. While Hennik seemed as if he were about to burst, Lady Jakabitus directed an uneasy look at Barsparse, who did her best to convey through subtle facial expressions that the unease was justified. Lady Jakabitus turned and beckoned to Wollard, who had been standing in the background with Phee. Wollard came forward, and he and Lady Jakabitus exchanged words.

"So—" Barsparse said, watching Her Ladyship and the Master of Formalities talk, "—without further delay . . ." Her Ladyship motioned to Hennik, who still looked terribly pleased with himself.

"It's high time . . ." Barsparse said, each word coming more slowly than the last.

Wollard nodded at some comment made by Her Ladyship and said something in reply. Lady Jakabitus bit her lip and turned to face Barsparse. She nodded. Barsparse tilted her head, as if asking if she were sure. Both Her Ladyship and Wollard nodded this time.

"To make some Skolash," Barsparse finished. "It's a uniquely theatrical dish, and is made in front of those to whom it will be served. My sous chef, Ebbler, will do the honors. He's a fine young man, who is only following orders. I will talk you through the process, which is also part of the Skolash tradition. Ebbler?"

Ebbler entered the hall pushing a silver grav-platter piled high with some large mass and draped with a cloth. His chef's whites and cap were identical to Barsparse's, and he was much more powerfully built than she was, but anyone could draw two conclusions at a glance: she was very much the one in charge, and he was more than fine with that.

Barsparse pulled out her papers and began reading from a prepared text.

"The recipe for Skolash calls for the whole carcass of a prode, a creature indigenous to the Hahn Home World. Prodes do not live on Apios, and we have no examples in Her Majesty's zoos, so we had to find the closest analog: a flunt, which, as you all know, is a medium-sized scavenger that lives off the leftovers and *leavings* of more evolved predators."

Ebbler remove the cover, revealing the flunt carcass. Several assistants ran toward him to set up what appeared to be a large, clear tent, attached to an apparatus and a high-pressure tank.

"Of course, no flunt was harmed for your meal. We scanned a living specimen and replicated it after some necessary modifications. The recipe calls for the animal to be killed by smothering, so that its skin is left unbroken, and then left out in the elements for three days. We didn't have time to do this, so the scan of the live flunt was tweaked by biologists from Her Ladyship's university to approximate the effect as closely as possible. Now, Ebbler takes the carcass into the preparation chamber."

Barsparse watched Ebbler, who pushed the grav-platter into the tent without hesitation. As an afterthought, she said, "Ebbler, don't forget your goggles."

Ebbler thanked her and quickly pulled on his goggles.

"He seals the chamber, which is airtight. While he does that, I'll read the traditional Hahn pre-Skolash statement, which I'm told has been read by chefs for centuries prior to the preparation of this dish.

"*We, your servants, present to you this Skolash. We prepare this food for the same reason most of you will eat it, because we must.*"

Barsparse looked up from her papers. "Sums it up nicely, I think. Now, Ebbler makes an incision along the creature's abdomen. Note that the . . . *ingredients* . . . are under considerable pressure, so they essentially remove themselves."

The machinery on the side of the tent sprang noisily to life. "The chamber captures the various gasses and aromas released," Barsparse said, shouting to be heard over the machinery, "and collects them for later use."

The machinery fell silent, and the audience was equally quiet. Barsparse wasn't sure if they were dumbstruck from the horror of what they were seeing, or if they were lying low, hoping she would forget they were there and thus not serve them. Either way, she could hardly blame them.

She paused again to check on the progress of the assistants, who had scurried back into the room with a new mechanical apparatus, this one featuring a large crank and a glass front. Behind the glass there was a confusing jumble of circular cams and meshing metal teeth. Beneath the glass, a large nozzle protruded, hanging at a shallow angle, ending inches above the floor.

Barsparse continued, narrating Ebbler's actions as he completed them. "Now Ebbler gathers the *ingredients* in his arms and carries them out to the traditional Skolash grinder. My thanks to the workers at Her Ladyship's machine shop, who fabricated this machine on very short notice. Ebbler feeds the ingredients into the top of the grinder and turns the crank. The grinder's unique transparent exterior, and the fact that it slowly rotates as it grinds, makes it possible for all in attendance to watch the grinding action. The raw Skolash is extruded at moderate pressure from the grinder and falls directly to the floor, from where it is collected in a large metal pan. The palace utilitics have been specially programed not to interfere with this part of the process. Once all of the raw Skolash is fully ground, it is cooked."

Ebbler walked back to the tent and removed the high-pressure canister.

"The creature's own flammable gasses are combusted," Barsparse read, "producing a greenish-blue flame and an unforgettable aroma. The flame is run over the surface of the Skolash, scorching it unevenly. The Skolash is now ready for serving. It is traditionally presented without garnish or seasoning. It is simply divided onto plates and served. Ebbler has prepared enough for each member of the ruling family, including Master Hennik, who I remind you, requested this dish, and one extra serving, which will be scanned and bulkfabbed, so that you all may *enjoy* it as well."

Ebbler and an assistant carried four plates piled high with smelly blackened mush to the Jakabitus family table, placing them in front of the members of the ruling family.

Hennik beamed down at his plate of Skolash, then turned to Lady Jakabitus.

"This has made me very happy," he said.

"Good, Hennik," Lady Jakabitus said unenthusiastically. "Please, take the first bite, and tell us if Barsparse has done your favorite dish justice."

Hennik said, "I'm not hungry."

PART 3

It is poor form to accuse someone of being a liar.

It is far poorer form to lie.

The mark of a skilled liar is the ability to convince others that the inverse is true.

-Excerpt from *The Arbiters' Official Guidelines Regarding Formal Accusations, Declarations of Wrongdoing, and Assorted Nonverbal Expressions of Reproach*

18.

Wollard skimmed over his papers and said, "Know that two thousand, one hundred, and seventy-one conventional years have passed since the Terran Exodus. Today is the sixty-third and final day of the third month. We meet on the planet Apios, in the servants' hall of Palace Koa, the ancestral home of House Jakabitus and its matriarch, Lady Joanadie Jakabitus. I am Wollard, Master of Formalities for House Jakabitus, and I am currently delivering the daily meeting to the palace staff."

Wollard was relieved to see bored faces looking up at him. It meant that equilibrium was being restored. It was rarely a sign that things were going smoothly when the staff showed a keen interest in the daily briefing.

"To start on a positive note, I think we can all agree that our newest addition, Kreet, has adapted well to his role as deliverer of edibles. While Kreet deserves congratulations, part of the credit goes also to Ebbler, who has been serving both as his trainer and as Chef Barsparse's sous chef since he received his promotion six days ago."

Sincere but disinterested praise was mumbled at Kreet from all directions. Kreet was a strapping, sleepy-eyed young man who had impressed everybody but Shly with his willingness to work and his unwillingness to talk.

Wollard moved on. “Her Ladyship is keenly interested in Master Hennik’s progress. She has asked that we all be extra attentive to his needs, his moods, and particularly his actions, watching for any indication of how well, or poorly, he is adjusting to life here. From my admittedly limited vantage point, Master Hennik appears to have accepted the situation. Of course, Migg is the person in the best position to verify that, but as we all know, members of the palace staff are sworn to never violate the trust of a member of the ruling family. I would never ask any of you to violate that trust. As such, as has become our custom, I will now ask some innocent questions and make some carefully worded, innocuous statements, to which Migg may respond as she wishes. You will all be present to *innocently overhear* the conversation. We are free to infer from her responses, or lack thereof, some hint of Master Hennik’s mental state.”

Eyes rolled, but everyone turned their attention to Migg, who was focused on Wollard. She had started wearing the standard uniform of a member of the palace staff, but she still seemed out of place. Everybody recognized that she was trying to fit in and be useful. Indeed, this daily farce was her idea. It could be argued that she and Wollard were still breaking the spirit of the oath, but after the banquet debacle, even the Master of Formalities saw the necessity of creating new protocols for dealing with Hennik’s behavior.

“Good morning, Migg.”

“Good morning, Wollard.

“Master Hennik seems to be adjusting well to life here in the palace.”

“It does seem that way. Master Hennik has been making a great effort to fit in and help his new family . . . relax,” Migg said.

“How are you today?” Wollard asked.

“Today is not my best day,” Migg responded.

“I’m sorry to hear that. Do you need medical assistance, or perhaps some other form of help?”

“Not at the moment. If that changes, I will let you know.”

“I see,” Wollard said.

"One way or the other, I expect the problem will have passed by tomorrow."

"I see. Please do let me know if your condition changes."

"I will try."

Everyone took a moment to fully digest what they'd heard, then Wollard continued with the briefing as if nothing had happened.

"We must all be on our toes today. Most of Her Ladyship's agenda is taken up by a vitally important summit with Lord Ment Pavlon, ruler of the planet . . . *Sheud.*

Wollard took care to pronounce *Sheud* properly, which meant saying *shee-ood* slowly, with his lips puckered. The information he'd received from the Arbiters had stressed the importance of using the correct pronunciation. They'd included the advice that the more wrong the word felt as it left your mouth, the better your pronunciation probably was.

"Lord Pavlon will meet with Her Ladyship in Her Ladyship's offices, then join the Jakabitus family for lunch. There will be a second round of meetings in the afternoon, after which he will depart for his home planet . . . *Sheud.* His world lies in close proximity to Ophion 6, and while the people of . . . *Sheud* have always maintained neutrality, they could be a powerful ally in our ongoing war with the Hahn."

Umily raised her hand. "Query."

"I recognize Umily, tender to personal needs."

"Has the intensity of the fighting died down at all?"

"Sadly, as you know, I cannot say," Wollard said. "Any information I may glean from Her Ladyship's daily greetings must be held in strict confidence. You are actually in a better position to answer than I am. Have you received any letters from Gint recently?"

"I got one the day before yesterday."

"Splendid. And has he been," Wollard cleared his throat, "regenerated recently?"

"No, not since those first four times."

"Well, that's good news. It seems we might be able to surmise that the fighting has eased."

Umily shook her head. "I don't know. I think he's just better at not getting killed now."

Wollard said, "Either way, a positive development."

With that, Wollard called the morning briefing to a close. Glaz made her standard declaration about the quality of the day and the copiousness of the work to be done, then everyone separated into small groups, squeezing in just a bit of conversation before getting on with their duties.

Migg approached Hartchar hesitantly, which was how most people approached Hartchar until they got to know her. Once they knew her, they approached cautiously.

"Hartchar, may I have a word?" Migg asked.

"Yes."

"You and Master Rayzo are having a regular sports practice today, right?"

"Yes. Why?"

"I was just wondering," Migg said.

"I understood that you asked because you were wondering. I wanted to know why you were wondering."

"Ah. Sorry. I'll get to the point. Do you have anything out of the ordinary planned for practice today?"

"No," Hartchar said. "Why do you ask?"

"No reason."

Hartchar said, "I'm glad we had this talk," and started to walk away, but she paused when Migg spoke again.

"I am sworn to keep the confidence of all members of the ruling family," Migg said. "Particularly those with whom I work closely."

"So you are," Hartchar agreed.

"I also feel a debt to those who have been kind to me, and I don't want to see anyone suffer unnecessarily."

"Migg, is Master Hennik planning something?"

"I couldn't say. If he were, it certainly wouldn't be anything dangerous. His usual goal is to disrupt and antagonize, not to cause anyone physical harm."

"How would he disrupt or antagonize me, hypothetically?"

Migg bit her lip. "I'm sorry, Hartchar. I've probably already said too much."

"You've said almost nothing."

Migg said, "*Almost nothing* is *something*."

On the other side of the room, a few members of the junior staff had gathered to talk.

"Well, Kreet," Ebbler said, "you're on your own."

"Or, if you'd feel better about it, Shly could keep an eye on me," Kreet said.

"There's no need for that. Remember, if you have any questions, I'll be in the kitchen."

Kreet said, "Good." He turned to Shly. "Where will you be?"

"Doing my work," Shly said

"So, Ebbler, you must be excited to finally be the sous chef," Umily said.

"You know it," Ebbler said. "Who wouldn't be?"

Umily and Shly said nothing, but their smiles were a little too broad. Kreet said nothing and did not change his expression.

"What?" Ebbler said. "Shouldn't I be excited?"

"No, you should," Umily said.

"Of course you should," Shly agreed. "We know how badly you want this. We just wouldn't want it ourselves, is all."

"Why not? It's a huge honor to work with Chef Barsparse."

"Yes," Umily said. "No question! She's a great artist."

"Absolutely," Shly said. "She uses her talent to do the work of a bulkfab, but that's her decision."

Ebbler couldn't believe his ears. "How can you say that? I explained this to you before. No bulkfab can do what she does."

Shly and Umily both nodded furiously, then Umily said, "Well, yes, you have said that."

"So, what, you didn't believe me?" Ebbler asked. "Did you think I was talking nonsense?"

Shly said, "It's not like we're calling you a liar. We believed that *you* believed it."

"No, you just thought I was wrong," Ebbler said, sourly.

Umily said, "Sorry, Ebbler, but when you come down to it, she makes food. That's exactly what a bulkfab does."

"But . . . Umily . . . what?" Ebbler sputtered. "You're married to Gint! He was the sous chef before Pitt!'

"Yes," Umily said. "I am."

"Did you ever tell him what you thought of his profession before you married him?"

"No."

"Why not?"

"I wanted to marry him."

Ebbler gave himself a moment to cool down, then, in an even tone that sounded as if it took great effort to maintain, said, "Bulkfabs are soulless machines. They crank out the same thing over and over. Chef Barsparse has originality and creativity. No two meals or servings are the same."

"That's what a *faulty* bulkfab does," Shly said. "Ebbler, I'm sorry."

Umily said, "Look, we're happy for you. Barsparse is great, and we know how excited you are for this. We just don't understand it."

"Look, I gotta go," Ebbler said.

"Go ahead. Have fun," Shly said.

"You're gonna do great," Umily added.

Ebbler said, "Thanks, I appreciate that, but you really don't know what *great* means."

19.

Hennik opened his eyes a crack and looked at the wall of his bedchamber while his brain booted up. Once he felt ready, he started his day the way he started every day.

"Migg," he barked. "Have you let me oversleep?"

"You have not overslept, Master Hennik. There is ample time to dress before breakfast is served."

"Lucky for you," Hennik said. "You should thank me for waking up on my own, saving you from your own incompetence."

"Thank you, Master Hennik."

Migg was standing in the corner of his room, exactly where she'd been standing when he went to sleep. Back on the Hahn Home World, Hennik, like all members of the ruling family, had a special servant whose sole job was to stand in the corner of his bedchamber watching him while he slept, in case he needed something. Here, on Apios, Migg was the only proper Hahn servant assigned to him, and as Her Ladyship had refused to provide the stimulants necessary to keep Migg awake around the clock, Hennik was forced to make do.

Migg stood in the corner until Hennik was asleep each night and resumed her position before he awoke each morning. It was less than ideal, but at least he knew she was getting less sleep than he was.

Hennik sat up and looked blearily around the room. He slept without covers, in shorts. The temperature was set to his preferences, with the result that Migg—fully clothed and standing at attention—was quite uncomfortable, which was his preference.

Hennik turned and hung his legs over the side of the bed. Migg sprang into action, rushing to open the door of the attached restroom facilities and ensure the room was prepared to Hennik's standards. On the Hahn Home World, several servants would have been toiling and scrubbing right up to the last minute, waiting to scurry aside like frightened insects when the door opened, but the utilitics and four-a-day visits from Umily kept the room well stocked and in pristine condition.

Hennik staggered into the lavatory while Migg stood facing the corner.

"Did they speak of me at the morning briefing?" Hennik asked.

"Yes, Master Hennik. The Master of Formalities asked how you were."

"And what did you tell him?"

"I told him that you were trying to fit in, as you instructed, Master Hennik."

"And was there any discussion of Rayzo?"

"Master Rayzo's name was barely mentioned, Master Hennik."

"Good. In the short time I've been here, I've completely eclipsed the little worm. He's an afterthought in his own home."

"Yes, Master Hennik."

"Even during his ridiculous Apiosan sports practice, his father pays more attention to me than to his own son."

"Yes, Master Hennik."

"That fool Frederain barely looks at the mat anymore. He's too busy regaling me with stories of every single match he ever won when he was young."

"Quite so, Master Hennik."

"It isn't fun for me, sucking up to that old blowhard, acting like I respect his ridiculous wife. The way she struts around, pretending to be a proper ruler, like my father. She sickens me."

"I know she does, Master Hennik."

"It will all be worth it when my plan comes to fruition. They'll know I've been treating them with the ultimate disrespect by misleading them. They'll be as crushed as their son is now. I bet Rayzo actually misses having that old fop shout useless advice at him."

"I wouldn't be surprised, Master Hennik."

"I can't wait to see the look on Rayzo's ugly little face when I climb onto the mat today."

"Do you still intend to participate in practice today, Master Hennik?"

"Of course I do," Hennik said.

"I suppose it is an opportunity to receive physical training from a professional at your adversary's expense."

"What, Hartchar? No, I don't think that monster has anything to teach me. I'll participate because this is my last opportunity to prove my ultimate superiority to Rayzo before our escape."

"We still intend to escape, Master Hennik?"

"Of course we do. It's all we think about! We can't wait to get back to the Hahn Home World and put this awful place behind us." After a moment of silence, Hennik asked, "Isn't that right?"

Migg said, "Yes, Master Hennik, it is as you say."

"Yes, it is," Hennik agreed.

His business in the lavatory done, Hennik returned to his bedchamber and assumed his dressing stance, feet slightly apart, arms spread wide, and an impatient look on his face. Threading garments onto Hennik had become easier now that he'd grudgingly adopted Apiosan clothing, but Hennik always compensated for this by being less helpful in the dressing process.

"Should I assume," Hennik asked, "that since you were somehow uncertain of the status of our escape plan, you haven't gathered the things I ordered?"

"I apologize for my misunderstanding, Master Hennik," Migg said as she lifted his right foot to sheathe it in his pant leg. "But the items are available."

"Really?"

"Yes, Master Hennik."

"Where? Let me see!"

"I don't have the items here, Master Hennik. I didn't want to arouse suspicion. I have procured sources for all of the necessary pieces, though, and I can have them here today, should you decide to make an attempt."

"Migg, you dullard. I've already decided. We escape tonight. And we won't *make an attempt.* We will escape."

"Yes, Master Hennik. I'm sorry, Master Hennik."

"Go to your sources. I expect to find the things I need in this room this afternoon. We have an opportunity here, Migg, and I'm not going to waste it. Understand?"

"I understand, Master Hennik."

"Good."

Now fully dressed, Hennik took a moment to look at himself. In addition to being easier to put on and take off than Hahn clothing, Apiosan clothing tended toward brighter colors, more ornamentation, and was designed to flatter, giving the impression of a narrow waist and a muscular frame while concealing the parts of one's anatomy of which one might be less proud.

"Disgusting," Hennik said, inspecting his ensemble. "Don't you agree, Migg?"

"Yes, Master Hennik."

Hennik shook his head. "Even their clothes are dishonest. They start each day by cloaking themselves in falsehood. Migg, we need to get away from these people."

Hennik left. Migg waited a respectful interval, allowing him to put enough distance between them to be spared the undignified spectacle of Migg leaving to go to her quarters.

Once she reached her quarters, Migg spent a long time sitting on her bed with her eyes closed, imagining all of the various ways the day could play out.

Eventually she sighed and said, “I suppose it’s time to go to my sources.”

She used the bulkfab set into the wall of her quarters to start producing the items Hennik had specified. All of the servants had their own bulkfabs. Hennik didn’t know, and Migg hadn’t told him.

20.

Lady Jakabitus stood in the courtyard, waiting.

Wollard stood next to her, also waiting.

Phee stood next to Wollard, watching them wait.

They were not concerned about security. While it was true that Her Ladyship was standing out in a large open area during a time of war, that open area was surrounded by her own palace, which was itself surrounded by a zone of carefully protected space, through which, they were confident, nothing unwelcome could penetrate.

Wollard cleared his throat. "Milady, I should point out that it is not too late to summon the rest of the ruling family."

"Should you?" Lady Jakabitus asked.

"Milady, I'm merely trying to inform you of all of your options. In this instance, you still have the option of assembling your family and the staff to greet Lord Pavlon."

"I do have that option."

"Then shall I send Phee to—"

"No," Lady Jakabitus said. "You shall not."

"Lady Jakabitus, I apologize if I have displeased you. I would not be doing my job if I didn't remind you that greeting a visiting Lord without the entire family and staff is highly unusual."

"Unusual, but not unprecedented," Lady Jakabitus said.

"It is true, Milady, that under unusual circumstances, various rulers have, at times, entertained foreign rulers without introducing them to the household, but it is not the norm."

"This is an unusual situation, Wollard. You know that. Our war with the Hahn has only intensified, despite our *efforts*. The Hahn are still employing strategies that are so outdated we're only now beginning to remember how to combat them. Lord Pavlon is in a position to be a great help to us. It's important for him to perceive me as a tough-minded leader who is serious about securing his assistance. I don't think it's important that he see me as a loving mother and wife. Above all, I think it is of paramount importance that he not be exposed to Hennik, and you'd be the first to point out that to introduce the rest of my family but omit my *adopted son* would be bad form."

"Indeed, Milady."

The transport became visible in the distance, plummeting out of the stratosphere before leveling off on a trajectory that carried it over the city and straight through the palace's gates. As always, the craft turned sideways to give the honored guests the best possible view. Soon the craft was stationary, the ramp had poured into position, and the passengers emerged.

The first person out of the craft was a man, middle aged and trim. He wore a dark, dignified uniform. He paused, looked about the courtyard, then nodded almost imperceptibly toward Lady Jakabitus. The nod said that he knew it would be rude to greet Her Ladyship out of turn, but it would be equally rude to pretend that he didn't notice her. He turned back to the craft and extended a hand toward the open portal.

The next person out of the transport was a man of similar build and age to the first, but dressed very differently. He wore a bright orange robe with a shocking green hem, cuffs, and collar, all of which flared aggressively. His hands, protruding from the oversized sleeves, looked like clappers in a pair of church bells. His head was dwarfed by the collar, which extended well above his cranium, not that you could see his head, hidden as it was beneath a thick layer of white makeup and a towering hat that branched like a tree, tapering to several points, the tallest of which was an arm's length above his shoulders.

The two men stood by the transport as Wollard and Phee approached.

Wollard bowed and said, "Know that two thousand, one hundred, and seventy-one conventional years have passed since the Terran Exodus. Today is the sixty-third and final day of the third month. We meet on the planet Apios, in the palace of the ruler, Lady Joanadie Jakabitus. This is the palace's inner courtyard. I am Wollard, Master of Formalities for House Jakabitus, and I am honored to welcome you, Lord Ment Pavlon, ruler of the planet . . . *Sheud*, for a state visit."

The man in the orange and green robe bowed slightly. His hat loomed over Wollard as if it were in danger of falling on him. The man's eyes darted to the second man, who nodded.

The man in the robe said, "Greetings Wollard. I am Lord Ment Pavlon, as you said."

Wollard bowed.

"This man," Lord Pavlon said, gesturing toward his companion, "Is Soodon, my valet. I travel with him, my valet, Soodon."

"Very good, Milord," Wollard said.

"He accompanies me when I travel, as my valet, but he has no further significance."

"As you say, Milord."

Lord Pavlon leaned toward Wollard, looking him in the eye. "During our stay, if you could extend Soodon the level of hospitality appropriate to a visiting Lord's valet, I would be most grateful."

"Of course, Milord." Wollard bowed toward the valet. "You have my assurance that we will afford him every courtesy."

"But only those courtesies that are due a valet," Lord Pavlon interjected. "Which is what he is."

Wollard said, "Indeed, Milord."

Wollard led Lord Pavlon and Soodon across the courtyard to Lady Jakabitus. "Please allow me to present Lady Joanadie Jakabitus, ruler of the planet Apios. Lady Jakabitus, this is Lord Pavlon, ruler of the planet . . . *Sheud*."

Both rulers bowed.

"Welcome, Lord Pavlon," Lady Jakabitus said. "I do appreciate you taking the time to meet with me."

"It's my pleasure, Lady Jakabitus. I should introduce my valet, Soodon, who is my valet, and travels with me."

Phee tugged at Wollard's sleeve. Noting the silent question in her eyes, he leaned in to speak to her discreetly. "His Lordship is traveling without a Master of Formalities. It's not uncommon for a ruler to seem . . . *unsettled* in such circumstances."

Wollard refocused on the conversation in time to hear Lady Jakabitus say, "We have much to discuss, but we'll get to that soon enough. First, I wonder if you'd like a quick tour of the palace?"

Lord Pavlon glanced at Soodon, who nodded.

"Yes," Lord Pavlon said. "That sounds fine."

"Good. While we do that, your man can get your belongings settled in your quarters. We know you don't intend to stay the night, but we thought you'd appreciate having a space of your own where you can rest and refresh yourself while you're here."

"He will need quarters too," Lord Pavlon blurted. "To wait in, while I'm in meetings. Servant's quarters, of course."

Soodon gritted his teeth, then quickly adopted a more neutral expression.

"Of course," Lady Jakabitus said. "I'm sure Wollard can make the necessary arrangements."

"They are already made, Milady," Wollard said. "Soodon, this is my protégée, Phee. She will show you first to His Lordship's quarters, then to your own."

"I think that should work," Lord Pavlon said.

"Certainly," Soodon agreed.

"Yes," Lord Pavlon said with greater conviction. "That will be quite satisfactory."

21.

“And this is where you’ll be staying,” Phee said, leading Soodon into one of the spare rooms in the servants’ quarters. Long ago, the servants in Palace Koa had slept in a sort of barracks, separated by gender, with only the senior staff getting any real privacy. But as the staff had greatly diminished over the past few hundred years, and the palace had been modernized several times, the space had been reconfigured into generous private living accommodations for all of the staff, with rooms to spare for visitors.

The room assigned to Soodon was a large and well-appointed, with a sleeping area, a dining area, its own bulkfab, and an attached lavatory. All of the furnishings were high quality and well maintained. It wouldn’t be ideal for raising a family, but it was quite comfortable for one person. Indeed, by most standards it would have been described as *luxurious.*

Phee watched Soodon inspect the room, waiting for him to express amazement, gratitude, or preferably a mixture of both.

“Adequate,” Soodon said. “For servant’s quarters, quite adequate. Of course, the other room was much nicer.”

“Lord Pavlon’s room,” Phee said.

“Yes, that was quite nice. Quite nice indeed.”

"I'm glad you approve," Phee said. "Lady Jakabitus takes great pride in her family's treatment of her guests and their servants."

"As well she should. Phee, that is your name, Phee, right?"

"Yes."

"You're Wollard's protégée. That means that you are bound by the same rules as a fully-fledged Master of Formalities. Is that right?"

"Yes."

"Good. And if I were to tell you something in confidence, what would happen?"

"If precedent supported maintaining your confidence, I would be honor bound not to divulge what we discussed."

"Very good. Phee, who's in charge here?"

"Lady Jakabitus is the ruler of Apios."

"Yes, I know, but who's in charge of the palace staff?"

"That would be Glaz, the palace expediter."

"Excellent. I wish to speak with this *Glaz* immediately."

It didn't take long for Phee to locate Glaz and return with her. Soodon closed the door behind them and offered them a seat.

"Glaz, Phee, I apologize for the subterfuge, but what I'm about to tell you is to be kept in the strictest confidence. The fact of the matter is that the man I arrived with is not Lord Pavlon. He is a decoy. I am Lord Pavlon."

Phee was stuck; she couldn't think of the proper way for a Master of Formalities to request that someone repeat himself and preferably elaborate without sounding either rude or ill informed.

Glaz said, "I'm sorry. What?" She was not a Master of Formalities.

Soodon said, "He's a decoy, my chief bodyguard. I know it might sound strange."

"It very well might," Glaz said.

Phee rather enjoyed letting Glaz take the lead for the moment.

"It's dangerous to be the ruler of . . . *Sheud*. My life is in constant peril. That's why I, as the Ruler of . . . *Sheud*, choose to travel with a decoy."

"But surely your bodyguard shouldn't be meeting with Her Ladyship; you should," Glaz said.

"He's been well trained to act as my proxy. *Sheud* . . . sorry. Should some unforeseen situation arise, he'll consult with me before making any decisions. That's why we've cultivated his image to make him seem weak willed and uncertain."

"He did look to you for reassurance when you arrived," Phee said.

"Exactly," Soodon said. "We try to give the impression that he's being manipulated by his valet. It seems to work. Occasionally, whoever we're meeting will start dealing directly with me in the hopes that I'll sway Lord Pavlon's opinion, not knowing that I'm actually Lord Pavlon."

"Clever," Glaz said, "but I don't like it. It's disrespectful to Her Ladyship, and dangerous too. If someone attempts to kill your double, Her Ladyship will be in peril."

"But she'll be standing next to the finest bodyguard my planet has to offer," Soodon said. "She's probably safer right now than she's ever been before."

"Her Ladyship has excellent security of her own. You can't see it, but Palace Koa is a fortress."

"I'm sure it is," Soodon agreed. "But if, when I agreed to visit, I'd said that I was bringing my own security, you wouldn't have dropped all your defenses because *Lord Pavlon has it covered.* And when Lady Jakabitus travels, I'm sure she doesn't just take it on faith that the rulers she's visiting will keep her safe."

Glaz and Phee were quiet for a long time. Finally, they turned to each other, looking for a sign of what to do next. The clear message they both received was, *Don't ask me.*

Phee fell back on her training. She stood, bowed, and said "Lord Pavlon, I will—"

Soodon raised a finger and interrupted. "I'm sorry. It's very important that you never bow to me or refer to me as *Lord Pavlon.* I appreciate the gesture, but if you slipped and did that in public, even once, the whole ruse would be destroyed. Please, address me as an equal and call me Soodon."

"Yes, Soodon. I was just about to say that I would make Wollard aware—"

"I'm sorry, again, but you cannot tell Wollard, Lady Jakabitus, or anyone else. This has to stay with us. I'm trusting you with my life."

Phee caught herself starting to bow and stopped. "Of course, Soodon."

"Very good. And you, Glaz?"

Glaz said, "I'll keep your secret as well, but I don't like it."

"That's perfectly understandable. I thank you for your cooperation. Now that you know the situation, I'd like to talk to you about my accommodations."

"Is there something wrong with the room?" Glaz asked.

"No, there's nothing *wrong* with it, per se, I'm just curious if there isn't something a little more in keeping with my actual position."

Glaz said, "I suppose we could move you to one of the empty suites we hold for honored guests. It's irregular, but not unheard of."

"We could say that we did it as a gesture of good will toward our future allies," Phee offered.

"That's very smart, but really, it would be best if you said nothing about it at all. Also, please give me a suite that is as distant from my decoy's suite as possible. It will defeat the whole purpose of our ruse if we're placed too close to each other."

Glaz said, "That won't be a problem."

"Good! Good," Soodon said. "Now, what is your chef preparing for lunch?"

22.

“All right,” Hartchar said. “Back on the mat, facedown.”

Rayzo dropped to the mat and lay facedown, spread-eagled in his sports shorts. The instant he was at rest, Hartchar shouted, “Go!”

“Up! Get up, Boy!” Lord Jakabitus yelled from his mat-side seat.

Before Lord Jakabitus had finished uttering the first syllable, Rayzo had sprung back to his feet and was hunched in a defensive posture.

“Again, down,” Hartchar ordered. Rayzo dropped to the mat again. “Go!”

“On your feet, Boy!” Frederain shouted. Again, Rayzo was standing faster than his father could tell him to stand. As the practice wore on, Hartchar and Frederain continued the refrain they’d developed, as if in chorus with each other.

“Again. Hit the floor. Go.”

“Stand up!”

“Down again. Go.”

“Up Boy! Up!”

“Again. Go.”

“Get up!”

Hartchar clapped. "That'll do for now. Remember, everybody gets knocked down. It's part of sports. What's more important is how you get back up. Not everybody gets back up, and even fewer get back up well. If your opponent knocks you down, but you're back on your feet instantly, as if it never happened, it will be more demoralizing for him than getting knocked down was for you."

"Of course," Hennik added, "it's even more demoralizing if you knock your opponent down and never let him up again, wouldn't you agree, Lord Jakabitus?"

Hennik was sitting in his customary seat next to His Lordship. It was convenient, both for the view it afforded him of Rayzo's training and for its proximity to Lord Jakabitus's ear.

"Quite," Lord Jakabitus said. "Hartchar is a fine trainer, Rayzo, and I'm glad she's spent the day working on this with you, but in general, I'd rather see you training to win than learning to simply avoid losing."

"Milord," Hartchar said in a slow, controlled tone. "It's hard to argue with what you say, but one of the important things that we learn from sports is the skill of turning failure into success."

"Very true, Hartchar," Lord Jakabitus said.

"Still," Hennik added, "it's better to not have failed to begin with, isn't it, Lord Jakabitus?"

"Of course, Hennik. Nobody can argue with that, wouldn't you agree, Hartchar?"

"That success is preferable to failure? Yes, Your Lordship."

Hennik smiled benignly at Rayzo.

Hartchar got back to business. "Now Rayzo, we will work on—"

"Hartchar, I don't want to interrupt," Hennik interrupted in a meek voice, "but I was hoping that I might train with Rayzo."

"Splendid, Hennik!" Lord Jakabitus smiled so hard it altered the shape of his moustache. "I'd been hoping you'd decide to participate."

"Yes," Hartchar said. "Splendid. Be suited up for practice tomorrow, and we'll—"

"I was hoping I could start today," Hennik said.

"Good man," Lord Jakabitus said. "Why delay, eh?"

"Then why didn't you say so at the beginning of the practice?" Hartchar asked. Lord Jakabitus cleared his throat, and she added, "Master Hennik."

Hennik looked up at Hartchar, then over at Lord Jakabitus, then at the floor, and said, "Shy, I guess."

"Oh, there's no need for that," Lord Jakabitus said. "Go suit up. I'm certain Hartchar would be too happy to let you join in."

"Too happy," Hartchar agreed. "There are extra pairs of shorts in the preparation chamber. When you return, we'll run some drills for—"

"Actually," Hennik said, "I was hoping I could start by sparring with Rayzo. Sports just looks like so much fun. I want to get right to it."

Lord Jakabitus laughed, slapped Hennik on the back, and said, "Well done. Yes, quite so. I like your attitude. Go suit up."

Hennik smiled at Lord Jakabitus, then at Rayzo, then ran to the preparation chamber.

"Looks like you've got a fight on your hands, boy," Lord Jakabitus said. "Remember, he's a beginner."

"Yes, Father."

Hartchar put a hand on Rayzo's shoulder and led him as far from Lord Jakabitus's seat as they could get without leaving the mat. Rayzo was average height for a fourteen-year-old male Apiosan, but Hartchar was much taller. She kept her hand on the boy's shoulder and looked him square in the eye.

"As His Lordship said, Master Hennik is a beginner."

"Yes, Hartchar. I'll take it easy on him."

"Don't you dare, Master Rayzo."

"But Father said—"

"Disregard what your father said," Hartchar said. She nearly said, *in this instance,* but stopped herself. "Do you think, if roles were reversed, Master Hennik would take it easy on you? Do you think he intends to take it easy on you now? Can you picture Lord Jakabitus praising you for *narrowly* beating a first-time competitor?"

After a small silence, Hartchar said, "The answer to all of those questions is *no.*"

"I know it," Rayzo said. "But Mother says that we must show compassion."

"Yes, but your mother, Her Ladyship, has no interest in sports. In a moment, Master Hennik is going to come out here. He is going to do everything he can to defeat you in front your father. He expects to succeed, or he wouldn't be making the attempt."

"But, he's never competed before. How can he expect to win?"

"He's a year older, he's got superior height and reach, he's more muscular, he's more aggressive, and he's spent the last week observing your training, looking for weaknesses. He knows all of this, and it has made him overconfident."

"You're sure he's *over*confident?"

"Yes, because he's only seen you practice the fundamentals. He knows nothing of sports strategy. Approach him physically as a larger opponent, but mentally, think of him as a child. The moves that won you your first matches will earn you victory here. Now oil yourself up."

Hennik reemerged in a fresh pair of sports shorts. He was able to dress and undress rather quickly when he wasn't being assisted, and the sports shorts didn't take long to put on. Since it was his first match, Hennik was unranked, even within the palace, so his shorts were blank. He went to the oil dispenser to apply the last portion of the Apiosan sports regulation uniform. He looked to the time readout above the door and slowed down, taking a surprising amount of time to apply the oil. After nearly two minutes of thorough oil application, Hartchar asked, "Master Hennik, are you sure you want to do this?"

"Of course I do," he said, glancing again at the time.

"I only ask, Master Hennik, because you appear to be stalling."

"Nonsense," Hennik said, looking at the clock. He applied one last palm full of oil to his shoulder and said, "Yeah, that ought to do. That should be just fine."

He slowly stepped across the retractable bridge over the gutter and into the ring. Rayzo took his position for the advantage round. It occurred to Hennik for the first time that he wasn't sure where he was supposed to stand. It didn't concern him. He knew the basic structure of the game, which was laughably simplistic. If he found himself at a loss, his victory would be assured if he just did whatever Rayzo did, but better. If he did find himself in trouble, he had his secret weapon, but he was sure it wouldn't be necessary.

I've observed Rayzo, and I know his weakness, Hennik thought. *It's that he, like everyone else on this ridiculous planet, is weak.*

Hennik stood opposite Rayzo, an equal distance from the center of the mat, and assumed Rayzo's stance—hunched forward, weight on the balls of the feet, hands in front, ready to slap. Hartchar stood nearby, acting as a referee. Lord Jakabitus leaned in, not wanting to miss a second of the action.

"Advantage round," Hartchar said. "Fifteen seconds."

The palace's practice mat was, of course, a full, regulation competitive mat, and the floor pulsated as a cue that the advantage round was about to start. Then the mat turned bright red, indicating that the round had begun.

Rayzo slapped Hennik once hard across the face. Hennik had anticipated many fast, weak slaps. The one, immediate, stinging blow stunned him for an instant. His sudden blush of anger was replaced with contempt when he saw Rayzo immediately transition to a cowardly defensive posture, raising both forearms to cover his face. Obviously he had taken his best shot, and was now fearing the inevitable reprisal. Hennik laughed in spite of himself as he leaned in, whipping both of his hands toward the sides of Rayzo's head.

Rayzo pushed his forearms forward and out to shoulder width. Hennik's wrists hit the uprights of Rayzo's arms and stopped, his hands never making contact with Rayzo's face. Rayzo kept his arms bent and rained the sides of Hennik's face with a flurry of fast, light slaps, each of which raised Rayzo's score while blocking Hennik's graceless attempts to retaliate. Hennik's arms were trapped outside the protective bubble of Rayzo's arms, and were of no use.

Hennik had just enough time to realize that he was losing, then time was up, and he had lost. The advantage round went to Rayzo. Hennik hadn't scored a single point.

Lord Jakabitus clapped loudly. "Well done, Rayzo, Well done! And don't worry, Hennik. You're still new to this. Leave it to me, Hartchar, and Rayzo. We'll teach you, in time."

"Yeah, Hennik," Rayzo said. "We'll teach you. So, what's your dominant hand?"

Hennik thought for a moment, squinted at Rayzo, and said, "The left."

Rayzo smirked at this, knowing that it was a lie. "I think I'll take your right hand anyway."

Hennik put out his right arm, which Rayzo grasped with his own right hand. The mat pulsated. As soon as the challenge round began, Rayzo started circling quickly to Hennik's right. This forced Hennik to spin in place to keep Rayzo from ending up behind him. Of course, Hennik could have done the same thing, but Rayzo was in the driver's seat.

They spun around several revolutions, Rayzo walking in a circle while Hennik pivoted, becoming slightly dizzy. Hennik decided he needed to make a big move to break them out of this stalemate before he lost his balance. He launched himself hard to his right, toward the space just behind Rayzo, hoping to force his competitor to pivot, thus providing himself with an opening to wrest control of the situation.

As Hennik lunged, Rayzo unexpectedly let go of Hennik's wrist, which would have been most welcome if Hennik hadn't been expecting

Rayzo's resistance. Hennik lurched forward and rotated clumsily, off balance. Rayzo used all his force to shove Hennik's right shoulder with both hands, adding to Hennik's rotational momentum.

Hennik spun like a top, but fell to the mat in exactly the way a top wouldn't. He rolled onto the mat, felt his face make contact, and heard the chime signifying a point for Rayzo. Lord Jakabitus shouted something, but Hennik didn't hear it. He was too occupied with rolling onto his back and fending off Rayzo, who had dived with both hands for the waistband of Hennik's shorts.

Somehow Hennik managed to fend off Rayzo's attack and get a grip on both of the younger boy's wrists, but Rayzo swiftly moved past Hennik's head and started twisting, forcing Hennik to either let go or roll facedown again. Hennik chose to let go and clambered to his feet just in time for Rayzo to get a firm grip on his right wrist and start circling to his right once more.

Again, Hennik attempted to lunge behind Rayzo and take the upper hand. Again, Rayzo let go of his wrist and shoved his shoulder. Again, Hennik spun and fell, resulting in a point scored for Rayzo and another attempted pantsing attack.

Soon they were back on their feet, again, spinning as before.

"You can't win," Hennik grunted. "I know your tricks."

"I've done the same move twice," Rayzo said.

"Those are your tricks. The move, and then doing it twice," Hennik said. "Say, do you hear anything?"

In spite of himself, Rayzo noticed a sound coming from beyond the mat. Specifically, he heard a voice. More specifically, he heard Shly's voice.

"I apologize, Milord," Shly said. "I was told that you wanted your beverage early today."

Shly's here! Rayzo thought. *I'm winning the match, and Shly's here to see it! How long has she been here?* Just then, Rayzo felt a strong shove, and the next moment he was in the gutter.

"Well done, Hennik," Lord Jakabitus said. "Good effort, Rayzo. Don't feel too bad. He is older and stronger than you. You'll just have to learn to outwit him."

"Hey, look," Hennik said. "My shorts have updated. That's a number one, isn't it?" Rayzo kept his eyes closed, but he could hear the smile in Hennik's voice. "And Rayzo's have a two on them now. That's not so bad. Second place. Good for you, Rayzo."

"Perhaps a second round is in order, or a rematch tomorrow," Hartchar suggested, straining the words through her teeth.

"I don't think that's a good idea, Hartchar," Hennik said. "We should both spend some time training. We must let Rayzo improve, so he'll have a fighting chance."

23.

In the kitchen, lunch preparation was reaching a fever pitch. Items too numerous to count were being baked, cooled, stirred, rested, boiled, chilled, and checked by Ebbler. The fact that lunch was being served in three shifts and two separate locations had not done anything to simplify matters.

Barsparse was whisking a single pot at just the right speed, for the perfect amount of time, while keeping it from rising above a specific temperature, which was requiring so much of her attention and skill she barely had enough mental bandwidth left to supervise Ebbler.

He lacks Pitt's training, but I knew that when I promoted him, Barsparse thought. *His enthusiasm helps make up for it, and he handles stress more gracefully than Pitt ever did. Of course, Ebbler doesn't have to deal with the added distraction of the food deliverer constantly offering to help. I can't imagine Kreet willingly volunteering his assistance for anything.*

She looked at Kreet, standing motionless by the door with his grav-platter in hand, waiting for his moment to slowly shuffle into action. He was like one of the pieces by a student sculptor she'd dated; he had mastered anatomy, texture, and proportion, but hadn't quite figured out posture or expression. The end result had been beautifully rendered statues of what appeared to be awkwardly mounted corpses.

Shly walked in, looking dispirited. Kreet's eyelids lifted from half open to three-quarters open.

"Hello, Shly," Kreet said in his bland monotone. "It's good to see you."

"Why's that?" Shly asked, worried something was wrong.

"No reason," Kreet said. "It just is."

"Oh. Thanks," Shly said. She did not look grateful.

Ebbler hadn't looked up from his work, but was obviously listening. "You don't sound good," he said, shaking a pan to make sure its contents didn't stick.

"I just came from Master Rayzo's sports practice."

Ebbler chuckled slightly. "I guess he noticed you."

"Yes, while he was fighting a match against Master Hennik."

Ebbler groaned. Kreet shook his head. Barsparse's whisking slowed almost perceptibly.

"And?" Ebbler asked, just wanting to confirm what they all feared.

"Master Rayzo's shorts have a number two on them now."

"He can't be happy about that."

"Are any of us?" Shly asked.

Ebbler said, "Poor Master Rayzo."

Shly frowned. "I feel terrible. It's not my fault that he was beaten, but I hate that I had any part in it."

"You like Master Rayzo, don't you?" Kreet asked Shly.

"We all like Master Rayzo," Ebbler said.

"Well, of course," Kreet said. "But Shly, do you *like* him?"

"Yes, I like him. If you're asking if I'm interested in him, then no, Kreet, I'm not. He's far too young for me, and even if he weren't, I am not about to have a brief, doomed fling with the future ruler."

"Oh," Kreet said. "Good."

Shly and Ebbler both managed to hide most of their irritation.

Barsparse didn't even try to hide her smile; her higher status and age gave her perspective. Kreet's inability to see that if Shly wasn't interested in Rayzo, she probably wouldn't be interested in the guy who brought Rayzo his food, was slightly more amusing to Barsparse than it was sad.

"Ebbler," Barsparse said, "Don't forget, we're making an extra setting for lunch. Calculate your cooking times and portions accordingly."

"Yes, Chef."

"Why are we extending extra courtesy to Lord Pavlon's valet again?" Shly asked.

"Because Glaz told us to," Barsparse answered.

"Will he be eating in the formal dining room with Her Ladyship?" Shly asked.

"No," Kreet said. "He'll be taking his meals in his quarters in the guest section."

Shly scrunched her face. "Well then, what's the point?"

"I'm sorry," Barsparse said. "What do you mean, Shly?"

"Chef," Ebbler said, "I think what she means—"

"You concentrate on your cooking," Barsparse said. She smiled pleasantly at Shly, her whisk hand never faltering, and asked, "I'm not upset. I'm just curious as to what you meant, Shly."

"Well, I meant no offense, Chef Barsparse. I respect you very much, but we were talking to Ebbler this morning, and we were saying that we just don't understand how the food you two work so hard to produce can really be better than what comes out of the bulkfab. Ebbler tried to explain it to me before, but it still doesn't make sense."

For a moment, the cooking sounds seemed deafening, due to the lack of anyone speaking . . . or even breathing.

"But you respect me?" Barsparse asked, still smiling.

"Yes ma'am . . . Chef. Very much."

"Just not what I do." Barsparse said, laughing a bit, but not enough to make anyone comfortable.

"Sorry, Chef," Shly said.

"Don't be. You're in no trouble. It's good to get an honest picture of where things stand. Who all was included in this conversation?"

"I'd rather not say, Chef."

"Shly, I give you my word, I'm not angry. There will be no repercussions."

"Me, Umily, and Kreet."

"But I didn't say anything. I was just listening," Kreet added.

"I believe you," Barsparse said.

"I'm sorry," Shly said.

"Don't be."

"I feel bad."

"You shouldn't."

"You're sure you aren't angry?"

"Yes," Barsparse said. "I'm sure."

Shly wasn't convinced. "Um, I should go." She lingered uncertainly for a moment, then left as quickly as she could without running.

Barsparse peered into her bowl, watching her whisk interact with the contents. She slowed, stopped, lifted the whisk to check the consistency, and looked pleased with the result. She turned her attention to Ebbler.

"How's it going, Ebbler? Have everything under control?"

"Yes, Chef."

"You'd tell me if you didn't, wouldn't you?"

"Yes, Chef."

"The extra plate isn't throwing you?"

"No, Chef. I'm grateful for the extra practice."

Barsparse nodded. "Yes. Extra practice is always helpful."

24.

I wish you could've seen the look on his face," Hennik said, lounging on his bed, reveling in his triumph.

"I'm sure Master Rayzo was devastated," Migg said, standing in her corner of Hennik's bedchamber as she watched him revel in his triumph.

"He was," Hennik agreed. "He really was. It's perfect. His last memory of me will be of his humiliation and defeat in front of his father and that servant girl he's smitten with."

"So we still intend to make our escape tonight?"

"Of course we do. We just discussed it this morning."

"I was wondering if the plan had been reformulated since then," Migg said, "which is why I used the word *still.* You see, Master Hennik, the word *still* implies that there may have been a change—"

"I know what the word *still* implies," Hennik said. "It implies that you may not have procured the equipment we need, and are hoping it won't be needed."

"I apologize, Master Hennik. I didn't intend to give that impression."

"So, you *have* procured the equipment?"

"Yes, Master Hennik."

"Really?"

"Yes, Master Hennik."

"Here?"

"Yes, Master Hennik."

"Can I see it?"

"If you wish, Master Hennik."

"I wish," Hennik hissed.

"Very good, Master Hennik," Migg said without moving, "but first I should remind you that our resources are limited, and evading detection was of the utmost importance."

"And I remind you that you are my servant, and if you fail to please me, I can have you removed from that position."

"What do you think would happen to me then?" Migg asked, with a wide-eyed expression that Hennik mistook for fear.

"On the Hahn Home World, you'd be killed, or given a job so bad death would be preferable. These Apiosans are soft-hearted fools, so they'd probably just ship you back to the Hahn Home World."

"You really think they'd do that, Master Hennik?"

"Yes, they might, but of course, the shame of returning home without me would be worse than whatever hideous punishment my father would subject you to for deserting me. No, returning home without me might seem pleasant, but it wouldn't be."

"I agree, Master Hennik."

"So, let's see the equipment that's going to take us home," Hennik said.

Migg walked over to the exquisitely carved antique bureau where Hennik's clothes were stored. In any other home on Apios, it would have been the most fabulous item in the house, and probably more valuable than the house itself. Here, in the palace, it was good enough for a spare bedroom that was assigned to an adolescent boy. She opened the bottom drawer and pulled out a bundle of fabric.

"As I'm sure you remember, Master Hennik, you requested two stealth suits, one for each of us." Migg held up one of the stealth suits she had procured.

"That's not a proper stealth suit," Hennik said.

"Master Hennik, everything that comes into the palace is subject to scrutiny. I was forced to be creative, so I ordered things that would serve our purpose without arousing suspicion."

"It's white!" Hennik cried. "Everyone knows a proper stealth suit is black."

"Master Hennik, a proper stealth suit may start out black, but it changes colors, depending on the background with which one is attempting to blend. I couldn't get an active stealth suit without arousing suspicion. We will be sneaking out of the palace, and most of the palace's walls are made of polished Apiosan marble, which is white."

She held the garment up to the wall, and Hennik admitted to himself—though not, of course, to her—that the colors did match.

Hennik felt the fabric. "This isn't a jumpsuit. What is it?"

"It's Apiosan formalwear, Master Hennik. It consists of light trousers, a shirt, a vest, an undercoat, an overcoat, a midcoat, this thing—which is sort of a large, decorative belt—a sash, and a matching bag that attaches to the belt thing and hangs down in front. Also, there's a hat. All of it is in the same shade of white. It should blend in with the walls, as well as the other pieces within the palace. If my attempt to procure it was discovered, it would simply look like you were trying to assimilate to their culture. I also got matching shoes, gloves, and scarves to wrap our heads in. When the time comes, we will be covered head to toe in Apiosan garb. When we're en route, we'll simply look like we're trying to be dapper. And, should the escape attempt fail, you now have a nice set of formal attire."

25.

After lunch, the man Lady Jakabitus knew as Lord Pavlon quickly slipped away to his quarters to freshen up. When he emerged, he had exchanged his voluminous orange and green robe and headdress for a loose-fitting yellow jacket topped with a set of hard shoulder pads with great, arching sculptural elements that met above his head and merged into a shape similar to that of a hat; the notable difference was that it hung several inches above his head. Also, his thick layer of white makeup had been augmented with yellow circles around his eyes and matching lipstick.

When Lady Jakabitus commented on his change in attire, he described the new outfit as *more suitable for discussing business.*

Lady Jakabitus and Lord Pavlon retired to Her Ladyship's offices to do just that.

The group term *Her Ladyship's offices* was, in fact, used to describe a suite of many rooms, which had at one time housed both the ruler's office and workspaces for the large administrative staff that was needed to help the ruler make—and then carry out—decisions. As with most other forms of labor at the palace, those tasks were now carried out by either the invisible army of microscopic utilities that covered every surface, or the invisible army of full-sized people who worked in the palace's new addition, well out of the ruler's sight. As such, the whole complex of rooms had been remodeled to allow the ruler a selection of offices to use as the circumstances and the ruler's moods demanded.

Lady Jakabitus did the vast majority of her work, including receiving the morning briefings, from the primary office. It lent these occasions the sense of grandeur and spectacle that she felt the people of Apios deserved. This meeting was different, though. She was dealing personally with a Lord, the ruler of his own planet. Any effort to awe him would instead result in contempt or resentment. She wanted him to identify with her. As such she chose the *informal office.* It was intimate but dignified, unlike the *private office* her father had commissioned for *off-the-record audiences* with various *special advisors* who were all female, attractive, and had exciting plans to share with His Lordship regarding his anatomy. She'd only learned about that particular *office* after becoming the ruler herself, and it had forever altered her image of her father. It was certainly intimate, but it lacked any kind of dignity.

Lady Jakabitus offered Lord Pavlon a seat on a priceless antique settee, then settled onto the identical settee facing him. Wollard and Phee stood nearby, in case either ruler needed their assistance. Shly arrived swiftly, dispensed drinks efficiently, then left silently.

"Lunch was wonderful," Lord Pavlon said. "Thank you again for your hospitality. It is a shame your family couldn't join us."

Lady Jakabitus made a point of not looking at Wollard and said, "Yes. Perhaps on your next visit."

"Perhaps," Lord Pavlon replied, "if there is a next visit."

Lady Jakabitus carefully hid all of the many signs of irritation that were trying to rise to the surface. In all her years as ruler, she had seldom endured a more frustrating exchange than the ones she had been having with Lord Pavlon. The man had shown a profound commitment to being noncommittal.

"I, um, I trust my valet's needs have been seen to," Lord Pavlon said.

"I'm certain of it," Lady Jakabitus said, glancing at Wollard, who nodded.

"He's been given fitting quarters?" Lord Pavlon asked Wollard.

"Yes, Milord. My protégée Phee saw to it personally."

Lord Pavlon switched his focus to Phee. "Was he satisfied with his accommodations?"

Phee looked to Wollard for reassurance. It was highly unusual for a protégée to directly converse with a visiting dignitary when her mentor was present. Wollard nodded almost imperceptibly, and Phee spoke.

"Yes, Milord. Your valet was quite satisfied with his quarters."

"Was he?"

"He was, Your Lordship."

"You're certain?"

"Yes, Your Lordship. I saw to it myself."

Lord Pavlon stared at Phee for a long moment, then said, "Good," and turned back to Lady Jakabitus.

"Lord Pavlon," Lady Jakabitus said, "as you know, my planet has been locked in a wretched stalemate of a war with the Hahn for generations."

Lord Pavlon squirmed in his seat and said, "Yes. I know."

"Then you also know that the location of the fighting, and the prize we are fighting for, is the planet Ophion 6."

"Yes."

"Did you know that the Hahn have recently stepped up their offensive efforts, causing a drastic increase in casualties on both sides?"

"Yes," Lord Pavlon said. "I had reason to believe that was the case."

"And I am aware," Her Ladyship continued, "that since the first days of the war, both sides have coveted the permission of House Pavlon to use your planet, . . . *Sheud*, as a base of operations."

Lord Pavlon nodded. "The unfortunate result of being the only habitable world in nonwarp range of the battlefield."

Lady Jakabitus leaned forward. "It doesn't need to be unfortunate. If we were to come to an arrangement, I can assure you that the Apiosan military's impact on your world would be slight, and we're in a position to pay you for your tolerance in any number of ways."

Lord Pavlon grimaced, then leaned forward himself. "Lady Jakabitus, I suspect every child born on Apios is raised with the knowledge that this world is at war with the Hahn. Is that not so?"

"Sadly, yes."

"And children born on the Hahn Home World are raised with the knowledge that they are at war with Apios."

"Presumably."

"Did you know that every child born on . . . *Sheud* is raised with the knowledge that Apios and the Hahn are at war, and that both sides would love to use . . . *Sheud* as a base of operations?"

"I didn't know that my planet's problems loomed so large for your people."

"Lady Jakabitus, your problem is our problem. For generations, both of your worlds have exerted pressure on my ancestors in hopes of securing our cooperation. Apios has always wanted a base on . . . *Sheud*, but you've never offered anything in return that justified being drawn into a war."

"And I'm sure the Hahn have made all sorts of offers as well," Lady Jakabitus said.

"No. I believe the Hahn made one offer, at the beginning of the war. When we refused they started regularly attempting to assassinate each successive ruler of . . . *Sheud* in hopes that their replacement would see things differently."

"That's terrible."

"Maybe, but . . . *Sheud*'s security forces have gotten very good at protecting their rulers. Besides, the Hahn don't really make what you'd call a serious effort. They try just hard enough to remind us of their interest."

"If we've offered friendship, and they've been trying to kill you, then I'd think deciding who to side with would be easy, Lord Pavlon."

"We don't think it's a decision as to whose side . . . *Sheud* should take. The choice is whether to take a side at all. If we were to do so, of course it would be yours. We all know that the Hahn are loathsome, but the only reason you've given me to join you against them is that they've recently become more violent. I don't consider that a compelling reason to make them angry."

26.

Hartchar was not happy. She was a woman who valued discipline, honesty, and routine above all things. Migg's clandestine note, which had arrived only moments ago, had asked her to forgo her usual schedule, leave her customary evening workout, and meet here, on one of the New Palace's balconies overlooking the palace courtyard, to privately discuss Master Hennik's sports training. It irritated her on every level.

The appointed time had almost arrived. Migg was not yet late, but she was already not early, which Hartchar took as more reason for irritation.

If one were going to pick a place to waste one's valuable time waiting, Hartchar had to admit, this was a good choice. It was a pleasant evening. The sun was just about to set, but it was plenty bright enough for her to watch Lady Jakabitus and Wollard make polite conversation with a visiting Lord and his servant in the palace courtyard. Their business had, presumably, been concluded, for a warp transport sat before them. Lord Pavlon appeared to be wearing a large reddish-brown tube that left his legs exposed from the knees down. The contraption was bent at the top to display his head, which was presented in the circular frame of the tube. His head stood out against the tube's dark interior because of the white face makeup with yellow circles and red lines slashed randomly across his features. His arms extended through holes in the sides of the tube, and were themselves sheathed in smaller tubes.

Most people would see the desirability of their location as a good thing, but for Hartchar, every quality that recommended the balcony was another reason for Migg to already be there—and thus another reason for her to be irritated by Migg's absence.

Hartchar heard footsteps approaching from inside the palace. She nearly demanded to know why Migg was late. Instead, she looked back to see who was approaching, and was grateful that she had. It was Lord Jakabitus.

"Your Lordship," she said, bowing. "If you want the balcony to yourself, I'd be happy to leave."

Lord Jakabitus said, "Not at all, Hartchar. I think you're meant to be here. I received a message from Hennik's valet."

"Migg."

"Yes. She wanted to discuss something about Hennik's training. I assume she sent you a message as well."

"Yes, Milord."

"Where is she?"

"I don't know, Milord."

"I see." Lord Jakabitus looked around the courtyard, then the sky, then the city, then back into the palace. He nodded, sucked his teeth, and said, "I found Hennik's performance today rather promising."

"As was Master Rayzo's," Hartchar said.

"But Rayzo lost the match."

"He became distracted," Hartchar said.

"Yes. He did."

"I believe Master Hennik planned it."

"Of course he did. It's why he won. Like I said, Hartchar, it was a promising performance for Hennik, all in all."

"As you say, Milord," Hartchar said, cautiously, "but I believe Master Hennik's actions today betray a lack of respect for the rules and spirit of the game."

"Boys his age should disrespect the rules. It's only by breaking the stated rules that you learn what the real rules are."

"Rayzo doesn't break the rules," Hartchar said.

"No, he gets that from his mother. She worries about the rules, worries about what others think of her, which is a good thing for a person in power. It keeps her from becoming a monster. She'll do what needs to be done, but she suffers for it. I love Joanadie and Rayzo, but truth be told, my friends and I were more like Hennik as lads. We were awful. Rayzo isn't awful. He's the kind of kid we were awful to."

"Rayzo works very hard to please you."

"No question. I wonder, if I ever told him how thoroughly pleased I am with him, would he stop? He will rule this planet one day. Do we want a ruler who believes he's already good enough at age fourteen?"

"You seem willing enough to express pleasure with Master Hennik."

Lord Jakabitus smiled. "It gives Rayzo a reason to work harder and encourages Hennik to keep behaving exactly as he does, which fools nobody."

"I'm angry with Migg for calling us here, then not bothering to show up," Hartchar said, "but I'm glad we had this conversation, Milord."

"Yes, it might be nice not having you believe that I'm an idiot." Lord Jakabitus leaned on the railing and looked down over the courtyard. "I'm nothing but happy with the work you've done with Rayzo, Hartchar. Moving forward, I think we need to work on getting him to vary his techniques, be less predictable, and ignore any dis . . . trac . . . what the devil it that?!"

At first, Hartchar wasn't sure what Lord Jakabitus meant. Lady Jakabitus, Wollard, and Phee were still making conversation with Lord

Pavlon and his servant. The warp transport still sat in the same spot, ready to take the visitors back to their home world. Hartchar was beginning to suspect that he was testing her ability to ignore distractions, but when she squinted and followed His Lordship's line of sight, she saw it. Two figures, clad from head to toe in white clothes that blended in with the marble wall, were carefully edging their way around the outside of the courtyard.

The two figures stood on the other side of the warp transport from the other people in the courtyard. One of them had ventured away from the wall, which caught Lord Jakabitus's attention. The white outfit stood out against the darker mosaic of pavers.

"Master Hennik," Hartchar said, then arched an eyebrow and added, "and Migg."

"The very person who arranged for us to be standing on this balcony, at this moment," Lord Jakabitus said. "That is interesting. I suppose he means to sneak onto the transport and escape."

"Shall I intercept them, Milord?"

"In a moment. There's no rush. This will be a nice opportunity for Hennik to become better acquainted with the security system."

Hartchar nodded. She scanned the courtyard, where countless hidden hatches had silently slid open, revealing a wide variety of weapons.

The personal chambers of the ruling family, their guests, and their staff were kept strictly private, but any common areas, corridors, and certainly the courtyard, were subject to constant, inescapable surveillance. Neither Hartchar nor Lord Jakabitus had any doubt that security knew who Hennik was, where Hennik was, what Hennik was attempting, and exactly how forcefully to respond. Given Hennik's importance, and the fact he was attempting to flee without injuring anyone, Hartchar suspected that security would opt to simply subdue him with the utilitics. The two continued to watch as the scene unfolded before them.

Hennik took several more steps out from the wall, then, feeling emboldened, motioned for Migg to follow. As she stepped away from the wall, Hennik broke into a fast trot toward the transport. As predicted, he made it only a few steps before his feet slid out from under him. He fell hard, face first, to the ground. Migg also fell. Hennik tried to lift himself, but his hand slid out from under him as if he were on ice. The utilitics were using the same technique they employed to move inanimate objects to prevent Hennik, an all-too-animate object, from moving. Migg wisely chose to remain motionless.

Hartchar nodded, said "Your Lordship," then casually vaulted over the balcony railing. The New Palace wall tilted at a steep angle. At first Hartchar fell, then she slid, then her feet caught, and she ran several steps down the wall before redirecting her momentum and jogging to a stop on the ground. Lord Jakabitus hadn't needed a reminder of why Hartchar had been hired to train Rayzo physically, but he was reminded nonetheless.

Hartchar walked out to Hennik, who was still attempting to struggle to his feet, and Migg, who still was not.

"Master Hennik," Hartchar said. "My compliments. That's a very nice suit."

"How dare you detain me, servant?!" Hennik pulled the white scarf from around his face with one hand, the other hand still trying and failing to pull him from the ground. "What gives you the right to interfere with a member of Lady Jakabitus's family?"

"The family you're attempting to escape, Master Hennik?" Hartchar allowed herself a moment's satisfaction watching him writhe and squirm on the ground. "I'm not the one detaining you, Master Hennik. Security and the utilitics are doing that. And I don't have the authority to release you. As you say, I am just a servant. I can escort you back to your bedchamber, though."

Hennik grunted with frustration as he sagged onto the ground. His formal white hat fell off and rolled onto the ground next to him. "This is an outrage!" he shouted.

"I can tell you're frustrated, Master Hennik. If it's any consolation, the fact that you thought this plan would actually work is pretty insulting. It shows how stupid you think we all are. You can take some solace in that."

Hennik continued to lay facedown on the ground, determined not to give Hartchar the satisfaction of even acknowledging that he'd heard her.

"I think it's time I escorted you two inside, Master Hennik." Hartchar didn't address the security personnel directly, but she knew they were listening.

Hennik bared his teeth at her and started to hoist himself off the ground, only to immediately fall again.

"Don't bother standing, Master Hennik. Let the utilitics do their work."

Hartchar motioned toward the palace entrance. The two Hahn slid silently in that direction. Hennik took the lead, or rather, was given the lead against his will. He was followed by his hat and scarf, gliding silently in his wake, then Migg.

As Migg slid past Hartchar's feet she pulled the scarf from her face and smiled up at the trainer, who returned the gesture. Hartchar looked up at the balcony, nodded to Lord Jakabitus, and followed the escapees as they slid back into the palace. The three of them kept a comfortable distance from Lady Jakabitus and the others, all of whom silently watched them pass.

Lord Pavlon exhaled, turned to Lady Jakabitus, and said, "Adoptions are always difficult."

"Too true," Lady Jakabitus agreed.

"Thank you, Lady Jakabitus, for your hospitality," Lord Pavlon said, bowing his head, which moved freely inside the stationary, curved tube that covered his torso and framed his face. He turned to Wollard and said, "And thank you for your assistance to me and my valet."

Wollard bowed deeply. "It was my pleasure, Lord Pavlon, but it was my protégée, Phee, who tended to your valet's needs. I cannot take credit for her efforts."

Pavlon reoriented his entire body to aim his cumbersome clothing toward Phee, then nodded. "I thank you, Phee."

Phee bowed. "It was my pleasure to ensure that Soodon was afforded the courtesy he deserves, Your Lordship." She smiled at Lord Pavlon, but her glance flicked briefly to Soodon, who instantly clinched every muscle in his body.

Pavlon rotated forty-five degrees to look at Soodon, then rotated back to look at Phee, then back to Soodon, then to Wollard, Lady Jakabitus, and back to Phee. Finally he let out a long, exasperated breath.

"Phee," Lord Pavlon said, "did Soodon tell you that he was the real Lord Pavlon, and that I am a decoy?"

Phee leaned in closer, and, in a quiet voice, answered, "Yes, he did tell me, but I assure—"

"There's no need," Pavlon said.

Soodon raised his hands defensively and stammered, "Milord—"

"Soodon, wait in the transport."

"Lord Pavlon, I—"

"The transport. Now."

Soodon took a moment to scowl at Phee before slinking off to the transport.

"I do apologize," Lord Pavlon said. "This is the third time he's pulled this stunt." Pavlon shrugged. "What can one do?"

"You could punish him," Lady Jakabitus said. "Have him locked up, or terminate his employment, or demote him. You could dock his pay, or just stop traveling with him."

"All interesting ideas," Lord Pavlon said. "I will discuss the matter with him."

Lady Jakabitus said, "Of course."

27.

"What do you think this is about?" Shly asked.

"I don't know," Umily said. "Glaz asked us to meet her here, and said she had a special job for us. That's all I know."

Kreet shrugged, his eyes on Shly, his mouth—as usual—closed.

The three of them stood in the darkened servants' hall for a moment. It was late. The family was in bed for the night, and usually the staff would be preparing for bed themselves.

"How's Gint?" Shly asked.

"Regenerating again," Umily said.

"Oh," Shly said. She didn't know whether to say *good* or *I'm sorry,* so she said nothing, which also felt wrong.

Footsteps rang out from the hall, so they turned to look at the entrance and watched as Hartchar and Migg entered. Migg nodded and muttered an embarrassed hello. She knew that word of her and Master Hennik's little adventure had gotten out, but she didn't know how many of the details were common knowledge. When the three junior staff members smiled and greeted her more enthusiastically than usual, she got the idea that the entire story had gotten out, which was good news, as long as it never got back to Hennik.

"Anybody know what this is about?" Hartchar asked.

Shly, Umily, and Kreet all shrugged, then flinched when Barsparse said, "I'll tell you."

Everyone swiveled to look at the door to the kitchen at the far end of the hall. Barsparse and Glaz entered and approached them.

Barsparse said, "I wanted to talk to everyone about some of the challenges we've been facing. Please, have a seat." She motioned to an empty table. Everyone took a seat, Barsparse sitting at one end of the table with Glaz next to her.

"As you know, Ebbler recently took over as my sous chef," Barsparse said. "He's a keen young man, but he has no training. He's a knowledgeable novice. It'll take him many hours of hard work to get his skills to where they need to be."

Nobody said a word. Those who knew Ebbler thought highly of him, but couldn't argue with what Barsparse had said. Those who knew Ebbler less well were still disinclined to argue with Barsparse.

"That's one problem," Barsparse said. "Another is that some of you don't understand why we have a kitchen in the first place. You see it as a pointless luxury."

Barsparse paused to let the discomfort build. "That's understandable. You've all watched us cook and serve our food for years, but you've never eaten any. Your opinions are based on ignorance. Luckily, I have a solution that will fix both problems."

Barsparse clapped twice. Ebbler, Wollard, and Phee emerged from the kitchen, pushing grav-platters filled with plates.

"What you're about to eat," Barsparse said, "is not a full meal. You've had dinner already, and we don't want you to have trouble sleeping because you're too stuffed. Each plate holds a few single bites that'll give you the sense of an entire dish."

Ebbler, Wollard, and Phee placed the plates in front of the staff members. Each plate contained four items. There was a small bit of seared meat covered with a thin layer of some sort of shiny glaze; an assortment of brightly colored vegetables diced, cooked slightly, then pressed into an inch-thick cylinder; a perfect cube that appeared to be made from solid chocolate, but promised to conceal some sort of surprise; and a ceramic cup holding a few ounces of a clear, steaming, amber broth.

"Everything you see here was prepared entirely by Ebbler, under my supervision," Barsparse said. "The plan is to have these tastings once a week until I think Ebbler's ready to ramp things up. Then, perhaps, we'll move on to dinner once a week. We'll see."

Phee finished service by giving everyone a glass of water, then she and Wollard sat down to their own plates. Ebbler didn't have a plate. He stood behind Barsparse's chair, beaming.

Barsparse lifted her cup of broth and said, "Let's begin with the soup course."

When the tasting was over, the general consensus of the staff was that having a living, breathing, professional chef was a luxury, but it was not a pointless one.

PART 4

It is poor form to assume, but it is impossible to function without making assumptions. Thus, proper form dictates that you act on your assumptions without discussing them. Others may assume that you are making assumptions, but they will not mention it. To do so would be to show the world that they are guilty of poor form.

-Excerpt from the preface of the *Academy of Arbitration Instructional Supplement: Unspoken Mutual Understandings: The Force That Holds Societies Together/Apart*

28.

"Know that two thousand, one hundred, and seventy-one conventional years have passed since the Terran Exodus," Wollard said. "Today is the fifteenth day of the fourth month. We meet on the planet Apios, in the servants' hall of Palace Koa, the ancestral home of House Jakabitus and its matriarch, Lady Joanadie Jakabitus. I am Wollard, Master of Formalities for House Jakabitus, and I am currently delivering the daily meeting to the palace staff."

Wollard looked over the assembled staff. They seemed attentive and alert. Ebbler was sagging a bit, but everyone has off days.

"Today looks to be a fairly normal day at the palace. The most notable event on the schedule isn't actually going to take place here. I refer, of course, to the sports meet this afternoon, which will be Master Hennik's first. As always, the regular afternoon sports practice has been moved to the morning, and Lord Jakabitus and Masters Rayzo and Hennik will be away this afternoon. I know that we all wish them good fortune, and will be very interested to see how their ranks have changed at the end of the day."

The entire staff (including Migg) was hoping the meet would go well for Rayzo and less well for Hennik. It was common knowledge that since their first disastrous match two weeks before, Hartchar had not allowed a rematch. She and Lord Jakabitus agreed that being ranked below Hennik would motivate Rayzo to try harder. If Rayzo were to somehow lose a second match to Hennik, it would likely demoralize him, leading to poorer performance.

Hennik, for his part, never missed an opportunity to remind Rayzo that he was ranked higher. Nothing fosters enthusiasm for a game more than doing well at it. Hennik had even taken to wearing his sports shorts around the palace, reveling in the bold, black number one emblazoned on its front and rear.

Wollard transitioned from this expression of the unspoken communal dislike for Master Hennik to an expression of their shared distrust of him, in the form of his and Migg's prearranged loaded conversation.

"Good morning, Migg."

"Good morning, Wollard," Migg said, smiling.

Wollard squinted and said, "Master Hennik seems to be adjusting well to life here in the palace."

"Yes," Migg agreed. "He is particularly looking forward to today's sports meet."

"So I'd imagined." This would be the first time he'd left the palace since his arrival on Apios. It was a prime opportunity to either attempt another escape or to embarrass the Jakabitus family.

Migg said, "Master Hennik has been putting a great deal of effort into planning his . . . strategies for the meet."

"I see," Wollard muttered. "I certainly hope he hasn't planned anything that's against the rules."

Migg shook her head emphatically. "No, I can assure you, his sole focus has been on improving his ranking, and nothing he has planned is against the rules . . . yet."

"I see."

Wollard ran through the usual administrative filler, then the meeting was adjourned.

Glaz stood and said, "All right. It looks to be a good day, full of work to be done. We'd best all get to it." As always, the entire staff broke into small groups to converse for a moment before actually getting to work.

"Wow, Ebbler, you don't look so good," Shly said.

"What? No, I'm fine."

"Did you sleep at all last night?"

"Yes. Some. Enough."

"Why aren't you sleeping?" Umily asked.

"I am sleeping," Ebbler said. "But I'm also studying. There's just so much I don't know about cooking. I've been doing some reading in my spare time."

"And have you been learning a lot?"

"Yeah, but the more I read, the more I realize how little I know."

"Sounds like a good reason not to read," Kreet said. Umily and Ebbler chuckled weakly until they realized that he wasn't joking, then they chuckled nervously.

Shly changed the subject. "Of course, they had to move sports practice to the morning today. I was hoping they'd skip it altogether for once."

"I bet," Umily said. "You never thought you'd miss the days when the most you had to deal with was Master Rayzo making moony eyes at you whenever you came into the room."

"It wasn't fun, but it was better than watching him look disgusted while Master Hennik tries to flirt with me."

"Doesn't he realize you're not interested?" Ebbler asked.

"You aren't, are you?" Kreet pressed. "In either of them. That's what you said."

"Of course I'm not, and yes, I think Master Hennik knows it. I don't think it makes any difference." Shly thought for a moment, then said, "I take it back. I think it makes it better for him, if that makes any sense."

Ebbler and Umily subtly shook their heads. Kreet nodded.

Shly said, “It’s time we get to work.”

They heard Glaz say, “Yes, it is,” from across the hall. They all quickly turned, bowed, and went their separate ways. As luck would have it, Shly and Umily had to go the same direction anyway, so they still had a moment for more conversation.

“Heard from Gint lately?” Shly asked.

“Got a letter last night.”

“What’s it say?”

“Dunno. Haven’t read it yet.”

“Why not?!

Umily looked terribly sad. “I’ll read it. I just have to work up to it. Does that make sense?”

“Sure.”

“I’m not a terrible person, am I?”

“No, heavens no! I’m sure this has been very hard, for both of you.”

“I don’t know, Shly. It was hard for him at first, but now it’s like he’s not the boy I fell in love with anymore.”

“War changes people, Umily.”

“This one sure has.”

29.

Wollard stood to the side and tried to remain positive while Lady Jakabitus received her daily briefing.

The wallpaper Wollard used as a bellwether to divine Her Ladyship's state of mind had gotten consistently darker and more foreboding with each passing day. Wollard suspected that the patterns were making increasingly less subtle attempts to tell him something.

He'd thought that today's pattern showed a large healthy tree surrounding and silhouetting a smaller leafy sapling in the foreground. All of this was rendered in one shade of gray against a field of black, but despite the bleak color scheme, he'd hoped the pleasant nature scene was a promising sign. It was only in retrospect he realized that what he'd thought was a tree was, in fact, a mushroom cloud, and what he'd thought was a leafy sapling was a tall, thin man, not unlike Wollard himself, with flailing arms.

The leaves were flames.

The news from the war on Ophion 6 was getting bleaker at a faster pace than the wallpaper. The Hahn seemed determined to harass Her Ladyship's forces. New countermeasures had been installed, and were as effective as her generals had promised, but the Hahn had answered by sending larger waves of soldiers to overwhelm the defenses. The death toll was appalling on both sides, but Lady Jakabitus knew that her soldiers' deaths would not concern Kamar Hahn, and she'd come to suspect that his own soldiers' deaths probably meant little more.

General Kriz did point out (while wiping his eyes) that thanks to the success of their loss-retardant measures, the death toll numbers were misleading. Most of the soldiers had died many times at this point. Also, the lessons learned by each successive death, and the automatic retraining that was imprinted in the soldiers' minds with each regeneration, were resulting in more effective fighters. This did little to brighten Lady Jakabitus's mood.

Of course, she had any number of devastating weapons she could use to wipe vast swaths of the Hahn's ground forces out of existence, but doing so would give Kamar Hahn the excuse to do the same, claiming she'd forced the violence. Indeed, Her Ladyship's Minister of Information—an important position that encompassed the duties of both a pollster and a spymaster—reported that the consensus among the citizens of the civilized galaxy who bothered to keep up with current events was that the recent increase in hostilities was probably caused, or at least exacerbated, by Lady Jakabitus's *adoption* of Kamar Hahn's only son.

Lady Jakabitus made a point of not looking at Wollard during this report; Wollard, in turn, made a point of not looking at her not looking at him. Instead he watched Phee read her papers.

Phee pulled out her stylus and hastily scribbled a note. Wollard leaned slightly to see. She was editing someone else's CV. Her addition read: *Keln, you really should stop sending me these messages. You're going to get me into trouble.*

Wollard whispered, "Instead of *going to get,* you should probably write, *have gotten.*"

Phee's face went red. She squeezed her eyes shut and dropped her hands, and the stylus and papers with them, to her sides.

"I'm so sorry, Wollard," she whispered.

"I can imagine," he replied.

"I was writing that the messages have to stop."

"Yes. Now. After weeks of warnings."

"I'm sorry. I've said that it has to stop before, but Keln won't listen."

"Then you should stop telling Keln anything. If someone won't listen, the best course is to stop talking. For example, you clearly haven't been listening to me. I could stop burdening you with my unwanted advice and find a protégée who listens."

"I'm sorry Wollard, did you have something to add?" Lady Jakabitus asked in the most serene tone of voice she could manage.

"My apologies, Milady," Wollard said. "I didn't mean to disrupt your briefing."

"I'm curious, Wollard, would carrying on a conversation during your ruler's war briefing be considered good form?"

"No, Milady. I'm mortified to have done so, and I beg your pardon."

"You know, Wollard, if you find these briefings tedious, you could stop attending them."

"Milady, I would never suggest such a thing."

"You wouldn't have to. I just have."

"Lady Jakabitus, again, I apologize for the disruption. My protégée and I were discussing important business, but that is no excuse. I feel strongly that I can be of great use in these briefings."

"You were certainly instrumental in the briefing before I chose to adopt Hennik," Lady Jakabitus said.

"Quite. These are difficult times, Milady, and in such times, guidance in relation to the Formalities is more valuable than ever. I will cause no further disruptions."

"See that you don't."

"Yes, Lady Jakabitus."

Wollard stood silently nearby as the briefing continued, neither being asked for input nor offering any out of turn. Finally, the paintings turned back into paintings, and Lady Jakabitus turned to face him.

Good, he thought. *Her Ladyship is understandably irritated with me, and after my disruption she couldn't turn to me for counsel in front of her generals without losing face, but now that they are gone, she'll want to know what the Formalities dictate.*

Lady Jakabitus said, "You're both dismissed."

Wollard didn't understand. "I'm sorry, Milady?"

"Yes, as you've said several times already. You heard the briefing, Wollard, at least parts of it. I have a war on my hands that is not going well, and I need to think with the minimum of unnecessary distractions."

"Indeed, Milady."

"So, I want you and Phee to leave."

"Yes, Milady."

"Now."

"Yes, Milady."

Wollard and Phee started toward the door, but Wollard stopped just short of actually leaving. He stood next to the door and cleared his throat.

Lady Jakabitus asked, "What is it?"

"One thing, Milady. I promised Lord Jakabitus that I'd remind you that Master Rayzo has a sports meet today, and that Master Hennik is going to compete as well."

"And now you have."

"Quite so. I just thought, Milady, that it might help you get your mind off the war if you were to attend the meet."

Lady Jakabitus considered this. "Wollard, I just told you that I want to think about the war without distractions, and you have deliberately offered me a distraction."

"I see your point, Milady."

"And the distraction you've offered to keep my mind off the war is an event you already know I detest."

"It is the most popular spectator event on Apios, Milady."

"One, I might point out, where young men fight."

"I . . . I am sorry, Mila—"

"You're dismissed," Lady Jakabitus said, turning her chair to face away from the door.

30.

The morning sports practice was proceeding without incident. Rayzo and Hennik were standing opposite each other on the mat, knees bent, shoulders hunched, each holding his dominant right hand forward to simulate having that hand held immobile by an opponent's grip. In this position, Hennik seemed only slightly taller than Rayzo, and Hartchar seemed almost twice as tall as either of them. "Right!" she shouted. "Left! Left! Right! Left! Right! Right!" With each order, Hennik and Rayzo did a shoulder roll in the indicated direction, maintaining their positions opposite each other, curving their trajectories so as not to go off the mat.

"Roll, boys!" Lord Jakabitus shouted. "Roll! No, not like that! Like a ball! A ball!"

The roll was an advanced maneuver, designed to either twist an opponent's arm or make him release his grip. If executed well against an unprepared opponent, the roll could position a competitor behind his opponent, holding his opponent's arm in a painful position.

Shly entered quietly, hoping to evade detection, but Hartchar saw her and decided not to risk any disruption of what had been a successful practice. She told Hennik and Rayzo to take a break. She and Lord

Jakabitus discussed the upcoming meet while the boys made conversation with Shly, who dutifully offered them cool drinks.

"So, Shly, sneaking in again to watch me practice," Hennik said.

Sadly for Shly, ignoring him was simply not an option. "No, Master Hennik. I've come to offer His Lordship his daily training beverage."

"Sure, of course, and I suppose the reason you creep in here so quietly and loiter in the shadows is because you hate coming in here so much, not because you enjoy watching me practice?"

"I have no interest in sports, Master Hennik."

"I didn't say you did. No, what I'm doing isn't important, as long as I'm the one doing it, preferably while wearing shorts, eh, Shly?"

"Master Hennik, my duty is to dispense beverages to those who want them, regardless of their attire."

"Ooh," Hennik said. "Did you hear that, Rayzo? Sounded like an offer to me."

Rayzo squinted at him. "That makes no sense."

"You'll understand someday, little brother." Hennik turned back to Shly. "Please ignore the boy. He doesn't understand these things. Do go on about how you'll serve whether I'm dressed or not."

Shly said, "Master Hennik, I assure you, I meant that I am duty bound to dispense beverages, nothing more."

"Sure, that's what you meant," Hennik said through a quease-inducing smile. "Look how upset she is, Rayzo. Obviously I touched a nerve."

"What you said upset her, but that doesn't mean it's true," Rayzo said.

"Right," Hennik said. "And that's why you're upset too, because what I said was wrong."

"Yes," Rayzo said.

Hennik smiled. "See, what you just said there Rayzo? It didn't upset me at all. That's because I know it's not true."

Lord Jakabitus called Shly over, cutting off Rayzo's response. She graced the boys with a perfunctory bow and took off like a shot. Hennik started to amble after her, but stopped when Rayzo grabbed his upper arm.

"Don't bother her," Rayzo said.

"Why not?" Hennik asked. "You're not going to."

The tension was partially defused by Hartchar, who suddenly loomed over them and said, "Master Hennik, His Lordship feels that I should warn you about what to expect at the sports meet today."

"I already know what to expect. I attended the last one, remember?"

It was true. Lord Jakabitus had brought Hennik along as a spectator to Rayzo's last meet. Rayzo had done well, but Hennik had been very vocal about the many ways in which he hadn't done quite well enough.

"That's not what I mean, Master Hennik," Hartchar said. "You'll be starting at an artificially high level, because you've only fought one actual match, in which you defeated a skilled opponent who's ranked quite highly for his age."

"Thank you," Rayzo said.

Hennik scowled at him. "You're welcome. It was my pleasure to beat you."

"No, I'm thanking Hartchar. She paid me a compliment."

"She paid *me* a compliment. Saying that you got beaten shouldn't make you feel good, little brother."

Hartchar took a moment to remember her place, then said, "Master Hennik, Master Rayzo is right to be proud. He has worked very hard to achieve his current ranking."

"But I just started to play sports, and I already outrank him," Hennik said. "So what does that tell you?"

"You tricked me," Rayzo said.

"Yes, easily," Hennik agreed.

"With all due respect," Hartchar said, "up until the moment Master Rayzo became distracted, he was dominating you, Master Hennik."

"Or so it would appear to the unsophisticated eye. I had him right where I wanted him the entire time."

"That's not how I remember it, Master Hennik."

"I'm not responsible for your faulty memory."

Rayzo chose that moment to leave the conversation. His only option was to go talk to his father, who was enjoying his beverage as Shly took her leave. Before she had quite made her escape, Rayzo said, "Shly, I'm sorry about him."

Shly curtsied and said, "It's not your fault, Master Rayzo."

"Maybe it is, maybe it isn't. Either way, I'm sorry."

She curtsied again before leaving the room. Rayzo watched her leave. He didn't see Lord Jakabitus smile, and the smile was gone by the time he turned back to face his father.

"Son," Lord Jakabitus said, "I know this has been a difficult time for you."

"Yes, Father. My performance has not been as good as you would like, but I know I can do better."

"That's not what I meant, son. I mean, of course, you could do better."

"As you always say."

"Yes," Lord Jakabitus said. "Look. You're right. You can always improve. I do say that."

"I am trying."

"I know you are, son."

"So you're saying I should try harder?"

"Rayzo," Lord Jakabitus said, "I'm not talking about sports."

Rayzo looked perplexed. "Father, I'm sorry. Have I displeased you outside of sports as well?"

Lord Jakabitus didn't know what to say, so he stuck to what he knew. "No, not at all. We'll talk later. I shouldn't be distracting you from sports on the day of a meet. Go back and listen to Hartchar. Whatever she's telling Hennik might be of use to you as well."

Rayzo reluctantly wandered back to Hartchar and Hennik and tried to pick up the thread of the conversation. It seemed they had decided to stop debating the quality of Hennik's performance and Hartchar's memory, and had moved on to a discussion of the rules.

"Yes," Hennik said. "I understand that feet are out, but what if I hit them with my hands?"

Hartchar said, "No, Master Hennik. You aren't allowed to strike an opponent in the genitalia with your hands either."

"Knees?"

"No, Master Hennik."

"Elbows?"

"No, Master Hennik."

"Head?"

"No, Master Hennik. It is strictly forbidden to strike your opponent in the genitals with any part of your body. To do so results in a very large points deduction. It's one of the first rules that was added, and Dilly Glifton himself came up with it. If not for that rule, sports would be little more than an exercise in battering the opponent's reproductive organs."

"We can't have that. It might make Apiosan sports fun to watch. Okay, tell me this: If I were to punch myself in the crotch during a match, would my opponent be docked points?"

Hartchar thought about it. "I don't know, Master Hennik, but I would very much like to see you try it."

31.

Wollard walked around the palace, looking for anything that might be out of place. Phee followed him, feeling out of place, but she was the one thing Wollard was not looking at.

Not long ago, they would have left the briefing with a list of things that Her Ladyship felt needed Wollard's attention. Lately her Ladyship was finding fewer and fewer things for which Wollard was needed, which meant he had more time to tell Phee about the job. Unfortunately, the job was getting smaller every day, and Wollard increasingly didn't feel like talking about it.

He hadn't at all mentioned the unpleasantness during the morning briefing. Phee wished he would. It was not going to be a pleasant conversation, but it couldn't be more unpleasant than the silence.

Phee said, "I'm so sorry, Wollard."

"I don't want to discuss it."

"I just want you to know how bad I—"

Wollard stopped walking. "I don't want you to discuss it either. I want there to be no discussion of the subject we're referring to as *it*."

Wollard stared down at Phee, who said nothing. After a moment, he began walking again, muttering, "It's your predilection for discussion that gave us this problem in the first place."

"Us?" Phee asked, regretting it instantly.

Again, Wollard stopped. "Yes, Phee. *Us. We* both have a problem. It's a bigger problem for you than it is for me, but we still have it together. You are going to be punished, Phee. That's your problem, and you can't avoid it. My problem is that I have a gifted and promising protégée, and I must punish her. I have no choice. If I don't punish you, I'm just as negligent as you've been."

"I understand," Phee said. "What are you going to do?"

"I don't know," Wollard said, resuming his pace, partly to avoid looking at Phee's face. "Something that is proportional to your offense, but won't permanently do damage to your career. I honestly don't have any idea what that would be, Phee. I should probably rebuke you."

"Would you do that?" Phee asked.

"After you've repeatedly ignored me? I don't want to rebuke you, I really don't, but I have to pick an appropriate penalty, or else *I* could be rebuked. The Formalities allow me a limited amount of time to think of an alternative. If I don't assign a suitable punishment by tomorrow night, I myself will likely be punished for indecisiveness. Stalling, after all, is never good form."

"Maybe I can help you think of something."

"Yes, splendid idea. And later, when I am accused of being too lenient, I can just say that the leniency was your idea."

"Is there anything I can do to help?"

"Me, or yourself?" Wollard asked. Before she could answer, he added, "Never mind. You can help us both by not bringing it up again. Let me think. Bothering me is not going to leave me predisposed to kindness. Am I understood, Phee?"

"Yes, Wollard."

"Good. I'll tell you when I've decided. Until then, we will not speak of it again."

Wollard stalked through the servants' hall and the kitchen. Everything seemed in order, and he had no messages from Her Ladyship to impart, so he maintained a steady stride, offering tight-lipped greetings to anyone he passed, which was most of the staff, since lunch service was about to begin. Phee followed in his wake, nodding to anyone who made eye contact and silently cringing otherwise.

When Wollard and Phee had left, Shly said, "Brrrr."

"Yeah," Umily said. "Poor Wollard. He doesn't seem happy lately."

"Poor Phee," Shly replied. "She has to follow him around, watching him be unhappy."

"It's probably an important part of her training," Ebbler said, chopping some large, woody, stemmed vegetables with a sharp knife. "One needs to know how to mope about without exhibiting poor form," he added, in a pretty good impression of Wollard's voice. Ebbler's sense of humor always ratcheted up when he was tired and his inhibitions were low. Today he was practically asleep on his feet, so he was in rare form. Shly and Umily laughed openly. Barsparse kept her back turned, fussing with an alarming number of occupied burners, but she smirked as she did so. Kreet, as was his wont, remained silent.

Ebbler looked at Shly and Umily, his two best friends in the palace, laughing at his joke. He smiled, then yelped with alarm when he looked back down to his chopping. Among the sliced vegetables, he saw a severed half-inch of his left index finger. Even more alarmingly, there was a thin slice of finger next to it, like a coin made of meat and bone.

Shly and Umily shouted. Kreet snorted. Barsparse looked over Ebbler's shoulder and said, "I'll need to bulkfab more vegetables. That lot's ruined. Okay, how do we treat a cut?"

"A cut?" Shly said. "His finger's off!"

"Yes," Barsparse agreed. "He cut it off. How do we treat it, Ebbler?"

Ebbler, who was suddenly wide-awake and in no mood for jokes said, "For a minor cut, we clean the wound and stop the bleeding. For a serious cut, we clean the wound, stop the bleeding, and seek medical attention."

"And would you consider this a serious cut?"

"Yes, Chef."

"So would I. Get to it."

In a home that wasn't powered with utilitics, Ebbler would have washed the wound with antiseptic, then applied a bandage, but the utilitics could do a more thorough job of both of those tasks than any person. Of course, people weren't constantly coated with utilitics. They found the idea unsettling. Instead, Ebbler pressed the bleeding knuckle of what was left of his finger against the nearest wall. Utilitics automatically streamed onto him, sterilizing the wound and clotting the blood. The parts of him that were still on the cutting board had been coated with the invisible machines the instant they were separated from him, and had bled very little. What little blood had managed to escape was already on the move, being shunted to the floor and out of sight like any other refuse.

Ebbler gathered up the severed fingertip and the extra finger cross-section, then walked to the kitchen entrance. Two white-suited members of the palace medical staff were already waiting. They had clearly been dispatched from their facilities in the palace's new addition the instant the injury occurred, if not before. The palace staff knew that the utilitics and the staff in the palace's new addition worked together, but if asked how they worked together, the best answer any of them could offer would be, "Seamlessly."

Barsparse busied herself with cleaning up Ebbler's abandoned station. "Sloppy," she muttered. "Careless and sloppy."

"I'm amazed that he kept chopping after he cut his finger off," Umily said.

"Yeah, well, it goes to show that perseverance isn't a virtue if what you're doing is wrong," Barsparse said. "I don't know, girls. He got off to a good start, but if he's already losing focus, maybe this isn't the career for him. You don't belong in the kitchen if you don't have the passion for it."

"Why would you think Ebbler's losing focus?" Umily asked.

"Or that he doesn't have passion?" Shly added.

"You don't cut your finger off by paying too much attention," Barsparse said, as she went back to her too-full cooktop.

Shly said, "Come on, Chef, you must have noticed that he was half asleep."

"Exactly my point. He knows he needs his rest, but instead he stays up late. It's not the first time. It shows a lack of commitment."

"He's studying," Shly said. "He feels like he doesn't know enough about cooking, so he stays up late reading up on it."

Barsparse looked at Shly, trying to figure out if she was serious.

"It's true," Umily said.

Barsparse returned her attention to her pots, stirring one while smelling another. "If there are things he feels like he needs to know, why wouldn't he tell me?"

"Maybe he's afraid you'll decide he doesn't belong in the kitchen," Shly said. "Why did you assume he was staying up late, goofing around?"

Barsparse thought for a moment, then smiled at Shly and Umily. "Because when I was a sous chef, that's what I did."

32.

"Here we are, boys," Lord Jakabitus said, shouting slightly to be heard over the street noise outside the competitors' entrance. "Remember, do well. Rayzo, keep an eye on Hennik in case he needs help."

Great, Rayzo thought. *His only goal in life is to make me miserable, and now I'm responsible for helping him do it.*

Rayzo and Hennik joined the queue, got registered, had their bodies scanned, were issued their shorts, and were finally assigned their lockers. Rayzo helped guide Hennik to the lockers, which were adjacent, since they'd been next to each other in line.

All of the other competitors watched Rayzo and Hennik intently unless either of them was looking, in which case the competitors tried to act like they hadn't noticed members of the ruling family were present. Rayzo was used to that, and knew nobody would bother him for fear of drawing the attention of the Jakabitus family's infamous and invisible security forces.

There was a subtle change in the tenor of the others' attention. Lady Jakabitus could officially declare Hennik a member of the family, but that didn't alter the fact that he was a Hahn. Many of the competitors knew someone who was fighting in the war. Many would be fighting soon themselves. When Rayzo was alone, the other competitors pretended not to be interested in him. With Hennik present, they were pretending not to be hostile. Rayzo could feel the difference in his bones.

Hennik felt it too, or so Rayzo gathered by his smile. The bureaucracy, the crowds, the Spartan décor, the stifling odor of hundreds of uncomfortable young men, and the unspoken resentment had all seemed to invigorate the Hahn. He was in his element.

The morning after his failed escape attempt, Hennik had emerged from his room a seemingly different person. This new Hennik was not only resigned to staying on Apios, but happy about it. He had continued his practice of nauseating suck-uppery toward Lord Jakabitus, and indeed, expanded it to encompass pretty much everyone but Rayzo. When Lord Jakabitus asked Hennik about his change of heart, Hennik said that when he realized that his escape plan was going to succeed, he suddenly knew that escape was not what he wanted, so he'd deliberately sabotaged himself to stay at the palace without losing face.

After listening to that story, Rayzo had learned that he was able to roll his eyes hard enough to cause physical pain. He feared he might have twisted his optic nerve.

Aside from his smug attitude and his aggressive attempts to pursue Shly, Hennik's behavior since the escape attempt had been exemplary. It was just a ploy to make everyone drop their guard, but it was having the opposite effect, at least on Rayzo. Hennik was a ticking time bomb, and every moment that he didn't go off brought them closer to the inevitable moment when he would.

Rayzo put on his officially assigned sports shorts and watched as his ranking appeared. He'd had a good run at the last meet, resulting in mumbled congratulations from his father and relatively few pointers from Hennik. His rank was #4,231. He allowed himself a moment to enjoy it. Then he looked at Hennik, who had beaten Rayzo in the one and only sports match he'd ever played. His shorts read #4,230.

Hennik saw Rayzo's expression and said, "Don't worry little brother. I'm sure your rank will be as high as mine someday."

Both Rayzo and Hennik were relieved when they were split up and sent to separate holding lounges to wait for their first match. Constantly coming up with new ways to antagonize Rayzo took a great deal of concentration, and Hennik was grateful to set aside his efforts and focus on his strategy for winning. He stood with the other competitors to watch the recitation of the prophecy on the big screen feed. The announcer's words were piped in remotely, but at the end, the sound of all the fathers in the stands saying, "It is the prophecy," carried through the tunnel and into the lounge as a barely audible pressure wave Hennik felt vibrating in his chest.

While waiting for his match, Hennik pretended not to notice the other competitors talking about him behind his back, using voices that were pointedly just loud enough for him to hear. He understood the Apiosans well enough to expect resentment. They didn't understand the Hahn well enough to know that they used other people's resentment as fuel.

Finally, Hennik's number was called, along with the number 4,056, a competitor ranked nearly two hundred spots higher than him. This gave Hennik much to think about on his pod ride to the mat.

He'll be far more experienced than I, Hennik thought, *and a more worthy adversary than Rayzo. That's good, though. If I beat him . . .*

For an instant, Hennik saw his father's face. His thoughts immediately took a different turn.

When! When I beat him, my rank will go up quite a bit. If, by some freak accident, I lose, my ranking won't take too much of a hit. I should still end the day ahead of Rayzo. I won't lose, though. I've been making a plan for days. All that's left is to act out the play I've written.

Hennik reached the mat. After a few seconds, his opponent arrived. He might have been older than Hennik, but he was definitely larger, both in height and in mass. The opponent recognized Hennik on sight, which made Hennik wonder just how famous he was on this planet. Of course, he'd suspected that the ruling family adopting the child of a sworn enemy would be news, but it would be interesting to know just how familiar his image had become to the people of Apios.

The opponent's father arrived, followed by Lord Jakabitus. His Lordship made polite one-sided conversation with the other man as Hennik and his opponent faced off for the advantage round.

Hennik made an effort to outslap his opponent, but his plan for this match didn't hinge on having the advantage, so he didn't give it his all.

Lord Jakabitus shouted encouragement and advice, suggesting that Hennik should try to land a slap, and he might want to consider targeting the opponent's face.

Predictably, the opponent won the advantage round. He asked Hennik to declare his dominant hand, and predictably, Hennik lied. The opponent failed to foresee this, and grasped Hennik by his left wrist, leaving Hennik's right hand free to enact his plan.

As the time counted down, Hennik thought, *Everything hinges on the next thirty seconds. I have to do this right. It must seem real. Any hint that I'm faking would ruin the whole plan.*

The round began. Hennik and his opponent circled each other warily for a moment, then Hennik shouted, "Hey, watch this!"

The opponent gave him a puzzled look. Hennik capitalized on this confusion by making a fist with his free hand, and bringing it down as hard as he could into his own crotch.

Some say that pain is less intense when it's self-inflicted. The idea is that if you're in control of the pain, it is perceived as an unfortunate necessity rather than an emergency. Hennik knew as soon as his fist made contact that this was not true. Hennik sank to one knee, pressing his belly with his free arm, as if it would somehow help ease his condition. He heard his opponent gasp, then curse, then laugh. More importantly, Hennik did not hear any score chimes, meaning that neither of them had scored when he struck himself in the crotch. Hennik had suspected this would be the case, but he'd wanted to be sure for his future matches.

Now, he just had to finish this match.

His opponent was standing above him, confused and laughing. It was just the opportunity Hennik needed. He swept his opponent's legs, and when the boy landed hard, Hennik quickly pinned his arms and rolled him onto his front. Hennik ran out the clock sitting between the opponent's shoulder blades, keeping him immobile. Toward the end, when it was clear that Hennik would win this round on points, the opponent said, "Okay, fine. You won this time, Hahn, but do you really think that trick will work against everybody?"

Hennik said, "I only needed it to work against you."

When the time was up, Lord Jakabitus seemed more bewildered than proud. He walked out to the mat and stood next to Hennik, who was still slightly hunched over from the residual pain. Lord Jakabitus held Hennik's hand aloft and said, "It is the prophecy," but his voice rose in pitch at the end, as if in question.

Hennik rode the pod back and tried to contain his glee as he reentered the holding lounge. He wanted to rub his victory in every face he saw, but he knew that he needed to play it cool for his plan to work. While he waited for his next match, he stood facing one of the displays. His eyes were watching the big-screen feed, but his ears were scanning the mass of competitors behind him, listening for the words Hennik, Hahn, and any synonym for the word *crotch*.

Hennik figured that news of the ruling family's adopted Hahn winning his first match by assaulting himself would spread about as fast as news possibly could. The more time that went by without Hennik hearing any whispers about his performance, the better he felt. He wouldn't have minded the story of his first match getting out, as it would have caused future opponents to underestimate him. But he did not want anyone to guess what he intended to do in his second match.

Hennik watched several matches on the feed before he heard his number called again. He felt confident as he rode to the mat, and this time he didn't think about much of anything, letting the spectacle wash over him.

His opponent and his opponent's father were already waiting at the mat. The boy was older, larger, and ranked a little over a hundred points higher than him. Hennik saw recognition and confidence on their faces, but no amusement.

Neither of them had heard the story yet, Hennik thought. *Did these people not talk to each other?*

Lord Jakabitus was the last to arrive. The scheduling algorithm always allowed for fathers who had more than one son competing to attend all of their sons' matches. The algorithm was quite good, but it still sometimes led to a hectic day for the father in question.

Because Hennik wasn't worried about winning the advantage round, he was free to experiment, and because he hadn't been raised with sports, he had no preconceived notions about how the game should be played.

The orthodox strategy for the challenge round was to keep the elbows apart and barrage the sides of the opponent's head with fast, light slaps, though one might block an opponent's arms with one's own. One could feint slapping low, then instead slap high. There were endless variations in the high-speed chess game of the advantage round, but the basic forms and strategies were honored.

The round started, and the opponent landed several light slaps in quick succession on the sides of Hennik's face. Hennik put his hands together in front of his chest and thrust them straight up, between the opponent's arms. He then opened his hands and smeared them into the other boy's face.

His opponent was stunned. He had difficulty seeing and breathing because his eyes, nostrils, and mouth were all either partially or totally clogged by Hennik's hands. His rational mind shut down altogether, and he stopped slapping, instead struggling to push Hennik's hands away from his face. He grappled and struggled and pulled at Hennik's arms, but Hennik had superior leverage.

The opponent finally managed to pull Hennik's left hand back, using both of his hands to do it. Hennik retaliated by slapping the opponent as hard as he could with his right palm. He landed several harsh, stinging blows before the opponent released his left hand and brought his arms up around his head to shield himself from further attack. He shouldn't have bothered. He had barely started cowering when Hennik won the round.

The opponent said nothing, nor did the opponent's father, nor did Lord Jakabitus. Hennik thrust both arms high into the air and walked a lap of the mat shouting, "Yes! Yes!" He took up his position for the challenge round, laughing and hopping up and down to stay loose.

"What's your dominant hand?" he asked.

The opponent started to answer, but Hennik interrupted, shouting, "It doesn't matter! I'll take your right!"

The opponent looked uncertainly toward the VIP box. His father and Lord Jakabitus both shrugged. He extended his right hand to Hennik, who took it in his own right.

The round started. Hennik immediately dropped to the floor and scurried between the other, taller boy's legs, still holding his opponent's right wrist in an iron grip. Hennik employed the technique that Hartchar had taught him and Rayzo, springing instantly back to his feet and pivoting. Hennik was now standing behind his opponent, who was hunched forward with his right arm extended back between his own legs, giving him no leverage to break free.

Hennik pitched his weight forward to tug back on the opponent's arm, then pulled upward sharply, bringing the unfortunate boy's forearm up between his own legs. As Hennik's earlier experiment had shown, the score was unaffected. Instead, the opponent instinctively rose to the balls of his feet, putting himself even more off balance.

Hennik kept applying upward pressure with his right hand, then shoved the boy forward with his left. His helpless opponent essentially tiptoed to the edge of the mat under his own power, with Hennik exerting only minimal effort to keep him moving. Once they reached the edge, Hennik used all of his strength to pull up, sending the boy headfirst into the gutter.

Hennik ran in circles and jumped and spun as energetically as he could while laughing.

"Undefeated!" he cried. Un! De! Feated!"

Lord Jakabitus said something to the opponent's father, then bent down into the gutter to speak to the defeated opponent. Hennik didn't know what he was saying, and didn't care. He was too busy sending a message to everybody to listen to anybody.

"This is my first meet, and no one can touch me! I'm amazed! I knew this game was ridiculous and stupid, but I had no idea it was so easy!"

Lord Jakabitus walked to the middle of the mat and took Hennik's hand. Hennik thrust both arms into the air, dragging Lord Jakabitus's hand up with them, and shouted, "It is the prophecy!"

Lord Jakabitus said nothing.

◆ ◆ ◆

Rayzo was under the mistaken impression that he was having a good day.

His matches had been challenging, but not so much so that he hadn't won all of them. The matching algorithm took into account not only whether or not you won your match, but also how difficult it had been. The easier one match was, the more challenging the next would be. As such, Hartchar's instructions were to win, but not too quickly; that way Rayzo would get extra *real-world* practice, avoid getting matched with a much higher-ranked opponent who was beyond his skill level, and continue to increase his standing in a controlled, sustainable manner.

Lord Jakabitus was far less vocal than usual. Instead of shouting encouragement at Rayzo to do whatever he was already attempting to do, His Lordship made polite conversation with the opponent's father in the VIP box before the match, then sat in silence while Rayzo competed.

After Rayzo's first win of the day, when Lord Jakabitus came out to raise his son's hand and invoked the prophecy, Rayzo asked how Hennik was doing. Lord Jakabitus had just enough time to say, "He won his first match, but I doubt that his strategy will work long term."

At each of his subsequent matches, Rayzo had repeated the same query, only to be answered with increasingly terse recitations of the sentence, "Don't worry about Hennik, son. Concentrate on your own matches."

Rayzo wasn't stupid. He could read between the lines. Hennik must be getting destroyed. Clearly his father was afraid that telling him so would be a distraction. It would also explain His Lordship's subdued demeanor. The old man had been hoping that Hennik would be a strong competitor.

Rayzo understood, but he didn't feel much sympathy for either of them. Hennik had gotten off to a good start, but the honeymoon was over, and he and Lord Jakabitus both needed to understand who was the best son and the best sportsman. The fact that he was having the best single day of sports in his career just drove the point home.

Rayzo won his final match of the meet, taking great care to do so slowly. Lord Jakabitus moped out onto the mat, held Rayzo's hand aloft, and quietly invoked the prophecy. Again, Rayzo asked how Hennik was doing. Lord Jakabitus bit his lip, put a hand on Rayzo's shoulder, and said, more gently this time, "Concentrate on your own game, son."

As he rode his pod back to the holding lounge, Rayzo thought, *Wow, Father is taking Hennik's failure awfully hard. I hate to see him unhappy, but I must say, it serves him right. You can't let your self-esteem get wrapped up in someone else's performance.*

Rayzo stepped out of the pod with more than a little swagger in his step. As he made his way through the crowd, he noticed an unusually high level of chatter in the room. It was late in the meet, and it wasn't unusual for rumors to have started spreading about what had happened during competition.

Rayzo looked around. Everyone was talking at once and stealing glances at him. He was a Jakabitus. He was used to people behaving this way. Almost everybody did. But this wasn't *almost everybody.* It was *everybody,* and they were all doing it at once. Somewhere in the sea of furtive mutterings, Rayzo clearly heard someone say, "Hahn."

"What's happened?" Rayzo asked.

The entire room went silent. A young boy said, "I'm sorry, Your Lordship. You are Rayzo Jakabitus, aren't you?" His shorts bore a ranking in the 9,000s. He was small, thin, and too young to know that he should be nervous.

"I'm not a Lord," Rayzo said, crouching to put himself on the boy's level, as he'd seen his mother do more than once when addressing children. "Officially, you'd call me *Master Rayzo,* but I'm not worried about it. What's your name?"

The boy smiled and said, "Mank, sir, uh, Master Rayzo."

"Hello, Mank."

"Hello. Um, I was wondering, you came here with the Hahn, didn't you?"

"Yes," Rayzo said.

"Is it true that he's developed a secret sports technique?"

"I don't know of any," Rayzo said.

"They say it makes him unbeatable, Master Rayzo."

"I . . . I don't think that's true," Rayzo said.

"Have you ever beaten him?" the boy asked.

Rayzo hesitated just long enough for someone to shout, "He's on the big screen! The Hahn's fighting on the big screen!"

Rayzo didn't have to make his way to a display. They were everywhere in the lounge. Hennik was standing hunched forward on a mat, preparing for the advantage round. Opposite him was a competitor who was larger in every measurable way, yet Hennik looked supremely confident.

The round began. The opponent tried to use his superior reach to his advantage, leaning back slightly and slapping at Hennik with his fingertips. Rayzo smiled to himself, which was exactly when Hennik lurched forward and mashed his palm into the opponent's face, pressing against his nose and blocking his mouth and eyes. The opponent instinctively grabbed Hennik's arm with both hands and tried to pull it off his face. Hennik capitalized on his mistake by striking the competitor repeatedly, as hard as he could, in the ear.

The opponent tried to block Hennik's blows with one arm while holding the other hand away from his face, but Hennik had the initiative, and he easily landed enough fierce blows to win the advantage round. He celebrated by running laps of the mat with his arms raised in triumph.

Hennik stopped celebrating with barely enough time to take his position for the challenge round. His opponent offered the information that his right hand was dominant. Hennik grasped the proffered right wrist grudgingly, snarling that he didn't care and it wouldn't make any difference.

When the round began, the competitor's arm shot forward like an arrow, trying to grasp Hennik by the neck. Unfortunately for him, Hennik's neck was not there.

Hennik had already dropped to the mat, and was halfway between his opponent's legs. A moment later, he sprang up behind the other boy and in one—now well-practiced—motion, ground the challenger's meaty forearm into his most sensitive weak spot.

As instinct dictated, the opponent sprung up on his tiptoes and pitched his weight forward. Hennik easily steered him across the mat. The opponent's legs kicked pathetically as he landed in the gutter, but the feed didn't linger on the defeated opponent. It followed Hennik as he once again started running laps of the mat, celebrating his victory.

"This is my first meet! My first, and I'm already the king of Apiosan sports! I'm undefeated! I'm undefeatable! All this time, all you needed was a Hahn to come and show you how your own idiotic game should be played!"

Lord Jakabitus slunk onto the mat and held Hennik's hand aloft. Before Lord Jakabitus could open his mouth, Hennik screeched, "It is the prophecy."

It was a revelation for Rayzo. After all these years, all the time spent worrying that he was a disappointment to his father, he now realized this was the first time he'd ever actually seen his father genuinely ashamed . . . and it wasn't at him. Rayzo nearly wept from the joy of it, but his happiness was short-lived.

Hennik started thrusting his pelvis forward and pointing at it with his free hand. He was drawing attention to his ranking.

Up until that moment, Rayzo had been proud of his own ranking. This had been his most successful sports meet ever, and he'd progressed from #4,231 to #3,856.

Hennik's ranking was difficult to read, as his attempts to call attention to it had made it a moving target, but then he spun and bent over so that the rear display of his rank would be clearly visible: #3,320.

I don't look forward to talking to Hennik tonight, Rayzo thought. *Oh well, why should tonight be any different than usual?*

33.

Umily pushed her grav-platter into the servant's corridor. She had just delivered the linens for Master Rayzo's postmeet shower.

Both Master Rayzo and Master Hennik would have cleansed themselves at the arena after the meet, but Rayzo always did it again once he got home. He'd once said that it took extra time to *feel clean* after a meet, which Umily didn't understand, but she didn't let it bother her. Working at the palace, you got accustomed to not understanding things.

The point was: there was reason to expect that Master Hennik might want extra linens, and Umily delivered them to his still-empty room without having received a request, which was her job. Of course, she made sure Master Rayzo was well cared for before tending to Master Hennik's needs. This was just one example of the countless ways in which Master Rayzo was getting preferential treatment, even if he was unaware of it.

Umily took no satisfaction from having done her job well, because she knew she hadn't done it well enough. She had cut the timing far too close. The letter from Gint, which she still had not read, was a lingering distraction.

She knew that the longer she put off reading it, the harder it would be to start. She also knew that Shly would ask about the letter at dinner, and admitting that she hadn't read it yet would likely lead to an uncomfortable conversation.

Umily had the time, she had the letter, and she had to get it done, so she left her grav-platter outside her quarters, sat on the corner of her bed, pulled out her papers, and started reading.

Umily,

I hope things are good for you. They've gotten better here.

I have been killed in combat twice since I wrote last, but that's good. Every time I die, I come back a better soldier, and I hate the Hahn more.

They are lower than animals, Umily. They throw themselves against us, wave after wave of them, climbing over their dead comrades as if the corpses are nothing but obstacles. They don't use bulk-guns. Some of them have fission grenades (as I've learned the hard way a few times), which they only detonate to keep from being captured alive. At first I thought it was because they were conserving their bulk-ammo, but the commander says it's all part of their plan. She says that they know Her Ladyship won't let us use arms against an unarmed force, on account of it being monstrous.

I'd like to see Her Ladyship and her generals face a few waves of bloodthirsty Hahn coming after them with sticks and clubs and murder in their eyes. Then we could have a nice talk about what is or isn't monstrous.

None of us likes it, but we abide by the treaty because those are our orders, and just like at the palace, the utilitics are always watching.

Oh! Here's something interesting. The other night, the commander came and had drinks with us. She told us stories about the old days. Did you know that at one time utilitics were weaponized? Apparently you could make them swarm and kill people. She said she didn't know how it worked, just that the enemy would breach your perimeter, take two steps, and then fall down dead. They even experimented with sending the utilics into enemy camps. There was no way to see them coming and no way to defend against them.

Of course, we can't do that anymore either, because some Jakabitus signed a treaty. I can't see why. It seems like such a great way to win a war. You could send the tics into an enemy base at night, then make your move come morning. The utilitics would even cart away the bodies like they do Barsparse's kitchen scraps.

How is Chef Barsparse? I hope she's well. She was always good to me. Please tell her I asked.

I should go. Some of the boys and I are working on a new weapon. It looks like a club, but after you hit a Hahn in the head, you keep the club pressed against their skull. It emits radiation that increases the pressure inside their head until the stuff that's inside comes out, either by exploding or finding a hole to squirt through. There's no treaty against that yet.

We're ready to start testing. I almost can't wait until the Hahn attack again.

Take care of yourself. I miss you.

Gint.

Emily folded her papers, put them back into her pocket, and silently mourned for her husband, who was not, at the moment, dead.

34.

“You should’ve seen it,” Hennik said. “There I was, on the big screen, pointing at my shorts and laughing.”

“You paint such a vivid picture, it’s as if I were there, Master Hennik,” Migg said.

Hennik lay on his bed, smiling up at the ceiling, trying to relive his victory in his mind. Migg stood in her corner of Hennik’s bedchamber, also trying to use her mind to go elsewhere, though with less success.

“And to think,” Hennik said, “you told me I shouldn’t apply moves from spak in Apiosan sports. You said it was a bad idea.”

Spak was a Hahn sport, wherein a skilled athlete would select a spak partner, usually someone smaller and weaker, and force them into some humiliating physical position without warning and against their will. The name derived from the sound made when an unwitting participant was slapped very hard on the back of the neck, a popular opening gambit. Spak was a very popular spectator sport. Many of the top spakers were quite famous on the Hahn Home World, although fans seldom approached them on the street.

"With respect, Master Hennik, I didn't say that it would be a bad idea. I said that it would be wrong."

"Then you probably shouldn't have brought it up, Migg."

Migg said, "Quite right, Master Hennik," then attempted to change the subject. "How did Master Rayzo do?"

Hennik sat up, excited. "I can't believe I forgot to tell you. That's the best part! He was pathetic! Absolutely terrible!"

"I'm sorry to hear he didn't do well."

"No, Migg, you dummy. That's what makes it so great! He had his best day ever; it just wasn't nearly as good as mine! He won all of his matches, but he was slow and had no style, so his ranking only went up a little while mine exploded. He tried to make some lame excuse about strategy and setting himself up for success. I told him he wasn't doing a very good job of it."

"Well said, Master Hennik."

Hennik shrugged and shook his head. "I can't get over the dishonesty of these people, Migg. I mean, either he was lying to me, or he was lying to all his opponents by pretending to be worse at sports than he is. Either way it's shameful."

"I must remind you, Master Hennik, that you are currently deceiving the Jakabitus family, pretending to have accepted life here while secretly maintaining a hostile attitude."

"But that's different, Migg. I hold them in contempt. I mislead them as an insult. They mislead each other as a basic form of communication. It's disgusting."

"Yes, Master Hennik. Clearly, from what you say, Master Rayzo is beneath contempt. In a way, it's lucky that you were adopted by his parents rather than the other way around. He would have been a complete waste of your father's time."

Hennik studied Migg for a long moment, then relaxed, clearly satisfied with whatever he saw.

"No, Migg. Wrong again," he said. "Rayzo is not without skill, and he's still young enough that he hasn't been entirely poisoned by his own culture. My father, or any good strong Hahn, might be able to make something of Rayzo."

Migg said, "It's a shame that's not possible, Master Hennik."

"Why not? The Formalities allowed the Jakabituses to take me. Why couldn't the Hahn take him?"

"It's not a matter of the form, Master Hennik. It's a matter of access. Master Rayzo never leaves the planet Apios, so no Hahn will ever have access to him."

Hennik stood and advanced on Migg. "I'm a Hahn, Migg. I'm the son of Kamar Hahn, ruler of the Hahn, and I have access to the Jakabitus whelp every single day."

"True, Master Hennik," Migg stammered, "but you are an adopted member of the Jakabitus family, you're only a year older than Master Rayzo, and your movements are restricted to the palace. If you were to try to forcibly adopt Master Rayzo, it would cause a tremendous amount of confusion and unpleasantness."

Hennik considered it, then muttered, "Yes, you're probably right."

35.

While most of the cleaning after a dinner service was handled by the utilitics, there were still some tasks that were done by hand for no better reason than tradition.

Barsparse silently watched Ebbler wipe his cutting board reverently, as if he were polishing his most prized possession.

"I think dinner service went well," Barsparse said, keeping her voice casual.

"Yes, Chef, I think so," Ebbler agreed.

"You seemed on top of your game."

"Thank you, Chef. I try my best. After I abandoned you at lunch, I knew I had to work harder to redeem myself."

"Really, you think that was it?" Barsparse asked. "Not the nap the medics ordered you to take after they fused your finger back together?"

Ebbler's shoulders slumped and his head hung down. "How did you know that they prescribed a nap?"

"I'm the one who told them to. Seriously, Ebbler, have you ever had a medic prescribe a nap before?"

"I suppose not."

"So, whose work have you been reading at night?"

"Shly told you," Ebbler moaned.

"Yes, she and Umily did. Kreet kept your secret, which is not to his credit. You should thank the ladies, Ebbler. I know you lack certain knowledge, but I like that you're diligent. Hiding things from me, however, is unacceptable. I could've terminated you because I thought you didn't care enough about the job to get a good night's sleep. Understand?"

"Yes, Chef."

"Good. Now, you've been reading in your off time to supplement your knowledge. Who have you been reading?"

"Garleth Senior."

Barsparse moaned. "No wonder you were sleepy."

"It wasn't while I was reading that I was sleepy," Ebbler said.

Barsparse cut him off with a wave of her hand. "At least you picked the right Garleth," she said. "Garleth Junior was a better writer, but didn't know anything about cooking. He just traded on the old man's name."

"Yeah," Ebbler said. "He was good at describing how dishes looked and tasted, but he never really told you how to make anything."

"Because all of his instructions would have been *have a father who's a great chef, and let him do the cooking.* Look, Ebbler, I like that you're studying, but I don't like what you're studying. If you want to continue, I'll suggest things for you to read."

"You'd do that?" Ebbler asked.

"Of course. That way I know you'll learn what I want you to learn, and you won't pick up any bad habits. Make sense?"

"Yes, Chef."

"Good, because you've got one seriously bad habit that you need to break: keeping secrets from me. I can't teach you if you won't tell me what you need to know."

PART 5

Should a party succeed in executing a complex scheme, proper form demands that said party be allowed to explain said scheme in granular detail. The joy of explaining is part of the reward. Often, the most satisfying part.

-Excerpt from *The Arbiters' Official Guidelines Regarding Etiquette for the Defeated, Vanquished, and Demoralized*

36.

"Know that two thousand, one hundred, and seventy-one conventional years have passed since the Terran Exodus," Wollard said. "Today is the sixteenth day of the fourth month. We meet on the planet Apios, in the servants' hall of Palace Koa, the ancestral home of House Jakabitus and its matriarch, Lady Joanadie Jakabitus. I am Wollard, Master of Formalities for House Jakabitus, and I am currently delivering the daily meeting to the palace staff."

Wollard looked up from his papers to survey the assembled staff. He had walked in looking at the floor and launched into the greeting immediately. Now, he took a moment to select his next words.

"Why are there multiple people missing?" he asked.

Kreet raised his hand and said, "Aren't you supposed to start your question with *query*?"

Wollard regarded Kreet silently, raising an impatient eyebrow.

Kreet grimaced, then said, "Query."

"Recognized."

"Aren't you supposed to start a question with *query*?"

"You're supposed to. I, as the chair of the meeting, have the power to ask questions at will, as long as they are pertinent to the matter at hand. As such, I ask again, why are there multiple people missing?"

Wollard had been delivering the daily meeting to the palace staff since the day the Arbiters had assigned him to Palace Koa, and in all that time, there had never been more than two staff members absent from any one meeting, and he had almost always been warned in advance as to who would be absent and why. Now he found himself looking at three empty seats with no warning or explanation. Of course, Glaz was the person who usually alerted Wollard of these absences, and she was one of those who were absent, along with Hartchar and Migg.

Three key staff members were lost, and the remaining staff appeared to be at a loss. They looked back at Wollard with puzzled expressions, and no one came forward with new information.

Wollard turned to Phee and asked, "Would you please see if you can find any of them? I'd suggest starting with Glaz."

Phee nodded and left. The day before, she had made Wollard angrier than she had ever seen him, and he had promised to decide on her punishment before this day was out. So she was alternating between trying to be the perfect protégée when he needed her and being invisible when he didn't.

"Well then," Wollard said, "while we're waiting for Phee to return, there's no reason we can't press on. As you all may know, both Master Rayzo and Master Hennik had successful outings at the sports meet yesterday. Normally, I would suggest congratulating Master Rayzo after a strong match, but in this case I recommend that you avoid discussing the topic with either Master Rayzo or Master Hennik. My understanding is that one of them has taken the events of yesterday very badly, and the other has taken them far too well."

The portion of the staff that was present listened attentively, but Wollard could tell they were distracted. He couldn't blame them. He was having difficulty focusing on the morning briefing too, and he was the one presenting it.

Wollard continued. "At this time I'd like to congratulate Ebbler on the quality of the food served at last night's staff tasting. I know I speak for everyone when I say it was both delicious and instructive." Wollard took a moment to consider his next comment, but not long enough of a moment.

"I'm also absolutely certain that the dishes you prepared are not the cause of the absent staff members this morning."

Wollard was embarrassed by his words as soon as he'd spoken them. He didn't often indulge in overt attempts at humor, and could tell that on this occasion it had been ill-advised. He looked up from his papers and smiled apologetically, but his audience, mercifully, hadn't been listening. Every single head was turned toward the door.

"Ah, has Phee re . . . turned?" Wollard asked, turning to look. He trailed off at the sight of Phee standing next to an ashen-faced Glaz.

"Wollard," Glaz said, "there's an emergency."

"Of course, Glaz. If someone needs medical attention or there's a security breach, I'm sure the new addition—"

"No," Glaz interrupted. "It's an emergency of a more . . . social nature. It's a problem of etiquette. We need you, Wollard. We need you to tell us what to do."

◆ ◆ ◆

Glaz moved across the Grand Gallery at a speed that was just a touch slower than a run, then rode to the second floor. She was followed by Wollard and Phee, who were followed by the rest of the staff. In the large servants' hall, the group felt small. Here, in the vast gallery, they seemed miniscule.

They found Hartchar pacing like a caged animal in front of the closed door to the training room.

"You see? It's like I said," Glaz explained. "He's barricaded himself in the training room, and he refuses to come out. He says he'll only talk to you or Lady Jakabitus."

"Wollard," Hartchar said, her eyes afire with delight at seeing him. "Tell me, how much force am I allowed to use against Master Hennik? I assume it would be bad form to break bones, but is there anything I can sprain? There are several parts of him that I'd very much like to sprain."

Hennik's muffled voice from the other side of the door shouted, "Is Wollard here? Good. Bring him close."

Wollard put his head next to the door and shouted, "Master Hennik? It's me, Wollard. I'm here. What did you wish to say?"

"Only that I refuse to talk to anyone but Lady Joanadie Jakabitus, ruler of Apios."

"That was stupid," Ebbler muttered.

"It was good form," Phee said quietly. "Essentially, *Master Hennik* just declared his position that Wollard is merely a means of communication, and that anything he says to Wollard from this point forward is meant to be related to Lady Jakabitus, and anything Wollard says back will be interpreted as Her Ladyship's official position."

"Okay, it's not stupid," Ebbler said, "but it's confusing."

"The Formalities often are," Wollard said, making it clear to Ebbler that he and Phee weren't being as quiet as they thought. "That's why people like Phee and I are necessary."

Wollard made fleeting eye contact with Phee, and while he didn't smile or even nod, it was clear to her that he'd approved of her explanation enough to make him momentarily forget that he was unhappy with her.

Or maybe, she thought, *he's so unhappy with the rest of his life right now that he seems happy with me in comparison.*

Wollard returned his attention to the door. "I understand, Master Hennik. Is there anything you would have me tell Her Ladyship?"

"Yes. Tell Lady Jakabitus that I am formally reasserting my belligerence."

"I think you mean *hostility,* Master Hennik."

"Shut up! Tell Lady Jakabitus that having invaded Apiosan territory more deeply than any other Hahn in history, I have officially claimed this gymnasium, along with its attached sanitary facilities, as Hahn territory."

Shly said, "He can't do that!" She looked to Hartchar, Glaz, and Barsparse, all of whom remained grimly silent.

Phee said, "All he's done so far is block a door and declare some things. He can declare anything he wants. It doesn't mean he'll get away with it."

Wollard said, "I will relay your message to Her Ladyship, but I shouldn't expect a positive response if I were you."

"And you shouldn't expect me to care if you were you," Hennik's muffled voice replied. "Also tell her that shortly after I annexed the training room, I caught an Apiosan encroaching on this newly sovereign Hahn territory. His name is Rayzo Jakabitus. As the prisoner is a minor, and I am a member of a hostile world's ruling family, which is greater in years, wisdom, and every other sense to the Jakabituses, I will show Lady Jakabitus the courtesy of raising young Rayzo as my own son."

"Master Hennik," Wollard said. "I urge you, for your own sake, not to harm Master Rayzo. If you already have done any harm to him, I suggest you open this door immediately and allow us to offer assistance."

"Wollard, I'm shocked at the very suggestion that I would harm my adopted son. Shocked and offended."

Wollard grimaced, but said what he knew he needed to say. "I apologize, Master Hennik. I meant no offense. I am certain that you have not harmed Master Rayzo, and that he is available to send greetings to Lady Jakabitus."

"I was never offered the opportunity to send greetings to my father," Hennik said, "but the Hahn are not heartless. Migg, remove my son's gag and bring him here."

There was the faint sound of a chair being dragged across the floor, then, from beyond the door, Rayzo said, "Wollard, will you please tell this idiot that he can't get away with this?"

Phee remembered what Wollard had told her. *We never tell members of the ruling family that they can't do a thing, because that would not be true. They can do anything they can get away with, no matter what the Formalities say, and if they remember that, we lose all power over them.*

Wollard sagged onto the door, letting it carry his weight. "I am sorry, Master Rayzo, but it's not my place. Are you hurt?"

"They have me gagged and tied to a chair, but they haven't hurt me."

Wollard said, "I'm pleased to hear it," then turned away from the door and said in a quieter voice, "Phee, please go brief Her Ladyship at once."

Phee left at top speed.

Wollard turned back to the door. "Master Rayzo, if I may ask, who is in there with you?"

"It's just me, Hennik, and his valet, Migg. Honestly, Wollard, if you just broke open the door, Hartchar could come in by herself and—"

"Migg, I think the boy's getting a little overstimulated," Hennik interrupted. Migg's voice said something quiet in an apologetic tone, then Rayzo's voice was muffled, replaced by the sound of a chair being dragged off into the distance.

Wollard said, "Master Hennik, it's going to be rather difficult, living the rest of your life and raising an adopted son entirely in the training room."

"It's less than ideal, I admit, but war sometimes forces us into uncomfortable positions."

Wollard resented the fact that he could relate so well to that statement.

"Besides," Hennik said, "it's not so bad. We have plenty of room for three people. We have sanitary facilities. The mat will give us a means of passing the time and remaining physically active, and will serve as a place to sleep."

"What about food?" Wollard asked. "There are no bulkfabs in the training room."

"An interesting question, Wollard. I wonder if there is any precedent in the Formalities regarding the supply of food to a small, hostile population, which is completely surrounded by a superior force."

Wollard turned to face rest of the staff. They were looking to him for some sign. They got it, but the sign didn't say anything they liked.

37•

Wollard walked slowly to Lady Jakabitus's offices. Though his body had not changed, he seemed to have lost several inches of height in recent weeks. His formal black uniform was still impeccable, and his hair was still perfectly styled, but he was disheveled on a spiritual level, and it showed. He looked at the wallpaper in the vestibule and was impressed. He wouldn't have thought it possible to make a graceful, tasteful-looking wallpaper pattern that incorporated elements that flashed bright red.

He opened the door. Lady Jakabitus was sitting behind her desk in her dressing gown, her hair pulled back and clipped in place. Clearly, Phee had found her while she was still preparing for her day. Even unprepared, Lady Jakabitus looked more formidable than any other person Wollard had ever met.

Phee was standing before Her Ladyship's desk, but she retreated as soon as Wollard entered.

"Ah! Wollard," Her Ladyship said. "I am glad to see you."

Wollard bowed. "Milady, it's always a pleasure. I am, however, sorry about the circumstances of our meeting this morning."

"Whatever do you mean?" Lady Jakabitus asked, smiling angrily, a difficult trick that she appeared to have been practicing. "This is a joyous occasion."

"Milady?"

"I can see why you're confused, dear Wollard. I'll admit, this isn't how I envisioned becoming a grandmother." Her smile smoothly faded into a snarl as she spoke. Wollard was so focused on her voice that he barely noticed her rising to her feet and leaning forward across the desk.

"Who could have guessed," she continued, "when I adopted Hennik to be my son that he'd go on to adopt *my other* son. With a single stroke, he has made himself a father, me a grandmother, and Rayzo his own uncle! I do hope Rayzo realizes that he'll be expected to occasionally give himself gifts."

"An interesting turn of events, to be sure," Wollard said.

"Yes! I know I'm interested," Lady Jakabitus said. "Specifically, I was just telling Phee . . . oh, by the way, I'm very impressed with how Phee handled the task of breaking the news to me this morning."

"I'm not surprised, Milady. I knew Phee could be counted upon to impart the information swiftly and clearly."

"Oh, she did, but what really impressed me, Wollard, was that she had the good sense to look fearful and ashamed!"

Wollard froze.

Lady Jakabitus smiled. "That's more like it. Now, I was just telling Phee that I looked forward to hearing whatever precedents your archivists would dig up for this situation."

"I contacted the Arbiters as I made my way here. No precedent springs to mind, but as you say, the archivists are investigating. In the meantime, we must prepare ourselves for the possibility that the situation is, in fact," Wollard coughed, "unprecedented."

"I'm sorry," Lady Jakabitus said, directly contradicting her facial expression and posture. "Did you say that this might be unprecedented?"

"It may well be, Milady."

"I believe this is the first time since I became ruler that I've faced an unprecedented turn of events."

"Indeed. After hundreds of years of Arbitration, across hundreds of worlds, there is little that the archivists have not seen before. That said, even without a firm precedent, the Formalities will suggest—"

Lady Jakabitus held up a hand and gave Wollard a look that instantly cut him off. "Wollard, this is the first thing you've told me in weeks that has pleased me. Don't ruin it."

Wollard nodded.

Lady Jakabitus gave him a thoughtful look. "If there turns out to be no precedent, that means I'm free to act as I see fit, and I will *set* the precedent."

"You are always free to act as you will, Milady. *If* it turns out that there is no precedent, it will mean that I am able to offer you little guidance from the Formalities."

Lady Jakabitus sat back down and spun her chair to face the stunning view of the capital. Then she rotated to look at the portraits of her ancestors, many of whom had ruled the planet before her.

When she spun back to Wollard, her face had changed. Her eyes were still keen and intense, but her expression was serene, confident, and unmoving, as if she were wearing a lifelike mask that was forged from steel.

"How long before we know for sure if there's a precedent?" she asked in an even tone.

"The archives are vast, but archivists are efficient," Wollard said. "If they haven't found anything within twenty-four hours, you can reasonably act without fear of seeming rash."

"I wouldn't want to seem rash, would I? Fine. We wait a day, for form's sake. Then, if we've heard nothing, I'll simply have security move in and subdue Hennik and his valet."

Wollard's training was screaming at him to speak up. His sense of self-preservation was screaming at him to keep quiet.

"Milady," Wollard's training said, "that course of action might be ill-advised."

Lady Jakabitus's steel mask did not crack, despite her eyes' attempts to bulge through it.

"Ill-advised?" she asked.

"Perhaps, Milady."

"Ill-advised," she repeated.

"It is possible, Your Ladyship."

"Ill," Lady Jakabitus said, then stared at Wollard for a full five seconds before finishing, "advised. What a fascinating way to describe my actions. *Ill-advised.* Perhaps you could advise me, *Wollard*, as to whom the outside observer would describe as my primary advisor?"

For weeks, Wollard had felt like he was sinking. Now, he felt like he was fully sunk. In his desperation, he reached out for the Master of Formalities' most dangerous weapon: *facts.* When in fear of losing an argument, say things with which no honest person can argue.

"Lady Jakabitus, sending security in could reinforce the mistaken view that Master Hennik is a hostage, not, as you have stated, an adopted member of the family."

"If word gets out," Lady Jakabitus said.

"Milady, your rule has been lauded for its transparency and honesty. The general schedule of life in the palace is a matter of public record. Any deviation is noticed. Indeed, I'm certain the postponement of breakfast has already been noted. If you were to clamp down on the flow of information now, it would take what seemed like a mundane anomaly and make it interesting, almost as interesting as calling in armed guards."

Her Ladyship pondered this grudgingly, then said, "Frederain and I could go in and discipline him ourselves. If word did get out, it would simply seem like normal parenting."

"Or an undignified spectacle, Milady. On many worlds you and His Lordship choosing to personally berate or actually assault Master Hennik would not be seen favorably."

"We could employ the utilitics to unblock the door and drag him out."

"Which, I fear, would be a spectacle that is both undignified and amusing, and would not result in less attention, Milady."

"I could simply wait for him to get hungry. How long could that take?"

"Not long, to be sure, but whether he is considered a prisoner or a member of your family, denying him food would be very bad form indeed, and could result in a great loss of face."

Lady Jakabitus sneered but did not speak, which Wollard interpreted as a sign of reluctant agreement. Wollard glanced back at Phee, who was reading her papers. Wollard knew that there was a chance she was exchanging messages against his wishes, but he didn't believe that to be the case. Phee looked up from her papers, saw that Wollard was staring at her, and tipped her papers forward slightly, as if inviting him to look, even though he was fifteen feet away. He interpreted the gesture as a sign that she had sent him something. He quickly dug out his papers and found her message.

Wollard read the note and the attached precedent. After several moments of silent reading, Lady Jakabitus asked, "What is it, Wollard?"

"I do apologize for the delay, Milady. I will be with you in a moment."

"Is it something important?"

"I wouldn't put you off otherwise, Milady."

"Is it from the archivists?"

"No, Milady, it's something Phee found."

"Then Phee can tell me about it while you get up to speed."

"I think," Phee said, "that it would be best for Wollard to tell you, after he's determined if it is relevant."

Well done, Phee, Wollard thought. *Your survival instinct will serve you well. It is a shame it is not doing anything to help me.*

Wollard said, "Milady, I believe I'm ready to report. Phee has found a precedent that can offer a small bit of guidance for one aspect of the current situation."

"She found something standing here in this room that your archivists haven't dug up?" Lady Jakabitus asked.

"They are seeking precedents for the specific situation of an adopted child declaring himself a combatant and then forcibly adopting his former sibling, which, as you can imagine, is a rare occurrence."

"Not rare enough."

"Indeed. Phee, quite brilliantly I must say, has instead sought out well-established precedent for the aspect of the current situation that possesses the most pressing challenge: Master Hennik's decision to barricade himself in the training room and declare it Hahn territory."

"And what has she found?"

"If a hostile force seizes territory and notifies the opposing Great House that controls said territory, the Great House must act to take back the territory in a swift manner. Failure to do otherwise can be seen as tacit admission that the territory has changed hands."

"So I have to flush Hennik out of there right now, or else the training room really will become part of the Hahn Empire?"

"Not just yet, Milady. There is a complex calculus for determining what may be considered *a swift manner.* It calls into account the size of the invading force, the size of the territory seized, and the relative ease or difficulty with which the original ruling house can expect to reclaim its territory."

Lady Jakabitus looked at Wollard with an expression of tired contempt, as if she had been losing respect for him for so long that she was beginning to find it boring. "And what, pray tell, would constitute *a swift manner* in this case?"

Phee cleared her throat.

"Phee, have you completed the calculation?" Wollard asked.

"I have," Phee said.

"How much time do we have to act?" Lady Jakabitus asked.

"Four hours, Milady."

"Really? That long?"

Phee aimed the bow of her boat directly into the oncoming tidal wave of Lady Jakabitus's sarcasm and forged on. "Yes, Milady, assuming that the invading force consists of an adolescent male and a single adult, neither of whom has any military training, and the disputed territory is inside the most well-protected building on the planet, and said territory consists of two rooms which are devoid of weapons, one of which is partially padded, the formula suggests decisive action should be taken within the next four hours."

"Wonderful," Lady Jakabitus said. "Neither of you can tell me what to do, but you can tell me when I have to do it."

"I am sorry, Milady," Wollard said.

"Don't be," she said. "I'm genuinely pleased. This means that if he doesn't come out on his own within the next four hours, I have to send in the guards."

"Perhaps, Milady, but it would certainly be preferable to avoid that."

"Certainly," Lady Jakabitus said, smiling. "I can imagine how unpleasant it would be to have armed guards drag Hennik out of there, kicking and screaming."

"Indeed, Milady. So, I would—"

"Wait," Lady Jakabitus said. "Give me a moment. I'm imagining it." She closed her eyes and took a long, deep breath.

Wollard said, "I would suggest that we pursue all available diplomatic options to defuse the situation before resorting to the guards."

"Of course you would. I suppose you want me to go talk to him."

"In fact, no, Milady. We don't want to be seen as caving into his demands. He knows that I am your official envoy. I would suggest that any communication continue to go through me."

"But you've already spoken to him. It doesn't seem like it did much good."

"No, Milady, but perhaps I can wear him down over time."

"Four hours."

"I'll try to work fast. Also, that would be only one of the possible diplomatic solutions Phee and I would pursue."

"Really?" Lady Jakabitus asked. "Who else do you intend to talk to, his valet?"

"His father, Milady. I would suggest trying to open a back channel to Lord Kamar Hahn."

"What could that possibly accomplish, save for giving Lord Hahn a good laugh?"

Wollard said, "I know Lord Hahn gave you the impression that he does not care about Master Hennik, but I do not have to remind you that the Hahn armed forces have grown more and more aggressive since Master Hennik came here. It is possible that Lord Hahn has been trying to apply pressure in the hopes of regaining his son."

"You're suggesting that there may be a way to rid ourselves of Hennik and end the current Hahn offensive in one stroke?" Lady Jakabitus asked.

"It may be possible, Milady. The only way to know is to open some form of communication. I should also point out that we would have to be very careful to conduct this maneuver in such a way as to avoid a loss of face for House Jakabitus."

"Of course," Lady Jakabitus agreed, "but stopping the offensive and getting rid of Hennik might be worth losing a little face. If Lord Hahn wanted Hennik back, wouldn't he have made some statement to that effect?"

"Your Ladyship, Lord Hahn is Hennik's father. I'm certain that he wants Hennik back. He may simply have a hard time expressing his more tender feelings. Fathers can be prone to that."

38.

"Open the door this instant, you little snot!" Lord Jakabitus bellowed through the training room door.

Hennik was sitting in a priceless antique chair, which was resting on its back two legs against the door. His arms were folded, and he had a smile on his face. His head was tilted forward. He had been resting his head against the door, but Lord Jakabitus had proved to be a bit of a door-pounder.

"Temper, temper," Hennik said. "You wouldn't want the help to get the idea that you weren't a patient and loving father."

"Don't you talk to me about being a father," Lord Jakabitus shouted. "My son has been taken hostage. Any good father would be angry, Hennik, or would at least have the good sense to act angry."

If that comment upset Hennik, he didn't show it. "But what about your other son, Your Lordship? I'm your son too, or so you've said, and I'm barricaded in an enemy stronghold, fearing for my life."

Hennik winked at Rayzo, who was one of the three people in the galaxy who knew that Hennik's *barricade* consisted entirely of a sturdy cord securing the doors shut and the chair on which Hennik was sitting.

During one of the brief intervals when Rayzo was not gagged, he had asked if Hennik really thought it was enough to keep anybody out.

"No, cowardice will keep your parents and their staff out," Hennik had explained. "If they decide to call in the armed guards, nothing I can do would keep them out, so anything more than the flimsiest token resistance would be overkill."

Hennik's low estimation of Rayzo's family and staff had stung, and with each passing minute of his ridiculous captivity, it stung more.

"I'm not sure it's wise to antagonize His Lordship," Migg said.

"Please, Migg," Hennik said in a hushed tone, lest Lord Jakabitus hear him. "If I avoided doing things just because you didn't think they were a good idea, I wouldn't have done any of the things I've done since I got here.

"What about it, Father?" Hennik said over his shoulder, to the door. "Aren't you worried for my well-being?"

After a long silence, Lord Jakabitus said, "Nobody wants to see you harmed, Hennik."

Rayzo, still bound and gagged, and Migg, who was standing by him, ready to ungag or untie him the instant she was ordered to do so, exchanged a look that said that neither of them agreed with Lord Jakabitus on that point.

"I hope that's true," Hennik said in his most angelic voice. "But the fact that you've expressed so much concern for my little brother and so little for me speaks volumes. A good father never plays favorites. I intend to dote on my adopted son, little Rayzo."

Rayzo's eyes grew wide upon hearing Hennik refer to him as *little Rayzo.*

"My son and his future siblings will be the center of my universe."

Migg's eyes grew wide at the implication that Hennik might expect to sire children, seeing as she was the sole female inhabitant of Hennik's makeshift Hahn colony.

"Enjoy your little game while you can, Hennik," Lord Jakabitus said. "When you do come out of that room, and you *will* come out, you'll find that everything has changed. You've burned off the last pretense of good will anyone on this planet had for you."

"Pretense?" Hennik said. "Are you saying that you've been misleading me?"

Rayzo had seen enough of Hennik's attempts at acting to notice the sincere surprise in the Hahn boy's voice.

"Haven't you been misleading us?" Lord Jakabitus asked. "Pretending to adapt to life here while planning this ridiculous farce of yours?"

"That's different," Hennik said. "I was misleading you as a demonstration of my disrespect for you."

"And we let you believe it was working for similar reasons," Lord Jakabitus said.

"But the difference, Your Lordship," Hennik said, biting off each word as if it were spelled in letters made of gristle, "is that I was right to disrespect you."

Once he was done laughing, His Lordship said, "Well, *son*, we'll discuss that once you get sick of cowering in this little play fort you've made. Eventually you'll get tired and hungry, or you'll wise up and realize that you have no choice. Then, we'll talk about how one goes about earning respect."

Hennik muttered, "How would you know, you married into it," but Lord Jakabitus didn't hear. His laugh grew distant as he walked away from the door.

Hennik smirked at Rayzo and Migg, as if to say, *you saw me win that argument, right*?

Rayzo looked up at Migg, then rolled his eyes downward and nodded his head, indicating his gag as best he could. After Hennik gave her a glum shrug, Migg pulled the gag out of Rayzo's mouth and left it hanging around his neck.

"Are you comfortable, Master Rayzo?" she asked.

"No, but that's not your fault," he replied. Then he addressed Hennik, "Okay, fine, you've got me. You asked me to meet you here first thing to discuss sports strategy, and then you ordered your valet to help you subdue me and tie me up. Well done. Now, how do you see this playing out? Do you really think we're going to spend the rest of our lives living in this room as father and son?"

Hennik shook his head. "Of course not. I expect you'll leave home when you've come of age. I've adopted you, but that doesn't mean I plan to support you for the rest of your life. You need to be your own man."

39.

Phee had difficulty keeping Wollard's pace as she followed him through the palace. She'd never seen anyone walk so slowly. When people walked, they were usually either trying to get to somewhere or get away from somewhere. Phee knew that Wollard hadn't liked being in Her Ladyship's office, but he was perhaps equally apprehensive about talking to Hennik. As his distaste for his destination was barely beaten out by the discomfort that would have come from remaining where he'd been, the net result was a leisurely walking pace that gave him plenty of time to think, which at one time had seemed like a positive thing.

The process of crafting the unofficial message to Kamar Hahn had not gone smoothly. In times past, it was the kind of task Lady Jakabitus would have simply asked Wollard to handle. He would have shown her a draft, which she would have glanced at with a cursory *thank you.* This time, she had insisted that Wollard compose the message in her presence. Her Ladyship had questioned, challenged, and demanded changes to every word of the message. In the end, she'd declared that it would have been easier and less irritating if she had left Wollard out of it and written the message herself.

Wollard had said, "Yes, Milady," out of reflex, but was disturbed to find that he meant it.

Wollard slowed to a stop just before he reached the training room, in front of the all-too-familiar door to the library. Without speaking a word, he pushed the door open and entered. Phee followed.

She knew he was still unhappy with her, and was certain he was about to tell her what her punishment would be.

The night before, she had sent Keln one last message, saying that it was just that—*one last message*. She didn't blame Keln for her predicament. She had chosen to answer the messages. She did blame Keln for sending the messages, thus putting her in a position to have to choose.

Wollard walked silently to one of the bookcases and looked at the spines of the ancient books. Phee made certain the door was closed behind them, then took a single step into the room and stood there silently. If Wollard had already decided, it wouldn't help for her to say anything in her defense. If he hadn't, there was a good chance she'd say something that did more harm than good.

"Phee," Wollard said, still facing the books.

"Yes, Wollard?"

Wollard bowed his head and said nothing for a long time. Phee considered repeating herself, but she knew he'd heard.

He turned to face her then, and she'd never seen him look so sad. She'd never seen him look sad at all, for that matter. The entire time she'd been his protégée, his emotional range had seemed limited to cheerful satisfaction at one end and benevolent disapproval at the other. The sight of Wollard's eyes moistening upset her, but it was his frown that disturbed her most. She simply hadn't realized his mouth could bend that way. Though she should have been concerned about what this meant for her punishment, she was much more concerned for Wollard than she was for herself.

Her concerns were well founded.

Wollard asked, "What went wrong, Phee?"

She stammered for a second, then said the one thing she was sure of. "I don't know."

"Did I make some mistake? Phee, you're smart. You were here the whole time. Did I do something wrong?"

"Not that I saw," Phee said.

"We had precedent on our side, right?" Wollard asked.

"Yes. We both saw the precedents."

"It was a peaceful means of ending the war with the Hahn," Wollard said. "It had worked before."

"In the short term," Phee said, "but that's the only way peace plans ever seem to work."

"There was nothing in the precedents to warn us of what a fiasco this would be."

"No," Phee said. "None of the precedents specifically covered adopting a Hahn."

Wollard said, "Still, form dictates that Master Hennik should have either openly fought and struggled with all his energy or assimilated himself into daily life at the palace, if only for the sake of his own comfort. That's good form! That's what the Formalities are all about! Who is he to fight that?"

"He's a Hahn," Migg said.

"Hahn is supposed to be a fully arbitrated, civilized world."

"But Hennik has shown us that the one thing we can count on the Hahn to do is the opposite of what they're supposed to do."

Wollard exhaled heavily. His shoulders sagged. He seemed to age twenty years in the course of a few seconds.

"If the archivists don't come up with something," Wollard said, "she's going to send in armed guards."

"I think we're lucky she's decided to wait the four hours," Phee said.

"Agreed. For a moment I thought she might send them in early just to spite me."

"How bad would that be?"

"Disastrous. When word gets out, I can't think of a way to package it that won't lose face for House Jakabitus. There's no way Her Ladyship can come out of it without looking cruel. She doesn't seem to realize that."

Phee said, "I think she does, but she also suspects that Hennik has already made her look weak and foolish. She'd prefer to seem cruel."

Wollard closed his eyes and said, "Of course, you're right."

"And how does this play out for Master Hennik?" Phee asked.

"The best case scenario is *badly.* If he gets his way, he lives out the rest of his life as lord and master of the gymnasium."

"Surely he's just hoping that if he makes Her Ladyship miserable enough, she'll let him go home."

"And he's partially correct," Wollard said. "She'll let him go to prison. He will be dragged out kicking and screaming, and then treated as a prisoner. His best hope is that I can convince him to come out peaceably and say that this has all been a joke."

Phee shook her head. "Her Ladyship will probably have him carted off anyway."

"Almost certainly. That's why we never predicted he might do this. No rational person would have forced the issue like he has."

That's exactly why we should have predicted that he might, Phee thought, but chose not to say.

"Really though, this situation is only a problem if people find out," Phee said. "There has to be some way to keep it quiet. I know the staff won't talk."

"As I told Her Ladyship, the disruption of the normal routine will have already been noticed. If we say nothing about the disruption, it will be suspicious. If we lie, it will look worse when the truth ultimately comes out. Even if we camouflage the disruption, and the palace staff and security team keep the secret, Hennik will eventually tell someone the story, and he's certain to put Her Ladyship in the worst possible light."

Phee considered what Wollard had said. "So, if Her Ladyship sends in the guards, Master Hennik will have the ammunition to make her look like a liar if he's ever allowed out in public again. If, on the other hand, he is *not* seen in public again, she'll still look like a liar. The only way for her not to lose face is if she doesn't have to root him out with armed guards."

"Which she is going to do with a smile on her face, in a little under three hours," Wollard said.

"Unless the archivists find something. Do you think they will?"

"Phee, have you ever sent a request to the archivists that took less than three hours?"

"So it's hopeless," Phee said.

Wollard stood up, straightened his suit, and said, "Never. It's not hopeless, Phee. Indeed, the way forward is clear. I simply must go to the training room and talk Master Hennik into cooperating."

Wollard walked out of the library with new purpose in his step. Phee followed, listlessly.

40.

Shly walked quickly out of the service lift and through the servant's corridor to the kitchen. Kreet followed close behind, giving her further incentive to maintain her pace.

Kreet said, "You must be excited."

"Must I?" Shly asked.

"Yeah," Kreet said.

"If you say so."

Kreet still barely made a sound if anyone other than Shly was present, but when it was just the two of them, he came out of his shell. As a result, Shly tried her hardest to make sure there was always someone else around. Occasionally that was not possible, and this was one of those occasions.

"I just mean, you're going to get to see Master Rayzo and Master Hennik."

"I see both of them every day, Kreet. So do you."

"Yeah, nobody's seen either of them today."

"I doubt the time away has changed them much," Shly said.

"Which of them are you more excited to see?"

"I'm not excited to see either of them, Kreet."

"Yeah, yeah, so you say, but which one are you more excited to see? You must like one more than the other."

"Everybody likes Master Rayzo more than Master Hennik."

"So, Master Rayzo's the one you're excited to see?"

"Kreet, I've told you, I am not interested in either of them. I'm just not. It's my job to serve them drinks and be friendly. I have no interest in any romantic relationship with either of them. Do you understand?"

"Yes," Kreet said, smiling. "I understand."

"Good."

"But if you were interested, it would be in Master Rayzo, right?"

Luckily, they were almost to the kitchen, so Shly only had to ignore Kreet for a few seconds.

Barsparse and Ebbler had finished the postbreakfast cleanup and were just launching into preparation for the lunch service. Breakfast had apparently been a tense, quiet affair, with Lord and Lady Jakabitus determinedly not discussing the reason for the boys' absence.

"Pardon me, Chef Barsparse. Wollard has asked me to borrow one of your portable catering-grade bulkfabs."

They didn't really need one of Barsparse's machines. Any bulkfab was perfectly capable of producing food. Even the one Umily used to create fresh towels and bed linens could just as easily produce a hot meal for a family of twelve. The bulkfabs that the palace staff referred to as *catering grade* were mechanically indistinct from any other bulkfab, but they were specially designed for members of the ruling family and their guests to use. Each was housed in an ornate polished silver casing with contrasting brass handles and decorative flourishes that spoke of elegant, artistic craftsmanship, not the mere creation of things. Their menus had been limited to only allow the production of those fully finished dishes that met Chef Barsparse's standards, namely exact copies of dishes she herself had prepared. Like most of the devices that were used directly by members of the ruling family, these bulkfabs were simplified and streamlined to ensure a positive experience through enhanced decoration and limited choice.

"Done," Barsparse said. The chef set down her knife and walked to a large door that rolled up into the ceiling at her approach, revealing shelves covered with identical shining bulkfab units. They were kept on hand for special events, and sat unused the rest of the time.

"What do you need it for?" Barsparse asked. She was simply curious. Shly could have told her that they intended to use it as a battering ram to bust through the training room door, and Barsparse wouldn't have minded.

"I'm to take it into the training room for Master Hennik, Master Rayzo, and Migg."

Barsparse touched one of the devices and gently guided its movements as it lifted itself from the shelf and floated effortlessly out into the room. "If I turn off its grav-field, we can make the utilitics carry it in," she offered, hoping to keep Shly out of harm's way.

Ebbler said, "Or they can just open the door and you can shove the bulkfab in their direction."

"Master Hennik specifically requested that I bring it in."

"You and Kreet," Ebbler said, motioning to Kreet, who was standing next to Shly.

"No, just me," Shly said.

"Oh, so why are you here, Kreet?"

Kreet shrugged.

Ebbler shrugged at Shly, who shrugged back.

Well," Barsparse said, "that's some real good shrugging, but my sous chef has work to do, and so do you, Shly. Kreet, I expect you'll be leaving with Shly."

"Yes," Kreet said.

"Yes, well, off you go then. Good luck, Shly. I don't envy you."

"Dealing with Master Hennik?"

"Or any other part of this."

Shly guided the hovering bulkfab out into the servant's corridor and walked as fast as she could to the lift.

"So," Kreet said. "About Master Rayzo and Master Hennik—"

"I told you Kreet, I'm not interested in them."

"I know. I believe you."

"Good, because it's true."

"Sure. I was just going to say, since you're not interested in either of them, there's no reason you and I can't get something going."

"What do you mean, *get something going*?"

Kreet said, "I think you know what I mean."

"I think so too, but I want to be clear. Do you want some kind of romantic relationship with me, Kreet?"

"Yeah, I guess. Why not, right?"

Of course, she'd known all along that this was what Kreet wanted, and she'd been anxiously waiting for him to ask. She couldn't decline something that hadn't yet been offered.

Shly stopped walking, pulling lightly on the bulkfab to stop its momentum. She looked both directions up and down the hall to make sure nobody was there to hear.

"Kreet," Shly said, "I'm sorry. It wouldn't work."

"It sounds like you wish it would, though."

"I'm not interested in having a relationship with anyone right now."

"But you may be in the future, right?"

"I'm not looking for a relationship."

"Sometimes a relationship finds you."

"I don't want a relationship."

"I understand," Kreet said. "It's all right, Shly. I get it."

"Really?" Shly asked.

"Yeah. I don't really need a relationship right now either."

"Good."

"Yeah, so I figure we could just casually—"

"Kreet!" Shly interrupted. "I'm sorry, Kreet, but I'm just not interested."

Shly resumed walking. Kreet followed.

"Shly," he said miserably. "Shly, talk to me."

"I did. I'm sorry that you didn't like what I said, but making me repeat it won't help."

"I really think we could be great for each other."

"But I don't."

"But if you'll just hear me out—"

"Kreet, you can't talk me into wanting you."

"How do you know if you won't let me try?"

Shly kept walking.

"Come on," Kreet whined. "Shly. Shly. I'm talking to you, Shly!"

Shly hoped that if she just stayed silent and kept walking, Kreet would stop following her. She got her wish. Kreet ran ahead then stood in her way. She tried to step around him, but he grasped the bulkfab machine and held it firmly in place.

"Why are you being so cruel?" Kreet hissed.

"Because you're forcing me to be! I don't want to say these things. I don't want to have this conversation. I just want you to stop bothering me and let me do my job."

Shly tried to wrest control of the hovering bulkfab machine away from Kreet, but he had a good grip and would not let go.

Kreet's eyes and voice softened. "Shly. Beautiful Shly. Why won't you let me love you?"

"Because I don't want you to, and nothing you can do will change my mind." She yanked sharply on the bulkfab machine and it broke free.

Kreet stood stunned, in the middle of the corridor, as Shly walked around him. Before she entered the service elevator, Shly turned back to Kreet and said, "It's like I said, I'm just not interested in getting involved with anyone. Not you, Master Rayzo, Master Hennik, or Ebbler, and that's not going to change."

Shly entered the lift, and as the doors closed, she heard Kreet ask, "Hey, who said anything about Ebbler?"

Shly finally reached the training room door with the bulkfab machine. Most of the staff had dispersed, having gone back to their work. Only Hartchar, Wollard, and Phee continued their vigil by the door.

Wollard was trying to talk Hennik into coming out peaceably, with predictable results.

"Master Hennik, it really would be best for everyone if you simply opened the door and ended this."

"I don't care what's best for everyone," Hennik shouted through the door. "I only care about what's best for me."

"Isn't that a rather selfish way to go through life, Master Hennik?"

"Not at all. I think everyone else is being selfish, always thinking about what's best for everybody else, not me."

"I don't think that's quite what the word *selfish* means, Master Hennik."

"Yeah, well, who decided that?"

"I'm not sure I understand the question, Master Hennik. Are you asking me who coined the word *selfish?*"

"No, dullard, I'm asking who decided what it means, and since you can't keep up with the conversation, I'll answer the question for you. Everybody. Everybody decided what *selfish* means, and I already told you what I think of *everybody* and their ideas about my behavior."

Shly cleared her throat, hoping to get Wollard's attention, which she did.

"Ah, good," Wollard said. "Master Hennik, Shly has returned with the bulkfab you requested."

"I requested nothing," Hennik said. "I demanded a bulkfab, and you acquiesced."

Wollard made a small, strained smile and said, "It is a semantic argument, Master Hennik."

"Which I've won," Hennik said. "Now stop wasting everybody's time and send the girl in with the machine. I know you won't try anything while the door is open."

"I wouldn't consider it, Master Hennik."

"No, you really wouldn't, would you?" Hennik laughed. "All right, I'm going to disassemble the barricade and let her in. It'll take a minute."

Wollard, Phee, Shly, and Hartchar stood in silence, listening for sounds of exertion on the other side of the door, which they did not hear. Hartchar squared her shoulders toward the door, crouched slightly, as if preparing to rush Hennik as soon as he opened the doors, and looked to Wollard with an expression that seemed to say, *How about it?*

Wollard shook his head.

Hartchar narrowed her eyes, as if to ask, *Really?! Why not?*

Wollard frowned and shook his head again.

Hartchar's expression hardened. She looked at Wollard, then at the door. She was obviously considering rushing Hennik anyway. She looked back at Wollard, who was shaking his head more emphatically now. She looked at Phee, shrugged, then rose up out of her crouch. Wollard looked at Phee and saw her shaking her head, which was clearly the thing that had actually convinced Hartchar not to act.

While Wollard was grateful to Phee for intervening, he was mortified that it had been necessary.

Finally, the door opened a crack. Then it opened a bit further. Then it opened enough for Hennik to poke his head out.

He looked around, then said, "Okay. Good. It was wise of you to not try to take me by force. Weak, but wise."

He sneered at Hartchar as he pushed the door open a bit more and motioned for Shly to come forward.

After Shly pushed the gleaming bulkfab into the training room, Hennik shut the door behind her and quickly retied the *barricade*.

The training room looked exactly as it always did, except that Rayzo was gagged and tied to a chair. Shly curtsied and said, "Hello, Master Rayzo."

Rayzo attempted to return the greeting, but his words came out as a muffled tangle of wet consonant sounds.

Shly turned to Migg, who was standing next to Rayzo's chair, looking embarrassed.

"Migg," Shly said.

Migg nodded and said, "Shly. It's good to see you."

Hennik said, "No greetings for me, Shly?"

Shly turned, faced Hennik, and performed the most reluctant looking curtsy he had ever seen, which he respected.

"Master Hennik. I've been instructed to bring you this bulkfab machine."

"Yes," Hennik said. "Instructed by me."

"And where would you like me to put the bulkfab, Master Hennik?"

"Next to my son."

Shly considered pretending not to know that Hennik was referring to Rayzo, but she had been instructed not to antagonize him, just to drop off the machine and get out. She guided the bulkfab over next to Rayzo, who rolled his eyes, which was so unexpected it almost made her giggle.

Migg said, "Thank you, Shly."

Shly nodded to Migg, then turned back to Hennik.

"There," she said. "The device is delivered, Master Hennik. If there's nothing else, I'll be on my way."

Hennik leaned against the doorjamb in a way he hoped looked nonchalant. "There is one other matter," he said.

"Yes, Master Hennik?"

"I wanted to talk to you about operating the device."

"Bulkfabs are not complicated, Master Hennik, and this one's interface has been streamlined to make it easy to use."

"Yes," Hennik said, "but it would be even easier if you stayed here to operate it."

"You already have Migg here. She's your valet. I should think she'd be able to operate the machine for you."

"But you forget, there's also my newly adopted son who needs tending. I fear that assisting me and raising my son would be too much work for Migg. No, it would be better if you stayed on with us."

"I serve Lady Jakabitus and House Jakabitus," Shly said. She started toward the door, but Hennik blocked her path. She stopped just inches before walking into him.

"Look, Shly, I understand," Hennik said, smiling sickeningly. "You're worried that you'll get stuck taking care of the boy. Don't worry, Migg will be assigned to little Rayzo. You'll be in charge of meeting my needs."

"I serve House Jakabitus," Shly repeated. "If you are, as you say, no longer a member of House Jakabitus, than I have no duty to serve you, but do have a duty to get back to my work."

Hennik said. "I can't let you leave. You're on Hahn soil, and as the ranking Hahn, I am in charge here."

"I'm not on soil. We're standing on a floor."

"Yes, but it's the Hahn's floor."

"Master Hennik, are you going to let me leave?"

"No."

Shly leaned a bit to the side. At first Hennik thought she was going to kiss him on the cheek, but instead she shouted at the closed door. "Wollard, are you hearing all this?"

"Yes, Shly."

"Am I allowed to use force to remove myself from this room?"

"That would be suboptimal, Shly."

"But can I do it?"

"It is within your power," Wollard said, "but you would almost certainly be terminated."

Shly looked at Hennik's smug face for a moment, then shouted, "Would I be given a good reference?"

Wollard said, "I can't speak for Her Ladyship or Glaz. I should think they would speak glowingly of your service, as you have always been quite dependable and a delight to have about, but I can tell you that word would eventually spread that you were terminated for assaulting a member of the ruling family."

She took another moment to study Hennik.

"Would people know which member?"

"I can't guarantee it," Wollard said.

Shly groaned. "It might still be worth it. I'll have to think about it, but I suppose I might as well think about it on this side of the door."

41.

Wollard remained by the door, keeping the communications flowing, trying to talk Hennik out of his folly.

Hennik remained in his chair against the door, pretending to listen to give Wollard hope, then occasionally dashing that hope for his own amusement.

Rayzo wished Wollard would stop. He appreciated the effort, but Rayzo had known Wollard his whole life, and the man didn't sound good. He was talking faster and higher than usual. It gave his words a frantic quality that made Rayzo uncomfortable.

Rayzo looked back and forth between Shly and Migg. He wished he could ask them if they were sensing it too, but he was gagged, and even if he could talk, he wouldn't want to encourage Hennik.

Shly was simmering with rage. Migg was listening intently.

On the other side of the door, Phee, Hartchar, and Glaz stood by silently while Wollard continued his efforts to reason with Hennik.

"I really do think it would be best if you came out, Master Hennik."

"Oh, you *really do* think that," Hennik said. "That's quite an upgrade from two minutes ago, when you just *thought* it would be best if I came out. That's real progress. At this rate, it won't be long until you're *absolutely certain.*"

"I apologize for repeating myself," Wollard said, wincing, "but you're forcing the issue. Master Hennik, you've made your point. I suggest that you come out of there before things take a nasty turn."

There was a long silence. Wollard leaned in closer, almost pressing his ear to the door.

Quietly, Hennik said, "Do you really think I've made my point, Wollard?"

"Yes, Master Hennik, I do."

"What is my point, Wollard?"

"Master Hennik?"

Hennik's voice grew back to normal volume. "You said I've made my point, Wollard. If that's so, you should be able to tell me what that point is. If you can't, why should I listen to anything else you have to say?"

Lady Jakabitus said, "The boy's got a point."

Wollard stiffened, then turned to face Her Ladyship. Phee, Glaz, and Hartchar were already standing at attention.

Lady Jakabitus and Lord Jakabitus were both present, standing in the hallway flanked by five armed and armored palace guards.

It was rare to see a palace guard in person and up close. The theory was that they were a more menacing presence if they were invisible and unknowable, but being this close to five of them, in their hulking, light-blue battle armor, grimacing protective masks, and high-velocity arm-mounted bulk-guns tied to the obscenely oversized ammo-bulk tanks strapped to their backs, made Wollard doubt that theory.

"Your Ladyship, again, I must tell you that I think using force is not the most advantageous course of action."

"Yes," Lady Jakabitus said, "and again I must disregard your opinion."

Wollard looked as if he'd been slapped. For an instant, Phee saw a glimmer of regret on Lady Jakabitus's face, but it was gone too quickly to be sure.

Wollard smiled, as if trying to use his own face to convince his brain that she'd been joking.

"Milady, I don't think the guards will be necessary. We've been making progress."

"Yes, I hear Hennik has taken another hostage."

Hennik's muffled voice called out from beyond the door. "She's not a hostage. She's a servant. *My* servant. Tell Lady Jakabitus to show a little respect, or I'll be forced to break off all diplomatic relations."

Wollard grimaced. "Milady, as we discussed, the repercussions if you send in armed guards will—"

"There will be negative repercussions, Wollard, but the situation now is inherently negative, and the consequences if I don't act decisively will be far worse."

"But the Formalities—"

"Say that I have to act within four hours. That's what you told me. Phee, when are the four hours up?"

Phee glanced at her papers and said, "In a little over six minutes."

"Please, Your Ladyship," Wollard pleaded, "please don't send in the guards. I know I can make Master Hennik see reason."

"You've got three minutes," Lady Jakabitus said.

"But the Formalities say there are six."

"The Formalities say we have to have it done before six minutes are up. We could wait five minutes, but I don't like to leave things until the last second."

Wollard turned back to the door and shouted, "Master Hennik, Lady Jakabitus has arrived with a contingent of armed security personnel. She intends to send them in."

"Yes," Hennik said. "In three minutes. *Very decisive.* How many are there?"

Wollard counted, then, in a quieter voice, asked Lady Jakabitus, "Why did you bring five, Milady? Surely that's overkill."

"In this case, Wollard, there's no such thing as overkill. When they drag him out, there will be one guard to hold each of his limbs and one to secure his head, in case he tries to bite or spit," Lady Jakabitus answered.

"And I'll go in as well," Lord Jakabitus said. "To watch."

"To make sure that Master Hennik's not harmed," Wollard said.

"To see it if he is," Lord Jakabitus corrected him.

Wollard turned back to the door. "Master Hennik, Her Ladyship has brought—"

"Yes, yes," Hennik interrupted. "Five guards. Tell her to send them in now. I could use them to help protect the borders of my sovereign territory."

"They're not coming in to help you, Master Hennik."

"But they will. I'll talk them into staying, just like I did the drinks girl."

"Her name is Shly, and you didn't talk her into staying. I advised her to stay," Wollard said.

"Fine. I persuaded you to instruct her to stay, let's not quibble. And as for her name, she has responded occasionally to *drinks girl,* so that shall be her name here, in my realm."

Wollard nervously glanced back at Lady Jakabitus. The mixture of disappointment and disgust he saw in her face made him long for the good old days when she'd just been angry. Wollard knew it was far too late to take a hard line with Hennik, and it was not his place in any case, but perhaps he could level with Hennik and make him see reason.

"Look. Master Hennik, you've had your fun. You've inconvenienced Master Rayzo and several members of the staff, and you've made me look foolish. I'm sure you're very proud, but if you're smart, you'll open the door, come out here, and say that this was all a joke."

"I think I'd rather stay in here and say that Lady Jakabitus is a joke."

"If you don't come out, Her Ladyship is going to officially accept your declaration of hostility and send in the guards. They will drag you off to one of Her Ladyship's prisons."

"She wouldn't dare," Hennik said.

"She would," Wollard said. "She will. I actually believe she's looking forward to it."

"Good," Hennik said. "Then let her. Send them in. It'll be delightful to see the look on her face when I beat them all down."

Wollard bit his lip. "That's . . . highly unlikely, Master Hennik."

"And yet it will happen."

"I doubt it, Master Hennik."

"You're wrong again, Wollard."

Phee placed a hand on Wollard's shoulder. She wanted to pull him away from the door, or at least distract him for long enough to calm him down, but he shrugged her off and put up a hand to indicate she should stop interfering. "Master Hennik," he said, "they are trained, experienced guards!"

"So what? I'm undefeated."

"You've never fought five grown men!"

"Five grown men have never fought me. That makes it even, I figure."

"Master Hennik! You won those matches by doing the same trick over and over again!"

"And I can do it five more times."

Lady Jakabitus said, "Wollard, I think—" She stopped abruptly when Wollard waved his hand at her exactly as he had at Phee.

"This is not a sports match, Master Hennik," Wollard shouted. "These men are armed."

"Meaning that they're encumbered, and probably overconfident."

"Master Hennik, please open this door! I don't see a way for you to prevail."

"Come in with the guards and you will."

"Hennik!" Wollard snapped. "This is folly! Folly, I tell you! There's no way to win! You can't go through with this!"

Everyone on Wollard's side of the door was shocked and unnerved, not by what Wollard had said, which seemed perfectly reasonable, but at Phee's audible gasp in response to what she'd heard Wollard say: *can't.*

Wollard heard her as well, and the sound snapped him out of his anger. He mentally replayed the last few seconds and turned to Phee with horror in his eyes.

Phee gave him a look that said, *we're in a bad situation, but we're in it together,* which he found reassuring.

Glaz, Hartchar, the guards, Lord Jakabitus—all of them looked confused. Lady Jakabitus was the only one who bothered to ask, "What? What is it, Wollard?"

Wollard was about to answer when Hennik's voice rang out from the far side of the door, saying, "What?!"

A female voice spoke, quietly enough that no one could make out who it was or what she was saying, but she spoke for quite some time, and when she was done, Hennik said, "Okay. We're coming out. Have the guards stand down."

The door trembled slightly as the *barricade* was removed, then it swung open.

In the background, Shly was untying Rayzo. Hennik stood off to one side, looking flushed and angry, while Migg stood in the center of the doorway. Her posture was straighter than usual. Her shoulders were thrown back. She was recognizably herself, yet she seemed utterly different.

Migg faced Wollard and said, "Know that two thousand, one hundred, and seventy-one conventional years have passed since the Terran Exodus. Today is the sixteenth day of the fourth month. We meet on the planet Apios, in the palace of the ruler, Lady Joanadie Jakabitus, in the corridor outside the training room. I am the person you have heretofore known as Migg, Master Hennik Hahn's personal valet."

Wollard blinked several times, then said, "I acknowledge and return your greeting, but must inform you of my intent to formally protest your implied subterfuge."

Migg smiled and nodded. "As you should. I, in turn, invoke my right to limited and prudent subterfuge in the interests of self-preservation."

Wollard's upright posture reaffirmed itself, but his expression conveyed the sense that his mouth was working on autopilot and his brain was paralyzed with stress and confusion. "I recognize the aforementioned right," he said, "and withdraw my threat of protest, pending the revelation of your actual identity and position and the affirmation of an imminent existential threat."

Migg smiled again. "Most gracious of you. I hereby apologize for said subterfuge."

"And I, on behalf of House Jakabitus, accept your apology, but remind you that acceptance does not indemnify the issuer of the apology from possible negative consequences," Wollard replied.

"Keeping that in mind, it is with great relief that I, the person heretofore known to you as Migg, personal valet and servant to Master Hennik Hahn, formerly of House Hahn and currently of House Jakabitus, am in fact, Migg, former Master of Formalities to Lord Kamar Hahn, patriarch of House Hahn and unquestioned ruler of the Hahn and the Hahn Home World."

Wollard's mouth opened and closed several times, but he made no sound.

Migg bowed deeply toward Lady Jakabitus.

Lady Jakabitus looked at Migg, then at Wollard, then turned to Phee and in a tone that was more plaintive than angry, asked, "What just happened?"

Phee said, "It would appear, Milady, that when he was captured, Master Hennik was not traveling with a member of House Hahn's household servant staff, as we've been led to believe, but was, in fact, traveling with Lord Hahn's Master of Formalities, Migg, who, having reasonable cause to fear for her safety should her true rank be discovered, chose to exercise her right to self-preservation by posing as a lower-ranking member of the Hahn organization."

"Indeed," Migg said. "Well done, Phee. Your poise and skill speak well of your mentor." She nodded to Wollard, who blinked at her, his mind still paralyzed with shock.

"And we're just supposed to believe this?" Lady Jakabitus asked.

"Milady," Migg said, "I would never presume to tell you what you should or should not believe. It is, of course, your prerogative to make up your own mind. I do, however, offer as evidence of my true identity a copy of my official charter from the Arbiters, my official invocation of necessary subterfuge, and the formal declaration of my intent to reveal my true identity, which I filed with the Arbiters while in this room. These items should be waiting in both Wollard and Phee's papers even as we speak."

Wollard snapped out of his stupor, furiously dug his papers out of his pocket, and started ruffling through them like a man possessed. Phee produced her papers as well. They stood reading in silence until Lady Jakabitus asked, "Is this true?"

Phee glanced at Wollard, who was reading as quickly as he could, his lips moving slightly as he attempted to fully internalize every letter of every word.

"Uh, Yes. Yes, Milady," Phee said. "Migg's statement appears to be accurate."

"Wait a minute," Lord Jakabitus said. "Did I hear right? She told the Arbiters that she was lying to us?"

Migg said, "Yes, Milord, I—"

"I wasn't asking you, whoever you are," Lord Jakabitus snapped.

"My name remains Migg, Your Lordship. That much has not changed."

"Good," he said. "Shut up, Migg. Phee, did the Arbiters know?"

"Yes, Milord," Phee said. "As you are aware, we file reports to the Arbiters reflecting all of our activities."

"And neither of you were told?" Lord Jakabitus asked, motioning toward Phee and Wollard.

Wollard was still reading and digesting every word of the documents provided, looking for any reason to dispute or distrust them.

"No, Milord," Phee said. "Those reports are read by the Arbiters and sent to the archives. We are only given the information we are supposed to have, not, necessarily, the information we need."

Migg said, "The role of the Arbiters, and the Masters of Formalities, is to smooth and lubricate the course of history, not direct it."

Wollard finally lowered his papers. He exhaled, turned to Lady Jakabitus, and said, "I have read every word of the supplied documents twice over, and they are in order." He turned to Migg, bowed, and said, "I recognize your credentials and welcome you, Migg, Master of Formalities to House Hahn."

Migg returned the bow. "I thank you, Wollard," she said. Migg rose from her bow, then bowed even more deeply to Lady Jakabitus.

"What did you say to Hennik to make him stand down?" Lady Jakabitus asked.

"He just learned that his father issued a standing order for him to do as I advise in matters of great importance. I deemed an imminent, and justified, assault by armed guards to be sufficiently important."

"And nothing that's happened up until that moment was sufficiently important?"

"This was the first situation in which his actions threatened to do permanent harm. Also, any attempt to directly guide his actions earlier would have exposed my identity."

"And we couldn't have that," Lady Jakabitus said.

"Sadly, no, I couldn't. I apologize most humbly for misleading you, Milady. I am now convinced that my safety was never in doubt, as your treatment of both me and Master Hennik has been unfailingly generous and benevolent. I thank you."

Lady Jakabitus looked askance at Wollard and Phee. Wollard's eyes were locked on Migg, and Phee just shook her head, which Lady Jakabitus found less than helpful.

Lady Jakabitus said, "You are welcome. We welcomed you and Hennik into our home with no intention of doing either of you harm."

"I don't doubt it," Migg said. "And as such, it is with a heavy heart that I must officially issue Wollard a rebuke."

"A rebuke?!" Wollard asked in a tiny, frightened voice.

"A stern rebuke."

Phee gasped again.

"You have violated our most sacred principle," Migg said. "Any lesser punishment is contraindicated."

"What are you talking about?" Lady Jakabitus almost shouted.

Migg said, "Wollard, I move, given the nature of the situation, that Phee should explain, as she is both trusted and not directly involved."

"Sensible," Wollard mumbled.

Migg said, "And I remind you, Phee, that while one usually does not discuss the directive in question with the uninitiated, as those present witnessed both the offense and the rebuke, you do have latitude to go into some detail in this matter."

Phee didn't know whether to nod to Wollard or Migg, so she nodded to a point in space equidistant between them, then turned and addressed Lady Jakabitus. "A Master of Formalities may never, under any circumstances, tell a member of a ruling house that she or he cannot do a thing. A ruler is free to do, or attempt to do, whatever she or he chooses. Our place is not to dictate, but to advise as to what the consequences are likely to be. Wollard, unfortunately, told Master Hennik that he could not win. Not that it was unlikely he could win. That he could not."

"But he couldn't," Lord Jakabitus said.

"Yes, I could!" Hennik shouted.

"No, you could not!" Lord Jakabitus shouted back.

"Be that as it may," Phee said, "it was not for Wollard to tell him what he could not do, just that his course of action was highly, if not almost entirely, unlikely to end in success. In light of Wollard's error, Migg, who we have just learned is of equal rank to Wollard, has issued a stern rebuke, meaning that Wollard is suspended from his duties and all the privileges that come therewith, and must make his way to the Central Authority to have his actions scrutinized."

Everyone looked upset by this, but Lady Jakabitus looked a bit less upset than Wollard might have hoped.

"So," Lady Jakabitus asked, "does that mean you get a temporary promotion until a replacement can be dispatched, Phee?"

"No, Milady. The privilege of assuming Wollard's duties falls automatically to the highest-ranking Arbitration official on the planet, and since her paperwork appears to be in order, that would be Migg."

Wollard noted with some satisfaction that Lady Jakabitus now looked quite upset indeed.

PART 6

To glory excessively in victory is poor form.

To wallow excessively in defeat is equally poor form.

Often, the safest policy is to avoid discussion of past results, instead shifting focus to future endeavors.

-Excerpt from *The Arbiters' Official Guidelines Regarding Etiquette for the Triumphant, Victorious, and Understandably Confident*

42.

Migg glanced at her papers, then looked up and, in a clear, loud voice, said, “Know that two thousand, one hundred, and seventy-one conventional years have passed since the Terran Exodus. Today is the seventeenth day of the fourth month. We meet on the planet Apios, in the servants’ hall of Palace Koa, the ancestral home of House Jakabitus and its matriarch, Lady Joanadie Jakabitus. I am Migg, Master of Formalities for House Jakabitus, and for the first of what I hope is many times, I am delivering the daily meeting to the palace staff.”

Migg was happy that the staff and the Jakabitus family finally knew the truth. It felt good to reassume her role as Master of Formalities. Of course, dealing with the staff here on Apios would be different from handling the staff back on the Hahn Home World, but she’d cross that bridge when she came to it.

Rather than the staff uniform she’d slouched around in up until the previous day, Migg stood in front of them dressed in the traditional stiff black suit of a Master of Formalities, which accentuated her slender frame and ramrod-straight posture. Her hair was slicked down in the same manner as Phee’s, and Wollard’s before her, and it looked brown now instead of the sandy blonde it had been. Such a transformation would have naturally engendered distrust, even if all who were gathered before her hadn't known how she'd come to be wearing the suit that day.

"Good morning, everyone," Migg said brightly.

Nobody replied. The entire staff stared back at her, unified in their resentment.

Maybe it won't be so different from the Hahn Home World after all, Migg thought.

The lack of interaction left Migg with no graceful option other than to continue with her presentation.

"The schedule for today should seem fairly familiar. This morning Lady Jakabitus has her regular briefing. Lunch will be at the usual time, and it will be attended by Her Ladyship, His Lordship, and Master Rayzo. After lunch, Master Rayzo will have sports practice."

Migg had deliberately omitted any mention of Hennik, hoping to goad one of the staff into asking her a question. The staff deliberately chose not to do so. It would have given her a sense of legitimacy in her new position that they simply did not want her to have.

Migg graced the staff with another pleasant smile, then said, "I'm sure you are wondering where Master Hennik will be. In light of his recent behavior, Lady Jakabitus has ordered that he be confined to his room. Chef Barsparse, Her Ladyship has asked that for the time being Master Hennik be served the same dishes as the Jakabitus family. This is to keep up appearances while Her Ladyship decides his fate. But though you have strict orders as to what to serve him, how much of it you serve, how promptly you deliver it, and how much care you put into preparing it are all entirely at your discretion."

Migg gave a sly smile as she said this, but received no encouragement from Barsparse or any other member of the staff.

"This concludes the reading of the schedule," Migg said. "Unless anyone has any questions?"

Again, there was another piece of information that Migg knew they wanted, but this time, she was going to make them ask for it. She cocked her head to the side and looked questioningly at the assembled group.

"No questions?" she asked. "Nothing? Don't be shy. This is your chance." She waited a moment, then said, "All right then. Since there are no questions, this concludes—"

A female voice called out, "Query."

Migg hid her irritation. "I recognize Phee, my protégée."

Migg had assumed all of Wollard's duties. That included mentoring Phee. So far, the mentorship had consisted of two brief chats—one the previous afternoon, wherein Migg gave Phee the rest of the night off, and one prior to the morning meeting, in which they discussed the schedule. So far, Phee had been unfailingly courteous and professional, and had done an admirable job of almost hiding the loathing and anger she felt for Migg. During the entire morning meeting, Phee had stood dutifully by her new mentor's side, expressing her displeasure by showing no emotion at all. Now, by putting forth the query Migg had guessed was coming, Phee would effectively demonstrate her allegiance lay with the staff and Wollard, not with Migg.

Phee said, "While there has no doubt been talk, I'm certain that the staff would like to know, officially, where Wollard is, and what will happen to him."

Glaz, the staff's nominal leader, smirked faintly and nodded, a sign of approval and support that would have been almost imperceptible if every other member of the staff hadn't done the exact same thing at the exact same moment.

A man they trusted is gone, Migg thought, *and their trust has transferred not to his replacement, but to his former pupil. Understandable. I will either have to convince all of them by winning her over, or convince her by winning them over.*

"Of course," Migg said. "I know that many of you think very highly of Wollard. I myself consider him a kind man and a skilled Master of Formalities. I am also certain that all of you have by now heard some incomplete account of yesterday's events. Those who were there have been sworn to secrecy as to the details, but can, without breaking said vow, attest to the fact that poor Wollard was under a great deal of stress. As a result, he made a mistake that, while it seemed quite minor, may well have dire consequences for his future. As such, he has been removed from his position as Master of Formalities. Shortly before his removal, my position as a Master of Formalities had been revealed, and as such, form dictated that I should take over in his stead."

Sensing their reaction to that last part, she chose to digress. "On a personal note, I want to say that I regret having misled you all. While my actions were in keeping with etiquette and protocol, and were, I assure you, in impeccably good form, your feelings of betrayal and distrust are understandable."

She surveyed the staff, looking for signs that her words were winning them over. She found none, as expected.

"I realize," Migg continued, "that it is hardly reassuring for a person who has misled you for weeks to give you her word. I cannot express to you how grateful I am for the way all of you have treated me up until now, and proper form prevents me from expressing my distaste for the Hahn—their behavior, their society, or their ruling family, to whom I was assigned by the Arbiters. For what little it's worth, I can give you my word that I will serve Lady Jakabitus to the best of my ability until the day I am replaced as her Master of Formalities. To save you the trouble of asking, the soonest that can possibly happen is two standard weeks. That's the minimum amount of time it will take for the situation to be analyzed, for a replacement to be selected, and for that replacement to make his or her way here . . . and it's an optimistic timeframe. The gears of the Arbiters grind slowly."

Ebbler asked, "And what will happen to Wollard?"

Under normal circumstances, Migg would have made him raise his hand and call, *query*, before answering, but she chose to let that formality slide on this occasion.

"None of us knows for sure what will happen to Wollard," Migg said. "The best case scenario is for him to be found without fault and simply reassigned to a different great house for a fresh start, although that outcome seems unlikely, given what Wollard did."

"Aren't you supposed to say *allegedly did*?" Ebbler asked.

Migg said, "Ebbler, in the future, please preface all questions by saying *query*. As for the content of your question, I think it would be not only better form, but also an excellent training exercise to have my protégée, Phee, answer."

For a moment Phee stood silent and motionless, an act designed to hide her emotions, which—unfortunately for her—accomplished the opposite effect. Finally, she said, "Were Migg discussing the actions of a second person as reported by a third person, then you would be correct in your assertion that she should have prefaced her reportage of the second person's actions with the descriptive, *alleged*. In this case, however, as Migg is relating the actions of a second person, Wollard, that she herself witnessed, she is the person doing the alleging. She does not need, therefore, to describe Wollard's actions as *alleged*. She merely has to allege, which she has done, and continues to do."

"Well put, Phee," Migg said. "I would ask for one point of clarification. Were you not also present when the events that I have alleged took place?"

"Yes, I was," Phee said flatly.

"Are my allegations in any way inaccurate?"

"No," Phee said. "They are not."

Migg made an expression that was meant to convey twenty percent sadness, fifty percent resignation, and thirty percent hope for the future. "So there's the situation," she said. "To his credit, Wollard has already left the planet without making a scene or subjecting anyone to awkward good-byes. Next, he goes to the Central Authority, the Arbiters' home world and headquarters. He'll plead his case to the Arbiters and face their reprimand. He is unlikely to ever return to Apios. If he does, it will be in his new role as Master of Formalities to some other dignitary. In the meantime, I shouldn't worry about Wollard. He is tougher than he seems, there were extenuating circumstances, and I doubt his punishment will be too severe."

43.

The confinement was terrible, but Wollard had found ways to cope. He tried as best he could to quiet his mind. He stifled the urge to stand, to spread his arms, to stretch, to scratch that itch in the middle of his back that had asserted itself the instant he'd realized he wouldn't be able to scratch an itch in that exact spot.

Food was a welcome distraction, but it was delivered with disdain, and was of such poor quality and in such meager portions that he suspected a great deal of study and discussion had been spent in deciding exactly how small a serving could be for the recipient to still grudgingly refer to it as a *meal.*

Wollard was surprised to find that the worst part of his situation was the emotional component. The helplessness. The hopelessness. The knowledge—not *suspicion*, *knowledge*—that he was no longer a person. He was an object. A commodity. Really, he was an inconvenience.

The fact that he was surrounded by, and often pressing up against, countless others who were in the exact same position did not make it better. There was no *esprit de corps.* Certainly, nobody was banding together to ease this difficult ordeal. Instead, many of those present were trying to make things a little better for themselves by making them much worse for the people around them.

None of this surprised Wollard on an intellectual level. He knew that anything the wealthy were willing to pay outrageous sums to avoid, and the nonwealthy were willing to lie and cheat to escape, would not be a pleasant experience, but no amount of mental preparation could have prepared him for the grim realities of traveling third class.

It wasn't the first time Wollard had traveled interstellar distances inexpensively. It was the second. The first had been when he was much younger, back when both his body and his expectations were much smaller.

Up to that point, Wollard had never left his home world, a bucolic backwater called J-Harris 5. The name signified that it was the fifth planet orbiting the star J-Harris, which had been named centuries before in honor of a man named Joshua Harris, whose mother had celebrated his birthday by paying a small sum to have a random star named in his honor.

Like most of the more sparsely populated planets, J-Harris 5 (the locals pronounced it quickly, as one word: *Jarrisvive*) contributed to the galactic economy mostly through bulk-farming, bulk being the genetically engineered crop that supplied all bulkfab-based technology with the raw molecular material to fabricate any number of useful, tasty, or lethal items. It was a warm, simple, slow-paced world, and the people who lived there suited it perfectly, but Wollard had never felt any sense of belonging. When, at age twelve, vocational testing identified him as a desirable candidate for work in Arbitration, he leapt at the chance and left the planet immediately.

That time, as with this one, there had been few good-byes. The tests tagged him for Arbitration, he accepted the offer, and three hours later he was leaving his parents. Yesterday, he'd been sternly rebuked, and within three hours, he'd packed, fabricated a traveling suit (he was no longer allowed to wear the formal blacks of a Master of Formalities), and left for the spaceport, where the Arbiters had booked him passage on the cheapest available flight.

Of course, back then he'd been setting off for the Academy of Arbitration, with a glorious career ahead of him. Now he was going to the Central Authority, and for all he knew, his glorious career was behind him.

Being rebuked itself hadn't been so bad. He'd experienced it as if he were watching it happen to someone else, someone he did not envy. Only later, when it was over and done, had the true horror of it sunk in.

Good form had dictated that he do everything in his power to prevent his departure from turning into an undignified emotional scene. He wished Migg good fortune in her new role. He told Phee that she had a bright future ahead of her, and he'd been lucky to have her for a protégée. He thanked Lady Jakabitus for having allowed him to serve her, and she in turn thanked him for his service and offered to have one of her interstellar transports take him to the Central Authority for old time's sake. He'd declined, as to accept would have been poor form, which was ironic because the form his cramped third-class seat was contorting his body into could also be described as *poor*.

Of course, due to the energy required, the building and maintenance of the transports, and the sheer logistics of the endeavor, interstellar transportation was astronomically expensive. Only the wealthy and powerful, or those doing important work on behalf of the wealthy and powerful, could afford to have their own transport and travel directly to a destination. Everyone else had to pay for the privilege of packing into an immense transport that traveled via predefined routes, and often got you close to your goal without actually bringing you to it.

On the rare occasions that Wollard had accompanied a member of the Jakabitus family on a commercial voyage, they had, of course, traveled first class. They waited in a smaller craft, more lounge than vehicle, which then attained orbit and docked with the interstellar ship. After it had successfully docked, they transferred into a large, open space with ample room, comfortable seating, and an atmosphere more like a private club than a mode of transit. Aside from the view out the floor-to-ceiling windows, the only reminder that one was traveling was a catwalk suspended from the ceiling, which the second- and third-class passengers shuffled through on their way to their seats. The catwalk itself was opaque, but it was suspended from the ceiling by sheets of transparent material that sealed out sounds and odors, while allowing an unobstructed view both ways.

Wollard had always considered the catwalk a strange design decision, but now, having just walked through one, looking down at the first-class passengers, he realized it served a purpose. Making the second- and third-class passengers miserably file past, with looks of undisguised envy on their faces, instilled in passengers of every class the desire to fly first class whenever possible.

Wollard tried to focus on the positive, and the fact that there was so little positive on which to focus made the effort all the more worthwhile. He craned his neck forward to get a peek out the window, a round portal about the size of a slice of Barsparse's bread, set into the wall five seat-widths away.

I'm traveling, Wollard thought. *That's always nice. And I'm going to the Central Authority. I've always wanted to go there someday. Of course, I'd hoped to go there to receive a promotion, but you can't have everything. Also, while this leg of the journey is on one of the older, smaller cruisers, the next leg is on one of those newer, larger ones with the greatly increased capacity. That should be interesting. Really, this trip is going to be an excellent opportunity to get used to not having everything. That's not the brightest of bright sides, if I'm being honest. Perhaps I need to adjust my expectations to prepare myself for dimmer bright sides.*

Wollard became aware that he was frowning rather intensely, which he told himself was due to the amount of effort he was putting into remaining positive.

44.

Phee followed the Master of Formalities, a tall, slender figure in the traditional formal blacks, walking at an improbably high speed through the dazzling Grand Gallery of Palace Koa, as she did every morning, yet the very act of following Migg felt like a betrayal.

Of course, Wollard's last words to her had been, "Do your job, Phee. Follow the Formalities and serve Her Ladyship. Give me something of which to be proud." One might think that would have helped, but it didn't. Instead, it covered her with a second layer of guilt. She felt guilty for doing her job, then she felt guilty for feeling guilty for doing her job.

For a moment, in her mind's ear, Phee heard her mother admonishing her not to beat herself up. Her mother would no doubt be disappointed in her, but she chose to ignore that thought, sensing the danger of starting a self-sustaining chain reaction of guilt.

"Phee," Migg said without turning or even slowing her stride, "I would ask you what's bothering you, but I fear it's too broad a topic. Instead, I'll ask you to pick the most pressing issue weighing on your mind, and we'll start there."

After a few silent steps, Phee said, "You didn't give them your word."

Migg considered this, then replied, "Excellent. Thank you for your candor. I now have three follow-up questions. They are *when, who,* and *what?*"

"During the staff meeting, you told the staff that you *could* give them your word that you'd serve Lady Jakabitus, not that you *did* give them your word. That you *could.*"

"Ah, you do have sharp little ears, don't you Phee?"

"Yes, and you're not supposed to mislead people. Our entire role is built on the reliable and precise communication of complex concepts."

"And that's exactly what I did, Phee. Nothing I said was inaccurate."

"But it was misleading."

"Have I failed to serve Lady Jakabitus in any way in the time since I uttered that sentence?"

"No, not yet."

"Then I haven't broken the word that you claim I never gave. In a sense, I'm being more honorable than if I *had* fully given my word. I'm keeping promises I didn't even make."

Migg looked over her shoulder at Phee and grinned, then asked, "Is there somewhere nearby where we can speak without fear of the staff or the ruling family overhearing?"

Phee was bound by duty to say, "The library is on the second floor."

Once they were alone in the library, and Migg had taken a moment to marvel at the most spectacular collection of books, art, and furniture she had never seen, she addressed Phee's concerns.

"You're right. I chose my words to the staff carefully. They are good, smart people, and making promises to good, smart people is always dangerous. The problem is that their definition of *serve* might be very different from mine. The loophole in my speech means that if I am someday forced to do something that serves Her Ladyship's long-term interests but does short-term damage, I will merely look slippery rather than seeming like an outright liar."

"Is that better?" Phee asked.

"Much. You only look like a liar if you get caught lying, which means you're not even a good liar. If people think you're slippery, at least they think you're clever. Either way, it's a fallback position. The hope is that it will never come to that. If it makes you feel better, Phee, because of your training and the precision with which you parse words, I can make you a solid promise. I promise you that I will do everything in my power to serve Her Ladyship's long-term goals."

Phee considered her words.

"Did you notice that I said, *in my power,* not *that I can*?" Migg asked.

"Yes," Phee admitted. "The word *can* is open to interpretation. *In your power* includes things you don't want to do. I did notice that."

"So, are you satisfied with my promise?"

"Yes," Phee said.

"Good. While we're on the subject, I've had limited exposure to Her Ladyship. How good will she be at detecting subtle verbal evasions?"

"Very good. Lady Jakabitus is the smartest person I've ever met. If you're less than honest with her, she will know it."

"I don't doubt it. Life is a little easier if I can allow myself a loophole or two, but they are not strictly necessary."

"I must point out that Wollard never felt the need to allow himself loopholes."

Migg opened the door, inviting Phee to precede her out of the room. As they resumed their journey to Her Ladyship's offices, Migg asked, "Wollard genuinely cared what the staff thought of him, didn't he?"

"Yes," Phee answered.

"And did he care what Her Ladyship thought of him?"

"Very much so."

"And he wanted you to think well of him?"

"I think so."

"And he's not here anymore, is he?"

Instead of answering the question, Phee said, "If you want me to think well of you, that was the wrong thing to say."

At that moment, they mounted the escalator, allowing Migg to stop walking and turn and face her new protégée as the slab of polished stone on which they stood floated in an upward spiral around the inner perimeter of the Grand Gallery atrium.

"I know, Phee, and that helps me prove the point I'm about to make. This is the first official lesson I'm teaching you as your new mentor. It may be the most important, and it's one Wollard couldn't teach you. Phee, people who care will always be at the mercy of people who don't. Wollard was deeply concerned about making sure everything went perfectly, all of his efforts met with success, and everybody liked him. It was a lot of pressure he didn't need, and in the end he couldn't handle it."

"And you only cared about usurping him, and you were willing to do it at the expense of everybody's respect and trust," Phee said.

"I am here to do my job. I'd like it if you, the staff, and Her Ladyship were to think well of me as a person, but at the end of the day, it's not critical."

"You're saying that it's better to care less? That can't be true."

"Why not?" Migg asked.

"Because it's awful!"

Migg nearly laughed. "You're probably right. After all, we all know how *wonderful* the truth is."

They rode the rest of the way to the top floor in silence, looking out through the copious windows at the city and the ocean, and down into the dizzying atrium of the Old Palace.

When they arrived at their destination, Migg looked around the vestibule. "You know, I've never actually been to Her Ladyship's offices before."

"Is it everything you hoped it would be?" Phee asked.

"Oh, it's marvelous. The whole palace is. The architecture, the furnishings, the ornamentation, all exquisite. I didn't expect the walls of Her Ladyship's offices to be jet black, though. Shall we go in?" Migg asked.

"Yes," Phee said. "Let's."

45.

Lady Joanadie Jakabitus sat behind her desk. The office was a veritable master's thesis on all of the various colors, shades, and light qualities that could be described as *dark*. The walls of the office, like those in the vestibule, were as black as the surface of a pool of ink. The immense windows were darkened to the point of almost total opacity, with only thin slivers of clarity running vertically along the entire height of each window, creating razor-sharp blades of light that scythed through the darkness, painting burning lines on the floor. The lines emphasized the darkness, exaggerated the size of the room, and silhouetted Lady Jakabitus.

"Come in," the Lady-Jakabitus-shaped shadow said. Her voice was courteous and businesslike. It made the hairs on the back of Phee's neck stand on end.

"Good morning, Milady," Migg said as she walked into the office, Phee trailing behind. "I hope the day finds you well."

"To be honest, I'm a bit tired. I was up late last night, reading the Charter of Arbitration."

"Rather dry bedtime reading, I should think."

"Yes, but fascinating. It really is a very carefully worded document. Quite ironclad. So much so that I'm more than a little surprised my predecessors agreed to it."

"Indeed," Migg said, "but happily, the leaders of all of the civilized worlds saw fit to ratify the charter."

"All of the civilized worlds," Lady Jakabitus repeated. "What, exactly, constitutes an uncivilized world, Migg?"

"The uncivilized worlds, Your Ladyship, are defined by the Arbiters as those inhabited planets that are either ungoverned, ungovernable, or whose rudimentary governments are too backward to yet participate in civilized commerce and political interaction."

"Which describes all of the worlds that have not ratified the charter," Lady Jakabitus said.

"I suppose it would," Migg said.

"And as such, the leaders of those worlds are not required to, I quote, *have a senior Master of Formalities, or another official representative of the Arbiters, present to advise and consult them whenever they are conducting or discussing any official business of state pertaining to any interaction, formal or informal, between their government and the ruling family or elected governmental agencies of any other world.*"

"Your knowledge of the Charter of Arbitration is most impressive," Migg said.

"More so today than yesterday, perhaps," Lady Jakabitus said. "In fact, my experiences with you and Wollard have caused me to see Arbitration in a new light. It has always been presented to me as a means of simplifying interworld politics, but I now see that, if abused, it could be a means of controlling it."

"Too true," Migg said. "Sadly, any tool can also be repurposed for use as a weapon. That is why the charter takes great pains to specify that you are not required to follow the advice of any Arbitration official."

"Which brings me to my point," Lady Jakabitus said in a slightly louder voice. "You are now the senior Arbitration official on this planet, and the charter says that I have to keep you here or else risk having my planet declared *uncivilized,* which would be economically ruinous. That doesn't, however, mean I have to listen to a single word you say. My morning briefing is about to start. You will stand against the wall and you will not say a word unless I am about to breach good form or you are spoken to, neither of which will happen. If, for some reason, you do feel a need to communicate with me during the briefing, I suggest you do so through Phee, as she is the only member of your organization who has any of my trust at the moment. If you understand, signify by slinking off into the shadows."

Migg bowed, then slunk off into the shadows along the wall. Phee followed, feeling more than a little smug.

Images of generals and ministers replaced the paintings on the wall. Their expressions were all grim, which set the tone for the entire briefing. The Hahn had not grown any less belligerent. Causalities were mounting and the supply of soldiers was beginning to run low. Every time a soldier had to be reconstructed, the military removed three months from that soldier's term of service. It was a way to thank the soldiers for having given their lives to the cause, if only temporarily. Now, many of the soldiers had been reconstructed enough times to be automatically discharged.

The loss-retardant measures had kept the soldiers from dying, but they were not keeping them in the military.

It was suggested that the soldiers' terms be unilaterally extended, but Lady Jakabitus dismissed the idea out of hand, which was a good thing, as to do so would have been very bad form, and would have required Migg to speak up. Instead, Lady Jakabitus assigned a general to research ways to motivate soldiers to reenlist voluntarily.

The briefing ended. The paintings reverted to their normal subjects. Lady Jakabitus reverted to sitting silently in her darkened office, acting as if Migg were beneath contempt.

She swiveled her seat to face Migg and Phee, still standing silently in the shadows along the wall.

"I suppose," Lady Jakabitus said, that same professionally conversational tone that made Phee cringe, "that Kamar Hahn must be rather pleased with himself."

"I suspect so, Milady," Migg said.

"And why is that?" Lady Jakabitus asked.

"No specific reason, Your Ladyship. Lord Hahn is pleased with himself as a general policy. It is always a safe bet to state that he is pleased with himself."

Lady Jakabitus was in no mood for levity from anybody, least of all Migg, but the comment had nicely confirmed her own opinion. It was at Lord Hahn's expense, so she allowed a sneering half-smile before asking, "What do you want here, Migg?"

"I will happily answer your question, Milady" Migg said, "but first I must point out that the far more important question is *what do you want, Your Ladyship?*"

"I disagree," Lady Jakabitus said. "My question is far more important, because I asked it."

"Point taken, Milady. I want nothing more than to do my job, and my job, as I perceive it, is to help you, Lady Joanadie Jakabitus, and only you, attain your major goals."

"That's very . . ." Lady Jakabitus paused, glancing down at her desk, "specific. Only my major goals?"

"I would be pleased to also help you attain as many minor goals as possible, Milady, but as we both know, the less important must often be sacrificed to attain the more important."

Lady Jakabitus nodded. Her eyes lingered on her desktop for a moment before she spoke. "That's certainly what I want to hear, but why should I believe a word of it?"

"Because it has the ring of truth to it, Milady, and also because every surface in the palace is covered with microscopic devices that, among other things, can no doubt sense my brainwaves and tell you if

I am lying. I suspect that if a lie is detected in this office you will receive a signal, most likely some visual cue in the design on your desktop."

Lady Jakabitus looked up from her desktop with an undisguised look of disgust. "You think you're clever, don't you?" she said.

"Milady, I know that I'm clever. It's the one real gift I have, and I want nothing more than to put that gift at your disposal."

Lady Jakabitus leaned back in her chair and studied Migg for a long moment. "As you say, all of the staff's brainwaves are monitored for subterfuge as a routine part of the palace's standard security measures. You managed to defeat it the entire time you've been here. How?"

"I defeated the lie detectors, Your Ladyship, by not lying."

"You somehow manage to make that sound dishonest."

"I fear it was dishonest, Milady. I kept my statements deliberately vague and played into people's expectations, tacitly encouraging them to lie to themselves on my behalf. I said that I worked in Lord Hahn's household, which I did. I said I was a low-level servant, and I promise you, that is exactly how Lord Hahn saw me."

"And the stress of keeping up this charade didn't register?"

"Milady, for the first week or so that I was here, I'm sure I manifested clear signs of being quite uncomfortable, even fearful. I assume the monitors simply interpreted this as the stress of working in a new place, as a servant to Master Hennik."

Lady Jakabitus shook her head. "You amaze me."

"Thank you, Milady," Migg said.

"That was not a compliment," Lady Jakabitus said. "You stand here explaining how you've misled every person you've met since before you arrived on this planet as if you think it's a reason for me to trust you."

"It is, in my opinion, Lady Jakabitus. As you've seen, I have one gift, and that's my ability to cleverly choose my words. As such, if I make an unequivocal statement, it is not by accident."

Lady Jakabitus considered this, then said, "Go on."

"We Masters of Formalities are discouraged from speaking ill of our former rulers, but in this case I am comfortable with telling you that I always found Lord Hahn, his government, and his culture distasteful in the extreme. Lord Hahn is of the opinion that you want nothing more than to end the war on Ophion 6 with as little fallout as possible. He sees that as a weakness. I disagree. I see the war as a foolish, wasteful, pointless conflict, and while I would not presume to claim that I understand you, I can imagine that were I in your place, I would want it to end as soon as possible. Still, I would want to do it in a way that did not lose face for my House and my planet or relegate me to history as the ruler who lost a multigenerational war for which my people have already sacrificed terribly."

Lady Jakabitus said nothing.

"Not long ago," Migg continued, "I conceived a plan. This plan, if successful, would allow you to end the war with honor, while also saving me to leave the hateful position in which I was stuck. So far, this plan has worked."

Lady Jakabitus stared a hole in her desk as Migg spoke. She looked at it for a long time, not moving. When she finally sat back, the walls lightened from pitch black to a very dark blue, fading to lead gray toward the ceiling.

Lady Jakabitus asked, "And was Wollard being rebuked part of your plan?" Phee had been wondering the same thing.

"The plan was flexible enough to allow for Wollard's cooperation, had I deemed him apt to participate, or at the very least, not interfere. Upon meeting him, I deemed him a bit too rigid, too brittle, for want of a better word, to do what will have to be done. My report to the Arbiters of yesterday's events describes his efforts in positive terms, emphasizing exactly how far and how hard Master Hennik had pushed him. There are no guarantees, but I hope that he will be reassigned to another great house with little unpleasantness."

Lady Jakabitus seemed to accept that answer a bit more readily than Phee did.

"What is the next part of this plan of yours?" Lady Jakabitus asked.

"For now, Milady, it's best for you not to know," Migg said. "You have not agreed to anything, and I will not make any moves that will affect your standing or interests without your approval, but now that you know who I am and understand my motives, I can put the last few pieces into place."

Lady Jakabitus nodded.

"There is one detail you should know, however," Migg said. "Lord Hahn still believes that I am working for him."

The blue color on the walls suddenly took on a repeating pattern of black thorn bushes. Lady Jakabitus noticed this, smirked, then said, "You should know, the walls of this office and the room outside change dynamically to reflect my mood."

Migg said, "I suspected as much, Milady." She looked down at Phee, who noticed there was no anger in Migg's expression, just amusement and respect.

46.

Lord Frederain Jakabitus sat in his customary seat in the newly reclaimed training room. On the mat, Hartchar and Rayzo were tied into a flailing knot of twisted limbs, slowly spinning as they struggled against one another.

Migg and Phee entered, paused for a moment to watch the practice, then quietly approached Lord Jakabitus.

"Hello," His Lordship said. "Welcome to the training room, or, I guess I should say, welcome back."

Migg bowed. "Thank you, Lord Jakabitus. Yesterday's events were . . . *unpleasant.* I am sorry that you and your family had to be subjected to them, especially your son, who, if I may say, handled himself with great dignity given the circumstances."

"Yes," Lord Jakabitus said, watching his son grapple with Hartchar on the mat. "I'm quite proud of my boy. Of course, it would have been better if he'd never been captured to begin with, but none of us expected Hennik to do what he did." He paused to look sideways at Migg before adding, "Except you. I suspect you might have seen it coming, right about the time he explained his plan to you."

"Milord," Migg said, "again, I'm not at all proud of the part I played in yesterday's events."

Lord Jakabitus waved her off. "It's in the past, Migg."

Migg said, "I must say, Milord, you're being much more understanding about this than I might be in your situation."

"You were under strict orders to assist Hennik, and you were bound to keep his confidence. I'm not happy about it, but I understand. Rayzo says that you were kind to him after the actual assault, and if security had deemed you and Hennik to be a real threat, we would not be having this conversation right now."

"I believe that is true."

"Good, because it is. As far as your new position goes, I liked Wollard personally, but his downfall was largely self-inflicted. You loaded the gun and handed it to him, but he shot himself in the foot. And he did advise Joanadie to take in that little turd Hennik. He lost her trust when he did that, and you don't have it in the first place, so I figure it's pretty much a wash."

"I believe the proper response to that, Milord, would be: *fair enough.*"

With that, Lord Jakabitus returned his concentration to his son's exertions. Migg glanced at Phee and arched an eyebrow. Phee shook her head, which only made Migg smile.

The three of them watched Rayzo and Hartchar struggle against each other. A great deal of effort was being expended, but there was precious little motion to show for it. Hartchar was taller, more muscular, and more experienced than Rayzo, but the boy seemed to have established a stalemate.

"Master Rayzo certainly seems to be giving it his all," Migg said.

"Yes," Lord Jakabitus agreed. "He came in here with a real head of steam today. He said that after yesterday, he never wants Hennik or anybody else to get the best of him again. He and Hartchar started early. They've been working on countermeasures to Hennik's ridiculous trick;

now they're running through the various permutations of how such a match could play out."

"Master Hennik's signature move has been outlawed in official tournament play," Migg said, "but that certainly would not stop him from using it against Master Rayzo here. Wise of you and Hartchar to develop countermeasures."

"It was Rayzo's idea."

"Excellent," Migg said.

"You aren't going to warn Hennik about this, are you?"

"Yesterday, my job was to serve Master Hennik. I didn't want to help him attack Master Rayzo, but I did. Today, my job is to serve House Jakabitus, and when Master Rayzo surprises Master Hennik with his countermeasures, I want very badly to be here to see it."

"Yes," Lord Jakabitus said, studying Migg. "I thought you might."

Just then, Lord Jakabitus and Migg were distracted by a discreet cough. At first Migg thought Phee was attempting to get her attention, but upon turning they discovered that Shly had arrived with His Lordship's training beverage.

Lord Jakabitus smirked. He looked at his son, still struggling, oblivious to the world beyond the borders of the mat. In a much louder voice than necessary, Lord Jakabitus said, "Hello, Shly. It's always good to see you, Shly. I am ready for my drink now. Shlyyyyy."

If Rayzo heard his father, he didn't let on. He and Hartchar continued to grapple with each other as if nobody had said a word.

In a much lower voice, Lord Jakabitus said, "Okay, Rayzo, I think it's time you took a break."

Rayzo immediately said, "Yes, Father." He and Hartchar stopped pushing and pulling against one another, relaxed, and slowly disentangled, dropping, panting, to the mat.

As they lay there struggling to catch their breath, Rayzo turned his head, and in as cordial a tone as he could manage, said, "Hello, Migg, Phee, Shly."

The fact that he had the presence of mind and the maturity to greet them in order of rank despite his exhaustion and the events of the previous day impressed Migg. The fact that he noticed anyone other than Shly impressed Lord Jakabitus, Hartchar, Phee, and Shly.

Migg said, "Master Rayzo, this is the first opportunity I've had to say how sorry I am about my part in yesterday's events."

Like his father, Rayzo waved off her apology. "What happened yesterday happened yesterday. I've learned several lessons, and I've moved on."

"And what lessons have you learned?" Lord Jakabitus asked.

"That Hennik's weakness is that he believes himself superior. My weakness was that I believed him. One of us is stronger now."

"I didn't tell him that," Lord Jakabitus said, smiling. "He came up with that all on his own."

"Waiting for others to tell me what lessons I should learn was another of my weaknesses," Rayzo said.

47.

Wollard sat in the departure lounge, waiting to board a transport for the second leg of his journey. While working with Lady Jakabitus, he had seen more travel than the average person, but he had never truly understood how thoroughly insulated he had been from what most people considered the experience of traveling.

For one thing, he had not set foot in a second- and third-class departure lounge since he was twelve, and he was shocked to see how little they had changed. The wall of windows offered a wonderful view of the planet below, and most of his fellow passengers were taking advantage of this view, because it was by far the most pleasant thing to look at.

Wollard wouldn't have called the departure lounge ugly, but no living creature would have called it pretty. Like many public spaces, it was designed to offend nobody's sensibilities, and as such, it didn't do much to excite anyone either.

People were also making a point of not looking at the transport, floating outside, waiting for boarding to commence.

When Wollard first left home, interstellar travel had been a dreary, utilitarian affair, a fact that had been reflected in the design of the ships. Wollard had been under the impression that great efforts had been undertaken to make interstellar travel more aesthetically pleasing for the traveler. Now he saw that things had only improved for some of the passengers. The first-class passengers, specifically.

Like the orbital transports that delivered dignitaries to Palace Koa in such a way as to maximize the view, Her Ladyship's official transport had always approached commercial interstellar transports nose on, so he was accustomed to only seeing them from the front. Now, looking at the transport he was about to board, he understood why. The front was gloriously designed, with a gleaming exterior and immense windows through which one could see the flight deck and lavish first-class accommodations. Behind the nose section, the decoration ended abruptly, replaced with a bewildering tangle of struts and cables, so densely packed as to obscure the actual bulkhead they were presumably there to support. The vast preponderance of the fuselage resembled a prickly cylinder. It was engineered to be light, strong, and easily reparable. It did not need to look good, and it didn't.

At boarding time, Wollard lined up with the rest of the people in the departure lounge. He knew that on multiple levels, in countless identical lounges, other passengers were lining up to board the same transport. He was curious to see how they would all find their seats on the new, extra-large vessel.

The line moved through a door, down a hallway that twisted and descended, and into a room that held a surprise.

Wollard had expected to walk through a gangway, as he had on older vessels, but instead he entered a huge space that contained row after row of seats. They were organized like the seating in an auditorium, except that instead of all facing the same direction, the rows alternated so they faced each other. The seats were fastened together, side by side, in clusters of ten, but while they appeared to be quite solid and stable, they were not attached to the floor.

The passengers filed in and, at the insistent direction of the attendants, sat down in as orderly a manner as possible.

Wollard took his seat, marveling at the brilliance of the system. *Why take our seats on the ship, where space is limited, when we can just take our seats here, where there's plenty of room. Then, presumably, the rows of seats will be transported onto the ship. Quite civilized. And the seat's not bad. It's a shame I don't have my own armrests, but I'm sure the strangers sitting on either side of me will let me have them for at least part of the trip.*

The only thing that puzzled Wollard was that while each seat featured a built-in view screen, the screen was mounted on a stalk on the armrest, and seemed to be positioned away from him at an angle that made it impossible to see. He puzzled over this, fiddling with it to see if it could be readjusted, but finally concluded that it must be there to convey information to the attendants, not the passengers.

An attendant walked down the line of seats, handing each passenger a small pouch and a cup of fluid.

Ah, Wollard thought, *snack service before we've even boarded. The offerings seem rather meager, but still, very nice.*

The attendant handed Wollard his pouch and disposable cup. The cup appeared to contain water. The pouch was marked "Complimentary Repressors," and contained five pills of differing size and shape.

Wollard turned to the woman in the next seat, who was tearing her packet open while keeping her elbows stubbornly rooted to her armrests. "Pardon me," Wollard said. "Can you please tell me what these are?"

She looked at him and said, "Repressors. Complimentary." Her eyelids were at half-mast, as if mourning the death of her enthusiasm.

"What do they repress?" Wollard asked.

She started popping pills into her mouth. Between each pill she stated their purpose, as if calling attendance. "Appetite. Nausea. Urinary function. Bowel function. Panic."

Wollard looked down at his repressors while she tossed back her cup of water and swallowed. "How long will they work for?" he asked.

"If you're lucky, almost the entire trip."

"What if I don't want to take them?" Wollard asked.

"It's an eighteen-hour trip," the woman said. "You wanna take 'em."

When Wollard looked around, he saw that everybody was taking the pills, so he did as well. The empty cups and pouches were thrown on the floor, where they started their utilitic-assisted trek to eventual recycling. A prerecorded voice rang out clearly above the collective mumbling of the passengers.

"Thank you for traveling with us today," the voice said. For your safety and convenience, there will now be a ten-second countdown before your seat's inertial safety restraint system is activated."

As the voice counted backwards from ten, Wollard noticed the other passengers were adjusting their clothing and scratching themselves with an odd, frantic intensity. Just seeing it made Wollard's nose itch. Thoughtlessly, he lifted his hand to his nose. The count reached zero, and suddenly Wollard felt much heavier. At first he thought he was accelerating upward at a forty-five degree angle, then he thought his seat had fallen backward, but his eyes told him that the seats were not moving. His right arm weighed more than the arm itself could lift. He struggled to keep it aloft for an instant, then gave up. Unfortunately it slammed down painfully into his gut. His other hand had been on his lap, but was pulled into the crevice between his thigh and the seat's armrest. His right arm, now relaxed after having been used to punch himself, also crammed itself into the space between his leg and the armrest. He looked down to either side and saw his seatmates were both gripping the armrests. They didn't look comfortable, but they looked quite a bit more comfortable than he was.

The prerecorded voice resumed. "All passengers are secure. Ambient artificial gravity will be deactivated, and final boarding will commence."

Wollard felt no lighter, but the bank of seats to which he was held drifted gracefully into the air, as did all of the others. The row across from Wollard started moving toward him. It remained perfectly parallel with his bank of seats, but appeared to be on a collision course. As the seats drew closer, Wollard realized that they were staggered so there were no passengers directly across from him. Instead, he was facing the space between two passengers.

The opposite bank of seats drew so close that Wollard braced himself for a collision, but at the last second the bases of both rows stopped moving and the seats tilted forward. Wollard's knees were mere inches from those of the two people opposite him. The heads of the passengers in his row and the opposing row had meshed like the teeth on a zipper. Wollard's head slotted neatly into the empty space between the heads of the two passengers opposite him; if he looked up, he saw shoulders and if he looked to the side, his eyes were four inches from an ear. If he looked forward, most of his field of vision was taken up by the view screen mounted to the arm of the seat opposite him, an arrangement that suddenly made sense.

The two rows of seats, locked into formation, maneuvered as one piece, joining a line of seating units to drift out of the room, down a long gangway, and into the ship through the first-class section. Despite the obvious motion, Wollard still felt as if he were simply lying in a chair that leaned back while the entire orbiting terminal, gangway, and transport ship maneuvered around him. He was glad he had taken the nausea repressor.

Most of Wollard's field of view was blocked by the blank view screen and other people's laps, but he could sense the vast empty space within the ship. Beneath him, there were already countless seating units like his own. Only the backs of seats and the backs of heads were visible as he glided past. Then Wollard saw a line of backrests and heads seem to rise up beneath him as his block of seats lowered into position and locked into place. After another moment, he felt another row of seats take position directly above and behind him.

With great effort, Wollard moved his head to look around his view screen at what was beneath him. The back of another passenger's head was roughly five inches in front of Wollard's ankles. Then they reclined their seat, coming to a stop not quite touching Wollard's shins.

Wollard's view screen blinked into life, showing an image of wide-open farmland, a fresh crop of bulk-stalks swaying gently in the breeze. It was a serene and comforting image. Wollard attempted to lose himself in it, but was distracted when the passenger who was simultaneously opposite him and next to his head said, "Hi."

Wollard turned. It was hard to get a full impression of the man when viewing him from a distance of only a few inches, but he appeared to be middle-aged. He had unruly hair and a broad smile that might have been only a little off-putting if his face weren't so very close to Wollard's.

"Hello," Wollard said.

"Where are you headed?" the man asked.

"The ship is going to Aquillus," Wollard said.

"Sure is," the man said. "Is that home, or are you just visiting?"

"It is only a layover."

"Oh, so where's your final destination?"

The question posed a problem for Wollard. He could answer it, admitting that he was on his way to the Central Authority, which would be very interesting to the stranger, and would lead to more questions. Or he could refuse to answer, which would be mysterious, and would lead to more questions. Lying would be bad form, and was not an option. Wollard took a moment to think, a moment too long, it seemed, as the man said, "Hey! I asked you a question. Why don't you wanna answer? Come on, don't be rude."

Wollard said, "I'm sorry. I don't mean to be rude, but I'd planned to spend most of this trip asleep."

"But now you don't have to, 'cause I don't mind talking!" the other man said. "So, where are you headed?"

I decided I was going to remain positive during this journey, Wollard thought. *Perhaps this is a blessing in disguise.*

He looked at the man again.

A masterful disguise. Still, I've been leading a sheltered life. This person is exactly the kind of individual from whom I've been sheltered. Perhaps I should embrace this opportunity to interface with my fellow man. My trip to the Central Authority should prove an interesting topic. Perhaps he'll have some insight that hasn't yet occurred to me.

"Actually," Wollard said, "since you've asked, I'm going to the Central Authority."

"Oh," the man said, "the Central Authority. Huh."

"Yes," Wollard said. "It's the galactic headquarters of the Arbiters, the keepers of the Formalities and the employers of the Masters of Formalities."

"Yeah," the man said. "I'm aware of the Arbiters."

"I expect you are," Wollard said. "Everyone is. I already knew of them when I was selected to work for them when I was twelve. That's when I took the aptitude test."

"Yes," the man said, looking down at his screen. "We all took the test."

"Indeed, and mine showed that I was suited for the Formalities. I was thrilled."

"Yeah," the man said without looking at Wollard.

"Of course, they took me away for training. I've worked for the Arbiters ever since, but I've never been to the Central Authority."

"Yeah," the other passenger mumbled. "Good for you."

"Um, yes," Wollard said. "Anyway, I've always wanted to see the Central Authority. You know, they say that all Arbitration is still handled from the same modest building the great houses built for the Arbiters back when they ratified the Charter of Arbitration. I'm told the rest of the planet is left in its natural state as a reminder both of the chaos of a world left—"

"Look, pal," the other passenger said sharply, looking up from his screen, "I know your business trip is fascinating to you, but I'm not interested in the Arbiters, okay?"

"Oh," Wollard said. "I'm sorry."

"Yeah," the man said. "I think it would be best if we just tried to get some sleep."

"Of course," Wollard said.

The man nodded and returned his attention to his screen.

Wollard said, "I wanted to sleep in the first place."

The man jerked his head up to glare at Wollard.

Wollard said, "Sorry," then leaned his head back, closed his eyes, and tried not to think about how much he missed the palace.

48.

Dinner service for the Jakabitus family was complete, but instead of the usual postdinner cleanup, Ebbler was busy preparing one more meal. It was to be served to Hennik in his quarters, which for the time being was also his cell. Kreet and Shly stood by silently, waiting to deliver the prisoner's meal. Glaz watched, as always.

Barsparse had wanted to serve Hennik bulkfabbed food, but Migg had reminded her that the Formalities required a hostile prisoner who was also a member of a ruling Great House to be served food of the highest quality available, within reason.

When Phee agreed with Migg's report, Barsparse pivoted into a debate as to the possible interpretations of the word *reason.* In the end, it was decided that he would be served the same dishes as the Jakabitus family, but he would be served later, as Migg had suggested from the beginning. They also agreed that his food would be prepared entirely by Ebbler, who needed the practice anyway.

Ebbler plated Master Hennik's meal, then turned to get Barsparse's opinion of his work.

Barsparse looked displeased.

"Not good?" Ebbler asked.

"Better than I'd hoped," Barsparse said, shaking her head.

"As you both know," Glaz said, "our work is a reflection of ourselves, and as such, we cannot tolerate any degradation of quality . . . usually."

Ebbler nodded and pushed the plate across the table to Kreet, who sneered and muttered, "Took you long enough," as he grabbed it and placed it on his grav-platter.

Ebbler was taken aback, but Barsparse, oblivious to any of the implied drama, said, "Actually, I wish it had taken a bit longer. In fact, you and Shly might want to walk slowly as you deliver the meal to Hennik. If you were to do so, the food might get cold."

A voice from the doorway said, "To suggest deliberately sabotaging Master Hennik's food would be very poor form."

All eyes turned to see Migg and Phee standing in the doorway.

"Fortunately," Migg said, smiling, "you didn't actually suggest that they do any such thing. You simply stated the unarguable fact that they might want to. Indeed, Kreet and Shly might very well want to dawdle, knowing full well that Master Hennik is waiting with his customary lack of patience, and that absolutely nobody will ever check to see if they dragged their heels or not. No one here is suggesting that you two commit this completely unprovable breach of etiquette no matter how much joy it might bring yourselves and everyone else, myself included."

"Well, don't worry," Kreet muttered, glaring sideways at Shly. "I want this over with as quick as possible, and I'm sure she can't wait to get back here to the kitchen."

Shly glared at him, but said nothing. Migg was certain there was a story there, and equally certain she didn't want to get into it at the moment.

"You both brought lunch to Master Hennik as well, yes?" Migg asked.

"We did," Shly said.

"How was he?"

"His usual self," Shly said. "He claims he's won. He says he wanted his own domain where he'd be left alone, and he's tricked Her Ladyship into giving it to him."

"Yes," Migg said. "That does sound like him. Thank you, Shly."

As Kreet and Shly left with Hennik's dinner, Migg turned to Phee and said, "And thank you, Phee, for all of your assistance. Your first day as my protégée is officially at an end. I'm off to my quarters." She bowed to the group and said, "Thank you all for your tolerance and patience. I know this situation has not been easy. Good night."

Migg departed for her quarters, leaving Phee, Glaz, Barsparse, and Ebbler in the kitchen.

"You were with her the whole day, Phee?" Glaz asked.

"Yes, Ma'am."

"Can we trust her?"

Phee muttered the word, "can," then said, "Certainly we *can* trust her. The question is, should we?"

Glaz understood what she meant and said, "I suppose the question I really want to ask is *do you*?"

Heavy silence filled the room while they awaited Phee's answer, so Umily drew everyone's attention when she entered the kitchen. Her shoulders were hunched forward, and she was clutching her papers to her chest. Her lower lip was trembling, and her eyes were filled with tears.

"Um? What's wrong?" Ebbler asked.

"I got a message," Umily said, struggling to get the words out, "yesterday. Didn't read it until now."

"Is it Gint?" Glaz asked.

Umily nodded, then, while choking back tears, said, "He's coming home!"

Glaz, Ebbler, and Barsparse rushed her, hugging her and telling her how happy they were. Umily cried some more.

"When?" Glaz asked. "When will he come home?"

"He's on his way. He'll be here tomorrow," Umily said.

That triggered a fresh round of hugs and congratulations.

Barsparse handed Umily a kitchen towel to dry her eyes and sighed, "Aw, tears of joy."

Umily took the towel, pressed it to her eyes, and kept crying.

49.

Migg returned to her quarters. She fought the urge to look up and down the corridor before entering. There was absolutely nothing suspicious about entering one's quarters at bedtime, but she was about to engage in clandestine communications, and the instinct to do so surreptitiously was strong.

Despite the changes in her position, and in other people's perceptions of her, Migg's quarters remained unchanged. She had the right to move into Wollard's old quarters, but she had opted not to—at least, not yet. The family and the staff harbored enough resentment over her usurping Wollard's position. She didn't want to look too eager to take his personal space as well.

She was absolutely certain that her quarters were not being monitored. To monitor any person's private quarters was egregiously bad form. Besides, even if Lady Jakabitus had ordered for her quarters and communications to be monitored, anyone listening in wouldn't hear anything Lady Jakabitus hadn't been warned to expect.

Migg sat on the corner of her bed, facing a framed painting of clouds, cliffs, and the ocean. She pulled out her papers, accessed a specific document she'd been saving since before her arrival on Apios, and initiated a secure, unofficial line of communication. The landscape painting faded out and was replaced by the sneering visage of Lord Kamar Hahn.

"Your Lordship," Migg said, bowing her head to the image. "Know that it is—"

"Skip the formal greeting," Lord Hahn said. "I don't have time for ephemera. Just tell me the important things."

"Of course, Your Lordship. First, your son Hennik is healthy, and is being treated well."

"I assumed as much. I said to tell me the important things."

"Of course, Milord. I am sorry."

Lord Hahn glared at Migg as if his patience was being sorely tested. "Again, I assumed as much. You're wasting my time."

Migg stiffened, looked Lord Hahn in the eye, and said, "I believe I can talk Lady Jakabitus into it."

"Of course you can," Lord Hahn said. "I wouldn't have deployed you and Hennik if I weren't absolutely confident that her stupidity ran deep enough that even you could exploit it."

"Indeed, Milord," Migg said.

"Still, it is amazing that she would give up something that seems so precious to her."

"She hasn't yet, Milord, but I believe she will, because she won't perceive it that way. She won't think that she's losing anything, just risking it, and she'll believe she's getting something even more important in return."

PART 7

Self-improvement is to be encouraged, as long as all parties involved are in agreement as to the definition of "self," and what constitutes "improvement" and "encouragement."

-Excerpt from the *Academy of Arbitration First-Year Instructional Text: "Adventures" in Semantics*

50.

"Good morning," Migg said brightly.

The staff, sitting as they did every morning for the daily staff meeting, looked at her, then at each other, confused.

Migg had anticipated their reaction, and had prepared an explanation. "The full formal greeting can be used at the beginning of regularly occurring meetings, but is only, strictly speaking, necessary if there has been a substantial change in the location, situation, or identity of the attendees since the full formal greeting was last invoked," she explained. "As the only change in the parameters defined by the full formal greeting is the date, which has progressed, predictably, by one day since we last met, I have chosen to dispense with the full formal greeting until at least one of the other parameters has changed as well, in the interest of saving time."

She looked down at the staff, then added, "One would hope that I will not have to explain the lack of the full formal greeting every morning, as the explanation proved substantially longer than the greeting itself."

Under different circumstances, Migg would have hoped for some outward signs of amusement—nothing so garish as outright laughter, but perhaps a smattering of smirks. Given the circumstances, the absence of contempt could be seen as progress, and she decided to take it as such.

Migg consulted her notes and continued. "Today looks to be an eventful day here at Palace Koa. The primary official event of note is a visit from a Lord Kank, ruler of the Cappozzi. He and his Master of Formalities are traveling to a conference, and will stop here on Apios to greet Lady Jakabitus to discuss their possible participation in the war. They will be here for lunch and a brief meeting with Her Ladyship, but they are expected to be on their way before dinner, meaning that Barsparse will only have to tailor the lunch menu to their distinctive palate. The Cappozzi are a stoic people, and their cuisine reflects their character."

Migg paused, smiled as she read her notes, then said, "That's the most notable piece of official business for the day. I think everyone here will agree that the most important event planned is the homecoming of Gint, Umily's husband, and Barsparse's former sous chef."

Now Migg got the positive response she had wanted. It wasn't really news to anybody, of course, but the fact that a gentle, thoughtful, well-liked, artistic young person returning from a war zone alive was good enough to warrant repetition. There were many smiles, pats on the back, and quiet congratulations for Umily, who seemed embarrassed by the attention.

Migg said, "Kreet and I are the only people in this room who haven't met Gint, but I do know that you all think very highly of the young man. I look forward to meeting him, and I'm certain you look forward to welcoming him back. He is expected to arrive sometime this morning. We will make sure everyone has an opportunity to say hello, but it is suboptimal to make too large a spectacle out of a soldier's return. The conventional thinking is that he has had quite enough excitement, and would prefer to ease back into his life. Umily will be given the rest of the day off, of course, as well as the next two days. Phee and I will be happy to pitch in to help where help is needed."

"Is he going to get his old job back?" Kreet asked while smiling sideways at Ebbler, who currently had Gint's old job.

"I'm sorry," Migg said. "Did somebody have a question?"

Normally, a junior staff member would be chagrined to have to repeat a question, but Kreet welcomed the chance to ask again. "Query," he said sweetly, raising his hand.

Migg said, "Query denied," which caused a visceral reaction in the staff. Wollard had never denied a query. They hadn't actually realized it was possible.

Migg said, "Any decisions regarding Gint's future employment are a matter for Gint, Barsparse, and Glaz to determine. I would point out, however, that if Gint were to supplant Ebbler in his current position, there's an excellent chance that Ebbler would then supplant the person filling his former position, Kreet."

This last missive received a subtle, but undeniably positive, reaction from the staff members who weren't Kreet. Migg was delighted. She had established that she was intolerant enough of disruption to threaten a staff member's job, yet the staff thought better of her for it.

I owe Kreet a thank you, Migg thought. *In private, of course. Thanking him publicly would undo most of the good he's done.*

51.

Wollard's journey to the Central Authority was almost complete. He had tried to frame the journey in his mind as an adventure filled with exotic sights and new experiences, seasoned with a little fear of the unknown.

Instead, he had seen the insides of various terminals, lounges, and transport vessels, and experienced institutional indifference in its many forms, seasoned with fear of the all-too-well-known.

Currently, he feared death in a fiery orbital transport accident, which didn't actually happen that often, but was spectacular enough when it did that most people pictured it happening to them whenever they boarded an orbital transport.

Wollard had spent the entire eighteen hours of his trip on the new, extra-large interstellar transport reassuring himself that he would be riding on a smaller craft for the third primary leg. The thought had given him a great deal of comfort . . . until he actually saw the smaller craft in question.

After Wollard's seats had deplaned, and Wollard had then de-seated, he made his way to the terminal's main concourse, feeling as if he were teaching his limbs how to move again. He went directly to use the facilities he now needed.

His complimentary repressors had not all worn off at the same time. For all he knew, the nausea repressor was still going strong, and he would never know for sure it had stopped working until the day he once again became nauseous. The urinary and bowel-function repressors had started to lose their effect during the final half hour of the flight. The panic repressor wore off while he stood in line at the terminal restroom.

Once that awful business was done, he set about locating his connection for the last leg of his journey. He was not in the Central Authority's star system yet, but he was as close as he was going to get via mass transit. The Central Authority was a world shrouded in mystery, and commercial carriers seldom ran regular transportation services *into the unknown.*

Wollard looked at his papers. His instructions were to make contact with a liaison from the Central Authority. That was the end of the instructions.

There's such a thing as being too succinct, Wollard thought. *It is not a sin of which we in the Formalities trade are often accused, but in this case, I fear the shoe fits. I am to make contact with someone, but I know not how or with whom. Perhaps this is a test of some sort.*

The idea that his skills were being challenged roused some of the spirit that the experience of traveling had buried deep within Wollard. He folded his papers decisively, determined to find this liaison, wherever he or she was hiding.

"Are you Wollard?" the liaison asked impatiently, having spent several seconds watching Wollard read his papers. He was a short, sallow man, wearing loose-fitting black overalls that were made of a sturdy fabric, but which had the unmistakable lapels and cuffs of a Master of Formalities.

Wollard bowed hastily. "Yes. Know that two thousand, one hundred, and seventy-one conventional years have pa—"

"I know," the man in the coveralls said. "Follow me."

The man walked quickly through the crowded terminal. Wollard struggled to keep up.

"My name is Wollard," Wollard said.

The man said, "We established that when I asked if you were Wollard, and you said *yes*."

"And you are?" Wollard asked.

"Your pilot. I'm to fly you to the Central Authority to be scrutinized. My duties don't include making conversation, but I am under orders to supply you with information I deem *useful*. For your information, my name is Prindle. You'll find it useful to know my name when you tell people about your trip later on. You'll be able to say *Prindle seemed unhappy. Prindle didn't want to talk. I kept nattering at Prindle anyway. Finally, Prindle threatened me.* And so on."

Normally Wollard would have responded to an introduction by saying, *Nice to meet you,* but he chose not to in this case.

They walked in silence to the distant, unfashionable end of the terminal, where the crowd and the carpet were thin. Without breaking his stride or even looking back to be sure Wollard was still with him, Prindle turned and started down a gantry way leading, presumably, to his transport.

Wollard could see the transport docked outside the window. What he saw didn't fill him with confidence.

The craft looked to be in good repair, but it was small and its design reflected the tastes of a bygone era. The garish stripes down the side and the decorative exhaust vents that served no useful purpose were a dead giveaway to its age. It would have seemed outdated decades before Wollard was born, but the laws of physics hadn't changed with the fashions. If it had been capable of interstellar travel and orbital reentry when it was made, there was no reason to suspect it wouldn't be now. Indeed, its silver skin was dulled and discolored from countless reentries.

The craft's interior was small and cramped, but Wollard had the entire passenger compartment to himself. The seats, floors, and ceiling had been cleaned regularly and repaired when necessary, but never updated or replaced. The cockpit was separate, and as Prindle closed the door behind him, Wollard wondered if that was the last he'd see or hear of his pilot. He was no sooner done thinking this than he heard Prindle's voice broadcast through a public address system.

"We're looking at about two hours of travel at interstellar speeds, then reentry at the Central Authority. Try to relax."

Acceleration to interstellar speed was not as smooth as it was in larger or newer transports. Wollard didn't know if the antique craft's inertial compensators were in disrepair, or if Prindle had merely decided against fully engaging them. One thing Wollard did know for sure was that his nausea repressor had definitely worn off.

Wollard stayed awake. Between his excitement at seeing the Central Authority, his fear of what might happen to him once he got there, and his much more immediate fear of what might happen to this relic of a craft to prevent him from ever arriving, sleep was not an option.

As the transport began its reentry, Wollard listened to its support struts groan and its outer skin flex and warp. When the ride finally smoothed out, he peered out the window. Beneath him, he saw puffy white clouds and a sparkling blue ocean. The craft lost altitude quickly, then leveled off at a cruising altitude low enough that when it finally reached the shore, Wollard could count the people enjoying themselves on the beach and the patrons of the open-air cafes that always seem to spring up wherever water meets land.

The transport drifted inland, floating over meticulously manicured green spaces. Lakes, trails, and bridges cut through a dense but obviously well-managed forest. Occasionally there were clearings covered in an even coating of grass, and in these spaces there were invariably a number of people engaged in some group recreation.

Wollard felt the transport bank and turn, and as the ship tilted, his view out the window panned upward, showing him what Prindle was changing course to avoid: a vast, gleaming city. It rose out of the forest, a thick mass of individual spikelike spires, each one a mammoth building. Any one building would have been the largest on Apios, much larger than Palace Koa, but they were lost in a mass of equally tall, graceful towers, sharing the same basic design vocabulary, all of them connected by a dizzying web of bridges.

Prindle brought the craft in on a spiraling trajectory, slowing as the radius of the turns grew tighter. Wollard looked down between the towers and saw rivers of vehicles, all traveling in perfect synchronicity.

The craft slowed practically to a stop, then landed on a flat surface several hundred feet above the ground, affixed to the side of one of the larger towers.

In the cockpit, Prindle shut down the transport's engines and flipped a few switches, one of which opened the passenger hatch. He spoke into the intercom, saying, "This concludes our flight. We have reached our final destination, the Central Authority, Scrutiny Division. Please exit the craft to your right and proceed inside, where you will receive further instructions. Thank you, and good luck."

Prindle waited a full minute, then rose from the pilot's seat and opened the door to the passenger compartment.

Wollard was still in his seat, waiting. "Where are we?" he asked, cheerlessly.

Prindle was disappointed. He had hoped that Wollard would be docile enough to simply do what he was told without explanation, but that clearly wasn't the case. Now Prindle would have to deal with him.

Prindle sat in the seat across the aisle from Wollard and said, "Like I said, we're at the Central Authority, Scrutiny Division."

"This can't be the Central Authority," Wollard said. "It's all wrong."

"Reality doesn't conform to your preconceived notions, so you figure it's reality's fault. Typical."

Wollard said, "I was always told that the Arbiters worked out of one austere building, and that the rest of the planet was allowed to exist in a state of natural equilibrium."

"All true," Prindle said.

"It looks like a vacation resort."

"Yes," Prindle said. "Humans pushed nature, nature pushed back, humans kept pushing until nature gave us what we wanted, and thus, equilibrium was attained. Why should this world be any different from every other world humans have inhabited?"

"But, but," Wollard sputtered, "this city—"

"Is one building," Prindle said. "Every single structure is connected. You can get to anywhere from anywhere without ever going outside. As such, the Arbiters consider the Central Authority to be one building, which has had extensive additions."

"It's not very austere," Wollard pointed out.

"The Arbiters call it austere, because they feel they deserve even better. Come on, you were a Master of Formalities. You've worked for the Arbiters for years. You can't be surprised to learn that they like to twist the meaning of their words until they almost snap."

Wollard looked out the window. "So, it's a lie. This whole time, it's all been a lie."

"No," Prindle said, "it's been something worse, a misleading truth."

"So," Wollard asked, "what happens next?"

"You get out of my transport and go through that door." Prindle pointed to a large open archway that led from the landing pad into the building. Guards stood just inside the arch. They wore black body armor with a stripe pattern painted on the chest plates that suggested the lapels of a Master of Formalities' formal blacks. Their helmets were molded in such a way as to suggest meticulously oiled and combed hair.

"What happens after I go inside?" Wollard asked.

Prindle said, "It's not for me to say."

Wollard stared at him, unblinking.

Prindle said, "I really don't know."

Wollard still had not blinked.

"I'm just a pilot. I have no way of knowing what will happen in there."

Wollard blinked once, slowly.

"But," Prindle said, "I have reason to suspect that you'll be taken into custody by those two guards, processed, then scrutinized, which is the whole reason you're here."

Wollard looked at the guards, then at Prindle, then at the guards again.

"So, they take me, I'm processed, then I get scrutinized?"

"So I gather."

"How long does processing take? A day, two days?"

"A few minutes."

"What?" Wollard cried. "I was told I'd have time to prepare a defense!"

"How long was your trip here?" Prindle asked.

Wollard's eyes and mouth all grew larger and rounder. He inhaled deeply, as if preparing to do some professional-caliber yelling, but he stopped short when Prindle held up his hands, signaling a preemptive surrender.

"I'm just the pilot, and I've only told you the truth as I know it. Being angry with me won't help either of us."

Wollard remained motionless, eyes bulging, mouth open, ready to bellow. He held that position for a full three seconds, then exhaled, seeming to deflate as he did so. He sagged back into his seat, a beaten man.

Prindle shook his head. "I'm sorry. I truly am."

Wollard moaned, "It's not your fault."

Prindle said, "True, but I hate giving people bad news. That's why I tried to avoid talking to you at all."

52.

The palace staff stood in their customary positions in the courtyard, awaiting the arrival of Lord Kank, ruler of the Cappozzi, and his Master of Formalities.

Lord and Lady Jakabitus and Master Rayzo stepped out of the palace's ceremonial entrance, followed by Migg and Phee. The Jakabituses and Phee all took up their customary places, but Migg bowed to Her Ladyship, then strolled over to where the staff was standing. Caught off-guard, Phee had to rush to catch up and follow her mentor.

Migg stopped in front of the staff, and took a moment to look at them before speaking.

"You all look marvelous," she said. "Very professional, which is good. Lord Kank is well respected, and his people are in a position to be powerful allies to Her Ladyship in the ongoing war."

Migg paused to make sure the importance of the situation was not lost on the staff. Convinced that it was not, she continued. "As I told you this morning, the Cappozzi are a stoic people. They value the ability and willingness to endure hardship. As such, their behavior may seem unusual, but I have no doubt Her Ladyship can count on you all to maintain the proper decorum. Are there any questions?"

A moment passed in which none of the staff gave any indication of speaking, so Migg bowed, thanked them, and returned to Lady Jakabitus's side.

They stood waiting for only seconds before the customary vibrant red vapor trail appeared high in the atmosphere, miles away, in a straight line from the palace gates. The line descended and flared before abruptly shifting in color from glowing red to billowing white.

The craft pulled out of its dive, leveled off, decelerated, yawed sideways, and coasted through the palace gates. This was Lord Kank's personal transport, and while it was the same basic size and type as Lady Jakabitus's personal interstellar transport, it had been subjected to an aggressive redesign. Where Her Ladyship's transports were all graceful curves and gleaming surfaces, this craft was all sharp edges, finished in shades that varied from *matte* to *dull*.

The ship silently slowed to a halt, and Migg bowed again to Her Ladyship and proceeded to the halfway point to await Lord Kank's Master of Formalities. Phee started to follow, but Lady Jakabitus stopped her with a hand on her shoulder.

"Is there a problem, Your Ladyship?" Phee asked, slightly alarmed.

"Phee," Lady Jakabitus said quietly. "That little speech Migg just gave the staff, warning them what to expect. Is that a common practice?"

Phee said, "I don't know that *common* is the word I'd use, Milady, but it is within the bounds of proper form."

"Wollard never did that."

"No," Phee said.

Lady Jakabitus looked at the staff, standing at attention, looking comfortable.

"Why didn't Wollard ever do that, Phee?"

"Wollard felt that people behave the way they do in the hopes of creating a specific impression. He felt it would be rude to do anything to interfere with that."

"So if someone wanted to surprise us, Wollard felt it was poor form not to let them?" Lady Jakabitus asked.

"Yes, Milady—or impress us, or delight us."

"Or offend us. I understand. I'm certain our visitors have appreciated Wollard's lack of interference. Particularly Hennik."

Phee said, "Milady, I feel I must—"

"That will be all, Phee," Lady Jakabitus said, stopping her cold. "You may go join your mentor."

Phee thanked her, then double-timed it across the courtyard to join Migg. While she had been talking to Her Ladyship, the Cappozzi transport's hatch had opened, and Lord Kank's Master of Formalities had emerged.

Lord Kank's Master of Formalities was neither a tall man nor a thin one. His hair was oiled and styled in the traditional manner and was gray at the temples, as was befitting a man of his age. His formal blacks were, of course, impeccable. There was nothing remarkable about him at all, save for his eyebrows, which were noticeable from a surprising distance. They were chaotic thickets of tangled, wiry hairs, extending in every possible direction from his brow ridge. His eyebrows overshadowed and dominated the rest of him, as if he weren't so much a man as an eyebrow delivery system.

Phee approached as Migg completed the formal greeting.

"I acknowledge and return your greeting," the visitor said. "I am Novich, Master of Formalities to Lord Kank, undisputed ruler of the planet Cappozzi."

Migg returned Novich's bow. That done, Novich stepped deftly to the side, flourishing toward the transport like a magician revealing a surprising number of live birds or foam balls. On cue, Lord Kank emerged.

Upon first impression, one might describe Lord Kank's demeanor as *severe,* but one would only do so in a whisper. He was an older man, but far from elderly. He was bald save for a single, one-inch wide, ruler-straight line of pewter gray hair that extended from one temple to the other around the back of his head and an impeccably trimmed beard. His head and facial hair were styled and groomed extensively. He clearly had to spend a great deal of time and effort on it; yet for all that work he was still, unquestionably, bald.

He wore a thick dark gray suit that lacked ornamentation, but boasted enough different layers, pieces, folds, pockets, and creases to make even Lady Jakabitus's most baroque uniform look clean and simple in comparison. He moved with great dignity and purpose, but with very little speed.

Migg bowed deeply and said, "Welcome, Lord Kank."

Lord Kank nodded and thanked her.

As Novich had done, Migg stepped to the side and flourished back toward Lady Jakabitus. Lord Kank walked over to Her Ladyship, and Migg introduced the members of the Jakabitus family individually, then the palace staff as a group. Novich thanked them all for their hospitality.

With these introductions out of the way, Migg and Novich faded into the background, and Lord Kank and Lady Jakabitus took the lead.

Lord Kank looked at Rayzo and Frederain, smiled knowingly, then said, "I was under the impression that you had adopted a Hahn."

Lady Jakabitus said, "Yes. We did take Lord Kamar Hahn's son, Hennik, into our household."

"But he is not here," Lord Kank said.

"No," Lady Jakabitus said. "Hennik is not available."

Kank nodded, as if this was perfectly understandable, but said, "Why not, if I may ask?"

Lady Jakabitus's smile became a bit brittle. She said, "Hennik is being kept separate from the rest of the family at the moment. There have been difficulties with his assimilation into life here."

Again, Kank nodded, this time more vigorously. "Please," he said, "allow me to explain my interest. I have had dealings with Lord Kamar Hahn, and have found him to be, without fail, acutely disagreeable. I can only assume this Hennik is much the same. When I heard that you, Lady Jakabitus, had voluntarily chosen to not only spend time in the presence of a Hahn, but actually adopt one into your family, I thought, *This is someone who does not shy away from adversity. This is someone I must meet.*"

Lady Jakabitus thanked Lord Kank with genuine gratitude. She clearly had not been prepared for anyone to understand what she and her family had been through. Then she offered Lord Kank a tour of the palace before lunch was served, if it pleased him.

"Of course," Lord Kank said. "And tell me, will the Hahn be joining us at lunch? I'm quite anxious to meet him myself."

53.

The staff returned to the kitchen in a rush. Barsparse and Ebbler had planned ahead for the formal reception, but they still had to execute a full meal in an unfamiliar cuisine. Ebbler was the first one through the door. When he came to a screeching halt, Barsparse couldn't stop in time and ran into his back.

Barsparse didn't ask why Ebbler had stopped. She saw the reason as clearly as he did. There was a large man in the field uniform of Her Ladyship's army standing in the kitchen, his back to the door.

Barsparse cleared her throat and said, "Can I help you?"

The man turned around.

Despite the fact that the man was now much taller and heavier, and a livid scar like a river delta started on his forehead, went around his left eye, and ended on his left cheek, Barsparse and Ebbler both instantly recognized him.

"Gint?" Barsparse asked.

"Yes, Chef," the man said in a deep, gravelly voice.

The rest of the staff filed into the kitchen, at first excited, then confused. Umily came in last, looking at the floor.

Gint shouted, "Babe!" He lurched forward, a blur of high-speed muscle. He grabbed Umily around the waist with one arm and pulled her off her feet in one smooth motion. Her toes hung a foot above the floor, and the front of her body was mashed tightly against the front of his. He kissed her with such force that he risked bruising the roof of her mouth.

The kiss seemed to go on forever.

Glaz cleared her throat.

Shly laughed.

Barsparse said, "Welcome home, Gint."

After a moment, she said, "Gint?"

Umily put her hands on Gint's shoulders and tried to push herself away from him. Gint used one hand to hold her face to his, the other to keep her waist locked to his own.

Glaz and Barsparse exchanged a worried look, then Barsparse barked, "You are in a professional kitchen, Gint. Have some respect."

At that, he finally let go of Umily, who fell to the ground and barely caught herself before her knees buckled.

Gint stood ramrod straight and said, "Yes, Chef! Sorry, Chef!"

"This is neither the time nor the place for that," Barsparse said. "Is that clear?"

"Yes, Chef!" Gint blurted. Then he glanced down at Umily, who was still trying to steady herself, and said, "There'll be plenty of time later."

Umily turned beet red and looked at the floor again.

"Well, Gint," Glaz said, "I'm certain I speak for everyone when I say we're all very happy to have you back, safe and in good health." Glaz started, realizing she may have made a terrible faux pas. "I . . . I'm sorry. I hope you're in good health."

"Yes, Ma'am," Gint said. "Thank you, Ma'am. I'm in the best shape of my life. Every time the Hahn scum killed me, Her Ladyship's science corps brought me back stronger," his eyes drifted over Ebbler, his old friend, as if he were looking at his own former self. "Much stronger," he concluded.

"Well, good," Glaz said. "In honor of your return, we've given Umily the next couple of days off so you two can, uh, catch up."

Umily cringed visibly, not that Gint noticed. He was being addressed by a recognized superior, and was looking straight ahead.

"Thank you, Ma'am. That's very kind, Ma'am. But if it pleases you and the chef, I would like to get right to work."

"Pardon me?" Glaz said.

"I'm here, Ma'am, because I work here, and that's exactly what I intend to do. I don't like to sit still. I am Chef Barsparse's sous chef. Work comes first, then pleasure."

"Well that's very . . . diligent of you, Gint, but I'm afraid there's a bit of a complication. You see, while you were away, Ebbler became the new sous chef."

Gint guffawed, then cast his eyes over Ebbler, slowly surveying him from the tip of his head to the ground.

"I see," Gint said. "No problem, Ma'am. Just allow Ebbler and me to discuss things alone for five minutes. I'm certain we can work this out among ourselves."

Kreet, and only Kreet, looked delighted.

Barsparse said, "That won't be necessary. Glaz, if you approve, I'll use them both for the next few days, until we make a final decision on how to move forward."

"That sounds fine to me," Glaz said. "Gint?"

Gint took another long look at Ebbler before muttering, "This is acceptable."

"Ebbler?" Glaz asked.

"Yeah," Ebbler said. "That'll be fine."

Kreet said, "Yes, it will."

Glaz shot Kreet a look that stopped his talking but did nothing to kill his smile.

"All right," Barsparse said, "We have a lunch to prepare. Shly, Umily, Kreet, go make sure the dining room is set."

Glaz, Shly, and Umily left. As they rounded the corner, Ebbler saw Shly put an arm around Umily's hunched shoulders. Though Kreet half-heartedly followed them to the door, he lingered there, not wanting to miss what would happen next.

Barsparse said, "Gint, you work for me. You and Ebbler are equals, but he knows the plan for this service, and I don't have time to reformulate everything, so he'll delegate half his duties to you for this meal. After that, you take orders from me. Understood?"

"Yes, Chef," Gint said.

Barsparse nodded, then retreated to the corner of the kitchen where she had the ingredients of a particularly tricky Cappozzian sauce ready for assembly.

Ebbler smiled up at Gint, nervously.

Gint smiled down at Ebbler with no nervousness whatsoever. He said, "I should introduce myself. I am Gint, Umily's man."

Ebbler looked shocked and hurt. "Gint, we're friends," he said. "We've worked here together for years."

"Oh," Gint said. "Sorry. When the science corps regenerated me, they gave me memories and skills that would help me survive, but removed memories that were useless. Clearly, they deemed our friendship useless."

Ebbler took a moment to glare at Kreet, who was snickering by the door, then turned back to Gint. "Let's get to work," he said. "If you'll julienne the onions, I'll get to work on the rice."

"Julienne?" Gint asked. "What does that mean?"

"Oh," Ebbler said. "I guess the science corps removed that. It's a way of cutting the onions. See you cut it in half, then you make dia—"

"Cut the onions," Gint said. "I understand."

"Well, there's more to it than that. It's not hard, it'll come right back to you." Ebbler stepped over to the cutting board and picked up an onion to demonstrate.

"It's cutting onions," Gint said. "I can cut onions. They might not look as fancy as yours, but what does it matter as long as the onions get cut up?"

Ebbler said, "It'll only take me a second to show you." He picked up a chef's knife, and then his world became a painful blur. In the time it took him to blink, his hand was in agony, he was on his back on the floor, and Gint was standing over him, holding the chef's knife.

Roused from her concentration by the noise, Barsparse looked over, then asked, "What happened? What's going on over there?"

Gint tilted his head slightly, never breaking eye contact with Ebbler, daring him to tell Barsparse anything.

Ebbler did not take the dare. Instead, Kreet, who had witnessed the entire thing, said, "Ebbler fell. Gint's helping him up." Kreet could barely contain his delight, but he wasn't trying very hard.

"Shouldn't you be in the dining room, Kreet?" Barsparse asked.

Kreet agreed, apologized, and went on his way with a smile on his face and a song in his heart.

Gint reached down with the hand that wasn't holding a knife, grabbed Ebbler by the collar, and hauled him to his feet.

"Are you hurt, Ebbler?" Barsparse asked.

Ebbler answered, "No, Chef." His eyes were locked on to Gint, who was looking down at him as if he were a bug.

"Good," Barsparse said, turning back to her sauce. "Be more careful. The kitchen can be a dangerous place. Now let's get back to work."

"Yes," Gint said quietly. He brought the blade of the chef's knife up between himself and Ebbler. "Do you still feel that I need instructions on how to use this?"

54.

Wollard would have been amazed at the efficiency with which he was processed, if he'd had the time.

He stepped out of Prindle's transport, took a moment to enjoy the cool air and magnificent view, then stepped through the arch to place himself in the guards' custody.

A door slammed down behind Wollard, sealing him inside with the guards. He started to recite the full formal greeting, but hadn't yet finished pronouncing the word *know* before one of the guards interrupted him.

"Disrobe," the guard said.

"I'm sorry?" Wollard said.

"Disrobe," the guard repeated.

"Don't you need to ask—"

"We already know. There's no information you can offer that we don't already have."

"But," Wollard sputtered, "I may—"

"No," the guard said, "you may not."

"It's poor form to interrupt," Wollard said.

"It's poor form to waste people's time. Disrobe."

Wollard did as he was told, slowly and miserably. There was still a glimmer of hope in his mind that *disrobe* didn't mean getting entirely naked. He took off his jacket, then looked to the guards to see if this satisfied them. It did not. He repeated this with every layer of his clothing until he was no longer wearing any. He felt terribly exposed and vulnerable, because he was.

One of the guards scooped up Wollard's clothing, removed Wollard's papers, and placed the rest of it in an unmarked canister.

"What's going to happen to my clothes?" Wollard asked.

As if to answer his question, a bright blue flame filled the canister, incinerating its contents instantly.

"Hey," Wollard cried, "those were mine!"

The guard said, "Yes."

Wollard turned to the other guard in the hopes that he'd be more reasonable, or at least less snide, but the second guard was no longer in the room. Woollard heard the first guard laugh, but when he turned back, that guard was also gone. For an instant he saw part of the wall moving as a well-camouflaged door closed behind the man.

Wollard had a quiet moment to examine the room in which he was now standing, alone and naked. The room seemed to be a perfect cube. The walls were lined with dark, polished stone tiles with straight seams and cracks that made it easy to hide various doors. The floor had a dimpled texture, like it was covered with tiny dents. He suspected they weren't dents at all, but small holes.

Wollard touched the wall. It was cold. So was the fluid that sprayed out of the holes in the floor with great force and absolutely no warning.

The pressure pushed Wollard into the center of the room. He closed his eyes and mouth tightly, but enough fluid got into his mouth, (either through his lips, or, alarmingly, his nasal passages) for him to taste it and know it was just water.

The barrage continued for several seconds, then ended as abruptly as it had begun. Wollard had time to take one good, deep breath before the nozzles began pumping more chilled, pressurized water at him, this time mixed with detergent. Wollard was instantly covered in thin greasy suds. Inevitably, he slipped and fell while struggling against the spray. He lay sprawled on the floor as the cold soap solution poured over him and drained through the floor.

The soap cycle ended, and Wollard had just enough time to groan before the next phase, which incorporated a fine grit into the spray, presumably to exfoliate his skin. Then he got another clean water rinse, followed by an onslaught of fast-moving hot air, which felt good at first, but then made Wollard's skin dry and tighten like old paper.

Wollard pulled himself into a seated position with his knees pressed against his chest. He sat there, just panting, trying to slow his heartbeat. Every square centimeter of his person felt clean and bruised.

One of the wall tiles above him tilted back, forming a ramp. A loose pile of fabric slid into the room and fell to the floor. Wollard picked it up. It was a rough beige sack. At first he couldn't understand why they would have given him such a thing, but then he saw that the sack had three large holes, one in the bottom and two in the sides, and it all became unpleasantly clear.

He stood up and pulled the sack on over his head like a shirt. It allowed his spindly arms and legs their full range of motion, and was just long enough to cover the parts of him he needed covered. It was a garment designed to spare his modesty, but not his dignity.

Several of the tiles along one wall folded inward, forming a door to a darkened chamber beyond.

Wollard looked around for any sign of where to address a question, then turned his head to the ceiling, because he didn't have any better ideas. "Am I meant to go in there?" he asked.

Nobody said anything to answer him, but the wall opposite the door started to slide toward him, forcing him forward.

Wollard walked through the door.

He emerged into a cylindrical room, fifteen feet across. The floor and walls were rough, cold stone. The ceiling was so far above him that he could only tell it existed at all because there was a single pinpoint of light beaming down, and logic told him it must be hanging from something.

Wollard looked up, shielding his eyes from the light, which, though dim, was by far the brightest thing in his universe. As he did so, something fluttered down between him and the light. Wollard recognized the rectangular shape and realized that it was a set of papers. Once he caught them, he saw the discolored spot where the official seal of House Jakabitus had been removed. They were his papers.

Wollard looked up toward the light and said, "Thank you."

The spot of light was instantly drowned out, lost in a solid disk of blinding brightness emanating from the entire surface of the ceiling. Now Wollard could discern that the curved stone walls surrounding him extended thirty feet above him, but ended several feet before the blinding white light. He shielded his eyes again, but he could see well enough to make out the shadowy forms of five people, or at least the heads and shoulders of five people, spaced evenly around the circumference of the circle, all looking down at him over the sides of the wall.

An amplified voice, presumably belonging to one of his observers, said, "You are Wollard."

"Yes," Wollard said, shouting to be heard by his distant audience. "I am Wollard."

"That was not a question," the voice said. "We know who you are, why you're here, and where you will go next."

"You have me at a disadvantage," Wollard said, which was a genteel way of saying that he wanted to know to whom he was speaking.

The voice said, "Yes, we do." It was a clear and effective way to say that they didn't care what Wollard wanted. "You, Wollard, have been summoned to the Central Authority to be scrutinized."

"Yes," Wollard said.

"We are the ones who will scrutinize you," the voice said.

"Ah," Wollard said. "Good. And how should I address you? What are you called? Do you have a title?"

"We are the scrutinizers, and that is all you need know."

"I see," Wollard said. "I apologize. I had assumed you'd have some more graceful title."

"You dare to start your scrutiny by criticizing our title?" the voice thundered. "Where do you get the gall?"

Wollard cringed. "I'm sorry. I meant no offense. Perhaps if you started the scrutiny with the full formal introduction—"

"And now you lecture us on civility and form," the voice blustered. "You who just openly mocked us?"

"I'm sorry!" Wollard cried. "I'm sorry!"

"Yes, you are sorry, and you will remain sorry. Wollard, you stand accused of breaking our most sacred rule, a transgression of which we already have incontrovertible proof. If you are found guilty by us of doing the thing we know you did, you will endure the loss of your rank as Master of Formalities and all of the privileges with which it comes."

"And then what will happen to me?" Wollard asked, squinting up into the light.

"You will be free to go about your life."

"That's it?"

"Yes, but I will point out that one of the privileges that Masters of Formalities in good standing share with all Arbitration officials is the ability to leave this planet."

"So, if found guilty, I'll be stranded on this planet with no friends or family and nothing to do for the rest of my life?"

"You're right about having no friends or family, but are mistaken about having nothing to do. You will be assigned a job."

"What kind of job?"

"A menial one. The kind of job one does not do voluntarily."

"That's if I'm found guilty."

"Yes," the voice agreed. "You stand accused of telling a blood member of a Great House that he could not do a thing. Did you do this?"

Wollard said, "Yes, I did."

"Excellent," the voice said. "Thank you for your cooperation."

"But!" Wollard shouted, "I can show that there were extenuating circumstances, and I can explain my reasons!"

"Fine," the voice said. "We will hear your testimony; it is only good form, after all. But be aware that having done something in a specific situation and for specific reasons does not change the fact that you did it."

55.

While smaller than the banquet hall, the palace's formal dining room was ancient, opulent, and designed on the general principle that the larger the table, the better the food tastes.

As protocol dictated, Lady Jakabitus sat at the head of the table, with Lord Jakabitus at her right hand on the longer side of the table, and Rayzo beside him. Had there been more people attending, Lord Kank would have been seated at the far end of the table to show Lady Jakabitus honored him highly, making it impossible for her to converse with him at all. As this was a smaller gathering, proper form allowed for him, as a guest, to sit wherever he chose, which was on Lady Jakabitus's left, across from Lord Jakabitus.

Novich stood along the wall behind Lord Kank, waiting to advise His Lordship should a question of protocol arise. Phee stood alone behind Lady Jakabitus, as Migg had been sent to fetch Hennik, whose presence Lord Kank had requested.

At first, the idea of exposing herself and her family, let alone a visiting lord, to Hennik had filled Lady Jakabitus with dread, but during Lord Kank's tour of the palace she had found him to be remarkably understanding and very pleasant company, despite his stern demeanor.

He listened, he understood, he commiserated, and instead of questioning her decisions, Lord Kank praised her fortitude in enduring the unforeseen consequences of those decisions.

"So, it was a kind of sausage?" Lord Kank asked.

"Yes, made from only the nastiest parts of a creature that was long dead," Lady Jakabitus explained.

"And it was prepared in front of the guests?"

"Yes, it was like a form of theater."

"The smell must have been horrendous."

"Worse than you can imagine," Lady Jakabitus said, surprised by how much the memory amused her.

"I wonder, could your chef provide Novich with the recipe?"

"Of course," Lady Jakabitus said. She thought it a fairly obvious joke, but an inoffensive one, and it was only good form to play along.

Lord Kank shook his head in disbelief. "I am most impressed. A lesser person would have done away with the Hahn long before it came to that, but not you, Lady Jakabitus."

Her Ladyship said, "It was tempting, but ridding ourselves of Hennik would have been counterproductive in the long term."

Lord Kank turned to Rayzo and said, "I wonder, young Master Rayzo, if you understand the strength your parents have shown. They could have dispatched this Hahn on a whim, but they did not, because the path to great reward often leads through great difficulty."

Rayzo thought for a moment, then nodded. "Yes, I think I know what you mean."

"Yes," Kank said. "I'd wager you do. You should visit Cappozzi, all three of you. I think you would find it quite worthwhile."

"Is it nice there?" Rayzo asked.

"No," Kank said, laughing. "The weather's abysmal, the terrain impenetrable, and the wildlife both ugly and vicious, but the people are marvelous. We've embraced adversity, and it has made us strong."

"Do you purposefully make your life worse to make yourself better?" Rayzo asked.

"Yes, my young friend. Well put. Why else would anyone wear this accursed suit?"

"You don't like your suit?" Rayzo asked.

"This awful, stuffy thing? It's miserable! People think we Cappozzi enjoy discomfort, but they misunderstand. We detest misery as much as anyone, but we enjoy growing stronger. Suffering breeds fortitude. That's why I requested that the Hahn join us, so I can endure his wretched company and be strengthened by it, as your parents have been."

Lord Jakabitus said, "And Rayzo as well. In many ways, he's suffered more than anyone since Hennik arrived."

Rayzo was happy to hear his father say that. "But I didn't do it by choice," he admitted. "It just happened to me."

Lord Kank leaned toward Rayzo. "I suspect that's not entirely true. I bet there were times when you could have avoided him and chose not to, or you could have backed down, and didn't. Even if I'm wrong, the great thing about suffering is that it makes us stronger whether we seek it out or not."

As if on cue, they heard the sound of Hennik shouting in the corridor. Migg entered, looking chagrined. The yelling continued, slowly growing louder.

Migg bowed. "Apologies, Your Ladyship. Master Hennik was reluctant to attend. It was necessary to involve security."

Lord Kank rubbed his hands together at the prospect of seeing guards drag Hennik kicking and screaming into the dining room, but Hennik entered the room in an altogether different manner. He was sitting on the floor with his legs and arms folded, shouting invectives as the invisible utilitics slid him into the room against his will.

"It's pointless for me to attend this lunch," Hennik shouted, "as the sight of each and every one of you causes me to lose my appetite! Not that your chef makes it any easier with the garbage she serves. It will be a race to see what makes me vomit first, the cuisine or the company!"

Lord Kank rose to his feet and spread his arms wide. "Ah, you must be Hennik, the scion of the Hahn Empire I've heard so much about."

The warmth of Lord Kank's greeting, paired with the grim nature of his attire, confused Hennik into a stunned silence as he glided around the end of the table. Only his confused eyes and furrowed brow were visible over the tabletop as he came to a stop behind the empty chair next to Rayzo.

Hennik looked up at the oddly welcoming Lord Kank, then over at Lord and Lady Jakabitus, both of whom were now also standing, looking down at him. He found the Jakabituses hateful, but they were at least familiar, and they might be able to explain the identity of this strange man to him.

He also wondered why everyone was smiling.

"Hennik," Lady Jakabitus said, "this is Lord Kank, ruler of the Cappozzi."

"Oh," Hennik said, still sitting sullenly on the floor. "I've heard of your people. My father says you're all twisted and perverse."

"Wonderful," Lord Kank said, delighted. "Please, Hennik, have a seat and tell me more."

Lady Jakabitus was still smiling, and Lord Jakabitus seemed to be stifling a laugh. Even Rayzo seemed happy as he pulled out Hennik's seat.

Hennik eyed his dining companions suspiciously, then turned his attention to Migg, who stood by the wall with her new apprentice, trying hard not to smile.

Hennik was not pleased with Migg. He had kept her secret and given her the honor of serving him, and in return she had destroyed his moment of triumph over the Jakabitus family by revealing his father's order, which she'd hidden from him for weeks. In some ways, he hated Migg most of all.

It went without saying that the happy atmosphere of the room was not at all to Hennik's liking. He looked up at Lady Jakabitus from his spot on the floor and said, "Of course, I always intended to come to lunch. I decided as much before you decided to invite me. I simply didn't care enough to walk here under my own power, so I manipulated your security apparatus to meet my needs."

Lord Kank said, "Very good," in a slow, awed tone, as if he'd just watched a great artist paint a masterpiece in a few simple strokes.

Lady Jakabitus said, "Of course, Hennik. Please, sit."

Hennik rose to his feet. He sneered at Rayzo, who was still holding out an empty chair for him, and yanked the chair out of Rayzo's hand, as if he intended to carry it rather than sit in it. Instead of reacting the way Hennik had hoped he would, Rayzo smirked at his parents and Lord Kank, who looked on with approval.

Hennik let go of the chair, then sat down slowly, as if he expected the chair to collapse out from under him.

Everyone else at the table was still standing, looking down at him expectantly. Hennik was lost, so he did what he did whenever he didn't know what to do. He imitated his father.

"Sit," Hennik said.

Lord Kank asked, "Lady Jakabitus, shall we sit?"

"Yes, Lord Kank, I believe we shall."

Lord and Lady Jakabitus, Lord Kank, and Rayzo all sat, but they continued to watch Hennik, particularly Kank.

Hennik beheld Kank with an expression that oozed contempt. "What are you looking at?" he snarled.

"You, Master Hennik."

"Why?"

"For my personal betterment. I believe I can improve myself greatly by observing you."

Hennik raised an eyebrow. "Quite right," he said. Clearly, this Kank character recognized the finer qualities of the Hahn bloodline and culture.

Rayzo turned his back to Hennik and shook his head.

Poor boy, Hennik thought. *He doesn't want me to see his anguish at having this visitor recognize my superiority. He probably realizes now that when my forced adoption of him was thwarted by his jealous birth parents he lost his best chance to learn from me.*

A chime rang out and Chef Barsparse, flanked by Kreet and Shly, entered the dining room. Kreet was guiding a large grav-platter loaded with five steaming plates. As Kreet delivered the beautifully composed dishes to the seated guests, Chef Barsparse explained that she and her sous chef had prepared indigenous Apiosan meats and vegetables in the traditional Cappozzian manner, by steaming and boiling the ingredients until they lost all flavor and structural integrity.

"Please correct me if I am wrong, Lord Kank," Barsparse said, "but the idea is to render the actual nutrients as bland and uninteresting as possible so they will not distract the diner's palate from the sauce."

"Quite so," Lord Kank said, rubbing his hands together in anticipation.

Shly silently filled everyone's glasses with whatever beverage they chose as Kreet made another lap of the diners, delivering ramekins of a thick blood-red sauce.

Barsparse continued. "The sauce," she said, "is called Chowklud, and is served with every meal on Cappozzi. It has a *strong* flavor, and I suggest you use it sparingly. You might want to start by lightly dipping a small portion of a single forkful in it."

Lord Kank dipped the tines of his fork into the Chowklud sauce, then put it in his mouth. He emitted a satisfied hum, then turned to Barsparse and said, "My compliments. Your Chowklud is quite authentic."

Barsparse bowed.

Lord Kank poured the sauce on his food, but stopped abruptly when Lady Jakabitus started to follow suit.

"You don't want to do that, Lady Jakabitus," he said. "I am accustomed to the flavor. You are not. I promise, there is no shame in showing restraint in this case. Please, try a small bit first, as your chef suggested."

Lady Jakabitus put down the ramekin, then dipped her fork as Kank had. She tasted the sauce, then after a long silence said, "Perhaps I will enjoy this sauce on the side."

"Perhaps you will," Lord Kank said as he poured his entire allotment of the sauce on his food. "It does no permanent damage, of course, but your nerve endings don't know that."

Lord Jakabitus tested a small amount of the sauce too, and openly grimaced. Hennik sniffed it, then set the entire container aside. Rayzo looked meaningfully at Lord Kank, then dumped all of his sauce on his food as the Cappozian had.

"Rayzo," Lady Jakabitus gasped.

Lord Jakabitus said, "Son, no, really. Don't."

Hennik smiled, and said, "You idiot."

Lord Kank sat motionless for a moment, then said, "Rayzo, you didn't have to do that."

Rayzo said, "I know. I chose to." He took a forkful of food smothered in Chowklud sauce, and without taking his eyes off Lord Kank, put it in his mouth.

Rayzo had tasted things that were sour, and things that were spicy, and things that were so cold they made his brain hurt. This was the first time he'd tasted something that stung. It was like having a mouthful of bee venom, only the bees were in his mouth with it. Rayzo's tongue and throat seemed to vibrate with pain. He struggled to reassure himself that his tongue and teeth were not suffering permanent damage, but the pain flushed all other thoughts from his conscious mind, leaving behind nothing but itself, and the will to keep chewing. It was important to chew thoroughly. For if eating the Chowklud was this unpleasant, he didn't want to even imagine choking on it.

Rayzo finished chewing, then swallowed and opened his eyes. He knew that the reward he was supposed to gain from his suffering was a long-term enhancement of his character, but the looks on his parents' faces was pretty rewarding in the short-term.

Lord Kank asked Rayzo, "Do you like it?"

Rayzo smiled, said, "No," and took another bite.

Lord Jakabitus turned to Barsparse, who was standing against the wall, looking on in amazement. "Chef, is this Chowklud something you could make again easily?"

Barsparse continued to watch Rayzo eat as she answered. "Making it from scratch this first time was tricky, Milord, but now it's in the bulkfabs, so Master Rayzo can get more anytime he wants."

Rayzo committed a terrible breach of manners by saying, "Good," with a full mouth.

"Very good," Lord Kank said. "Very good indeed!"

Hennik dipped a fork in his serving of Chowklud, then touched it to his tongue, emitted a strangled gagging noise, and spat the trace amount he'd sampled into his napkin, which he then used to wipe any remaining sauce residue off his tongue. As he watched Hennik, Rayzo swallowed his second mouthful and prepared a third.

Hennik said, "I'm impressed, Rayzo. You're so much dumber than I ever thought, and I thought you were pretty dumb."

"Why do you believe his intelligence is lacking?" Lord Kank asked.

"Because he's not smart enough to avoid pain. Even worms have figured out that essential concept. You and he are the only two who seem unclear on it."

"Ah, but Hennik, my people have a saying. *From suffering comes reward.* We believe that hardship makes us stronger."

Hennik rolled his eyes. "That's what losers always tell themselves. The truth is that not suffering is its own reward, and winning means you're already strong enough."

"I'd be careful if I were you," Lord Kank said. "You're coming dangerously close to insulting my people's most deeply cherished beliefs."

"The fact that you would be careful is precisely why you'll never be me," Hennik said, "and I'm not *coming close* to insulting your beliefs, I'm deliberately doing exactly that. My prerogative to do so is one of my culture's most deeply cherished beliefs."

Lord Kank remained motionless for a long time before finally saying, "If you were a man my age, I'd challenge you to settle this by combat, to the death."

"If you were a man, my age wouldn't stop you," Hennik replied.

"Novich," Kank said, "am I correct that it would be poor form for me to challenge, then assault and murder the young Hahn at this time?"

"Yes, Lord Kank, although I suspect my colleagues would agree that you have been provoked."

"Indeed," Migg agreed. "The age, size, and experience differentials would render trial by lethal combat untenable, as far as the Formalities are concerned."

"What if the combat were something nonlethal, and I chose a champion? Someone who has my respect, but is closer in age and size to the Hahn?"

Novich considered this. "If the combat were, as you say, nonlethal, and your champion participated voluntarily, I believe form would be satisfied. Do you concur, Migg?"

"Yes," Migg said. "That would be acceptable, and as I suspect I know which champion you have in mind, I might further suggest that you select Apiosan sports as the designated form of non-lethal combat. Both combatants would, hypothetically, be well acquainted with the rules, and we have the facilities readily at hand."

Without turning his gaze away from Hennik, Lord Kank asked, "What do you say, Rayzo? Will you be my culture's champion?"

Lady Jakabitus started to object, but stopped when she felt Lord Jakabitus squeeze her hand. She looked at her husband. He nodded with an air of great confidence.

Hennik said, "That's probably the only good idea you've ever had, Kank! What do you say, Rayzo? Are you brave enough to face me again?"

Rayzo swallowed the mouthful of food he'd been working on, then opened his eyes and loaded more food onto his fork.

"Sure," he said. "Just let me finish my lunch first."

56.

The kitchen was bustling. Rayzo and Hennik's sports match was a special event, and special events called for special refreshments, even if they happened right after lunch. Barsparse and Ebbler would have prepared finger food in any case, more because Barsparse preferred to be prepared for every eventuality than because the guests were likely to want it. In this instance, Barsparse suspected that the canapés would be appreciated, as Rayzo was the only person to have eaten much at lunch.

Barsparse and Ebbler were concentrating on producing these impromptu snacks while Gint butchered a carcass of some sort. It was a task to which he was still well suited, so Barsparse set him to work even though game meat was not actually on the evening menu. Glaz stood by at a safe distance, observing Gint's workmanship and trying to think of a job at the palace that might fit his new skill set. Umily stood near Ebbler and Shly, listening to their conversation in an effort to avoid Gint.

Kreet stood by the door, grav-platter at the ready, waiting and watching. He waited for the signal that the canapés were ready, and he watched as Ebbler delayed that signal by splitting his efforts between cooking and asking Shly questions about what had happened at lunch.

Sure, Umily was standing there too, but as usual, the conversation was all Ebbler and Shly.

"He ate the whole thing?"

"Yeah, every bit of it. Is it really that bad?"

"I tasted some when Chef was making it. Just dipping my finger in it was painful. Tasting it was like eating pure hurt."

The phrase *pure hurt* caught Kreet's attention. It was a good description for how he felt as he watched Shly and Ebbler. He'd been a fool not to see it before. Though he and Barsparse had watched the whole scene unfold as well, Ebbler had only asked Shly about it . . . and she'd dropped everything to tell him.

Kreet looked at the floor, where Shly's bulkfab sat neglected while she gossiped with her wannabe boyfriend.

It's a nice, cozy setup for them, Kreet thought. *Because they work together, they get most of the benefits of being in a relationship without having to do anything serious, like actually admitting how they feel to anyone, even themselves.*

He glanced down at Shly's bulkfab again and thought, *Yup, it's a sweet setup. Sweeter than they deserve.*

He looked at the lovebirds, engrossed in each other. Without anyone noticing, he bent down to make some adjustments to Shly's bulkfab, covering his action by fiddling with his shoe. That done, he casually strolled to a bare spot of wall several feet away and waited for the food.

Once the food was ready, Kreet placed the canapés on his grav-platter as quickly as Ebbler could finish them. He made a point of not looking at, talking to, or acknowledging the existence of Shly, and he only interacted with Ebbler as much as was strictly necessary to do his job. Once his platter was loaded, he spun on his heels and left at top speed.

"What's his problem?" Ebbler asked.

"I don't know how to answer that. I couldn't possibly narrow it down to one," Shly moaned.

"He's really getting to you, isn't he?" Umily asked.

"I try to ignore him, but then he tries to offend me by ignoring me, so it just magnifies the effect when I ignore him back. It's bad enough that I have to work with him at regular meals. I really didn't need an extra event thrown in."

"Let me cover for you," Umily said. "I know how to work the bulkfab. Besides, this way, you won't have to deal with Kreet, and it'll help me get my mind off . . . things."

Shly glanced at Gint just in time to see him attempt to remove a steak from the rear of the carcass by stabbing it off.

Shly called out, "Glaz, is it okay if Umily covers for me for a little while? I'm not feeling well."

Glaz had trouble hearing Shly over the racket of Gint grunting obscenities as he hacked away at the meat, but she managed to piece together what had been said, and replied, "That'll be fine. Go get some rest, dear." Though the words were carefully chosen and delivered kindly, the message was clear. *It's fine if you don't feel up to doing your work, but don't think you'll stay here talking instead.*

Umily picked up Shly's bulkfab machine, grabbed a stack of glasses, and headed to the training room.

Shly called out after her, "I leave it set to His Lordship's favorite. If you start with him, you'll look like a mind reader." She turned back to Ebbler. "If she's going to be a friend and cover for me, I might as well help her look good."

57.

The advantage round of the match was already in full swing when Umily ducked in through the training room door. Lord and Lady Jakabitus and Lord Kank were sitting in the ringside seats, watching the proceedings with great interest. Migg, Phee, and the visiting Master of Formalities stood behind them, while Hartchar stood sentinel at the far edge of the ring, exuding quiet confidence.

Kreet waited by the door with his platter of canapés. He glanced at Umily with obvious surprise. Umily smiled at him. *That's right,* she thought. *You won't get to make Shly uncomfortable this time.*

On the mat, Hennik was slapping Rayzo with great speed but little force. Rayzo was not lifting a single finger to defend himself. As the final seconds of the round ticked away, Rayzo lashed out with one forceful slap across Hennik's face that reverberated through the room and left a red handprint on the Hahn boy's cheek. It didn't change the outcome. Hennik had still earned the advantage, but instead of feeling triumphant, he was hurt and angry.

Umily capitalized on the brief pause between rounds to dart forward and offer the Lady and the Lords a beverage. Kreet had stepped toward her as if he intended to say something, but she didn't feel like discussing Shly with him, and besides, duty called.

"Would His Lordship like his usual?" Umily asked. Lord Jakabitus said yes and thanked her, but he was preoccupied, whispering to Lady Jakabitus and Lord Kank about the match as she poured his drink.

"He threw that round on purpose. He and Hartchar have determined that there's an advantage to letting Hennik start with the upper hand."

Lord Kank nodded as if he had known this without being told.

"He wants Hennik to be confident, but off balance," Lord Jakabitus said softly. "Hennik has won every match he's played so far, but always through trickery, and all but the first two by using the same trick. Hartchar and Rayzo figure he'll use it again now, and they have a plan for if he does. If he tries some different tactic, then it will come down to skill. Rayzo's been training. Hennik hasn't."

"I knew I wouldn't regret choosing him as a champion," Lord Kank said. "You must be very proud of the boy."

Lady Jakabitus usually avoided watching sports, finding it to be at once brutish and embarrassing, but Lord Kank's words and her son's behavior at lunch had framed this particular match in a much more noble light. She wasn't watching her son being forced to suffer through a mortifying ordeal. She was watching him choose to endure and triumph over a mortifying ordeal. "We are quite proud of him," Lady Jakabitus said, smiling.

"Yes," Lord Jakabitus said, making sure everyone heard, "we are very proud of Rayzo."

Umily handed Lord Jakabitus a tall glass of thick red liquid, which he took without so much as a glance. His attention was elsewhere. Umily offered both Lady Jakabitus and Lord Kank a drink as well, but they both declined, focusing instead on the match.

Hennik had a firm grip on Rayzo's right wrist in preparation for the challenge round. Hennik tipped his head toward the spectators. "They're trying to give you confidence," he said, sneering.

Rayzo made no reply.

"It won't work," Hennik said.

Rayzo said nothing.

Hennik said, "Shut up."

Rayzo said, "No."

The round began.

Hennik's signature move—the move that had officially been named after him—was to fall to the ground, then propel himself between the opponent's legs and spring up behind the opponent, using the opponent's own arm to immobilize him and cause him pain. The move had been outlawed in regulation play, but Hartchar had made a point of keeping it legal here, where she set the rules.

Predictably, Hennik dropped to the ground, but Rayzo had adjusted his stance so that his feet were aligned one in front of the other instead of shoulder width apart. Hennik couldn't scuttle between them, and would need to come up with an alternate plan.

Hennik thought, *I have to think fast,* but that was as far as he got.

Rayzo lunged into a spinning leap and landed with one foot on each side of Hennik's back, still holding Hennik's left arm in a painful twist. As soon as Rayzo dropped his weight onto Hennik's back, Hennik released Rayzo's wrist, a reflex reaction to make the pain in his shoulder stop, but he couldn't get his arm in place to support himself in time, so he fell gracelessly to the mat, face first.

A chime played, and the segment of the mat Hennik's face contacted lit up, signifying points scored for Rayzo. This was repeated many times as Rayzo lifted Hennik's head up and mashed it back down into the mat.

Hennik finally managed to get his arms in position and lifted his body, as if doing a pushup. It was a desperate bid to get his face away from the mat. Hennik was in an untenable position, and Rayzo could have easily pulled Hennick's arms out from under him or waited for his arms to give out under their combined weight. Instead he rolled backwards, down Hennik's back and legs, and landed just behind Hennik's feet. He grasped Hennik's ankles and lifted, preparing to drag Hennik into the gutter.

Hennik felt Rayzo lift his legs. He knew what was coming next, but he couldn't just passively accept this one-way trip to defeat. He had to do something, and he had to do it now.

Hennik pressed down with his arms again, lifting his torso from the mat. He was suspended like a table, his arms supporting his head and shoulders and Rayzo lifting the rest of him. Hennik pulled forward, struggling to resist Rayzo's attempt to fling him into the gutter.

To Hennik's surprise, Razo stopped pulling. He felt an instant of triumph, which was quickly shattered when Rayzo started pushing on his ankles instead. As his center of gravity shifted out over his hands, Hennik had a simple choice—move his hands forward or fall face first back onto the mat. He chose to move his hands forward. He did this repeatedly, and Rayzo pushed him around the mat like a wheelbarrow.

In a sense, Hennik had gotten what he wanted. He had chosen not to passively accept his defeat; instead, he was taking an active role in it.

Rayzo did not grandstand. Not much, at least. He pushed Hennik around just enough to prove that he was in control, then he steered Hennik into the patch of gutter directly in front of his parents and Lord Kank.

Hennik, of course, saw where he was headed and resisted enough to fall on the mat, scoring several more points for Rayzo as his face skidded off the mat and into the gutter.

Hartchar, Lord Kank, and Lord and Lady Jakabitus all cheered and congratulated Rayzo, who just looked relieved.

Lord Kank leaned forward and looked down into the gutter, from which Hennik glared up at him. Hennik was trying to think of a way to spin this turn of events to make it seem like losing and being humiliated had been his plan all along, but he was finding it difficult.

"Don't look so glum, young Hahn," Kank said. "Everybody experiences setbacks. You should think of this as a marvelous opportunity to better yourself."

Behind Lord Kank, Lord and Lady Jakabitus were still reveling in their son's victory. Lord Jakabitus had exhausted every positive adjective in his vocabulary and realized that, while cheering, he had shouted himself hoarse. Absentmindedly, he lifted his almost-forgotten glass to his lips and took a sip.

Everybody has had the experience of taking a mouthful of one beverage when they were expecting a different one. Everybody knows how disorienting and panic-inducing it can be, even if the surprise drink is something pleasant. Lord Jakabitus unexpectedly found himself with a mouth full of Chowklud. His instincts took over immediately, and he spit it out into the gutter.

He didn't deliberately aim for Hennik, so only about half of the Chowklud hit Hennik's face. Hennik shrieked, first from shock, then from the indignity of being spat upon, then from the searing pain in his eyes, nose, and open mouth.

"And here you've been given another marvelous opportunity!" Lord Kank said. "What a lucky day this is."

58.

"Where's Shly?" Umily asked, storming into the kitchen.

"I'm right here," Shly said. She had been leaning against the wall near the door, watching Barsparse and Ebbler work, making occasional conversation with Ebbler.

Of course, she was supposed to have gone to her quarters to rest, but Shly had explained the truth to Glaz. As Glaz understood why prolonged exposure to Kreet would make anyone feel ill, she'd let Shly off the hook just this once. After all, she had bigger problems. Watching Gint attack a fresh side of beef made that painfully clear.

Barsparse had attempted to correct Gint's technique, but his multiple regenerations had driven the capacity for subtlety out of him. Glaz was disturbed by the way he hacked at the meat, but what worried her more was the way he froze when he realized Umily was upset.

"Shly," Umily shouted, "you said you'd set the bulkfab to His Lordship's favorite."

"I did."

"Then why did it give him a glass of that damned Cappozzian pain sauce?"

Ebbler stopped working and Barsparse slowed noticeably, which was as close to stopping as she ever seemed to get. They were listening, but neither felt they would help matters by getting involved just yet.

Kreet trailed Umily in and stood along the wall, observing. Things hadn't worked out as he'd planned, but at least it would be entertaining to watch the fallout.

"You gave Lord Jakabitus a glass full of Chowklud?" Shly asked, incredulous.

"Yes! You think it's funny?" Umily replied.

"No, it's horrifying! Did you set it to Chowklud?"

"No! Why would I do that? You told me to leave the setting where you had it, and I did."

In the far corner of the kitchen, Gint slowly turned away from the side of beef he'd been butchering, still holding the knife.

In a low voice, Glaz said, "Gint, we'll get to the bottom of this."

Gint remained still.

"Are you saying that the bulkfab malfunctioned?" Umily asked.

"I don't know what happened," Shly said, "but I want to find out."

"As do I," Lady Jakabitus said as she, Migg, and Phee entered the kitchen.

The room went silent in an instant. Everyone, even Barsparse, dropped what he or she was doing and stood at attention.

Lady Jakabitus smiled disarmingly and said, "But before we solve the case of the surprise Chowklud, we have some more pleasant business at hand. I've been trying all day to find an excuse to sneak down here and welcome our Gint back from the front. Where is he?"

Gint said, "I am here, Milady." He was much taller, noticeably bulkier, and his face was far more scarred than when last she'd seen him. He was wearing a blood-smeared apron and holding a dirty butcher knife. He started to approach Lady Jakabitus, but Glaz put a hand on his shoulder and gently took the knife away. He proceeded to Her Ladyship and dropped to one knee.

"Gint," Her Ladyship said. "That's not necessary. Please stand up."

Gint said, "As you command, Milady," and stood at attention.

"You appear to have grown," Lady Jakabitus said.

"Yes, Milady, thanks to your science corps. Every time I got killed, they brought me back stronger than before."

"Every time," Lady Jakabitus said. "Here I thought you'd gotten so big from eating your own cooking." Lady Jakabitus was shifting gears, hoping to hide her discomfort behind humor. Unfortunately, nobody made any sound that could be in any way interpreted as a laugh, and like all unsuccessful camouflage, her efforts only drew more attention to what she was trying to hide.

"Not hardly, Milady," Gint said. "Your boys in the science corps got rid of most of my cooking knowledge. Cooking wouldn't help me kill the Hahn, Milady. Unless I were to poison them, that is."

"I see," Her Ladyship said.

"In fact, I have some ideas along those lines, if you've got a few minutes."

"That sounds . . . *interesting.*"

"Yeah, of course, making a lethal gas isn't really cooking, if you're being technical about it, but I guess it could be classified as an aroma."

"Thank you, Gint," Her Ladyship said. "I look forward to discussing your ideas, but I don't really have the time at the moment."

Gint's expression hardened. He looked away from Lady Jakabitus, staring off into the middle distance. "Sure, Your Ladyship. I understand. You have important business. No time to waste on a simple soldier who's died many times in your name."

Lady Jakabitus blanched, then looked as if she might respond. Migg cut in before she could, saying, "Milady, perhaps we should tend to the business at hand so we can get back to your guest."

"Yes," Lady Jakabitus said. "Quite." She cast her eyes around the room until she found the person she was looking for.

"Umily?"

"Yes, Milady."

"Why did you serve my husband a glass of liquid agony?"

While everybody else was focused on Lady Jakabitus and Umily, Glaz kept her eyes locked on Gint. He was standing at attention, but his knuckles were white, and he was watching and listening with terrible intensity.

"It was an accident, Milady. I would never do any harm to His Lordship on purpose."

"Well, you'll be happy to know that no real damage was done. As we speak, Lord Kank and his Master of Formalities are helping Frederain and Hennik wash the Chowklud out of their mouths and eyes. I am curious as to how an accident like this could have happened."

Shly stepped forward. "Milady, I am responsible, not Umily. It was my duty to dispense His Lordship's beverage, but Umily was covering for me. I had thought I'd left the bulkfab set to His Lordship's usual, but clearly I was mistaken."

Lady Jakabitus did not look angry, but she didn't look not angry either. "How could you possibly be mistaken about something so basic? Your entire job consists of working that machine. You must remember. Now, tell me honestly, did you set the machine properly or not?"

Shly grimaced. "I did, Milady."

"Good. I believe you. Umily. Did you change the setting?"

"No, Milady."

"Hmm. I believe you too. Not only do you both seem sincere, but the act itself makes no sense. It's so easily traced, and would so obviously cost those responsible their jobs."

Glaz saw the muscles in Gint's shoulders tense. She prayed that security could intervene in time if things turned ugly, because after watching Gint hack at the carcass, she knew she wouldn't be able to stop him.

"Someone must have done this deliberately," Lady Jakabitus said. "I would hate to think that the bulkfabs have started dispensing that awful sauce as a default."

Lady Jakabitus paused, enjoying the tension in the air before releasing it with her next comment. "If only security were able to review all of the events that transpired in the common areas of the palace," she said in a theatrically loud voice, "and could show us what happened."

Instantly, as if someone, somewhere, had simply been awaiting their cue, a square patch of one of the walls went black, then displayed a high-quality, close-up image of Kreet tampering with Shly's bulkfab. The perspective changed to a close-up of Kreet's hand as it reset the device to dispense Chowklud.

Lady Jakabitus was clearly going to have something to say about this, but she never got the chance. Gint darted toward Kreet and grasped him firmly by the wrist and upper arm, as if his limb were an axe handle. What he did next didn't seem like it was an attempt to hurt Kreet. It was more as if Gint were trying to hurt the wall by striking it with Kreet.

Kreet slammed face-first into the wall and sagged against it, groaning, while Gint reversed his grip and whipped Kreet around in a half circle to strike the wall again, this time with his back. Kreet's legs lost all strength, and he crumpled to the floor, but Gint still had his arm, and several creative ideas about what to do with it. He adjusted his footing and in one smooth motion turned his back, hauled Kreet up and over his shoulder, and leaned forward at the waist, creating enough momentum to send Kreet soaring through the air to slam down onto the floor in front of Gint.

Gint let go of Kreet's arm and reared back, preparing to rain blows down on the other man's head, but was stopped by the four security guards who had seemingly appeared out of nowhere. Gint struggled for a moment, stumbling around the room with the guards hanging from his upper body like poorly fitted garments, before they managed to tranquilize him.

Kreet, whom they also intended to apprehend, did not require tranquilizing.

59.

Lady Jakabitus walked, silent and glassy-eyed, through the Grand Gallery. Migg and Phee followed at a respectful distance.

It was dusk, which was widely considered the best time to be in the atrium of the Old Palace. Because of its height, you could stand on the ground floor, at which level the sun had already set, and look up at the towering column of windows to see the reddish-orange light of sunset suffusing the space above your head. Riding the escalator up, when timed properly, would not only provide a great view of the sunset, but would prolong the very sunset you were watching.

Her Ladyship noticed none of this as she rode the floating stone escalator to the palace's upper levels. Migg and Phee were on the next slab, having decided to give Her Ladyship her space.

"It's amazing, Phee," Migg said in a whisper. "Some things just want to happen."

"What do you mean?" Phee asked.

"Sometimes, you have the simplest plan, and nothing goes right. Other times, you have an idea that seems like it will take years of hard work and luck to implement, but everything just falls into place."

When they reached the second floor, Migg sped up to join Lady Jakabitus.

"Milady, I would suggest we stop for a moment so you can collect your thoughts before we reconnect with your guest."

"What?" Her Ladyship said. "Oh, yes, that's probably wise."

"Splendid, Milady. If you'll just follow me." Migg led Lady Jakabitus through the nearest door.

And of course it's the library, Phee thought as she followed them in.

Lady Jakabitus sagged into a chair. "He was the gentlest, sweetest young man," she said after a moment. "He was an artist. Of course, you never met him before, Migg, but Phee, wasn't he?"

"Yes, Milady," Phee agreed.

"I did this to him," Lady Jakabitus said.

"You didn't start the war," Migg said.

"No, but I haven't ended it, and I sent him into it. I made him what he is now, and he's just one of thousands."

"It's an ugly mess, Milady. All wars are."

"Yes, but this is my ugly mess." Lady Jakabitus looked on the verge of tears. Phee had never seen her so distraught.

Migg said, "Milady, you do have the power to end the war. Soon, bloodlessly, and without a loss of face for House Jakabitus."

"So you're finally ready to tell me your plan?" Lady Jakabitus asked.

"I think, Milady, that you're ready to hear it."

"Perhaps I am. Okay, Migg, out with it."

"We must arrange for Master Rayzo to marry a member of House Hahn."

For several seconds, Lady Jakabitus was silent, concentrating all her energy on simply looking horrified. Finally she gasped, "You can't be serious!"

"I am, Milady. It is a well-established technique that is almost certain to succeed." Migg paused, then said, "Phee?"

Phee had been rifling through her papers, and was ready with the pertinent precedents. "It is true, Milady. There are examples of great houses cementing alliances through marriage that reach back to well before the Terran Exodus."

"Of course I know that," Lady Jakabitus spat, "but he's far too young! He's only fourteen!"

Migg nodded, as if in agreement, but she said, "He will be fifteen soon, and there is precedent." Again, there was a moment of awkward silence before Migg said, "Phee?"

Phee continued to scan her papers as she spoke, "There is precedent. It is not uncommon on many federated worlds for marriages to be arranged and formalized, either by the betrothed or their families, years before the betrothed reach adulthood."

Her Ladyship shook her head emphatically. "I can't send my dear Rayzo away to the Hahn!"

Migg turned to look at Phee.

"Milady," Phee said, "according to precedent, sometimes the couple is legally married in every way except that the respective spouses each reside on separate worlds until both parties have reached adulthood, or sometimes long after."

Lady Jakabitus glared at Migg. "You ask a great deal."

"I ask nothing but that you listen. This is an opportunity to end the war that has caused so much waste and suffering, with a relatively minor sacrifice on your family's part."

"You call Rayzo a minimal sacrifice?" Lady Jakabitus shouted.

"You wouldn't be sacrificing Master Rayzo. He wouldn't die. He wouldn't even leave home for several years. Indeed, it's entirely practical to think that he and his spouse would live here or—at worst—split their time between this world and the Hahn Home World, depending on his spouse's responsibilities."

"But he'd be married to a Hahn!"

"Milady, I lived many years on the Hahn Home World, and I can assure you that not all Hahn are like Master Hennik or Lord Kamar Hahn. It's entirely possible that Master Rayzo would have a rewarding relationship with his betrothed, and even if not, they would hardly be the only people in the universe engaged in a marriage of convenience. While it is not ideal, there are ways to make that existence more palatable. There were rumors that your own father had . . ."

Migg trailed off, because Lady Jakabitus's expression made it very clear that she should.

"Would Kamar Hahn consent to this arrangement?" Lady Jakabitus asked.

"He already has, Milady. This is the endgame of the gambit that began with Hennik and me being captured."

"Is that how it began?" Lady Jakabitus asked. "Or did it start with the Hahn offensive?"

Migg looked at the floor. "Regrettably, you are correct, Milady. He came up with that wrinkle on his own, and would not be dissuaded. Still, you have the opportunity to ensure that all of the suffering he has caused your people isn't in vain."

Lady Jakabitus took a long, slow breath while staring at Migg. "So Kamar Hahn believes he's manipulating me."

"Yes, Milady."

"Then why would I let him?"

"Because, Milady, it is in fact you who will be manipulating him."

"I suspect it's you who are manipulating both of us," Lady Jakabitus said.

"You are correct, Your Ladyship. All three of those statements are true. The beauty of this course of action is that all parties will walk away victorious."

Lady Jakabitus sat and thought. Migg smiled at Phee, who took her time not smiling back.

"Who would Rayzo marry?" Lady Jakabitus asked. "I'm certain you have some idea."

Migg breathed deeply, then said, "The most appropriate candidate would be Lord Hahn's daughter, Master Hennik's older sister, Miss Shimlish Hahn."

"Is she not commonly referred to as *Shimlish the Pig*?"

"She is, Milady, but I have known Miss Shimlish for many years, and I can assure you that the honorific *the Pig* is not a reflection on her appearance, only her behavior, and even then it is greatly exaggerated."

"Exaggerated? I was told it was meant as a compliment," Lady Jakabitus said.

"Yes, Your Ladyship, but it's a compliment to the Hahn. In your culture, it would still work out to being an insult, I'm afraid."

"And you want to marry poor sweet Rayzo into that?"

"Only after properly preparing him, Milady. I had expected to spend years using Hennik as a training tool to get Master Rayzo ready, but as he has amply proved today, Master Rayzo is much stronger than I had dared hope. I fear we must move quickly before word filters back to the Hahn Home World that Master Rayzo is not the weakling Lord Hahn assumes he is."

"I'm going to need to think about this," Lady Jakabitus said bitterly.

"Of course, Milady, but as I said, time is of the essence. With your permission, I will start the preliminary planning. I will not do anything official, nor will I involve anyone besides Phee."

Migg glanced at Phee, and was displeased to see her furiously scribbling on her papers, oblivious to the conversation. There was no need for precedents at the moment, so Migg couldn't imagine what she was noting or requesting.

"Phee," she said sharply, "are you paying attention?"

Phee lowered her paper and stood at attention. "Yes, Migg," she said. "I am."

60.

"So I believe it's clear," Wollard shouted up to the impassive silhouettes of the scrutinizers, "that I am but a victim, an unwitting pawn in a sinister game I didn't even know I was playing."

The scrutinizers looked down at him; Woolard stood as defiantly as he could manage while at the bottom of a stone pit, wearing a sack. After a moment, one of the scrutinizers (Wollard still could not distinguish them) asked, "Are you done?"

"Maybe," Wollard said.

"Almost definitely," the scrutinizer said. "If we understand your position, Wollard, it is that you admit to committing the error of which you stand accused, yet you feel you should not have been removed from your former position because your successor outwitted you."

"I don't think I said that," Wollard sniffed.

"You did."

"Even if that is the way you choose to see it, I was not the only one to have been manipulated. She outwitted everyone."

"Perhaps," the faceless scrutinizer said, "but we aren't scrutinizing everyone, Wollard. Just you. Do you have anything further to say in your own defense?"

"Yes," Wollard blurted. He didn't know what else he could say, but he was certain that what he had said thus far had not worked, so he saw little harm in trying to come up with something else. He had counted on having some time to go through his journal and organize some notes. Without that time, he'd been forced to make his defense on the fly, skimming his notes and mentioning important points as he came to them. Now he ruffled and jabbed at his papers, scanning his journal in reverse order in a frantic search for anything he might have missed.

"What is it, Wollard?" the scrutinizer said. "What more would you like to say?"

"Um, I'm looking for it now. I'll have it in a second. Please bear with me," Wollard said without looking up from his papers.

"I'll tell you what, Wollard. I have a few things I'd like to say. I doubt you'll enjoy hearing them, so feel free to continue looking for this miraculous defense, which you neglected to mention at any earlier point. I will say my piece. If, by the time I'm done chastising you, you have not remembered whatever it is you would like to say, we will pass judgment. Agreed?"

"I have little choice," Wollard said.

"You have no choice," the scrutinizer corrected him.

Wollard signaled his agreement by returning to his search.

"Wollard," the anonymous scrutinizer said, "nobody denies that the Master of Formalities known as *Migg* has acted in a suspicious manner, manipulating the Formalities to suit her own ends and possibly the ends of her former ruler, Lord Kamar Hahn. That is the case you have made, and we find it convincing. That said, you yourself have pointed out that she's worked within the rules of proper form, which is the reason you are being scrutinized and not her."

Wollard shrugged his shoulders to signal that at least one hemisphere of his brain was listening while the other was still trying to save his skin.

The scrutinizer continued. "You should be grateful to Migg, Wollard. Because of her actions, the great unspoken truth of the universe is about to be revealed to you—a truth that she seems to grasp without guidance, but which you must be told. It's a shame you aren't paying closer attention. Wollard, the truth is that while the rulers of each individual planet make the decisions on which history is built, they almost always make the decisions we suggest. Knowing that, I must ask you who truly rules the galaxy, and since you're otherwise occupied, I'll answer for you. *We* do. We, the Arbiters, rule the galaxy."

This broke Wollard's concentration. "What?" he asked. "But we merely advise. The role of the Arbiters, and the Masters of Formalities, is to smooth and lubricate the course of history, not to steer it."

"Yes, but you can do a great deal of steering by lubricating some places more than others, creating a path of least resistance, and I advise you to keep looking at your notes. You don't have much time left. Wollard, the great houses abide by the Formalities because to do otherwise would be ruinous. To advise is to tell someone what they should do. To command is to tell them what they must do. We advise the great houses, but they follow our advice because they must. They accept our control because they don't perceive it as control. That is why we can't ever tell them that they can't do anything, even when they can't. You know this. You've given some version of this speech yourself, I'd wager."

"It didn't sound so malevolent then," Wollard said.

"Because you didn't perceive it as such, which only strengthens my point. Wollard, this can't really be a surprise. Why on earth did you think it took so long for the Arbiters to ever make a formal recommendation? If it were simply a matter of looking up information and sending it along, the process would be nearly instantaneous. We gather, catalog, analyze, and parse all of the information in the galaxy, then we debate everything and then prune the information like a tree until it conforms to the shape we want. I'll give you an example. We wanted Lady Jakabitus to adopt the captured Hahn boy because all of the precedents suggested that this would lead to increased tensions on Ophion

6. So, we edited the precedents to downplay the increased tension and emphasize the possible long-term gain."

"But why would you want to increase the tensions on Ophion 6?" Wollard asked, looking up from his papers.

"For the same reason we engineered the conflict so long ago, have maintained it ever since, and will see to it that it continues until everyone in this room is long dead. Because Apios and the Hahn Home World have the two most fully developed armies in their respective regions of the galaxy, and as long as we can keep them aimed at each other, they will remain safely stalemated until we need to direct them elsewhere."

Wollard sagged. He looked back down to his papers, but something told him that he was fighting to retain a position he no longer even wanted. He muttered, "I've been a fool."

"Yes, Wollard," the scrutinizer said, trying and not quite succeeding to sound sympathetic. "You're here today because of several failures of perception. You failed to perceive the Formalities' true purpose, you failed to perceive Migg's true intent, and you failed to understand the true purpose of your scrutiny. You've spent your time trying to convince us that you behaved properly in the past. We see everything. It often takes us some time to see it, and more time to act, but we always do. We already know how you comported yourself in the past. What we don't know, what you should have been telling us, is how useful you can be to us in the future. With that in mind, do you have anything to add?"

Wollard looked up, confused. "Have you already passed judgment?"

"No," the scrutinizer said. "I was just about to. You really should be listening, Wollard, I'm laying it all out here."

"It's just, my CV has been edited. You didn't do it?"

"No. We do things properly here at the Central Authority. I promise you, your CV will not be edited until you have been officially found guilty, and then it will be erased, and you will be given a job well below your former position, not that anybody will have any way of knowing that. Wollard! Are you listening to me?"

"Only as much as I have to. If, as you say, the maintenance of tension on Ophion 6 is important to you, then my former protégée has just sent extremely fresh information that will be of great interest to you. It may well demonstrate a way in which I can be of use, which, if I heard you correctly, should make you quite happy."

"Ecstatic," the scrutinizer said bitterly.

PART 8

A wedding between two people who love each other is a joyous occasion, and is to be celebrated.

A wedding designed to form a marriage of convenience is a convenient occasion, and is to be celebrated only so much as is convenient.

-Excerpt from *The Arbiters' Official Guidelines Regarding the Careful Control and Judicious Deployment of Enthusiasm*

61.

"Know that two thousand, one hundred, and seventy-one conventional years have passed since the Terran Exodus," Migg said, projecting so as to be heard throughout the servants' hall. "Today is the twenty-second day of the fourth month. We meet on the planet Apios, in the servants' hall of Palace Koa, the ancestral home of House Jakabitus and its matriarch, Lady Joanadie Jakabitus. I am Migg, Master of Formalities for House Jakabitus, and I am currently delivering the daily meeting to the palace staff."

The servants' hall was filled with people, the vast majority of whom seemed excited. The visible minority was made up entirely of the customary palace staff, who looked numb. Migg understood this. They had grown quite comfortable in the routine of their jobs, but in the five days since Migg had taken over as Master of Formalities they'd been fed a steady diet of surprising events.

"I want to start by welcoming all members of the auxiliary staff. As you well know, we have brought you in from every corner of the planet, on very short notice, to assist us at this exciting and stressful time. We of the permanent staff welcome you here, and believe me, we appreciate your help."

A polite laugh rippled through the crowd, diverting around the stone-faced group of permanent staff like waves flowing around a rock.

"It may interest you to know," Migg said, "that most of us were just as surprised as you all were when Lady Jakabitus announced the forthcoming wedding of Master Rayzo."

She chose not to mention who Master Rayzo was marrying. It was not a secret, but that didn't mean she needed to remind everyone.

Migg continued, "And I can assure you that the staff was probably more surprised than you are to hear that the actual nuptials would occur here, at the palace, tomorrow."

Phee looked down at her friends. Not one of them looked happy, and why should they? There was too little time and too much pressure for them to pull off an extremely high-profile event the following day, no matter how many auxiliary staff members had joined the team. Besides, everyone who knew the parties in question was certain it was a mistake.

Migg seemed confident, but then again, she always did. She claimed to believe the staff was up to the challenge, but Phee couldn't help but remember that Migg had gotten her current position by putting Wollard under great pressure then watching him fail. Phee looked out at the sea of eager faces in the crowd and wondered if Migg intended to recruit a new palace staff that would not remember who she was or how she came to inherit her position.

Migg said, "A wedding is always a happy occasion—a wedding joining two great houses, even more so. But this occasion trumps even that, because I am authorized to announce to you that as of last night, Lady Joanadie Jakabitus and Lord Kamar Hahn have agreed to a provisional cease-fire, halting all aggression between their houses on the planet Ophion 6."

The crowd roared its approval. This news was the logical next step after the announcement of the wedding, and most people had expected it, but the wedding had only just been announced, so they hadn't been expecting it so soon. Even the permanent staff was happy.

They're eager to trade the future of a promising young man for the lives of hundreds of strangers, Phee thought. *What does that say about them? Then again, what does the fact that I'm not willing to make that sacrifice say about me? Is it possible to be selfish on someone else's behalf?*

As Migg laid out the schedule for the coming day, Phee tried to distract herself by checking her papers, but no good news awaited her there. She hadn't heard back from Wollard. She didn't even know if he had seen the message.

Phee was so lost in thought she didn't even hear it when Migg dismissed the staff. Only the sight of them all standing up snapped her out of her daze.

She followed as Migg quickly made her way out of the servants' hall. Migg moved quickly every day, but usually not to this extent.

As they left the room, Phee took note of Umily talking to Gint, who was standing next to her in his new guard uniform. The captain of the guards had apparently viewed Gint's attack on Kreet as an audition rather than an assault.

By the same token, Lady Jakabitus had taken Kreet's sabotage of the drink-dispensing bulkfab as a resignation rather than an act of treason. He would recover in an infirmary somewhere in the Palace's new addition until he was well enough to be sent back into the general workforce. None of his injuries were serious, but they were painful enough that Lady Jakabitus felt that they, combined with the sting of being fired from his position at the palace, were punishment enough.

Despite his size, his fearsome armor, and the fact that he was talking to his own wife, Phee thought Gint looked rather like a boy introducing himself to a girl he fancied. Umily seemed as if she were a girl who was interested in the boy pursuing her, but was trying to decide if he was worthy of her trust. In a sense, this was exactly what they both were.

62.

After a morning that had shot by in a blur of frenzied activity, and a lunch for the Jakabitus family that had passed slowly in excruciating silence, the entire staff, auxiliaries included, lined up in the courtyard to await the arrival of honored guests.

The crowd of temporary help was abuzz with excitement until the Jakabitus family, including their *adopted* son Hennik, emerged from the palace in their third-finest dress uniforms, stepped down to the courtyard, and walked to their customary space in front of the main palace entrance, Lord and Lady Jakabitus in the lead, Rayzo and Hennik following behind.

Quietly enough so that only his wife could hear, Lord Jakabitus said, "I understand why you're doing this, Joanadie, but I don't like it."

Lady Jakabitus said, "I know, but arranged marriages are just a fact of life for people of our rank."

"Not always. You didn't have to submit to an arranged marriage. You got to marry whoever you wanted."

"Yes, Frederain, but I could marry anyone who met certain financial and social criteria, was fertile and of sound health, fell within a specific age range, and passed an extensive emotional stability test and moral background inquiry. Of the eight possible candidates, you were the clear choice."

"Well, it's not very romantic when you put it that way," he grunted.

Lady Jakabitus let out a sympathetic moan, then said, "But I do love you, Frederain, I love you very much. I fell in love the instant I saw your name and picture on the list my father had compiled."

Migg and Phee followed the ruling family at a respectful distance, as always, then broke away from the ruling family so that Migg could address the staff, filling them in on what they should expect when the honored guests arrived. She knew all too well what could happen when people were exposed to the Hahn ruling family without preparation.

Lady Jakabitus looked down at her son. "Rayzo," she said, trying not to sound sad, "are you excited? You're about to meet your future wife."

Rayzo neither looked at her nor said anything. Normally, she wouldn't tolerate this, but given the circumstances, she decided to let it slide.

"How about you, Hennik?" she asked. "Are you excited to see your family again?"

Hennik looked up at her without replying. He had just seen Rayzo ignore her question, and saw no reason why he should do any different.

This, Lady Jakabitus was not willing to let slide, and neither was Lord Jakabitus, but Rayzo spoke up before either of them could say anything.

"Are you excited, Mother?" he asked. "You're ending a war that has lasted generations, and all it's costing you is your son."

"Both of your sons," Hennik said.

Lord Jakabitus growled, "You're assuming your father wants you back."

"You're hoping he won't?" Hennik asked.

"Quite the contrary," Lord Jakabitus said.

"Hennik," Lady Jakabitus said, "it is my intention to offer your return as a token of good faith, but you should note that neither your father nor any of his representatives requested it. And as for your question, Rayzo, this is a great day for Apios and House Jakabitus, but there are parts of it I dread," she turned to look at Hennik, "even while other parts delight me to my core."

Hennik looked at her, delighted. Rayzo looked at her, full of dread.

Meanwhile, Migg was finishing up her brief address to the extended staff.

"While you are all bound to offer the same courtesy to the Hahn ruling family you would offer the Jakabituses," Migg said, "remember that whenever dealing with a member of the Hahn contingent that a Hahn's primary goal is to inconvenience you. When the Hahn are rude to you—note, I did not say *if*—when they are rude, showing any irritation back will only encourage them."

Migg paused, giving her words a moment to sink in before she continued. "The best reaction is to simply act as if you have not noticed. It won't be terribly satisfying for you, but it will be terribly unsatisfying for them. They may well escalate their behavior, which is their way of indicating that what you're doing is working. Thank you for listening. I know you will all serve Her Ladyship well."

Migg and Phee returned to their assigned spot behind and to the side of Lady Jakabitus.

Phee muttered, "I can't believe the Hahn agreed to such a speedy wedding."

Migg said, "Lord Hahn is his son's father. All I had to do was give His Lordship the impression that Lady Jakabitus didn't want a fast wedding, and he nearly insisted on it."

"Still," Phee said, "they're going to be here for almost a full day before the ceremony. What if Hennik tips Lord Hahn off to the fact that Rayzo isn't the weakling they'd hoped for?"

"Phee, can you see that happening? *Father, I want you to know that Rayzo Jakabitus is quite formidable. He bested me in a humiliating manner.* That's the last thing we have to worry about. Anyway, it's too late now. Here they come."

A trail of fire and vapor appeared in the stratosphere, signaling the imminent arrival of the Hahn transport. The auxiliary staff shuddered with excitement. They had never before taken part in the greeting of a foreign dignitary. The permanent staff exchanged uncertain looks. The transport was approaching much more slowly than usual. It seemed odd to think of an item that was emitting a trail of fire as moving at a leisurely pace, but relatively speaking, it was.

"Predictable," Migg said. "Apiosan Orbital Control assigns a precise entry point and time for entering transports, but after that, the details are left to the pilot's discretion, and this pilot is clearly following Lord Hahn's orders."

The transport seemed to come to a complete stop thousands of feet above the palace. After several seconds of perfect stillness, it started to make a slow descent, like a balloon filled with cool air sinking to the floor. The craft seemingly took an eternity to drop to the altitude of the palace, then it hovered for a few moments before drifting forward as if nudged by the wind.

While the Hahn transport took its time, the entire palace staff was standing idle on what was possibly the busiest day of their lives, and the Jakabitus family was experiencing the novelty of being kept waiting, a turn of events to which they were unaccustomed.

Hennik was pleased.

At long last, the transport wafted through the gates. It was an orbital transport of conventional design. It had probably come from the same coachbuilders on New-Oregon who built Lady Jakabitus's own transports. In the time since then, it had been painted with alternating irregular red and blue stripes, carefully designed to make a viewer's eyes hurt.

The transport twisted sideways, in adherence to protocol, and Lady Jakabitus could see the outlines of several people peering out of the vehicle's windows.

The craft drifted to a stop inside the palace's inner courtyard, then quickly spun one hundred and eighty degrees, so that the side of the craft without an exit was facing the palace entrance.

In the empty space beneath the craft, they could see the egress ramp pour into place on the far side of the transport.

Migg said, "Milady, good form dictates that I meet their Master of Formalities halfway, so we will have to walk a bit farther, but there is no requirement for anyone other than me and Phee to move at all."

A pair of feet could be seen leaving the ramp and circling around the transport. Migg and Phee set off at a brisk pace, and met the current Hahn Master of Formalities about two-thirds of the way to the craft. Lady Jakabitus had seen him before, via the feed in her office, and he was much as she remembered. His name was Kallump. He was tall and thin, as Masters of Formalities were wont to be; blond, as all Hahn were by Lord Hahn's decree; and dressed in the distinctive mottled brown clothing of the Hahn, modified with the cuffs and collar lapels of the uniform of a Master of Formalities.

Migg and Kallump worked through the formal greeting, complete with the various addendums and modifications on which the Hahn always insisted. After protracted negotiations, Kallump finally bowed, and more motion became visible on the far side of the transport.

The first person to round the nose of the craft was a Hahn servant, who was walking backward with great care, both hands occupied with manipulating some sort of boxy device that was strapped to his chest. A moment later, a pair of spindly mechanical legs emerged, followed by four more legs, and then the device to which they were attached. The six folding legs met at the base of an ornate metal chair, complete with armrests and footrests. Nobody needed to be told that the man riding in the chair was His Lordship, Kamar Hahn.

Lord Hahn's complexion was often referred to as *fair*, which really meant *pale white*. His hair was commonly described as *platinum blond*, which also meant *pale white*. His limbs were so long and thin that his knees and elbows jutted out even when he was sitting in his custom-made chair, giving the impression that he was not so much a person as a pile of mismatched person-parts thrown in a heap.

Lord Hahn's eyes were striking, even from a distance. It wasn't their light blue color so much as their intensity. They seemed to glow with energy. His smile was equally bright.

The chair's legs scrabbled wildly at the ground in their effort to keep Lord Hahn suspended and moving in the proper direction, but the chair's motion was smooth and gentle. It had been cunningly designed to keep Lord Hahn comfortable, but make everyone else uncomfortable.

Rayzo leaned over to Hennik and asked, in a hushed voice, "Did your father lose the use of his legs somehow?"

"No," Hennik said. "He can use his legs, he simply chooses not to. He says his legs are beneath him."

"Are all of your father's jokes that bad?"

"Yes, most are worse. Telling awful jokes and forcing people to laugh at them is a powerful demonstration of dominance, as is refusing to do the things everyone else has to do, such as walking."

"That doesn't prove dominance," Rayzo said. "It proves laziness."

"Hardly," Hennik sniffed. "He puts far more effort into not doing things than it would take to just do them."

"Did he tell you that?"

"Many times, at length. That's another way he asserts dominance. Take that chair: It took a great deal of time and resources to design and build it. It's made of exceedingly rare metals, hewn by my planet's greatest craftsmen and engineers. It's a one-of-a-kind work of art, and he controls it with his thoughts."

"Huh," Rayzo said, impressed in spite of himself. "Then what's that man walking backwards with that weird machine doing?"

Hennik rolled his eyes. "He's simply part of the apparatus. He anticipates what my father is thinking, then manipulates the chair accordingly."

"What if he fails to anticipate your father's thoughts?"

"He's scrapped and replaced, like any other faulty component."

By this time, Lord Hahn had reached Kallump, Migg, and Phee, and the requisite pleasantries had been exchanged. Migg bowed. Lord Hahn nodded, and the rest of the Hahn party emerged from around the transport.

Lady Inmu Hahn was predictably tall and unnervingly graceful. Her hair was a shade paler than her husband's white-blond hair, and actually verged on a metallic silver color. She wore a flowing gown made from a fabric that was the same mottled brown color as all Hahn attire, but the thin, sheer material flowed gently around her, like a drab, brownish mist. She was too beautiful, so beautiful that it pushed through into its own version of ugliness. She was like a painting by a skilled artist who knew no restraint and filled every square inch of the canvas with flowers, birds, and puffy white clouds. Looking at her for too long made one uncomfortable, then agitated, and in the end, angry.

Behind Lord and Lady Hahn came their daughter, heir apparent to the Hahn Empire, supreme commander of the Hahn armed forces, Hennik's sister, and Rayzo's bride to be, popularly known as *Shimlish the Pig*.

Rayzo studied her with understandable interest. She was shorter than either of her parents, but taller than Hennik. Rayzo knew her to be sixteen years old. She shared her mother's silvery hair and most of her facial features, but she had her father's intense eyes. She wore the most graceful, feminine battle armor Rayzo had ever seen. It too was Hahn brown, but the effect was more *practical camouflage* than *deliberate ugliness.* She carried a combat helmet under her arm. The armor was scarred and scuffed enough to show that it had seen action.

Rayzo was surprised to find that she was quite beautiful, though her beauty didn't make his forced marriage any more appealing.

The two female Hahn and Lord Hahn's chair walked across the courtyard to meet House Jakabitus.

"Lady Joanadie Jakabitus," Migg said, "it is my pleasure to present Lord Kamar Hahn, ruler of the Hahn Home World. Lord Hahn, I present Lady Joanadie Jakabitus, ruler of the planet Apios."

Lord Kank, who had quickly become a trusted adviser and friend, had helped the Jakabitus family carefully plan how they would react to Lord Hahn's inevitable remarks in the hopes of robbing him of any of the joy he'd gain from denigrating Lady Jakabitus and her family.

Lady Jakabitus bowed slightly and said, "Lord Hahn, it is an honor to welcome you to my home."

Lord Hahn smiled, bowed, and said, "I agree with your statement, Lady Jakabitus."

Lady Jakabitus let out a tiny, polite laugh, as if she'd expected Lord Hahn's joke. He smiled at her uneasily.

"I expected you would. Please allow me to introduce my husband, Lord Frederain Jakabitus."

Lord Jakabitus bowed.

Lord Hahn said, "A pleasure. It's so seldom I get to meet a man who is truly irrelevant."

Frederain said nothing.

"You have no reply?" Lord Hahn asked.

Lord Jakabitus shrugged. "If I am irrelevant, then any comment I might make would be equally irrelevant, would it not?"

"Quite," Lord Hahn said, furrowing his brow.

"And here are the boys," Lady Jakabitus said. "This is Rayzo, your future son-in-law, and of course you know Hennik."

"Yes," Lord Hahn said. "I must say, Rayzo, is it? I do hope you fit into my family as well as Hennik has clearly fit into yours. Yes, he looks right at home among your people."

"I haven't fit in at all," Hennik nearly shouted. "I've fought them at every opportunity."

"Oh, yes," Lord Hahn said, "I can see your defiance in the way you're standing here, silently, at attention, at the end of the line of reception."

All three members of the Jakabitus family felt a momentary pang of sympathy for Hennik. Not enough to speak up, of course. It would have done no good anyway. Having a Jakabitus stand up for him, even if it was to describe what a pain he'd been, would not have helped Hennik save face.

Lord Hahn took a moment to enjoy an extended sneer in Hennik's direction, then changed the subject. "I thank you," he said in a perfunctory, almost mechanical manner, "for your hospitality. Please allow me to introduce my wife, Lady Inmu Hahn."

Until that moment, Rayzo had been unaware that it was possible to bow sarcastically. Somehow, her bearing made it clear that any compliments delivered by her would have the opposite meaning.

After completing her deep, slow bow, Lady Hahn said, "I thank you, Lady Jakabitus, and your *lovely* family, for having us here in your *beautiful* home. I'm certain we'll grow to be *good friends.*"

Lord Hahn said, "And this, as I'm sure you've surmised, is my daughter and your future daughter-in-law, heir apparent of the House Hahn, supreme commander of the Hahn military, Miss Shimlish Hahn, known throughout the galaxy as *Shimlish the Pig.*"

Shimlish scowled as she bowed.

My lovely bride to be, Rayzo thought. *The very act of greeting me and my family is hateful to her.*

Shimlish's armor rattled slightly as she rose from her bow. She stood silently, her mouth clamped into a straight, tight line.

Neither Lord Hahn nor Lady Hahn turned to look at Shimlish, but Lady Hahn said, "Your *wonderful* future family has *graciously* invited you into their home. This is your chance to make a good first impression on these people who will be so *important* to you. Don't you have anything to say to them, Shimlish, *dear*?"

Shimlish exhaled heavily through bared teeth.

It pains her to even speak to us, Rayzo thought.

"Thank you," Shimlish said quietly, "for inviting us into what will one day be my palace. I wish to honor your family by starting our relationship with total honesty. I have consented to marry your son, and I will soon technically be a member of your family, but understand that if I have my way, once your son and I begin cohabitating, you will never see him or me on this planet again in your lifetime."

"I appreciate your candor," Lady Jakabitus said.

"Yes," Rayzo said, speaking out of turn. "And please allow me to be equally honest when I assure you that you will not get your way."

Normally, Lady Jakabitus would have scolded Rayzo if he'd said something impertinent to a visitor, but instead she was filled with pride. The visiting Hahn all stared at Rayzo, their faces registering differing amounts of surprise.

For an instant, Rayzo thought he saw Shimlish smile.

Migg tried to defuse, or at least redirect, the tension. "Lady Jakabitus, if it pleases you, I would like to direct your visitors' attention to the palace staff, who have been working so hard to make tomorrow perfect."

Migg motioned toward the small army of servants, as if Lord Hahn had simply not noticed them.

Lord Hahn looked at the servants and said, "Ah, yes. Indeed."

Rayzo saw the Hahn servant who controlled the chair flinch and move one of his hands on the controls. Instantly, Lord Hahn's chair scuttled sideways, like a crab, toward the assembled workers. One of the chair's automated legs nearly struck Shimlish, who had to leap backwards to avoid the collision. The chair operator cringed, but Lord Hahn did not appear to notice.

Lord Hahn's chair stopped in front of the servants. He cleared his throat, and it became obvious that somehow his voice was being amplified.

"We, the Hahn, are accustomed to the very best service. I will not, however, hold you to the same standard as I would my own palace staff on the Hahn Home World. To do so would be unfair to you, and an insult to them. I want you to know this because knowing it will deepen your shame when you inevitably disappoint me anyway."

The chair dipped forward slightly, simulating the bow that protocol demanded but Lord Hahn could not be bothered to deliver, and then Lord Hahn skittered back over to where his family, the Jakabitus family, and the Masters of Formalities were waiting. Migg announced that the customary next item on the agenda was a tour, guided by the Jakabitus family. Lord Hahn voiced no objections, and Lady Hahn said that she was *anxious* to see the palace in more detail.

They all walked through the main entrance into the Grand Gallery. Lord Hahn's chair operator walked ahead of them, backward, controlling His Lordship's chair while scouting ahead for obstacles. Migg dispatched Phee to help guide the poor man, lest he walk backward into a pillar, or off a balcony.

Hennik remained behind, waiting for the others to notice he was not following. He had to do something to demonstrate to his parents what a thorn in Lady Jakabitus's side he'd been. This was his chance.

To his chagrin, the group was beyond the door and well inside the palace before anyone said anything. He was a little happy Lord Hahn was the one to notice his absence, but that happiness evaporated when Lord Hahn told Lady Jakabitus, "Your adopted son doesn't seem to be following us."

"Hennik, dear," Lady Jakabitus called out, "is something troubling you?"

"I'm not coming," Hennik yelled back. He stood his ground, arms folded defiantly across his chest.

"Don't be silly, Hennik," she said. "Come along now."

Hennik shouted. "I said I'm not coming!"

Lady Jakabitus's smile did not dim. "Oh, Hennik, we've been through this before. We both know that you're going to join us. The only question is whether you'll do it voluntarily or not."

As if on cue, the utilitics beneath Hennik's feet started sliding him toward the palace entrance. He instinctively widened his stance and bent his knees, lowering his center of gravity, but he made a point of keeping his arms folded. Realizing that the resulting pose was somewhat less than dignified, he tried to walk backwards to counteract the forward motion, but the utilitics accelerated, and soon he was nearly running backwards with his arms still folded. The only results were that he slightly slowed his forward momentum and looked like he was doing some sort of folk dance. His parents were too far away for him to see their facial expressions, so he didn't know if he was impressing them. He hoped that from where they were standing inside they couldn't hear the staff, who were beginning to laugh.

Running backwards wasn't working, so Hennik stopped and let the utilitics propel him toward the entrance, which they did with impressive speed. He glided forward, doing his best to maintain his haughty posture, and did a fine job until his feet hit the incline that led up into the gallery. The incline caused his feet to slow. The laws of physics caused his head to continue at the same speed. The combination of these factors caused him to fall.

Hennik tumbled forward headfirst, spreading his arms wide. He landed on his face and slid forward on the utilics-coated stone floor, coasting to a stop at the feet of Lord Hahn's chair.

Hennik rolled over on his back, looked up at the unimpressed faces staring down at him, and said, "Okay, I've decided that I'll come along after all."

He sat up, then attempted to put his right hand down to lift himself to his feet, but his hand immediately slid out from under him.

"That's fine, Hennik," Lady Jakabitus said. "Stay seated. We don't want you tiring yourself out."

The tour continued, with Phee and the chair pilot in the lead, followed by Lady Jakabitus and Lord Hahn talking, Lord Jakabitus and Lady Hahn listening, Rayzo and Shimlish pretending to be oblivious to each other, Migg and Kallump waiting to be needed, and in the rear, Hennik, seated uncomfortably, scooting along the ground with his arms, once again, folded in defiance.

63.

The banquet hall was alive with furious activity. The permanent staff directed the auxiliary staff as they prepared the room for the evening's prewedding banquet.

Thanks to the utilitics, the tables and chairs could be shifted with ease, but they still needed to be arranged, set according to the agreed-upon plan, examined critically, rearranged, and reset in accordance with the new plan one person had devised on the spot, as was the customary manner in which all formal events had been staged since the dawn of human history.

Migg and Phee stood observing the preparations for a moment or two, then went to check on the progress in the kitchen.

"Chef Barsparse," Migg said, "how goes the preparation of the traditional Hahn drunesplop?"

"I wish every banquet was this easy," Barsparse said. "Of course, for an event of such importance, we're preparing everything by hand, so that's some work, but it helps that *drunesplop,* as you call it, is essentially the exact same dish as what we call tartare. It's just raw, seasoned, decontaminated ground beef. They present it differently, serve it without side dishes, and grind it more finely, but those are just details. This is the second Hahn dish I've prepared, and they've both involved grinding. Do they grind everything?"

"Most things," Migg said. "The Hahn find grinding to be a powerful metaphor for life, their society, pretty much everything, but the grinding of meat in general symbolizes Hahn culture."

"Really?" Barsparse asked.

"Yes. Disparate, dissimilar, and in some cases rather intransigent ingredients being persuaded through the application of pressure and force to become a uniform, homogenous whole. If anything, it's a little too on the nose, as metaphors go. I mean, you don't think I was dyeing my hair blond because it worked so well with my skin tone, do you?"

Barsparse smiled. Phee did not. It worried her that Migg might actually be winning the staff over. Phee knew one smirk at an amusing comment wasn't quite an act of betrayal, but that was how it started. A thanks for some assistance here, a laugh at a joke there—multiply that by a few hundred days, and before you know it two years have passed and nobody ever thinks about how Migg got her job or the look on Wollard's face when he was removed.

Migg asked, "Chef, do you ever find it odd that whenever some honored off-worlder visits, you end up cooking a dish from their home world?"

"That's what the Formalities dictate," Barsparse said, raising her eyebrow provocatively. "I should think you'd know that."

"Oh, I know that it's good form. I just don't pretend to understand it. Wouldn't this be a great chance for the visitor to experience top-notch Apiosan cuisine, instead of your attempt at a dish with which you are usually unfamiliar? No offense intended."

"None taken. I see your point. The thing is, people say they want adventure and novelty, but for the most part, they only like the exotic when it's served with a side order of the familiar. In this case, the Apiosan guests get an exotic dish prepared by a familiar chef, and the Hahn get a familiar dish prepared by an unknown chef."

Migg nodded. "An interesting point. It just goes to show, Phee, you never know what's going to happen."

"What? I'm sorry. Did you ask me a question?" Phee blurted, hastily putting her papers in her pocket and returning her attention to the conversation.

"No, Phee, I was just saying, you never know what's going to happen. For instance, when I got up this morning, I never would have expected I'd get a valuable lesson about proper form from the chef. Thank you, Barsparse."

"You're welcome," Barsparse said. "Now, if you'll excuse me, I should really get back to not cooking the beef."

Barsparse turned and disappeared into the depths of the kitchen, where she and Ebbler were overseeing several temporary chefs operating large grinders.

Migg walked silently out of the kitchen and into the palace's main corridor. Phee followed.

"So," Migg said, "any sign of the cavalry?"

"Pardon me?" Phee said.

"I already have. *Any sign of the cavalry.* It's an old, old expression. It means, *is help on the way?* I saw you reading your papers. I assume you were looking for some sign that somebody is coming to stop the wedding. It's fine, Phee. I'm not angry. You're loyal. Not loyal to me, but in general, loyalty is a good thing."

"I don't know what you're talking about," Phee said.

"You're not particularly honest, though," Migg said. "Phee, I know that you will never forgive me for what happened to Wollard, and I know that you don't want this wedding to happen. If I were the dangerous, manipulative monster you believe me to be, I'd accuse you of wanting to prolong the war."

"I don't like the war," Phee said.

"I'm certain of it, but I'm also certain that you don't like me, and that you've sent a message to the Central Authority telling them what's happening here in the hopes that they will put a stop to it."

"You have manipulated everyone," Phee said, changing the subject without admitting or denying what she'd done.

"True. I suppose it would be fair to describe me as a benevolent, manipulative monster," Migg said. "As for your message to the Arbiters, I admire your optimism, but we both know that the Arbiters are slow to act. They prefer to react. It takes less effort, and besides, it helps them maintain their carefully cultivated illusion of passiveness. I fear the best you can hope for is that several days after the wedding, an emissary, possibly a new Master of Formalities, will arrive. The marriage will stand, and I'll be displaced and recalled to the Central Authority for scrutiny."

"And you're betting that they'll approve of your actions," Phee said.

"Probably not. Phee, we, as Masters of Formalities, are constantly dissuading people from doing things by pointing out the potential consequences. One thing we seldom discuss is that there are times when the benefit is well worth the consequences."

"It's that important to you that Master Rayzo marries the Hahn?"

Migg said, "Is Master Rayzo's problem so large that you really can't see past it?"

Migg unexpectedly veered through an arch, outside, onto one of the New Palace's numerous balconies. It was late in the afternoon. The balcony was in the shade, but the sun shone down on the city, making the sides of the buildings glitter like the facets of cut gems. The airspace was thick with vehicles, swarming and buzzing like a cloud of gnats. Beyond the city, the sea extended to the horizon and merged almost seamlessly with the sky.

"It is a lovely city, isn't it Phee?" Migg asked.

"Yes," Phee agreed.

"I haven't seen much of it yet, but I'm told it's a beautiful planet."

"It is."

"Where are you from, originally, Phee?"

"Eurbia."

"Eurbia," Migg said, closing her eyes. "Mostly water. The landmass is primarily small islands. More coastline than any other planet its size. Very nice."

"You've been there?"

"No. Never seen it."

Migg waited patiently. She knew that Phee had little interest in her background, but she also knew that proper form dictated certain actions. If Phee were worthy of her position, she would eventually do what was proper.

At long last, and with little obvious interest, Phee asked, "Where are you from?"

Migg chuckled lightly, then said, "If you must pry, my family moved around a lot. I lived on seven different worlds before I was recruited by the Arbiters. Originally, though, my family came from Ophion 6."

"I didn't know there were people who were from Ophion 6," Phee said.

"Therein lies the problem, Phee. Everyone whose family lived on Ophion 6 is *from* there, not *living* there. Nobody lives there anymore. Plenty of people fight there, but that's not the same thing as living there. Not really."

"When did your parents leave?"

"My parents have never been to Ophion 6, and their parents lived their entire lives without ever seeing the planet. The story they told me was that my great-grandparents lived on Ophion 6. One day soldiers landed—whether they were Hahn or Jakabitus troops changes depending on who tells the story. They explained that Ophion 6 was unusually rich with a top-secret strategic resource, and they were there to secure the resource before the other side could."

"What was the top-secret resource?" Phee asked.

"They never said. It was top secret, after all. Anyway, both sides established a foothold, then fought to expand their control until the planet was as it is today, a sphere of smoking ruins with two parallel belts of fortification running around its circumference."

"None of the original inhabitants stayed?"

"The prudent ones fled right away. The brave ones stayed to defend their homes. After about two-thirds of the brave ones were wiped out, the remaining third decided that they'd rather be prudent after all."

"If a planet's worth of people fled, you'd think everyone would know about it," Phee said.

"It's a big galaxy, Phee. Ophion 6 was a small world, and it happened a long time ago. There are a few cities on a few planets where there's a population of people from Ophion 6. We call ourselves *Orphians.* For the most part, the galaxy just swallowed us up. We're spread out over a thousand worlds, so thin that nobody even notices us anymore."

"Okay," Phee said. "I think I get it a little better now. Wollard loses his position and Master Rayzo marries Shimlish the Pig, but as a result, the war ends and your people get their world back."

"You still haven't quite got the whole picture," Migg said, "but you're closer. When we go back inside, please remind me that I need to speak to Glaz about the seating arrangements."

"I notice you've changed the subject," Phee said.

"Did I?" Migg asked.

"Yes, but I'm changing it back. I guess I can see your reasoning," Phee said, "But I still feel terrible for Rayzo and Wollard."

"Perhaps the situation has been unfair to them. Perhaps. But if so, I'd point out that it's impossible to build something without destroying something else. Every statue represents a ruined piece of pristine, unused clay, which in turn represents a hole dug in the ground somewhere."

Phee considered this.

They stood looking at the city for a long moment, then Phee asked, "Do you intend to go back to Ophion 6?"

"No, Phee. Even with the war over, it will be many years before the planet fully demilitarizes, decades before it's truly habitable, and probably at least two generations from now before it's a place I would actually want to live."

"Then why do all this?"

"Because if nobody in my generation had, it would have been at least three generations."

64.

A line of transports hovered like an oversized dotted line extending from the palace courtyard through both gates and out over the city. With almost mechanical precision, the craft at the front of the line would land and disgorge its payload of overdressed aristocrats. The passengers would then make a grand entrance into the Grand Gallery, their names announced by a temporarily employed palace herald, while behind them in the courtyard their craft shot straight up in the air, making room for the next transport full of overdressed aristocrats who were awaiting their turn to make the exact same grand entrance.

The more insecure guests lingered among the grand columns of the gallery, waiting to see who else would show up and what they were wearing.

The guests who were surer of themselves traded greetings graciously, then made their way to the banquet hall to find their seats and decide what their seat's location meant.

Over time, the line of transports grew shorter, and the crowd inside grew larger. Emissaries from every planet within one day's interstellar transport range were present because that was all the notice the general public had been given. Some special guests had been given advance notice.

Lord Kank was present, of course. Between the promise of meeting the Hahn ruling family in person; the prospect of witnessing a young man he liked get married too young, and probably against his will; and the chance to endure endless wedding party chatter with the galaxy's upper crust, this was too great an opportunity for self-improvement to pass up.

The palace had more visitors than at any other time in living memory. Even with the small army of temporary help, the staff was having great difficulty keeping up. The kitchen was pumping out hors d'oeuvres. A squadron of young ladies with empty glasses and portable bulkfabs made their way through the guests, answering questions, dispensing drinks, and ignoring advances.

Most people had the good taste not to look, but if guests were to let their eyes drift to the side of the room where the wall and floor met, they would see an alarming parade of unnoticed crumbs, dropped morsels, dollops of spilled sauce, discarded napkins, and smudged glassware. Anything food-related that made its way to the floor or was left unattended for too long was claimed by the utilitics, and joined the great refuse migration along the walls and out the nearest door. The durable goods were cleaned and sanitized automatically by the time they arrived back in the kitchen to be stacked, redistributed, and used again.

The non-durable goods formed a steady stream that flowed into a cleverly concealed room where specialized utilitics in a large hopper broke down the waste into its constituent parts, which were then reformed into bulk, which could be used for further fabrications. Sadly, it was not a perfect system, and some matter was lost, thus keeping the bulk farmers in business.

The auxiliary staff was doing most of the actual work, but the permanent staff was managing the event, and that meant managing a tremendous amount of stress. After answering questions, directing staff, and putting out fires for what felt like both several hours and no time at all, Shly snuck back to the servants' hall to catch her breath. There she found Glaz, who seemed to have had the same idea.

"I'm so glad it's not like this every day," Shly said as she almost fell down into the chair next to Glaz. "I know I shouldn't tell you that, but it's the truth."

Glaz laughed. "Mentioning to your supervisor that you don't want to be busy isn't usually a great idea, but in this case I think you can be excused. I wouldn't want this every day either, but a little more often might be nice."

"I can see that," Shly agreed. "Maybe once a year."

"I was thinking more like once a month," Glaz said.

"No way," Shly said. "That would be way too much work!"

"Again, not a great thing to say to your supervisor, Shly. Don't worry. I understand. I wasn't speaking for everybody, just for myself. I wouldn't mind the extra work."

"I guess that's why you're the palace expediter and I'm not."

Glaz shook her head, then said, "No, Shly, it's not why I'm the expediter, it's because I'm the expediter. I hired a great staff, did my best to get them well trained, and now I watch as they do all the work. I don't know if you've noticed, but aside from sharing the occasional opinion and making the occasional informative statement, there really isn't very much for me to do."

65.

The guests were ushered into the banquet hall. There were two sets of immense carved stone doors at the far end of the room. Each door was a priceless work of art in its own right; the hinges alone were exquisite enough that on a lesser world an entire museum might be erected simply to display one of them. The set of doors on the left swung open silently, and Lord and Lady Jakabitus walked into the room with Hennik. They were wearing their second most-formal uniforms, and they could hardly move for all the brass and braiding. Lord and Lady Jakabitus bowed to the guests; Hennik barely nodded; then after a moment's confusion, they sat at a table to the left while the assembled multitudes applauded. The doors on the right opened, and Lord Hahn's chair operator entered, followed by Lord and Lady Hahn. Lady Hahn bowed slowly and deeply, with exaggerated hand motions and a facial expression that said *I hope you're satisfied.* Lord Hahn did not move, but his chair tipped forward, then back. While the guests emitted a polite amount of applause, Hennik watched his parents' every move with undisguised admiration. Lord and Lady Hahn sat at a table to the right. A staff member had to scramble to remove a chair that Lord Hahn clearly would not need.

Both sets of doors remained open, and at the exact same moment, Rayzo Jakabitus and Shimlish Hahn emerged, each from opposite sides, to thunderous applause. They bowed stiffly, walked toward each other, and sat alone at a table that was placed in the absolute focal point of the room. Like his mother, his father, and his adopted brother, Rayzo was wearing his second-finest formal uniform. Like her father and mother, Shimlish was wearing the same clothes she had arrived in, though she had adjusted the color of her adaptive armor to a reasonably bridal shade of white.

As the applause faded away, it was replaced with music, provided by a live orchestra that was strategically positioned on a terrace at the back of the room so few would see it, but its music filled every corner of the cavernous banquet hall.

Lady Jakabitus looked at her son, sitting alone at a table with a total stranger. She caught Migg's attention and called her over.

Migg was, of course, wearing her customary formal blacks. There was no more formal garment in existence, and as such, it was appropriate for every event. Migg leaned down and said, "Yes, Milady?"

Lady Jakabitus said, "I was not told that we would be sitting at separate tables."

"No, Milady?"

"No. In fact, I was told that we would *not* be sitting at separate tables."

"There is ample precedent for the betrothed to sit at their own table, as the focal point of the party celebrating their wedding," Migg said.

"Perhaps," Lady Jakabitus allowed, "but there's no precedent for such a fundamental change in plan occurring without my knowledge. How did this happen, Migg?"

"May I be blunt, Milady?"

"Yes, but you should also be careful."

"Always, Milady. I take full responsibility for the change. I only got the idea late this afternoon, and the seating arrangement hardly seemed like the kind of issue that was urgent enough to warrant bothering Your Ladyship."

"It's my son's wedding, Migg."

"And that is the point, Milady. Master Rayzo is marrying a young woman he has met once, whom he will not see tomorrow until the actual ceremony. This dinner is the only chance he and his bride to be will have to actually converse with each other, and I thought that said conversation might go smoother if her parents weren't involved. Sadly, form dictated that you could not be involved either."

Lady Jakabitus's expression darkened. She looked off into the distance and took several protracted breaths before finally saying, "I would have approved it if you had put it to me that way."

"Yes Milady, and I would never have made the change if I hadn't been absolutely certain of that fact."

"If you ever pull anything like this again . . ." Lady Jakabitus deliberately allowed her voice to trail off.

"I'm absolutely certain of how that sentence ends," Migg said, "and I'm equally certain that you mean it."

Lady Jakabitus looked at her son, sitting silently, avoiding all eye contact with Shimlish, who was avoiding him with equal concentration.

"What if it doesn't go well, the conversation between them?"

Migg said, "Then Master Rayzo will at least know what he's in for."

Before dinner there was a program of light entertainment. The orchestra was joined by a singer, then the large empty space at the center of the room was used to stage a demonstration by a group of former sports champions and crowd favorites who toured the globe performing under the less-than-subtle name, *The Apiosan Superstar Sports Squads.*

The four *Superstars* varied in age from their early twenties to their late forties, but all were in excellent physical condition, which was obvious given that their uniforms consisted solely of sports shorts, emblazoned with the highest rank they'd achieved and the year in which they'd achieved it. Three of the men's shorts had a number one on them. The shorts of the man who did all the talking bore a number eight. He acted as a sort of narrator. When the other Superstars were preparing for a demonstration, he told the audience what they were about to see. While the Superstars were engaged in their demonstrations, he explained to the audience what they were seeing. When the demonstration was complete, he cued the audience to applaud by reminding them, with great volume and intensity, of what they had just seen.

Lady Jakabitus had been against having the Apiosan Superstar Sports Squad as the predinner entertainment, but Frederain had been equally adamant. She argued that their act was far too undignified for such an important occasion. He counterargued that the occasion itself would lend more dignity to the Superstars' performance. She said that it wouldn't be nearly enough. He claimed that it was an opportunity to show dignitaries from across the galaxy what Apiosan sports was really all about. She took issue with his use of the word *opportunity.*

In the end, she let Frederain have his way, because she loved him, and if having grown men in short shorts cavort around before dinner made Rayzo's marriage any more palatable for him, it was a small price to pay.

The Apiosan Superstar Sports Squad warmed up with some synchronized tumbling, then moved on to demonstrations of their specialized skills.

One demonstrated how many times he could slap a practice dummy in fifteen seconds. His hands and forearms were a blur as he landed slap after slap on the dummy, which vibrated visibly and emitted a noise like a piece of paper stuck in a fan.

Next, a volunteer raced one of the Superstars a short distance, but while the volunteer ran on foot, the master moved in a series of diving somersaults. The volunteer lost the race, but was graced with a round of applause for his trouble.

The third Superstar displayed his legendary strength by ripping the shorts off a practice dummy with one hand, then slapping various objects in half.

The fourth Superstar, the one with an eight on his shorts, rounded out the show by picking a random member of the audience and demonstrating his signature move, taunting the opponent until he became angry and made a mistake, which in this case was crying.

The audience fell silent, feeling terrible for the crying man, except for Lord Hahn and Hennik, both of whom were giggling.

The fourth Superstar apologized and asked the crying man to stand so everyone could give him a round of applause. When the man stood, he ripped off his fancy clothes, exposing the fact that he too was wearing sports shorts. The fourth Superstar told the crowd that this man had gone undefeated in three consecutive meets owing to his amazing ability to cry at will, which confused and demoralized his opponents, allowing him to gutter them. Of course, the crowd loved this revelation, and the rafters rang with applause.

The fourth Superstar said, "Usually our demonstration would end here, but tonight we have a unique opportunity. There is a young man in the audience who recently swept a meet and is, I am led to understand, still undefeated in regulation play. He managed this feat on the strength of a move he invented, one so devastating that it was immediately outlawed following his first meet, and so unique it was named after its inventor. If Milady approves, could your adopted son please come show us the move that is known as a *Hennik?*"

Lady Jakabitus said, "If Hennik wishes it," but Hennik had already stood up. He stepped around the table and joined the shorts-clad men in the center of the room. He made a point of not looking at his true parents, knowing that they would likely disapprove of what appeared to be his cooperation, but Hennik was sure that once they witnessed the awful embarrassment he'd doled out to so many Apiosans, they'd be proud of him.

The fourth Superstar thanked him, then started the demonstration by asking if Hennik preferred to have the advantage or not.

Hennik said, "It doesn't matter. I'll win either way."

The audience oohed at this proclamation as the Superstar feigned exaggerated fear. Hennik did take the advantage, however, and he and the fourth Superstar squared off.

The fourth master shouted, "Go," and in less than a second, Hennik had dropped, slid through his legs, and popped up behind him, pulling the man's own arm up into his crotch, rendering him helpless. The crowd laughed and clapped as he steered the off-balance master around the room in this undignified posture. The fourth master played his pain and embarrassment for laughs.

Over time, the laughs quieted, and the Superstar said, "Thank you so much, Master Hennik, for this demonstration. Let's hear it for Master Hennik!"

The audience applauded, but Hennik maintained his grip on the man's wrist and continued to push the man around the room.

"Okay," the fourth Superstar said, all mirth drained from his voice. "Thank you Master Hennik. I think you can stop now."

"I know I can stop now," Hennik said. "I can keep going for as long as I'd like, and there's nothing you can do to stop me, isn't that right?"

The fourth Superstar said nothing.

Hennik pulled his wrist up a bit further and said, "Tell them. Tell them that I'm right."

"It's . . . it's true, ladies and gentlemen, once Master Hennik has his opponent in this position, he is quite helpless. That is why the move was outlawed."

"Yes," Hennik said. "Because it exposed a weakness. A weakness all Apiosans shared, which only a Hahn could see and exploit."

Hennik stood in the thick, oppressive silence of the room, soaking it in like a sponge. He gave the man's arm one last sharp yank upward, then released it and walked back to his seat. The silence was only broken by the sound of his shoes on the floor, and the sound of Lord and Lady Hahn, slowly clapping.

Rayzo glanced at Shimlish, who was sitting with her hands folded in her lap.

Lady Jakabitus shot the orchestra leader a look that he could clearly interpret even from all the way across the hall, and he quickly directed the orchestra to start playing again.

"Why didn't you clap?" Rayzo asked.

Shimlish said, "I wouldn't be caught dead encouraging that awful little troll."

Well what do you know? Rayzo thought. *We have something in common.*

66.

"It's just so typical of him," Shimlish said. "He thinks of the most brutal possible approach, then he keeps using it over and over until it stops working. Let me guess, I'm betting he's never defeated the same opponent twice."

"That's true," Rayzo said.

"See, that's just him. He keeps doing the same thing until he's absolutely sure it won't work anymore, then he sulks about it. You must have seen that for yourself. He may be undefeated now, but he would have lost eventually. He always does. Someone always thinks up a countermeasure."

Rayzo said, "Oh, he's not undefeated. He's undefeated in regulation play, but I've beaten him in an informal match."

"When?"

"A couple days ago."

"How'd you beat him?"

"I knew what his move was, so I thought up a countermeasure, like you said."

Shimlish said, "Good."

Well, there it is, Rayzo thought. *My first one-on-one conversation with my future wife, and it went pretty well. Of course, we can't spend the rest of our lives doing nothing but bad-mouthing Hennik.*

He scoured his brain, searching for a topic he could discuss with her. He was doing his best to hide it, but Rayzo found his future bride quite intimidating. She was older, taller, a seasoned commander from a famously hostile family, and to top it all off, beautiful.

He considered bringing up the topic of how attractive she was, but dismissed the idea immediately. They were being forced to marry, and while he didn't want to take it out on her, he didn't want to give her the impression that he was any happier about it than she was.

Still, he thought, *there might be something to talk about there. Most people's favorite topic is themselves.*

"Hennik did catch me off guard at first," Rayzo said, crafting the smoothest segue he could muster. "I'm sure he found me an easy competitor since his sister's a decorated soldier."

Shimlish rolled her eyes, and Rayzo braced himself for whatever sarcastic reply she'd make.

Before speaking, she looked at him, and then glanced at her parents. "I'm not supposed to tell you anything about, well, anything until after the wedding," she said, "but I figure the ceremony tomorrow is just a formality. I mean, we're going to be married no matter what either of us does, right?"

"Yeah," Rayzo said. "Pretty much."

"Right. So, the truth is that I'm no soldier."

"But you're the head of the Hahn military."

"Please, Rayzo. Am I pronouncing that right? *Rayzo*?"

"Yes, Shimlish. I'm getting *Shimlish* right, I hope?"

"Yes. It's a hard name to say, especially if you put Miss in front of it. *Miss Shimlish.* My father's idea, of course. Anyway, please, Rayzo. Think about it. I mean, would your mother yield control of her military to you?"

"No," Rayzo said, "but she has a general who handles most of the day-to-day business of the war and reports back to her. That's what we always figured you did."

"Really?" Shimlish asked, looking thoughtfully at Lady Jakabitus. "She actually lets Kriz The Weeper make decisions?"

"Yes, what did you think he did?"

"The same thing I do. Stand around in a suit of armor, drawing fire and preparing to be a scapegoat if Father makes a mistake."

Rayzo was amazed. "So, you're not the leader of the military, but you *are* a soldier?"

"Not really. I mean, I've trained, but not to be a good soldier, just to make soldiering look good. I can run an obstacle course with the best of them. My punches and kicks look great, but they don't have a lot of force, and my rifle technique looks dramatic, but I have a terrible aim."

"It's all for show?"

"Yes."

"Is the damage on your armor fake?"

"I wish. No, they scavenged all the pieces from the armor of soldiers who died in combat. They said it looks more authentic."

"But why you?" Rayzo asked. "You're his daughter."

"That's why. If things go well, people will assume he's advising me . . . and that I inherited my military genius from him. If things go badly, he looks selfless for punishing his own daughter. If I get assassinated, he can retaliate as violently as he likes and everyone will understand because he lost his daughter."

"That's the worst thing I've ever heard."

"That's my father. I've always been the odd one out in this family. I'm just not cut out to be a Hahn, and he knows it. He sure tells me often enough. He and Mother spent half the trip here making me recite that awful speech I made when we arrived."

"So, all those things you said, that's not really how you feel?"

"No. Those were Father's words. I told him it would be simpler if I just punched you in the face."

"What did he say?"

"To save that for after we're married."

Rayzo spent a moment trying to process what he was hearing, then asked, "If you're not cut out to be a Hahn, how did they end up calling you *the Pig*?" As soon as the question left his mouth, he regretted it.

If Shimlish was offended, it didn't show. "It was a punishment. I disappointed Father, so he started rumors about my hygiene and how I treated the servants. He ordered them to call me *the Pig*."

Rayzo said, "I was told that on the Hahn Home World, being called *the Pig* would be a compliment."

"If Father did it knowing that I wouldn't like it, can it really be considered a compliment? Anyway, it's hardly something all Hahn would consider a tribute. Look at my mother. Do you think she'd be pleased if you referred to her as *the Pig?*"

Rayzo looked at Lady Inmu Hahn, and had to concede the point. Not only was he certain that such a moniker would *not* please her, but he doubted he'd ever have the nerve to test the theory and find out. "What could you have done to deserve that?"

"I told him that I was interested in becoming a Master of Formalities, rather than taking over as ruler. The reputation he gave me was humiliating, and it made it impossible for me to ever seek a career in Formalities, like Migg."

"You and Migg were close?" Rayzo asked. He looked over to where Migg was standing along the wall behind his mother. He still thought of it as Wollard's spot, and probably always would.

He couldn't be sure, but he would have sworn Migg had been looking at him, and that she'd looked away the instant he looked back.

"Yes. I don't know how things are in your palace, Rayzo, but I don't have any real friends in ours. There's my family and the servants, who are rightfully terrified of my parents. Migg was really the only one

I could talk to. I was so sad when she and Hennik got captured after being sent on that ridiculous tour of the front. It would have been worth taking Hennik back if Migg had come back with him."

The band continued to play as Rayzo and Shimlish talked, and the servants took up positions around the perimeter of the room for the dinner service. Once everyone was in position, all attention shifted to Chef Barsparse, looking crisp and professional in her cleanest chef's whites, and flanked by Ebbler. Dressed as immaculately as his supervisor, he was guiding a large, covered grav-platter.

Barsparse ran through a greeting to all those in attendance whom proper form dictated she should acknowledge. It was an impressive act of memorization. Her ability to speak publicly and remember foreign names and pronunciations was what qualified her to be the head chef of a great house rather than the head chef of a great restaurant.

Now that Barsparse had explained whom she was serving, she could move on to the difficult bit, explaining what she was serving.

"Tonight's entrée is a dish from the home world of our honored guests, the Hahn. It is a preparation of beef, which has been inspected, trimmed, ground to a fine consistency, and will be served in its natural state, at the ambient temperature. On the Hahn Home World, there would be a sprinkling of various *pungent* indigenous herbs mixed in with the ground beef. These I have replaced with a variety of native Apiosan aromatics, some of which were pickled to heighten their unique flavors."

Barsparse looked at the faces of the guests, and for the most part, liked what she saw. Smiles.

These were not stupid people. Everyone had been caught unaware at Hennik's welcome banquet, but word had traveled fast in the aftermath of that meal (much to Lady Jakabitus's chagrin). This time, the guests had come knowing what to expect from Hahn cuisine; they were either counting on Barsparse to have found a cunning workaround or were planning to skip dinner.

Those who were skipping dinner didn't care what was being served. Those who were hoping for a pleasant surprise had listened with intense interest as Barsparse described the traditional dish tartare so clearly it could almost have doubled as a recipe.

"The dish," Barsparse said, "is called *drunesplop*. My sous chef Ebbler will now personally serve the members of House Jakabitus and House Hahn, in the traditional Hahn manner. Servers will be by with your portions shortly thereafter. As with all Hahn cuisine, the presentation is of paramount importance to the dining experience. I hope you enjoy your meal. It is our honor to serve you."

Polite applause accompanied Barsparse as she left the floor. Ebbler stood motionless until the noise died down. Once the room was silent, he turned with military precision and approached Lady Jakabitus's table, pushing the floating covered platter before him. Like all of the guests, she was seated in front of an empty plate and table silver.

Ebbler paused. Lady Jakabitus nodded in encouragement. Ebbler muttered, just loud enough for her and Lord Jakabitus to hear, "I'm sorry, Milady."

Lady Jakabitus said nothing, but nodded again.

His apology having been delivered, Ebbler squared his shoulders and raised his nose into the air. He grasped the decorative silver dome on his platter, lifted it, and violently cast it to the floor, making a startlingly loud gonglike sound.

The Hahn drunesplop sat on the platter, exposed for all to see. It was a glistening pink pile of raw ground beef with specks of green and dull red mixed in. While it was recognizably tartare, it was easily the least appetizing presentation of the dish any of the guests had ever seen.

Ebbler maintained his proud posture as he cupped his right hand, forming a crude scoop. He thrust his bare hand into the pile of drunesplop and pulled out a warm handful. As he withdrew his hand, a suction was formed that made a wet, squishing sound.

He held the handful of drunesplop aloft, muttered another nearly silent apology, then recited the traditional drunesplop delivery announcement, "And now you receive the meal you deserve."

Ebbler was stocky, with broad shoulders and thick arms. Usually his build had no effect on the performance of his duties, but his arm strength was a definite plus in this unique situation. He hurled the drunesplop down onto Her Ladyship's plate with enough force to make it flatten on impact, but not enough to make it splatter or fly apart.

Ebbler muttered, "I am so sorry."

Lady Jakabitus smiled at him and said, "Thank you."

Ebbler took one step to the right, stopping in front of Lord Jakabitus.

"Sorry," Ebbler moaned.

Lord Jakabitus nodded.

Ebbler took another handful, proclaimed, "And now you receive the meal you deserve," and hurled it at Lord Jakabitus's plate.

Lord Jakabitus thanked him.

Ebbler moved on to Hennik, who raised one eyebrow and in a loud, clear voice said, "None for me. I'm not hungry."

Ebbler started to move on to Rayzo and Shimlish's table, but paused in spite of himself when Hennik whispered, "What? Don't I get an apology?"

Rayzo accepted his drunesplop as graciously as his parents had. Shimlish quietly declined hers. Before Ebbler could move on, Rayzo, speaking every bit as loud as Hennik had, said, "I'll take hers."

Reluctantly, Ebbler flung another handful onto Rayzo's plate. Shimlish looked at Rayzo with a mixture of amazement and confusion.

Predictably, Lord and Lady Hahn were not feeling peckish. As Ebbler gratefully exited, the Hahns looked expectantly at Lady Jakabitus, waiting for her to have her first taste of drunesplop.

Lady Jakabitus took a dainty but not insubstantial forkful of the dish, placed it in her mouth, closed her eyes as she chewed it, and swallowed. She opened her eyes and looked at Chef Barsparse, who was still standing by, as was customary, and said, "Delicious. Well done, Chef."

Barsparse bowed and left for the kitchen. The temporary servers moved efficiently throughout the room, reciting the drunesplop introduction and dispensing servings overhand to the waiting guests, who all dug in eagerly.

Lord and Lady Jakabitus made pleasant conversation while they ate their drunesplop. Hennik watched them with open disgust. His expression was matched by his parents'. Lord and Lady Hahn's heads swiveled and their eyes bulged as they watched the guests devour the drunesplop with what appeared to be genuine pleasure.

Even Shimlish seemed confused by Rayzo's lack of reticence as he ate his double helping.

"What are you doing?" Shimlish asked.

"Eating," Rayzo said, enjoying her confusion.

"Drunesplop isn't for you to eat. It's for them to eat," Shimlish hissed as she motioned to the mass of guests.

"I don't understand," Rayzo lied. "It's a Hahn dish. You're a Hahn. You don't eat drunesplop?"

"No!"

"Why not?"

"Because it's repugnant!"

Rayzo looked at his double portion and laughed, because she wasn't wrong. It certainly didn't look appetizing. He looked to Lord and Lady Hahn's table, then to Lord and Lady Jakabitus's table, and when he saw that none of them were watching, he leaned slightly closer to Shimlish.

"You told me the truth, Shimlish, so I'll do the same. This stuff you call *drunesplop,* it's almost identical to a dish of ours called *tartare.*"

"You eat this *tartare* voluntarily?" Shimlish asked.

"Yes."

"Your parents eat it as well?"

"Yes. My mother would never ask her subjects to do something she wouldn't do herself."

Shimlish furrowed her brow. "That's all my father does, except he doesn't ask. The whole point of serving drunesplop is to make his followers eat it without eating it himself."

"So, when you serve drunesplop, what do you and your family have?"

"A snack later."

They sat in silence for a moment while Shimlish thought about things and Rayzo took another bite of his drunesplop.

"This dish you call *tartare.* You like it?"

Rayzo looked at his plate, then said, "Well, it's not my favorite or anything, but I don't mind it."

"Why did you ask for my helping, then?"

I've started telling her the truth, Rayzo thought. *Maybe that's not the kind of habit I want to break.*

Rayzo said, "Take a look at your parents and your brother."

Shimlish looked over at her family. Lord and Lady Hahn were still speechless with horror. While Lady Hahn was holding a napkin over her mouth, Lord Hahn was squirming uncomfortably in his chair. His chair was, in turn, squirming beneath him because his chair operator misunderstood the situation and was trying to adjust the chair's position to make Lord Hahn comfortable.

Hennik sat low in his seat, arms folded, sulking, with a look of disgust mixed with resignation.

Rayzo said, "We've been living with your brother for a while now. We've learned a few things."

"I see."

"Would you like to try a bite?" Rayzo asked quietly. "It's okay if you don't, but it would really drive your father crazy if you did."

"Yes," Shimlish said. "I expect it would."

Rayzo started to push his plate toward her, then stopped, "You know, it would bother him even more if I fed it to you."

"Yes," Shimlish said, "but I don't think I'm ready to bother him quite that much."

Rayzo pushed his plate toward his future wife. She took her unused fork in her hand, then said, "Why yes, I will try some."

Five heads (two of them Jakabitus and three of them Hahn) turned to watch as Shimlish took a small forkful of drunesplop and placed it in her mouth.

After chewing and swallowing, she said, "That's not bad."

Lord and Lady Hahn quickly looked away, unable to bear the sight any longer. Hennik returned to his sulking, but Lord and Lady Jakabitus watched for a bit longer.

When they had finally turned away, Shimlish quietly said, "It isn't very good either."

Rayzo whispered, "Like I said, it's not my favorite, but we all do what we must."

In a louder voice, Rayzo asked, "More?"

"Yes," Shimlish replied, taking another bite. She chewed it while watching her parents' table.

"Have you ever heard of a sauce called *Chowklud?"* Rayzo asked.

"No," Shimlish admitted.

"It's a Cappozzian dish."

"Will it make this stuff better?"

"Better, no, but definitely more amusing."

Rayzo called out, "Shly?"

Shly came forward eagerly. "Yes, Master Rayzo?"

"My betrothed and I would like some Chowklud."

Shly failed to hide her surprise. She bulkfabbed them a small bowl of Chowklud, and two tall glasses of water they had not requested.

Rayzo briefly explained to Shimlish how the Chowklud would taste and why someone would want to eat something like that in the first place. He took a large spoonful so she could watch his reaction.

Shimlish took her own spoon, and per Rayzo's suggestion, barely dipped the end of it into the Chowklud. She then put the spoon in her mouth. One of her eyes slammed shut while the other bulged. Her shoulders heaved, and her mouth formed an exaggerated frown. She maintained this expression for a full five seconds, then began to laugh.

When she was done laughing, she dipped her spoon in again and had another taste.

Lord and Lady Hahn were studiously avoiding any eye contact with their daughter's table. Hennik was staring, so Rayzo smiled at him. He did not smile back.

Rayzo looked out at the guests, and his eyes fell on Lord Kank, who was watching the events at Rayzo's table with great interest.

When he realized Rayzo had seen him, Kank smiled, raised both eyebrows, and lifted his glass to Rayzo, who returned the gesture.

67.

Dinner had been much better than expected for both Rayzo and Shimlish, but the next morning was not.

Down in the palace's Grand Gallery, where the ceremony would take place, preparations were progressing smoothly, or so Lady Jakabitus would have been told had she asked. Upstairs in the Jakabituses' private chambers, tension was in the air.

Rayzo stood in the center of his room while various temporary staffers helped him get dressed. Of course, Rayzo was ordinarily capable of dressing without help, even when wearing his third or second most-formal uniforms. For this occasion he was wearing his *most* formal uniform, a silver brocade jacket and pants adorned with so many epaulettes, aglets, and other bits of interconnected polished brass hardware that it was simply impossible for one person to don the entire outfit correctly without help.

When he was fully ensconced in his finery, the staff left Rayzo's room, and his parents entered to continue the argument they'd started over breakfast. They were both in their most-formal uniforms as well, so decked out in gleaming militaria that one almost suspected that the buttons and medals had been added primarily for their value as armor.

"Rayzo," Lady Jakabitus said, "I'm sorry that what I said upset you, but it's very important for you to understand that you can't trust Shimlish Hahn."

"So, you're sorry that what you said upset me," Rayzo said, "but you just repeated the thing that upset me."

"I'm repeating it because it's important, Rayzo. You can't trust her."

"I never said that I do," Rayzo said.

"But you haven't said that you don't," Lady Jakabitus countered.

"You two haven't spoken to her alone," Rayzo said. "She seems all right."

"She's certainly pretty enough," Lord Jakabitus said sourly, settling into a large wing-backed chair.

"No," Rayzo said, then stammered, "well, yes, of course she is, but that's not what I meant and you know it."

"Yes," Lady Jakabitus said. "You've seen past her pretty exterior and into her beautiful soul."

Rayzo narrowed his eyes. "Look, I know I've only really had one conversation with her. I'm not saying that we've fallen madly in love or anything."

"Good," Lady Jakabitus said.

"Yes," Rayzo agreed, "because it would be awful if I loved my future wife. Mother, you're making me marry her. I didn't want to yesterday, and I still don't want to today, and I'm absolutely certain that she feels the same way. I'm just saying that I've talked to her, and I think she might not be a monster."

Lady Jakabitus put her hands on her son's shoulders and looked into his eyes. "I know, dear. I understand, and I'd like to believe that too, but I can't. I'm just too worried it's a trick."

"I know, Mother, but I don't think it is."

"That just means it's the worst kind of trick."

"The kind that isn't a trick at all?"

"No, the kind you fall for."

◆ ◆ ◆

"I don't like it," Lord Hahn said, sitting in his chair as it paced back and forth, "And by *it*, I mean him!"

Shimlish said, "I know, Father." She didn't roll her eyes, but it was implied in her tone. She and her parents were in the room she'd been assigned. It was as opulently appointed as every other room in the palace, but larger than most. The idea was that Shimlish would need the space and the use of several servants to prepare for the ceremony, but her adaptive armor did not take long to program, so instead the room was a simply an extra fancy place for her parents to harangue her.

"That boy's a bad influence," Lord Hahn said, making eye contact with Lady Hahn as he passed. She was sitting perfectly straight with her hands in her lap, as if trying to minimize her actual physical contact with the priceless antique chaise on which she was forced to sit.

"All we did was talk," Shimlish said.

"And eat," Lord Hahn said. "And laugh!" Lord Hahn pointed at Shimlish and said, "Your instructions were simple." He continued pointing as the chair paced.

Lord Hahn paused, then glanced in the corner of the room, where the chair operator was standing with his hands on the controls and a large device over his ears, making it impossible for him to overhear their conversation. Though he was not allowed to listen to the private conversations of the members of House Hahn, he was still expected to anticipate and execute Lord Hahn's wishes. Lord Hahn felt that emphatically pointing at his daughter was a clear signal that he wished to stop pacing and approach her. Unfortunately, the chair operator's attention had lapsed, and the chair continued to pace. Lord Hahn waved his arms at the chair operator, which failed to attract the man's attention. Finally, Lord Hahn opened the small red door marked *Emergency* on one of the arm rests and pulled out a small device, which he threw at the chair operator's head.

The object made an audible *thunk* when it hit. The operator yelped and cringed, composed himself, took one look at the expression on Lord Hahn's face, and yelped and cringed again.

The chair came to an immediate halt.

Lord Hahn bared his teeth at the chair operator, then looked back to his daughter, pointed at her again, and said, "Your instructions were simple," then glanced at the chair operator. The chair approached Shimlish until it loomed over her menacingly.

Lord Hahn continued. "You were to either ignore and belittle the boy, or seduce and emotionally cripple him. You were not, under any circumstances, to befriend him."

"You never told me that last part," Shimlish said.

"It was implied," Lord Hahn yelled. "It's always implied! Have you completely forgotten the values we raised you with?"

"Father, I . . ."

"Silence!" Lord Hahn interrupted. "Do not speak! Do not talk back to me now, and do not talk to that Jakabitus boy at all. He's a bad influence, and you are not to speak to him ever again. Is that clear?"

"Is the wedding off?" Shimlish asked.

"What a stupid question. Of course the wedding's not off. I still mean to usurp House Jakabitus, and you're still the tool I will use, so no, the wedding is not off. You are going to marry Rayzo Jakabitus. You're just not allowed to talk to him."

"How am I supposed to be his wife if I can't talk to him?"

"It's called the silent treatment. Your mother can tell you all about it, but you'll have to wait until I leave the room. Isn't that right, dear?"

Lady Hahn pursed her lips and looked away.

68.

While dinner the night before had featured Hahn cuisine, the wedding itself was being held in the Jakabitus ancestral palace on Apios. The Formalities allowed Lady Jakabitus to choose between Apiosan and Hahn marriage customs. In the interest of being thorough, she had requested a briefing on the traditional Hahn ceremony, which she found fascinating.

Since the Terran Exodus, human cultures, belief systems, and customs had, of course, diverged. Many noted that when mankind went to the stars and found no aliens there, they set about making themselves as alien as possible. Marriage customs were no exception.

A wedding is usually one of the most positive, life-affirming rituals a culture has to offer. The Hahn, on the other hand, had systematically drained it of all spiritual and philosophical context. On the Hahn Home World, a wedding ceremony was treated solely as a legal arrangement. Responsibilities were explained, delineated, and legally conferred through the reading and signing of several lengthy contracts. The bride and groom were expected to invite, personally welcome, and provide food for virtually every friend and relative they had, and all of those people were expected to attend the wedding and watch as the contracts were explained and signed, standing each time a passage was initialed, kneeling each time it was signed and dated.

Lady Jakabitus opted for an Apiosan ceremony, which had its roots in ancient Terran traditions.

The Grand Gallery was lavishly decorated for the event. The main addition to the décor was an intricately woven netting of live ivy vines, which hung from the pillars around the periphery at a height of forty feet, giving seated guests the impression of being outdoors under the canopy of a forest while still allowing them to see well enough to remember that they were, in fact, in the Old Palace's atrium.

Hundreds of seats were arranged in two equal groups on either side of the gallery, facing an altar that had been erected in front of the wall of windows and its view of the seemingly endless sea.

The guests were already seated. The incredibly select group of people who were deemed important enough to merit witnessing the wedding in person were also intelligent enough to know how lucky they were, and responsible enough to be on time.

At the appointed hour, the palace orchestra began playing the processional march. At that precise moment, many miles away at the far end of the city, the procession began.

Koa city still kept one broad avenue that split the city and led directly to the palace, an anachronistic holdover from the days of ground transportation. It had been maintained specifically for occasions just like this. Today it was lined on both sides with throngs of citizens, all jockeying for a view of the historic ceremony in which the son of their beloved leader would marry the daughter of their hated enemy.

The first vehicle in the procession carried Lord and Lady Jakabitus, to signify to the people of Apios that their planet was of paramount importance.

Their antique coach had carried the planet's rulers to and from various weddings, coronations, and funerals for centuries. Any Apiosan who had studied history had seen countless images of this very coach, going all the way back to the days when it still rolled on wheels. In person, its gold surface blazed in the sunlight, burning itself into the memories and the retinas of the spectators. Lord and Lady Jakabitus waved, and tried their hardest to look pleased.

The second vehicle carried Lord and Lady Hahn, to signify to the people of the Hahn Home World that their planet was of paramount importance, as the Jakabituses had clearly been sent in first to test for snipers.

The Hahn coach had been fabricated especially for the event, according to Lord Hahn's specifications. It was a featureless cube of unpainted armor plating with no visible windows or doors. It was a craft carefully designed to deprive spectators of a view, and assassins of a shot. The only indication that Lord and Lady Hahn were inside was the stenciled lettering listing their names on each panel of the cube, like a warning label.

Next were two identical open-air coaches gliding side by side, to signify that the occupants were of equal importance. In one sat Rayzo, smiling and waving, resplendent in his most formal uniform. In the other sat Shimlish, unmoving, her adaptive armor set to a gleaming white. Her silver-blonde hair cascaded over her shoulders below her bridal helmet. Her lips and chin were visible, but her eyes were obscured, as her helmet's blast shield was partially lowered.

The procession slowly made its way up the boulevard, past the citizens, and through the palace gates. The guests inside all turned around uncomfortably in their seats to watch through the open doors of the palace as Lord and Lady Jakabitus stepped out of their coach which, now empty, lifted straight up and out of sight. The Jakabituses took their seats at the front of the audience, to one side of the dais. Hennik was already present, wearing the white formal ensemble he'd attempted to use as a stealth suit. He considered this break from the Jakabitus family to be an act of defiance, as was the fact that he'd only taken his seat in the first row after the utilitics had carried him into the Grand Gallery without any cooperation.

The Hahn's armored cube silently drifted up to the door, then dropped to the ground with a resounding *thud*. The side of the cube facing the door slid up, and Lord Hahn's chair operator, followed by Lord and Lady Hahn, exited the craft. They moved up the aisle and headed to the opposite side of the dais from Lord and Lady Jakabitus, where an empty seat and room for Lord Hahn's chair awaited them. As they entered the palace, the cube closed again and remained motionless. For a long time nothing happened, then Rayzo came into view, walking around the Hahn armored cube from one direction while Shimlish walked in from the opposite direction. The two met in the middle and entered the palace together as the music swelled to a crescendo.

All eyes were on the couple, neither of whom was looking at the other as they walked down the aisle.

Fourteen Masters of Formalities were gathered at the back of the room. Many of the guests had brought their own, and form dictated that they all be on hand in case they were needed. They stood in a ruler-straight line, black suited and poker-faced. Migg stood at one end of the line, next to Phee, who surreptitiously checked her papers one last time. As Phee put her papers away, Migg said, "I'm sorry you're unhappy, Phee, but I'm delighted by what's making you that way."

In the centuries since the Terran Exodus, religion, like every other aspect of human society, had splintered and evolved. There were few planets where all of the inhabitants agreed on one faith, and there were no two planets that couldn't find some bone of contention about which to disagree, argue, and in all too many cases, go to war. As a result, proper form dictated that all interplanetary state weddings be strictly secular affairs, officiated by the highest-ranking non-religious official available.

In this case that official's title was, ironically, Minister of Health.

On Apios, Minister of Health was the very highest position to which a non-Jakabitus could rise, as the official in this position was charged with maximizing the health of the planet's inhabitants, a charter so vague that the Health Ministry had annexed almost every part of the government over the years.

The Minister of Health was a wizened old man named Seibert Adler. He had won his position with his gentle, benevolent manner, and he'd kept it for fifteen years by mercilessly crushing anyone who got in his way . . . or anywhere near him.

Shimlish and Rayzo reached the altar. Minister Adler recited the full formal greeting, ending by welcoming the bride and groom and all of their parents, using their full names and titles. He then welcomed the honored guests, but showed restraint by only welcoming the first two rows' worth by name. The rest, he assured the global audience, would retroactively be welcomed in writing.

The greetings out of the way, he gave an extended speech about the nature of love, which was as stirring as it was irrelevant to the matter at hand, which everyone knew was essentially a business transaction.

Finally, nearly two hours after the official beginning of the ceremony, Minister Adler began the actual wedding.

"We are gathered here today to join two young people in the unbreakable bonds of eternal, irrevocable wedlock."

He could have worded that a bit better, Rayzo thought.

"On my right," Adler continued, "I have Master Rayzo Jakabitus, of House Jakabitus, the beloved son of our leader Lady Joanadie Jakabitus and her husband Lord Frederain Jakabitus." Adler motioned toward Lord and Lady Jakabitus, who were sitting beside the dais on Rayzo's side, looking deeply conflicted, though one of those conflicting emotions was definitely pride.

Adler said, "On my left, we have Miss Shimlish Hahn, of House Hahn, the beloved daughter of the leader of the Hahn Home World Lord Kamar Hahn and his lovely wife Lady Inmu Hahn." Adler gestured toward Lord and Lady Hahn, who were sitting to the left of the dais, Lady Hahn scowling as she felt the fabric of her chair's covering to judge its quality. Lord Hahn was reading his papers. He glanced up upon hearing his name, waved dismissively, and went back to his reading.

Minister Adler cleared his throat. "If there is anyone who has a reason for why these two people should not be married, let them speak now."

Wollard cleared his throat and said, "Pardon me."

Every head in the Grand Gallery swiveled violently. Shimlish turned hers so fast that it knocked her helmet and blast shield out of alignment with her face.

Wollard was standing, unperturbed, in the middle of the aisle. He was impeccably dressed in his formal blacks and looked utterly relaxed. Most would have assumed he'd simply strolled in, if he had not been accompanied by a heavily armored stealth combat automaton, painted in jet-black livery with subtle stripes that suggested a Master of Formalities collar and cuffs. It hovered behind Wollard, its brake thrusters still glowing bright red, its pincers extended from having just gently placed Wollard where he stood.

Wollard took no notice as the automaton reversed its thrusters and silently streaked out of the palace, deftly threading through the entrance doors and the twin glowing holes it had melted through the front and rear walls of Lord Hahn's armored cube on the way in.

"I regret," Wollard said, "that I must, under the auspices of my position as a representative of the Arbiters and in the interest of promoting proper form, object to this union on the grounds that it was conceived and executed due solely to unprecedented interference on the part of an Arbitration official. In cases such as this, proper form dictates that I consult with the highest-ranking actively involved Master of Formalities."

All eyes turned to the herd of black-clad Masters of Formalities. They seemed uncharacteristically shocked, except for Migg and Phee, who looked ashen and delighted, respectively.

The Masters of Formalities quickly looked at each other, muttered a bit, then one of them, having been hastily determined to be the senior, said, "We recognize your request, and ask that we be given time to determine whom among us is directly involved, and whom among them is the senior official."

"A reasonable request," Wollard said, "But unnecessary in this case. The Arbiters have already determined that the involved parties, aside from myself, are Kallump, Master of Formalities to Lord Hahn; Migg, Master of Formalities to Lady Jakabitus; and Phee, her protégée. Of those three, Migg is by far the senior official, as she served for many years as Lord Hahn's Master of Formalities before infiltrating House Jakabitus."

The wedding party and the gathered guests all expressed shock and confusion—shock at the revelation, confusion as to how such a thing was possible, and whether it, in fact, meant anything.

Migg, Phee, and Kallump met Wollard in the middle of the aisle.

Wollard said, "I move we dispense with the full formal greeting."

Migg said, "Agreed."

"Migg," Wollard said in a flat, professional monotone, "the Arbiters accuse you of acting in poor form; specifically, of manipulating the heads of two great houses in an unethical and unprecedented manner to achieve your own ends. Be advised that you have the right to a public recitation of the evidence against you."

"I waive said right," Migg said.

"Let it be noted that I, Wollard, the Arbiters' representative in this matter, understand and agree with your decision to waive your right. If you check your papers, Migg, you will find official written notice that you have been removed from your position as Master of Formalities for House Jakabitus and summoned to the Central Authority, where you will face scrutiny. This notice has also been forwarded to Lady Jakabitus, and to your former protégée, Phee."

Phee, her nose buried in her papers, said, "Yes, I have it right here."

Migg muttered, "Thank you, Phee. Well done."

"Yes, Phee," Wollard agreed. "Well done."

Lady Jakabitus said, "Whenever it's convenient, will someone please tell me what has just happened?" Her tone made it clear that it was convenient *right now.*

Wollard bowed to Lady Jakabitus, then looked expectantly at Phee and said, "My protégée will be happy to fill you in."

"Milady," Phee said. "Migg has been accused of impropriety. She has been removed from her position, and according to the official notice, replaced by Wollard."

"And what does that mean for the wedding?" Lady Jakabitus asked.

"The Arbiters have found evidence that the wedding was conceived in a manner not in keeping with the Formalities," Phee said, "and as such, to continue with it under the circumstances would be poor form."

"So the wedding is off?" Lady Jakabitus asked.

"Wait one minute," Lord Hahn shouted. "The Arbiters can't tell me what to do! I say the wedding is still on, and if it isn't, then the war *is*."

Wollard and Migg both glanced at Kallump, who looked panic-stricken. Wollard and Migg rolled their eyes, and Wollard spoke.

"If I may, Lord Hahn, you are correct that your actions are yours alone to decide. Ours is only to offer advice, and to warn of the possible consequences of your choices. In this case, you may proceed with the wedding, but following through on an arrangement made under questionable circumstances would reflect most negatively on both House Jakabitus and House Hahn, possibly resulting in both of your home planets losing recognition as civilized worlds."

"Then war it is," Lord Hahn said.

"That is also an option," Wollard said, "but I must point out that by agreeing to this marriage in the first place, House Hahn tacitly expressed a wish for peace. In the face of the wedding's cancellation, any return to open conflict could be interpreted as an act of petty revenge, and would almost certainly result in a loss of face for House Hahn. In that case, the Hahn Home World would likely lose recognition as a civilized world. Apios's standing would be unaffected."

"Wait," Lady Jakabitus said. "Are you saying that the war on Ophion 6 is over, but the wedding is off?"

Wollard smiled. "I am suggesting that the scenario you just explained is the optimal course of action for both House Jakabitus and House Hahn, Milady. Unless, of course, Master Rayzo and Miss Shimlish express an overwhelming desire to be married, in which case, it would be poor form to stop them."

Rayzo looked to Shimlish, who raised her blast shield to look back. They didn't say a word, but they were clearly in agreement. Rayzo turned to Wollard and said, "We regretfully announce that we've broken off our engagement."

"It is a mutual decision," Shimlish added, "and we thank the citizens of both of our worlds for respecting our privacy during this difficult time."

"Well," Lady Jakabitus said. "Huh. I see. Most interesting. I suppose I should start by saying welcome back, Wollard."

"I'm delighted to be back, Milady."

"And Migg," Lady Jakabitus said, then paused before continuing, "I honestly don't know what to say to you at this point."

"Good form dictates that you thank her for her efforts, regardless of the results, Milady," Wollard offered.

"I thank you for your efforts, Migg."

"And I thank you for the opportunity, Milady," Migg replied.

"And Lord Hahn," Wollard said, "I don't wish to step on Kallump's toes, but the Formalities would also suggest that you thank Migg for her efforts, as her apparent attempt to serve two masters at once would seem to be what has landed her in her current predicament."

Lord Hahn seethed at Wollard, then looked at the hundreds of seated dignitaries from around the galaxy who were hanging on every word of what had turned out to be the most interesting wedding they'd ever attended.

"Migg," Lord Hahn spat, every word seeming to cause him physical pain, "I also thank you for your . . . *efforts*."

Migg replied, "And I thank you for the opportunity as well," which did nothing to alleviate his pain.

After enjoying the sight of Lord Hahn uncomfortable for a moment, Migg turned to Wollard and said, "The Formalities have been satisfied. I understand and accept the notice you have delivered. I request leave to return to my quarters to collect my things for my journey to the Central Authority."

"That will not be necessary," Wollard said. "As the Arbiters sent me here directly via their own interstellar transport, and said transport must return to the Central Authority anyway, you are directed to proceed directly to the courtyard to board it."

"But I should at the very least change out of my formal blacks."

Wollard smiled. "There'll be time for that during your processing."

Phee said, "Pardon me, Wollard. May I please accompany Migg to the transport?"

Wollard agreed, and Phee and Migg walked up the aisle and around Lord Hahn's destroyed armor cube, which was still radiating heat. They approached the Arbiters' transport, which was sleek and smooth, and such a dark shade of black that it was difficult to discern anything else about it.

"Well, Phee," Migg said, stopping just before entering the craft. "How do you feel?"

"Conflicted," Phee answered. "I think someone I know put it best. She said, *I'm sorry that you're unhappy, but I'm delighted by what's making you that way.*"

"I'm not as unhappy as you might think, Phee. My goals were to end the war, improve Mistress Shimlish's position, and escape Lord Hahn."

"But you're going to be scrutinized."

"I don't know much about the scrutinizers, but I am sure that I'll prefer them to Lord Hahn. Good-bye, Phee. You've been a fine protégée."

"Good-bye, Migg. Working with you has taught me a great deal."

69.

The members of House Jakabitus and House Hahn retired to their personal quarters to recover from the day's events. Wollard and Phee personally expressed the gratitude and regrets of House Jakabitus to each and every dignitary as they left.

Once all the guests had been given their due and were on their way, the Hahn could safely vacate without the risk of an unpleasant public scene.

Lady Jakabitus, Lord Jakabitus, and Rayzo came to the courtyard to see them off, and were predictably kept waiting. When the Hahn finally did arrive, Hennik was trailing them, wearing the brown jumpsuit in which he'd been captured.

Lady Jakabitus opened her mouth to speak, but was interrupted by Rayzo, who asked, "If it pleases you, Lord Hahn, Mother, may I have a moment alone with the young lady I nearly married?"

Lady Jakabitus nodded. Lord Hahn looked away, which was as close to permission as he was likely to give. Rayzo and Shimlish walked a far enough distance to ensure they wouldn't be overheard.

Rayzo said, "I just wanted to let you know that I'll keep your secret.

I don't see any reason for telling my mother that you're not really the head of the Hahn military now that the war's over."

"Thank you," Shimlish said, "but it's not necessary. I've been removed from my position. In order to save face, Father intends to blame the cancellation of the wedding on me. Apparently, I was unable to fully seduce you because of my disgusting piggishness."

Rayzo moaned. "Shimlish, I'm sorry."

"Don't be. I'm happy. I lost my title in a way that allows me to keep breathing. Now that I'm no longer head of the military, I may be able to pursue my own interests without scrutiny and wear clothes that nobody died in. Besides, I'm still first in line to be ruler of the Hahn Home World someday."

"Sounds like you're coming out of this ahead," Rayzo said.

"Yes, how about you?"

Rayzo looked over at his mother and father, stiffly attempting to make conversation with Lord and Lady Hahn, Hennik making a point of standing next to his blood parents. Rayzo considered telling Shimlish that his mother was paying more attention to him these days, and that his father was paying him the *right* kind of attention, but instead he chose to say, "It looks like Hennik is returning home with you, so I'm pretty happy myself."

"Yes," Shimlish said. "I bet you are."

Rayzo took a moment to consider his next sentence. Once he'd examined it from every angle, he said, "You know, I'm happy that I'm not going to be forced to see you every day for the rest of my life, but I do look forward to seeing you again someday."

"Well put," Shimlish said. "I feel the same. I mean, after all, we'll be the heads of two great houses, and it's going to take decades for us to manage the reconstruction of a planet-sized demilitarized zone."

Shimlish and Rayzo rejoined their families. Formal good-byes were exchanged between Wollard and Kallump, Phee standing by, looking happy but exhausted.

As the Hahn, including Hennik, turned to board their transport, Lady Jakabitus said, “Hennik, I don’t recall Lord Hahn requesting that you return to the Hahn Home World with his family.”

Hennik said, “He didn’t.”

“And I don’t recall you requesting permission to leave.”

“I didn’t.”

Lord Hahn’s chair had paused and turned to watch the exchange, and for a moment, he looked almost proud.

Lady Jakabitus said, “If that’s how it must be, Hennik. I do hope you won’t miss us too much.”

Hennik said, “I won’t,” and both he and Lady Jakabitus knew that he meant it.

◆ ◆ ◆

The Hahn were gone. The Jakabituses had retired to their rooms. The rest of the staff was busy. For the first time since his return, Wollard and Phee had a moment to talk.

Wollard looked to Phee, nodded, then silently turned and walked at his accustomed pace, with Phee struggling as always to keep up.

They walked through the Grand Gallery, past the auxiliary staff tearing down the decorations, up the escalator, and to the library. Wollard held the door open for Phee.

Once they were inside, and the door was closed behind them, Phee rushed Wollard and hugged him. He stood ramrod straight and patted her back three times in quick succession. She let go, took a step back, and smiled at him.

“It’s good to have you back,” she said.

“It’s good to be back,” he replied.

Wollard looked around the library, as if seeing it for the first time, then sat in one of the chairs. Phee found the sight of Wollard sitting unsettling. She’d never seen him do so before. The rules allowed Masters of Formality to sit when alone, but Wollard never had in the past. He motioned for Phee to sit on one of the other chairs, which she did. The chair was comfortable. She was not.

"Thank you for the message," Wollard said. "It was instrumental in helping me regain my position."

"How did you manage that?"

"I used your message to get the Arbiters' attention, then once I had it, I groveled and simpered and lied. Basically, I told them that all I wanted was to serve them, and I'd do anything they asked."

"And that was a lie?"

"Yes," Wollard said. "I have no intention of blindly following orders anymore. I learned some things while I was away, Phee. Things about the Arbiters and the Formalities. Things I don't like."

"So why are you still working for them?" Phee asked.

"I had a choice. I could convince them that I was their man, or be discarded. I managed to convince them, but I don't really work for them. Not anymore. I'm my own man. I work for myself. Is that going to be a problem for you, Phee?"

Phee thought about her time working with Migg and said, "I've learned a few things while you were away myself. No. That's not going to be a problem."

"Good," Wollard said, "because as my protégée, you work for me too."

"Yes," Phee agreed. "I work for you every bit as much as you work for the Arbiters."

Wollard smiled. "You always have been a fast learner, Phee."

◆ ◆ ◆

On the planet known as the Central Authority, at the bottom of a stone pit, in a sack that had three strategically placed holes, Migg stood and looked up at the shadowy forms of her scrutinizers.

One of the shadowy silhouettes that looked down at her from the rim said, "Migg, what do you have to say in your defense?"

"Nothing," Migg replied.

The silhouettes looked at each other, then back down at Migg.

"Why will you not offer a defense?"

"Because there's no point," Migg said. "You know what I've done. You know why I did it. You know what you think of it, and you know what you're going to do about it. Anything I say at this point would be a waste of time for all of us."

The silhouettes looked at each other again, then returned their gaze to Migg.

"You stand by your decision to offer no defense?"

"I do."

"We thank you. You have made the next part much easier for us."

"Yes," Migg said, "I notice you haven't asked for time to deliberate."

"Indeed. Migg, former Master of Formalities to both House Hahn and House Jakabitus, you have subverted the Formalities to suit your own ends, manipulating those who trusted you, risking the careers of others, and taking an active role in directing the life path of members of two great houses and countless citizens, all to suit your own ends. Do you deny any of this?"

"I do not," Migg said.

Whichever shadow was speaking said, "Then you leave us little choice but to offer you a position as an Arbiter."

ACKNOWLEDGEMENTS

I'd like to thank my wife Missy, my friends Steven Carlson, Allison DeCaro, Jen Yates, John Yates, Mark Yocom, Rodney Sherwood, Leonard Phillips, Ric Schrader, Scott Adams, everybody at 47North, my parents, my brothers, and the readers of my comic strip, *Basic Instructions*.

I'd also like to thank all of my current friends and former coworkers at the tower. The original tower, the one true tower, not any of the later, lesser towers.

ABOUT THE AUTHOR

Scott Meyer has worked in radio and written for the video game industry. For a long period he made his living as a standup comedian, touring extensively throughout the United States and Canada. Scott eventually left the drudgery of professional entertainment for the glitz and glamour of the theme park industry. He and his wife currently live in Orlando, Florida, where he produces his acclaimed comic strip *Basic Instructions.*